Our Common Hatred of Florida Summers

Mitchell J. De Haan

The Rooster's Rest Collective — Zimmerman, MN
ISBN: 9798991883207
Library of Congress Control Number: 2024923004
Title: *Our Common Hatred of Florida Summers*
Author: Mitch DeHaan
Digital distribution | 2024
Paperback | 2024

Cover Art by Lauren Sohre

This is a work of fiction. The characters, names, incidents, places, and dialogue are products of the author's imagination, and are not to be construed as real.

Table of Contents

CHAPTER 1

The first thing anyone needs to know about me is that I hate Florida summers.

Okay, maybe not the *first* thing. The actual first thing people need to know about me is that my name is Jack Connors. No, not O'Connor. Not Connor. Not Corners. It's Connors, like a bunch of guys named Connor walked into a room. Connors. Jack Connors. I'm about six feet tall, one hundred and seventy pounds. I'm not exactly muscular and I'm not exactly fat either. 'Well balanced,' my mother always says. I have brown hair, but it's been getting blonder with how much time I've been outside in the sun. I tend to keep it around three inches long and use hair fiber to flip it to one side. The only two traits that stand out about me is that I've got bright green eyes and skin that tans well. Originally, my family is from Alaska. But we moved to Florida a few years ago.

Hence why I hate Florida summers. I genuinely despise this season in God's Waiting Room. One might ask oneself why I could possibly hate it as much as I do. 'It's super sunny!' they might say or 'There's always the parks!'

No. Just no. Stop. Those aren't good reasons. It's not a good season. Whatsoever. Period. End of discussion.

Let me explain.

As I mentioned previously, I grew up in Alaska. Born and raised near Juneau, I enjoy cool, moderate temperatures and lots of outdoors time. Yeah, winters are a bitch, but it happens. I prefer it up there. It never gets too hot and I can handle the cold. Here's what my grandpa always told me: "You can always put more clothes on if you get cold. But you can only get so naked before it becomes a problem."

Sure, if I'm in my bedroom or house, it's not an issue – I could take it all off. But I don't have to – I'm in my climate-controlled home so I can just crank the AC or chill in my boxers and tank top or jump in the pool. But I can't do that in public.

That's why I say I prefer it up in Alaska. But things have clearly changed for the worse. See, my dad, Simon, is a money manager. I can't really explain it better or simpler than this: if someone has money and wants more via investments or clever money-making techniques, my dad is their man. And my dad isn't just an average money manager – he's a freaking genius. His first job was with one of the largest financial firms in the country and based out of Juneau when he semi-applied. And I mean semi-applied because they didn't actually have a job opening for him and were hesitant even considering him because he was so young at twenty – my dad graduated college a year early to save money. I understand their hesitancy. My dad was from a small town and the son of a fisherman who came to the big city thinking he can make money in the seven and eight figures at his first crack at things. Hell, I would be skeptical to hire him and he's my dad! But, my dad is a stubborn son of a gun, he goes and tells them that they don't have to pay him a base salary – only pay him the percentage that all of the managers make on their accounts. They laughed at him, but hired him. They thought they might as well get some free help from him and some free money in the process.

But, oh, how they were wrong. My dad ended up making twice as much as the top agent of the entire company. Literally millions in his first year as a money manager. All of which was completely legal.

They promptly gave him a job after that first year.

With that job, my dad was able to marry my mom, Lydia. My parents were high school sweethearts and my mom always knew that my dad could make money. But she didn't know how much he had made. So, on their wedding night, my dad looked at my mom and told her that she would never have to work a day of her life if she didn't want to. She had laughed at him until he showed her the bank statements.

She kept laughing, but more out of disbelief and shock than anything else.

So, married to someone that told her she didn't have to work, she decided to paint. She painted Alaska as she saw it – everything from a busy day at the fish market to the sunrise over the glaciers. To be honest, my mother is one of the greatest modern painters in America. And she has commission pieces with the price tags to prove it.

So, my dad makes tons of money. And my mom makes lots of money. So, yes, I'm a rich kid. But not one of *those* kids. Trust me. I know some of *those* rich kids and I am nothing like them. Thank goodness.

About a year or so after my dad got his job at that Alaskan firm, they had me. They had always wanted a kid and had talked about it for a long time. My mom has some health complications so my parents knew it was going to be a challenge. But I don't think they knew how much of one it was going to be. In fact, my mom almost died giving birth to me. My dad jokes around and tells me that it was because of my 'big ass head,' but my mom told me she had preeclampsia and eclampsia. She basically was having seizures while pregnant and was forced to have an emergency early delivery. I was born about ten weeks early – a premature baby – and both my mom and I almost died. It was really scary at the time for my parents – and whenever I think about it now, I get a little freaked out – so they decided one was enough and I would be their only kid.

And that's okay. I sometimes wish that I had siblings, but I'm very introverted and haven't really needed anyone to be at peace with life, liberty, and the pursuit of happiness. Yes, I have friends and shit – I'm not some crazy loner. But I do enjoy spending time by myself with a good book or video game or whatever.

Anyways, back to Alaska to Florida.

My dad ended up getting some national attention and soon began to work for celebrities and other large-scale corporations – investing their "hard-earned" money to make more of it for them. He began to make so much money for these people that one of the largest entertainment corporations in the world – I can't say for *legal* reasons who he works for despite the fact I could say a few key words and everyone would know who it was – and they just had to have him working for them. They threw a literal shit ton of money at him, increased his commission by an absurd percentage, and paid for him to relocate.

To Florida.

Mom had always wanted to get out of Alaska. She has started to develop some early onset, rather severe arthritis. My dad, being the loving and caring husband that he is, was more than happy to make her happy. 'Happy spouse, happy house, son' is what he keeps telling me. Therefore, I had no choice in the matter. I packed up all my things—granted there weren't actually that many things because I'm somewhat of a minimalist – and said good-bye to some close friends, loaded the moving truck who had a nice long drive from *Alaska to Florida,* and got on a plane.

So, we moved. To Florida. In July.

For those who don't know, Florida lies in a humid subtropical region. Surrounded by oceans and filled with lakes, swamps, and wetlands, Florida's annual precipitation averages in the mid-double digits. Likewise, the warm ocean currents coming in from the Gulf and the Caribbean prevent the state from getting much colder than forty degrees. That's when Floridians begin to break out the Carhart jackets and parkas and complain about how 'the cold weather is not of God.'

Weak as shit. Try negative fifty out in the tundra, Karen.

Anyways, when we landed in Florida, I remember walking out of the airport to get into a waiting car to take us to our new house near Lake Nona. When warm air and the water cycle meet, their love-child is humidity. And Florida, by God, is like an armpit. The first time I stepped out of the climate-controlled airport and into the wild Orlando air, it honestly felt like walking out of a refrigerator and into a damn swamp. I quickly checked my phone before absolutely deadass sprinting to the waiting and, what I presumed, air-conditioned car. Ninety-nine degrees. Ninety-nine percent humidity.

'Kill me' was my immediate thought.

But that was my new reality. Florida. And that's been my reality for about three years now. My dad, of course, still makes rich people richer and my mom still paints. Instead of Alaskan sunsets and moose, she paints the ocean and gators. And I go to school.

I go to Hurston and Hemingway Preparatory High; we students simply call it H&H. It's named after Zora Neale Hurston and Ernest Hemingway, great writers and champions of intelligence in their own rights. It is seen by most in the Orlando area as one of the most prestigious schools in the nation. Most people at school have scored in the thirties on the ACT and in the 1400s and 1500s on the SAT. I already know a few people in my grade that have received full rides to Oxford, Cambridge, Harvard, Yale, and Stanford. It's highly competitive to get in and it's expensive to attend. There are scholarships and tuition cuts for those who can't afford it and those kids tend to be the ones that graduate with the highest GPA, valedictorian, and full rides to literally anywhere in the world.

I sit in the middle of the class. 4.0 GPA – though that doesn't really say anything at H&H. 1515 on the SAT. 33 on the ACT. I'm planning on getting into the engineering field and working on next generation transportation methods that are greener and cleaner for the planet. My goal is MIT. Or something equivalent to that. My dad is bummed I refuse to get into finance, but supports my 'gallant efforts in conservation and preservation.'

But that is during the school year. It's currently not the school year. It is the summer time. And in the summer, I try my best to do what I'm doing: survive.

I admit, I dramatize things a little, but I truly despise it. I'm eighteen and going into my senior year in high school. Last summer, I managed to get a job bussing and serving tables at Lucy's Tiki Bar in Cocoa Beach. It's about an hour drive, but I make my gas money for a couple months in tips alone within a week. Not to mention, I have a great car. 2006 Subaru Baja, full package. I absolutely love this car.

I keep getting sidetracked. My apologies.

This summer, retaining my position at Lucy's, I thought that I was going to have a better summer because of this job. The owner is a really cool guy by the name of Farrow McNiler. It's an odd name but he's honestly one of the coolest old guys I've ever met. And I think he likes me quite a bit too. Not in a weird way, more like a grandfatherly or uncle-ly sort of way. When I turned 18 earlier in June, he upgraded me to server full-time. And I can serve alcohol now too. 'Gotta give those beach ladies something sweet to look at, ma-boy!' he always tells me with a wink.

Now, note that I said I *thought* I was going to have a better summer. Past tense. Old news.

This summer has been miserable. My advice for any tourists is that if they decide to visit Florida in the summer, for the love of everything that is good and holy, don't be a dickhead about it. Tourists are the absolute worst thing not only for the environment, but for my mental health. I'm not sure what happened this summer, but there have been way more idiots in Cocoa and Orlando than normal. And, so help me, they are the worst. Sure, tips have been good, but the number of times I have either been called a racial slur – despite being white, just super tan – and hit on by women three times my age has been astronomical. I've even spent a couple of nights after work with Nick to try and clean up the beach around Lucy's because tourists apparently don't know what a trash can is and, if they do, they certainly don't know how to use it.

Never had this issue in Alaska. Now, it's a norm here in Florida.

Degenerates from up country, I swear.

It's about 4:00 pm now and I'm wiping down a table the busboy has missed – again. These new hires are morons. Except for Nick.

Nick is a friend of mine. One of the few I've made here in Florida, but undoubtedly the best. He's a little shorter than I am, around five foot nine, with buzzed black hair, pierced ears, and deep brown eyes. His jaw line could kill a man and spends much of his free time running. He's in the same grade as me and needed a job for the summer. I talked to Farrow and we worked something out. Nick almost quit the first day though. I don't necessarily blame him – Farrow kept using she/her pronouns. See, Nick is transmale. He's pretty confident on who he is, but every now and then he gets called 'she' or someone says something like 'you dress pretty boyish for a girl,' and that sets him off. I can't say that I understand because I don't think I ever could, being a cis-male and not having to work on that, but I try to empathize. Farrow felt pretty embarrassed because he had hired a Nicole as a hostess and got the two confused. 'I try to keep up with the times and respect everyone, but ya know how things get when you're super old like me!' Farrow had said, trying to get Nick to stay. I was able to talk Nick down and ever since then he's been really enjoying his job here. He and Farrow have really hit it off as well and it's been fun to have conversations between the three of us.

Nick and I met on the first day of school my freshman year at H&H. He found me like a hound finds a raccoon – sniffed me right out of the crowd. He had approached me and straight up introduced himself, fully informing me of his name, identity, and proper pronouns. I was taken aback at first – I grew up in a pretty conservative area. Neither of my parents are conservative and I frankly don't have the patience to deal with politics and the catastrophic bullshit that comes with it, but running into people of the LGBTQIA+ community in my area was very rare. Even rarer to find one so open and upfront about it. I stumbled through my introductions, included my pronouns, and finished with a sheepish smile. I think that's what got Nick. He instantly knew I was new and began walking me through the norms and routines of H&H. He helped me find my classes, introduced me to teachers, and assisted navigating and operating the cafeteria's complex system of getting food, paying for it, and choosing the appropriate place to sit. There, he introduced me to what is now my core group of friends – himself, Khalan, Mona, and Lisa. But Nick has been and will always be my best friend.

"Jack! New table! Outside! P3!" Nicole, the hostess, shouts to me. I smile and nod to her, grabbing my notepad and pens off the counter by Nick.

"How much we betting on this one?" I ask Nick, clicking my pen three times. We have this thing on slow days where we bet whether or not the customers will order something formidably basic or something unique.

Nick leans against the bar top. "Have you seen them yet?"

I shake my head.

He nods. "Five bucks says they order something basic as hell."

I extend my hand. "You're on."

He shakes it firmly before I head for the patio area. I look at Nicole. "What do I got?"

"Looks like three teenagers. One's wearing a big sunhat like she's fifty-something. But I'm pretty sure none of them are over eighteen. One even has a H&H tank top on, so your classmate, right?"

"Oh, the joys." I let out a deep sigh. I didn't really enjoy seeing people from school outside of school other than my friends. I put on my best smile and walk outside to the table. Sure enough, there sits not one but two of my classmates from H&H.

But the third girl is new. She is wearing a light blue crop top with no sleeves. Her hair is long and black, the braid going down to her waist. She's slim but very much in shape. Sitting down, I can't really tell how tall she is, but my guess is she is somewhere around five foot nine, five ten. The hat on her head is one of those obnoxious sun hats that old ladies wear on the beach, which seems odd since she is, again an estimate, eighteen. And she's wearing big sunglasses that shield her eyes to the point where I can't even see the whites of them, much less the color.

"Good afternoon, ladies! My name is Jack and I'll be your server today."

"Oh my god, Jack Connors! How are you?!" The first girl exclaims.

"I'm fine, thanks for asking!"

Is her name Shelly? Brittany? Polly?

Definitely not Polly.

"Z, this is Jack. He's the guy who plays piano we talked about!"

The new girl, Z, nods and looks up at me through her dark shades. "What do you have for soda?"

"Coke products – Coca Cola, Diet Coke, Dr. Pepper, Mellow Yellow, Sprite…"

"I know what Coke products are, thanks."

I can't spit in customers' food.

I can't spit in customers' food.

I can't spit in customers' food.

"What can I get you?"

"Diet Coke please," the girl – I'm pretty sure it's Shelly – says.

"Me too!" says the other – who, if it's actually Shelly, is most likely Adrianna.

"I'll take this, but virgin? Can you do that?" The girl named Z asks, pointing to something on the menu. I take a look and she's pointing at the Eastbound and Down, a tropical mix of orange, grapefruit, and limes which is typically served with rum.

Ironically, it's also my favorite drink to get here at Lucy's. Virgin, of course, but still. Very good.

"Great choice! It's my personal favorite."

"Great, so glad I got your feedback on that," Z says, tossing her menu on the table.

What the hell is this girl's problem?!

"Z, come on, that's rude," the one I think is Adrianna says before she looks at me. "I'm sorry about her, she just got here today from California. Jet lag, ya know?"

You don't get jet lag on a midday flight.

"It's not a problem. Will you want some food?"

They nod and begin talking to one another. I nod and make sure I have everything written correctly, before heading back inside.

"Nick! I need two DCs and an Eastbound and Down going the speed limit!"

"You got it! I'm not sure what that means for our bet though."

"Call it even?"

"Fair enough!"

I walk over to the counter to grab a fresh tray. "I'm pretty sure the two who want Diet Cokes are Shelly and Adrianna. They have a new girl with them and she's, uh, something."

"Shelly Anderson and Adrianna Moklin?" Nick asked.

"Dude, I don't know! I'm not good with names, you know this."

Nick shook his head. "Damn it, man. The one who you think is Shelly Anderson – blonde hair? Freshly cut and curled?"

"Yeah, pretty much."

"Shelly Anderson."

"How do you know this?"

"Instagram, bro."

I shake my head. "I don't check mine that often. And when I do, it's mostly memes."

"Who's the new girl?"

"They only called her Z. Don't know much else."

"How do you make such good tips, man! You need to be more personable."

I laugh. "Dude, I'm sexy. You better believe they like what they see."

"Farrow!" Nick calls out. "Did you hear that?!"

Farrow peaks his head around the corner. "I'm already grabbin' me mop, meh boy. I heard Jacky-boy drop a load of shite!"

The three of us laugh as I pick up the tray and make my way back outside, my smile a little more genuine than last time.

"Alrighty, two Diets and an East Bound," I say as I place the drinks in front of the appropriate drinkers. "Did we decide on any food?"

"That's pretty tasty!" Z exclaims after taking a sip before either of the other two could answer.

"I know, right! I love it."

Z leans forward in her chair. "So, you're the piano player?"

Her change in demeanor throws me a little. "I am, though, I'm stunned Shelly and Adrianna remember."

"Oh, he does remember our names! I told you, Shelly!" Adrianna shouts. "And of course, we remember you play – you played that piece at the talent show fundraiser. Shelly and I organized it so we were there in the back."

"Yes, you were so good!"

"Why, thank you, Shelly. I appreciate it."

I look back to Z, who is staring intently at me and it is starting to make me feel uncomfortable. Even with the big sunglasses on, I can feel her boring down on me.

"Where have you played?" Z asks.

"Here and there," I reply. "Mostly at universities since they like to host competitions and I've been all around the southeast. Made it to Berlin once. And London."

She nods. "Very impressive."

I nod back. I can't get a read on her. She's either very illusive or being very intentional about making sure I stay at arm's reach.

No matter. This is my job.

"What can I get you ladies for food? Or do you need another minute?"

"I'll have a Caesar salad with crispy chicken," Shelly replies.

Adrianna quickly follows. "I'll have the same but with grilled."

I jot down the orders and look back at Z. "And for you?"

"Well, I'll start with some of the cheese bites – if they're any good."

I hate that the South calls them cheese bites. They're cheese curds.

"Absolutely, some of the best on the beach. What kind of dipping sauce do you want?"

"Options?"

"Ranch, ketchup, blue cheese, sriracha ranch, sriracha honey, mustard if you're into the kind of thing, and a dip that is very similar to Chick-Fil-A's."

"Not that last one thanks. Can't stand Chick-Fil-A."

I laugh – not out of any sort of negative headspace, but out of surprise.

I also hate Chick-Fil-A.

Z doesn't seem to catch that.

"Something funny, piano boy?"

I quickly shake my head and change my demeanor. "No, just a little shocked. I don't find many people that share the same distaste for Chick-Fil-A."

She nods. "My apologies for snapping at you. It's been a… rough day."

I shake my head again. "Oh, no worries."

"What do you get with the cheese bites?"

"I normally go with sriracha ranch. I'm from Alaska and ranch is kind of a big thing up there but since moving down here, I've really been able to appreciate some heat in my food."

"I'll go with that, then. And then I'll just do a classic burger, no ketchup or mustard."

"So, lettuce and tomato and pickles? Do you want any other sauce?"

"Mayo?"

"You got it. Are fries okay?" She nods. "Anything else I can get you while I'm here?" The three shake their heads. "Okay, I'll get your order in and be back to check on your drinks in a bit."

They resume their conversation and I hear a quick jab from Shelly to Z. "Why are you being so rude? Is your boyfriend really bugging you that much?"

"Yes. I'm sorry. I just…"

"Don't apologize to me, Z. Apologize to Jack. He's a decent guy."

I don't hear anything past that once I enter the restaurant. I turn in the order to the kitchen where Raphael and Georgina, our two beach famous cooks, start getting the food ready. It doesn't take super long since we aren't busy and between the food being ordered and ready I refill the drinks once, but the three girls were too focused on the discussion at hand. I think it was back to Z's boyfriend, but I couldn't tell.

Once the three had finished eating, I bring them one last round of drinks.

"How was the food, ladies?"

"Good!" Shelly and Adrianna say in unison. They are always together and basically robotic twins, even at school. Freaks me out a bit.

"Burger was okay, but those cheese bites were to die for. I appreciate the suggestion on the sriracha ranch as well," Z says, handing me her plate.

"Just okay with the burger? Anything that you would want differently?"

"It was a little overcooked. I wasn't going to be that person though. I'm sure you have plenty of that with some of these other women here." Z says in a low voice, gesturing to the gathered customers at my other tables.

"Oh, don't worry about it. Next time you're here, I'll make sure to change that. That is, if you order the burger again."

"We'll see. Check?"

"Just one?"

"Yes."

"Z!" Shelly shouts. "You don't have to do that!"

"It's okay, I got this."

I go back inside, print the check, and return it to their table. Before I can take the payment method, a voice calls out from behind me.

"Jackie! Hey Jackie! Can you come here?"

Another table that needs my attention. Fun never stops.

"Coming!" I turn back to the three. "I'll be right back."

I go and help the table with their order despite that is phenomenally basic. One of the ladies as I walk away slides a ten into my hand.

"Come back quick, handsome."

Barf.

I turn back to Z's table, but the three of them are gone. I can make out Z's big hat walking down the beach towards the hotels. I walk over and pick up the black folder we use for checks and open it. Inside are two crisp one hundred dollar bills and a note made from a napkin. I'm shocked. I've never got a tip this big before. The first hundred would have easily covered the meal and left me with a substantial tip. The second was completely unnecessary.

I flip the napkin over and read the note.

The first $100 is for the bill and your tip. The second is an apology. Sorry about being rude. Rough day… - Z

The corner of the napkin has a wet mark. It's the size of a tear.

Now, I feel bad. I look up to see if I couldn't catch up to her before she disappeared, but it was too late. No sign of Z or her big hat.

The rest of my shift goes incredibly slow because the only thing I can think about is not trying hard enough to make Z's day better.

Wait, what? Why am I thinking that? I barely know her. She was rude to me.

She was having a rough day. There was that tear. Maybe that's why she wore the sunglasses. Maybe she had been crying. I force myself to focus on my orders and work my tables. When 9:00 rolls around, the twenty-something year-olds show up for their night shift. The night shift always has a riot and often will drink with customers, showing them how much fun they can have at Lucy's. It's a big reason why the tiki bar does so well.

I fist bump Nick as he heads to his car.

"See you, my man," he shouts behind him. "We still hanging out with Khalan tomorrow?"

"Da Vinci not back yet?" That's what we call Mona and Lisa. They have been dating since ninth grade and were one of the first open lesbian couples of our grade. They quickly adopted the couple name Da Vinci, for obvious reasons. They are currently on vacation with Lisa's dads somewhere in the Bahamas.

"Nope!" Nick calls back to me. "They'll be back in, like, three days? Maybe four? I can't remember and they aren't any good at replying to texts when they're together, much less on vacation. Still good with your place?"

"Yep! I'll let you know if my mom says differently."

Nick clasps his hands over his heart. "Uh, Lydia. Give her my love, will you?"

I shake my head. "Alright, will do, man."

I walk over to the Baja and I'm about to hit the unlock button when I do my routine scan of the beach. There are a few people here and there, more fishermen than anything. But one individual catches my eye. They are sitting alone, knees tucked up into their chest, and a big sun hat resting in the sand next to them.

Z.

I hit the lock button out of habit and start walking over to her. I intend to give the extra hundred back and apologize for being… something. I'm not sure. But I'm feeling almost drawn out to her.

As I approach, I can see her shoulders shaking.

Is she crying? Should I leave?

"Hey? Are you okay? Z?" I ask quietly.

I must have startled her because she jumps a little to the sound of my greeting. She quickly wipes her eyes and looks up at me. "Shit, piano man, you scared me."

"Sorry. I didn't want to intrude." I'm still a few paces away from her.

Turning away, she lets out a half-hearted laugh, almost like a chuff. "At least you're polite today."

She sniffles again. I grab the little package of tissues I keep in my back pocket in case of nosebleeds (had a lot of those when I was younger) and close the space between us.

"Here," I say, offering the small bundle.

She looks up at me and I see her eyes clearly for the first time. They are a deep shade of blue and the longer I keep eye contact with her, the more enchanting they become. I try my best to disarm the situation and crack a light smile out of the corner of my mouth. She returns my smile with an almost sad one, taking the tissues from my hand.

"Thanks," she says before she sobs again, returning her gaze back out to the ocean.

I don't really know what to do. Should I sit? Should I leave? Should I stay where I'm at until she's done with the tissues?

She blows her nose then looks up at me. "Aren't you going to sit down?"

I don't say anything. I just lower myself down next to her, copying her posture and wrapping my arms around my legs.

Neither of us says anything for a while. We simply watch as fishermen bring in an assortment of catches. I'm not sure why I'm staying. I don't really know her. But I don't want to go either.

I suddenly remember why I walked over in the first place. "Here," I say, taking out the $100 bill. "This wasn't necessary. No apology needed either."

Z looks at me with bewilderment. "I'm sorry, what?"

I tap her arm with the bill. "You didn't need to do this. I totally understand – you were having a rough day."

"You're giving me back the money that I tipped? Despite the fact that it's $100?"

I nod.

I see her demeanor change as her smile is wider, happier, and more genuine. "Shelly said you were a decent guy, but I think that was an understatement."

I can feel my cheeks burn as I smile back at her. "Thanks. Take it back. You can spend it the next time you come to Lucy's. Just make sure I'm working."

She gingerly takes the bill back. "And you're sure?"

"Absolutely."

"Okay." She bumps me with her shoulder. "Can we start over?"

"Yes, yes we can." I extend a hand to her. "Jack Connors. Not Conner. Not O'Connor. Not Corners. Just Connors."

"Kind of like a bunch of guys named Connor in the same room?"

My smile widens. "Exactly."

She takes my hand. "Well, Jack Connors. I'm Z."

"Just Z?"

"That's what all my friends call me. Thinking we skip the formalities. You've got one of those faces you can trust, ya know?"

I laugh. "Fair enough. I'll accept that. Why are you out here, Z? If you don't mind me asking?"

Her smile disappears quickly. "Boyfriend is being a dick."

I nod. "I figured that's what it was. I overheard a little bit at Lucy's. Sorry."

Z shakes her head. "Don't. It's our fault for talking about it so loudly."

"What's going on?"

Z stares out into the vast expanse that is the ocean for a long moment. "So, I'm not from around here."

"California, right? Flew in today?"

Z nods. "Near LA, to be exact. I wasn't a fan of it. In fact, I hated living there. But I was there due to some obligations and finally had the opportunity to leave, despite my parents not wanting me to. I was able to convince them to let me move in with my Uncle Simon to finish up high school. My boyfriend, who is originally from California, and I have been dating for a little over a year now and he had moved out here a few years back. So, I thought it was going to be nice. I was out here a couple weeks ago to just finalize stuff and connect with Uncle Simon and whatever. But my boyfriend's been a fucking asshole. I didn't move out here for him, but he's acting like I did and being super possessive and it's almost suffocating. Kind of like the damn humidity here."

I chuckle. "I also hate the humidity."

"Right?! Ugh, it's so annoying."

"I genuinely hate Florida summers."

"Me too! We seem to hate a lot of the same things."

I laugh. "Yep, we sure do."

Silence follows for a moment before I ask the next question.

"Why are you out here though?"

She jerks her head back to the hotel just a block away. "I'm here with his family. I just couldn't anymore, ya know?"

I nod. "I mean, kind of. I've never had a girlfriend, but my grandparents can be really suffocating."

She looks at me with a high eyebrow. "You've never had a girlfriend?"

"Nope, not one."

"That's actually really surprising."

"Oh?"

"You just seem like a really nice guy, Jack." She leans into me and her head gently rests on my shoulder. "I feel very connected to you, Jack. I appreciate you being so nice. Especially considering how much of a bitch I was to you earlier."

"You're good, Z."

We stay like that for a long moment. My heart is beating faster. She smells really nice. And the amount of vulnerability she had with me was unexpected, but welcome. I want to talk more, but I also don't want her head to leave my shoulder. I sit as still as I can, not adjusting or disturbing her resting place.

After what feels like a half hour, she takes a deep breath and picks up her head. "Okay. I should get back before he comes looking for me. Don't want you to deal with him. I wouldn't do that to you."

I quickly stand up before she gets a chance to so I can extend my hand to help her up. Z smiles and takes my hand. I help her to her feet and it is a little faster than what she expected. She stumbles forward and I quickly catch her.

"Oof, I've been sitting like that too long. My legs feel weird."

"You going to be okay?"

Her smile returns and this time it sends electricity down my spine. "Yes, I will be. Thanks."

She steps into my space and goes on her tip toes. I feel her lips brush my cheek and I freeze.

"Bye, piano man. Thanks. I hope we see each other again."

She starts to walk away and I still haven't moved. I can still feel the light kiss on my cheek like a hot iron.

Z claps her hands and spins around. "What am I doing! If I want to see you again, I need your number. Give me your phone."

I take my phone out of my pocket, unlock it, and hand it to her. I watch her put in her number into a new contact then text herself a simple message with my name.

"There. I'll text you, Jack!" She calls out as she starts to jog off back towards the hotel.

I'm still frozen by the time she's out of sight. It is only until then that I unfreeze and make my way back to my car, walking on clouds.

CHAPTER 2

It is always a good time when Nick, Khalan, and I get together. We talk a lot about everything and nothing all at once. We are sitting in my family's entertainment room, *The Office* playing as white noise in the background. It was one of Dad's favorite shows and he shared his passion for the shenanigans of Dunder Mifflin with me. I gladly share it with my friends and it is now our regular thing. Sometimes we watch it intently, sometimes we just have it playing while we talk much like today.

"Dude, I don't get it. Why do we have to go with you to do school shopping? We wear uniforms at H&H. There's no point in buying anything else," Khalan states, popping another piece of popcorn into their mouth.

Khalan is a special person and it's complicated to explain sometimes. At birth, Khalan's assigned gender was male. But, as time went on, Khalan started to feel less and less like a male, but also nothing like a female. They had traits and qualities that are typically assigned to one gender as well as the other. When they brought this up to their parents and started therapy, they discovered they were non-binary. And, on top of that, they also found out they weren't sexually charged either. So, Khalan is both non-binary and asexual. And Arab. And Muslim.

Like I said, very special person.

But, son of a bitch, can they punch. Khalan's not someone to pick fights nor start them, but they will damn well finish them. Khalan's been boxing since they were seven and they are *good*. They don't do a lot of big tourneys or competitions, but they like to compete locally and they're known throughout Orlando. They are also known at H&H for someone that should definitely not be messed with. I've seen a couple of guys bothering Zahra, Khalan's little sister, and the second, I mean the *second*, Khalan raised their voice, those guys stopped bothering her and never came back.

"Ugh, Khalan, you're always one to try to logic things out of happening," Nick replies. "I don't care about the uniforms, man. Will I still wear them? Yes, we have to, I don't want to get dress coded. But I will have style for school events, I will have style for after hours, and, by whatever deity is listening, I will have style for literally style's sake."

I laugh as Khalan rolls their eyes, turning their attention back to their popcorn.

"What is your opinion, Jack-in-a-box?"

As I consider my response, my phone vibrates. It's a text from Z. She and I have been texting basically every day. Nothing crazy serious, but still constant and fun.

Z: So, I listened to Guaraldi like you instructed. Love it. Love it like candy.

I smile. Z had asked me to give her some piano music to listen to that I like and Guaraldi is one of my favorites.

Me: I'm glad! Hope that he sounds familiar.

Z: Peanuts, right?

Me: Yes, nice! Who's next on the list?

Z: Rachmaninoff? I think that's how you spell it.

Me: Spot on.

Z: I wish I could listen to all this with you, piano man. I would love to hear everything you have to say about it. And I miss your niceness.

Me: Boyfriend again?

Z: Ugh, yes! Football practice started and now he thinks he's just the bee's fucking knees and wants me at EVERY practice...

Z's relationship is a big point of confusion for me. I constantly want to tell her that she should just leave him, but that's not my place and I don't want to ruin whatever is going on between the two of us. So, I decide to hold my tongue yet.

Again.

Me: Sorry to hear that. Anything I can do?

Z: When do you work next? Like, a night shift?

Me: You mean till 9? Friday.

Z: I just got my car. Beach after your shift again?

Me: Done deal. Looking forward to it.

Z: Oh, really? You missing me, piano man?

Me: I think your boyfriend would have a problem with my honest answer.

Z: Well, I won't tell him if you won't ;)

Something hits me on the side of the head. I'm pretty sure it's a fly so I just wave my hand to dismiss the irritating bug. But then multiple projectiles hit me in the face and popcorn falls on my phone. I jump and look up.

"What the hell!"

Khalan and Nick bust a gut laughing with Nick making a dramatic display to fall off his chair.

"Dude, who are you texting? We've said your name, like, fifty times!" Khalan asks, reloading their arsenal of edible missiles at the machine in the back.

"Oh, he hasn't told you!" Nick whips his head back to me. "Jack! You haven't told Khalan?! What the shit, dude?!"

"What is there to tell, Nick? She's got a boyfriend."

"Wait. Wait, wait, wait," Khalan jumps the row of seats to sit between me and Nick and wraps an arm around me. "Did you just say... 'she?'"

My cheeks begin to burn.

"You did! You son of a bitch, you did!"

"Hey!" Nick punches Khalan's shoulder. "You never address Mistress Lydia like that again, so help me gods."

Khalan puts their hands up in surrender. "My apologies. I would hate to be the target of thy wrath, Nicholas."

Nick popped a piece of popcorn in his mouth. "Damn right, you would. But, we digress, good person! Jackothy, tell Khalan about this girl."

"She's a girl I met at Lucy's a couple weeks ago. It's no big deal. She has a boyfriend."

"Ugh, you have no dramatic flair, Jackatthew. Khalan, she only goes by Z. She's never given him her full name. She doesn't tell him who her boyfriend is. She moved here from California to live with her Uncle Simon. She's as mysterious as the day is long. And I LOVE this drama. It is *juicy*."

I roll my eyes. "Like I said, Khal, there's nothing there. She has a boyfriend. They've been together for more than a year and were friends for a long time prior to them actually dating. He can be a dick sometimes, but she has never made any indication of breaking up with him."

Khalan thinks for a second. "Jack, you remember that I box, right?"

I roll my eyes and put on my best exaggerating voice. "No, Khalan, I completely forgot. Do you really box? Are you any good?"

Khalan hits my shoulder at maybe twenty percent effort. It still hurts.

"Don't be an ass when I'm trying to help you."

"My apologies, sensei."

Another hit. Another ounce of pain.

"In boxing, especially against a stronger or bigger opponent, it can be hard to see an opening. They could have the best guard in the world and no matter what you think or try, you can't get around it. But nothing is ever perfect. If you can bide your time, be patient, and wait for an opportunity to strike, you will be successful."

"What does that mean?"

"Dude, you're as daft as my sister sometimes," Khalan says, shaking their head. "Despite not being interested in other humans for romantic endeavors, I understand the concept and have seen enough to know that the relationship she describes won't last. That's where you come in. And I don't mean you push the relationship to end. You don't rush your opponent when you wait for an opportunity. You might ruin it. But you need to make a choice – is she worth waiting for or are you going to move on and just be friends?"

I nod slowly. They're right of course. Always are – they are very intelligent and in touch with the world around them.

"Thanks, Khalan. I appreciate that. You've given me a lot to think about."

"Always, my man. Always."

Nick dramatically twirls to his feet. "Enough of this depressing talk! I, my friends, have news! Some sweet, sweet tea, if you please."

"Oh, shit, here we go again," Khalan remarks with an eye roll, easing back into their seat.

Nick is obsessed with gossip. I don't really know why. It's not beneficial. It's counterproductive, in my humble opinion. But Khalan and I indulge Nick because he's… well, Nick.

"What do we have today, Nikolaj?" I asked, picking up my soda and taking a good draught.

"We have a new student joining us at the illustrious Hurston and Hemmingway Preparatory High!"

"Big deal," Khalan remarks flatly. "We get at least three newbies every year."

"Ah, but not a newbie like the one I'm referring to. Her name is Zendaya Thompson."

"Shut up! Are we talking about *the* Zendaya Thompson?" Khalan says, spitting out kernels of popcorn.

"You're damn right!" Nick shouted, clapping his hands.

"Nick. Please don't swear in my home," Mom calls from the door.

Nick bows. "Yes, of course. My deepest apologies, Lady Lydia."

Mom laughs. "Oh, Nick. You're ridiculous." She walks away.

Nick shakes his head. "I have brought shame upon my family. The queen is angry with me."

I kick his shin. "Anyways, back to this new student. Who is she?"

Both Nick and Khalan look at me with disbelief.

"I'm sorry, did you just ask who Zendaya Thompson is?"

I nod. "Yeah, is she a big deal?"

Nick throws up his hands. "Tell him, Khalan! Tell him his sins!"

"Jack, she's, like, one of the greatest actresses of our time. She's been compared to Keira Knightley due to her almost angelic performances in period pieces. She's been in a couple of movies, but she's best known for *A Pirate's Love*. It's the story of a young governess who falls in love with a newcomer into town. They're both, like, fifteen and live in different worlds. And, of course, the newcomer is a pirate. In the Age of Expansion, nonetheless! Pirates! The Caribbean! The romance! My good man, how have you not seen this?"

"I don't watch TV, you guys! Other than *The Office*, my knowledge of the small screen is very, very limited."

"Okay, pull up her picture on your phone and tell me what you think."

As I raise my phone to start my search of this infamous actress, the screen switches to an incoming call – Farrow McNiler. I swipe the answer icon.

"Farrow. What's up?"

"Jacko, I hate to call ya on a day off, but I'm down a server tonight. Any chance yer willing to come in today? Pick up an extra shift? I can switch ya with someone for yer Friday shift if ya want."

"How long of a shift?"

"'til 9."

I quickly open my wallet. Cash reserves are fine, but with Nick wanting to go school shopping tomorrow and only the stars know what else that might entail, it wouldn't be a bad idea to pick up another shift. Not to mention it's a Wednesday, so the likelihood of the shift being a rough one is little to none. Decent enough tips to make Thursday's expeditions more manageable, not busy enough to make me want to switch out my Friday shift. Not to mention, Z.

"Yeah, sure, I can come in, but I'll keep my Friday shift. I can be there in, like, an hour? Maybe a little more?"

"You're sure, lad?"

"Yes, Farrow, I'm sure. You need Nick?"

"Not unless he wants to."

"Give me a sec." I move the phone away from my mouth and cover it with my hand. "You want to work?"

Nick laughs. "Hell no, man. I've got a date tonight; I'm not rescheduling that."

I'm about to relay the message to Farrow before he interrupts me. "I heard. I'll see you in an hour and a half?"

"Yep, see you then." I hang up the phone.

Khalan runs their hands through their hair. "Goddamn it, Jack. I thought we were hanging out today."

"Well, if we're going school shopping tomorrow, we'll need this reprieve or we'll want to kill Nick."

Khalan thinks about this for a second, then points both index fingers at me. "Not a bad call, actually. But you're buying coffee tomorrow. No questions asked."

I stand up and elegantly bow. "As you command, my highborn friend."

All three of us leave the entertainment room after I turn off the TV. I shout to my parents that I picked up a shift. Mom makes a fuss about me not being home for dinner, but Dad quickly remedies the exaggerated catastrophe with the promise of a date night. I laugh at him as I change into my classic Tommy Bahamas short sleeve button up with the Lucy's logo and grab a new pack of pens I picked up the other day. My phone vibrates due to a text from Z.

Z: I'm. So. Bored.

Me: Ugh, that's the worst. Boyfriend busy?

Z: Opposite. Being a clingy asshole. Not how I want to spend my day.

Then why don't you just break up with him? I think to myself. I even type out the message, but choose to erase the whole thing and inform her of my change of plans instead.

Me: Well, if you're not busy, I picked up a shift today. Working until 9.

Z: OH! Beach after? Maybe take a little walk?

Me: Done deal. I'll grab a couple Eastbounds in to go cups.

Z: What a gentleman! See you then!

I smile as I shove my phone and billfold in my pockets, grab my keys from my dresser, and make my way downstairs.

"Bye, Mom! I promise I'll make dinner tomorrow night if you're not mad at me!" I yell as I make my way to the garage.

"Deal! Have a good shift, sweetie!"

"Make the big bucks, son!" My dad shouts from his office.

"Copy that, sir!"

My drive to Lucy's is pretty uneventful, traffic is only bad once I get closer to Cocoa. Once I get there, I quickly clock in and tie my apron around my waist. The shift is uneventful, as I predicted. There are a few customers that are, in a nutshell, the worst. But not the worst I have ever encountered. They don't ruin the shift, but they certainly don't make it. I get a good amount in tips – I don't typically count until I get home but my best guess is somewhere close to $200 – but I'm not really focused on that either. I'm mostly focused on the upcoming beach walk with Z. I'm almost jumping out of my shoes by the time 9:00pm comes around. When I finally get off work and have retrieved the drinks, I can see Z on the beach.

She smiles when I get closer, and my heart skips a beat. She's not wearing her big hat today, but has instead opted for a ball cap from the University of Alaska Southeast. She's wearing leggings and a long sleeve shirt, her hair loosely pulled back into a ponytail.

"You like UAS?" I ask, handing her one of the cups.

"I like the design. I collect college hats, actually."

I raise an eyebrow. "Oh? That's… not the oddest thing I've heard of people collecting."

Z hits my arm. "You were totally going to say something like 'that's an odd thing to collect,' weren't you?!"

I smile back at her. "I mean, possibly."

We laugh for moment and take sips of our drinks before walking south along the beach head.

"Decent drive out here?" I ask, not sure what to talk about.

Z shrugs. "Would've been nicer if my boyfriend stopped interrupting my music with a phone call every ten minutes."

"You didn't pick up?"

"I did the first few times. But he was being really unfair and pissing me off. So, I just sent him to voicemail from then on."

"What's this boyfriend's name?"

"I just call him Pete."

I almost spit out my Eastbound. "You're dating a guy named Pete? What, is he, like, fifty?"

She tries to playfully hit me again, but I dodge out of the way. It was extremely inelegant and Khalan would have been appalled, but they aren't here so I could get away with it.

"No, he's eighteen just like us! And, yes, it may be an older sounding name, but his name is Pete."

I shake my head. "Fair enough."

I laugh again but this time she doesn't join me. Her smile has quickly faded and she's staring at the sand as it shifts under our weight.

"I don't know what I'm doing with him, Jack."

My heart feels cold as I begin to panic. I have never had this conversation with anyone before. Nick basically lives his life with a revolving door of girlfriends. Khalan is asexual so literally no need there. Mona and Lisa have been going steady since they were in ninth grade and I've only seen them argue, like, once? Maybe twice? But never have I heard either of them raise any concern about being with the other.

"What do you mean?" I ask, my brain refusing to say anything else despite the fact I know exactly what she means. We've been talking consistently and she always complains about him. Sure, she has mentioned how sweet he is sometimes, but I don't focus on that. Maybe I should though… I mean, if I'm her friend, shouldn't I help her?

"You know what I mean, Jack… please don't play dumb," she replies, her voice soft and sad.

"I'm sorry… you're right, I know what you mean. Why did you get with him in the first place?"

She shrugged. "We were incredibly close in California. He helped me through some rather big… developments in life. When he moved here a few years ago, I was devastated and confessed that I felt something toward him. He then decided we should try long distance. I came out here every few months to see him since he was busy with school and I used to have a pretty flexible schedule since I was mostly online."

I nod. "But now?"

She's quiet for a moment too long and I look over at her. She has a tear streaking her cheek. "I don't know, Jack. He can be really sweet and charming and funny. And when we're in sync, it's almost magical. But… but now that I'm actually here in Orlando and we can see each other all the time, it's like he's a different person. I've become more like…"

"A possession rather than a person."

Z looks at me, a light smile on her face. "You remembered that text from this morning?"

I nod. "Yeah. It bothered me then and it bothers me now."

Too far, dude. Too far.

Z turns her attention back to the sand. "Sometimes I wish that he was… more… more like… I wish that he was different."

"Why don't you break up with him, Z?"

BRO, WHAT THE HELL!

Z sits down quickly in the sand, dropping her drink. Her hands fly up to her face and she starts sobbing into them.

I immediately feel like I've killed a kitten. The guilt washes over me like a riptide. I quickly get down next to her, pick up her empty to go cup, and try to hand her mine. She laughs in the midst of her sobs and leans against me, turning her head so her tears begin to stain the shoulder of my shirt. I don't move. Not with her being so vulnerable. If I move, I'll ruin everything. But something tells me I should rub her back, so I do and, over the next ten or so minutes, her sobs begin to subside and ease. All that is left is a few double breaths due to the hyperventilation of her cry. We stay like that for a while after as I softly glide my fingertips across her back.

"I don't know, Jack…" Z finally says.

"Don't know what?" I ask, completely forgetting the question I had asked prior.

"I don't know why I don't break up with him… maybe because of the history? Maybe because of how close our families are? I really don't know, Jack… I wish I did."

I nod. Again, I'm at a loss for words. I've never had a girlfriend. I've never even gotten close. My friends have never really needed that kind of advice. My parents have always been happy. I've been lucky that way. Quite fortunate, indeed.

But now I wish I had the words. I wish I had the ability to help her. I wish I could be there for her in a way that was more beneficial than whatever I was doing right now. I hate this feeling of helplessness. I hate this feeling like I am not doing anything – like I can't do anything. I want to hold her close and tell her everything will be okay. I want to tell her what Mom tells me whenever I'm down and out – 'It'll all be okay in the end. If it's not okay, it's not the end.'

I can hear her phone vibrating in her pocket and she sits up. Pulling the phone out, I see the contact briefly – Pete. She swipes the icon and lifts her phone to her ear.

"Hello… I'm fine, Pete… Cocoa… Because I was meeting up with a friend… No, I'm not going to come over… I can see you tomorrow… Okay, when is practice? … Okay, I'll just come over after that… No, I don't want to hang out with them… Because… No, it's not that… Because… No, Pete, would you let me finish? Because I don't like spending time with them and you at the same time… You're a different person when they're around… Need I remind you the last time they came over and treated me like a bar maid? … I'll only come over if it's just us… Thank you… Good night… You, too… Bye."

She hangs up the phone and looks at me, catching a glimpse of the small ring of damp cloth on my shoulder.

"I'm sorry about…"

"Don't apologize. Never apologize. I'm here whenever you need me."

Dude… how cheesy can I be tonight?

"I appreciate that, Jack." She touches my hand and my senses immediately become electrified. "You're a good friend. Sucks that I'm just meeting you now."

I nod. "I feel the same way."

"Help me up? I should go home."

I stand up and help her to her feet. She is more prepared the suddenness of it this time and doesn't fall towards me. Nevertheless, she steps into my space and hugs me tightly.

"Thank you."

I can only nod as I hug her back.

We walk back to our cars – she's only parked a few rows away from me. I open the car door for her when she unlocks it.

"First drinks, then the car door. A true gentleman, if I may say," she says, a genuinely bright and happy smile appearing for the first time since prior to the tears on the beach.

"I do try, believe me."

"I do."

We stand there for a moment, neither of us saying anything and just listening to the dinging of her car alerting us of an open door.

"Z," I finally say, breaking the silence, "Does Pete know about me?"

She shakes her head.

"I just feel weird about these secret rendezvous we have."

"So, you don't want me to come back on Friday?"

"No, that's not what I meant."

"What did you mean then?"

I think for a long moment. I don't really know what I meant. Knowing she has a boyfriend and knowing he doesn't know about me isn't sitting right with me. Not to mention that I can't stop thinking about her when I'm not with her. Not to mention that I often think about that simple kiss on the cheek a few weeks ago. I chastise myself often due to this incredibly corny, cheesy thing to do, but I can't help it. Maybe it's my personality or maybe it's just my ability to read into things way more than I need.

I can't think of an answer. "I don't know, I'm just tired."

"Long shift? Busy?"

I nod despite the fact it wasn't.

"I won't come on Friday if that would make you feel better?"

I can hear the touch of hesitation in her offer as well as the concealed sadness.

"No, Friday is fine. I can grab some drinks again. Want to try something new?"

"Sure! Nothing with coconut in it, okay? I hate coconut."

I let out a light laugh. "I also hate coconut."

Z smiles and my heart thuds a little louder without fail. It happens every time.

"I'm glad we are united by the things we hate. I'll see you Friday."

"See you Friday."

I shut her door once she sits down. She knocks on the window and blows me a kiss. I pretend to catch it and she laughs. I turn and walk away, hearing the start of the car's engine and the bass of a pop song resuming. I wave to her as she drives away and make my way to the Subaru.

I am crazy about Z. And this will be the death of me.

CHAPTER 3

With only a few days left until school resumes in full force, I get antsy. Part of me is going insane with the repetition of the summer, but the other part of me is not looking forward to the repetition of school. It's this weird paradox that really doesn't make any sense, but at the same time totally does.

It's confusing, I know.

It's a Thursday morning and I don't work tonight, which means I have most of the day free. Unfortunately, everyone else does not. Nick's moms are taking him down to the Keys for a long weekend, the last of the summer. Khalan is up in Tallahassee for a boxing thing, not sure if they said tournament or conference or training. Mona and Lisa just got back from their Caribbean trip and are insanely tired from all the relaxing they did (their words not mine). And Z is with Pete today. Not only is the possibility of seeing her completely gone, so is the likelihood she'll text me.

I'm incredibly jealous of Pete. I finally admitted that to myself a few nights ago. I knew that the feeling was there, but I finally accepted its reality and now need to make a choice on what to do next. I can either keep being patient like Khalan advised, or I can give up. It's not like I was or still am looking for a relationship. I mean, I have never been in a relationship. Sure, I've liked girls and girls have liked me, but I never do anything about it. Despite my parents being high school sweethearts, studies show that it is incredibly rare for high school sweethearts to get married. It makes sense, psychologically speaking. Brains aren't done maturing until most people are midway through their twenties. There is so much growth that occurs in college and the immediate years after. People grow differently and cut ties to the things that want to keep them in their old way of things. So, why would I put myself in the situation of getting heartbroken? It doesn't make sense logically and I would prefer to avoid heartbreak at all costs.

But Z is different. Whenever I talk to her, I feel a deep sense of connection. Whenever I see her, my heart flutters and races. Whenever our skin touches, electricity pulses through my body. She has been one of the fastest friends I've ever made and seems to understand how I feel or what I'm saying even when I don't.

Do I remain patient? Or do I surrender and change course?

I don't know. I think the best option is to move on. She's out of my league anyways.

"Jack!" Mom calls from downstairs. "Phone!"

For some odd reason, my parents still insist on having a home phone. Anyone's guess is as good as mine. Dad says it's because he doesn't like having his cell phone number just 'out there in the ether.' Mom likes old school kind of things. I wish we didn't have it. Like, I don't want to leave my room right now. What's in my room? My cell phone.

"JACK!" Mom yells.

"Yeah, I'm coming!" I get up from my desk chair and jog downstairs to take the receiver from her.

"Sounds like the main office at school," she says, handing me the phone.

"Okay, thanks," I reply, thinking of what reason the school could possibly have for getting a hold of me on a Thursday morning before school has even started. "This is Jack."

"Hi, Jack, this is Ms. Presley from the front office. How are you doing? Ready for school?" The sweet, melodic voice of the front receptionist rings in my ear.

"Hi, Ms. Presley. I'm doing well. And yeah, I'm ready for school. Excited for senior year."

"So great to hear! Say, I'm giving you a call because you indicated that you wanted to be a Teacher Assistant this year for Dr. Thurmond. Is this correct?"

"Yes, ma'am. I haven't heard anything about it though and it's not on my schedule."

"Would you still like to be his TA? He's indicated he's very interested."

I smile. Dr. Thurmond is the best teacher at H&H. He's been my favorite since the first day of freshman year. "Absolutely."

"Oh, wonderful! Instead of having a third hour study hall, you'll report to Dr. Thurmond's room to assist him. He requested I put you through if you accepted his offer. Do you have some time to chat with him?"

"Yes, for sure."

"One moment…" I hear some clicking on the phone's number pad and a brief pause before Dr. Thurmond picks up.

"Yes, Janice?"

"Dr. Thurmond, I have Jack on the line with me. Jack, are you still there?"

"Yes, ma'am."

"Alrighty then, I'll leave you both to it! See you on Tuesday, Jack!"

I hear her line disconnect and then a short silence.

"Mr. Connors," Dr. Thurmond states in his low, brassy voice.

"Dr. Thurmond, sir."

"How are you, my good man?! It's been some time."

"I'm doing well, sir. How about you?"

"Just fine, just fine. Looking forward to having the brilliant minds of my students back in the classroom."

"I look forward to AP Government with you, sir!"

"And I with you! Say, I wanted to talk to you about some expectations I have for you this year as my TA. Sorry it took so long to get back to you about that, old sport. I took my girlfriend to Europe for a few weeks before school got going again."

"No worries, sir, I'm just glad I heard from you at all."

"Do you want to do this over the phone? Or can you come in? Or do you not want to step foot in these hallowed halls until it is only absolutely necessary?"

I laugh. "No, sir, I can come in today."

"Marvelous. How long until you can be here?"

"Give me a half hour?"

"Can do."

"I'll probably stop at Wawa on the way there. Do you want anything?"

"If you are offering, a Diet Dr. Pepper would be marvelous."

"Right away, sir."

"See you soon, my young pupil."

I hear the phone click as I pull it away from my ear.

Senior year just got a whole hell of a lot better.

I quickly change out of my basketball shorts and t-shirt into something a little more professional to go to school in. Our uniforms are pretty sophisticated - matching black blazer (optional on hotter days) and dress pants, white button ups, and a black vest with a red and gray chevron tie. On Fridays we can wear jeans with a school logo shirt on. So going in my casual summer attire seems to be a little underdressed to go walking through those halls. I end up choosing a pair of my nicer jeans and one of my non-work Tommy Bahama's. I stop at Wawa - a gas station with a hot deli line in it for those who are not familiar with Southern convenience stores - and pick up a Coke and Diet Dr. Pepper.

I pull into the school about ten minutes earlier than anticipated and make my way inside. I'm met by Ms. Presley, who warmly greets me with smile while opening the door.

"I said I'd see you Tuesday, but here we are! Welcome back, Jack!"

"Thanks, Ms. Presley. I'm guessing Dr. Thurmond told you I'd be coming?"

"Indeed, he did, indeed he did. Come on in. You remember the way to his room I presume?"

"222 still?"

"Good memory! Have fun!"

I nod my thanks and wave at the other office workers. I see the principal and vice principal talking in the middle of the common area. I wave as to not interrupt them and they wave back without stopping their conversation. I've seen this before—Mrs. Julkowski and Mr. Balaban are in a very intense work mode. Once there, it's hard to get them to come out until their task is done.

As I climb the stairs to the second floor of the East Wing, I hear the heavy metal playlist Dr. Thurmond listens to while he works. I'm not really partial to the music, but it always makes me smile. Dr. Thurmond, after all, is the best teacher at H&H and is unapologetically awesome. I pick up my pace as I reach the second floor and hurriedly walk to the room.

"Dr. Thurmond!" I shout over the loud music.

Dr. Thurmond looks up from his laptop, turning down the music when he must realize who I am. "Mr. Jack Connors! Welcome!"

Dr. Ryan Thurmond, a Minnesota born transplant to Florida, is the social studies department chair and teaches AP Government, AP Economics, and AP World History. Standing six foot six with a shining bald head and long, brown beard often braided with Nordic runes, Dr. Thurmond is a certified badass. He graduated from Yale with his PhD when he was twenty-six, not taking a break between his Bachelor's at the University of Minnesota. He wrote a defining paper on the Viking civilization and he is recognized in the Scandinavian countries and Denmark as a true friend to their history. His passion for the subject is unrivaled and can make the most boring concepts of history the greatest thing any student would ever learn. He is undoubtedly the most respected and most liked teacher here at H&H. His classes are brutal, but fun. He is fair, but firm. He listens to heavy metal and has more compassion than a priest. He's the absolute best.

I enter the room with a big smile as he stands up and come around the desk. I stick out my arm and he slams his arm into mine in one of his classic handshakes. We chosen few who are recipients of this said handshake call them Thurmond's Titan Handshake – it's styled after old warrior handshakes where they clasped forearms instead of hands. Our forearms meet with a loud clap and his smile beams down at me.

"My good man, how are you doing?"

"I'm doing well, Dr. Thurmond. It's been a… decent summer I guess."

"Please, sit," Dr. Thurmond says, gesturing to a chair on the other side of the desk from his own. "Tourists bad at Cocoa this year?"

"That's a gentle way of putting it."

He laughs. "I've been meaning to come out to Lucy's one of these nights, but I've been busy with some work on my next paper."

"Still working on that Norse mythology piece?"

"Indeed, I am. Good memory, old sport."

I hand him the Diet Dr. Pepper I had in my plastic bag from Wawa as I crack open my Coke. "Any closer to being done?"

Dr. Thurmond takes a long pull and lets out a low belch. "I'm close. Probably twenty to thirty pages away from completing it. Thankfully, too. The lady isn't a fan on how busy it's been keeping me."

I laugh. He's never really told any of the students who he has been seeing for the past year or so, but I know she's roughly the same age as him and is really into the same nerdy things he is. "So, when do I get to know this infamous lady?"

Dr. Thurmond wags a finger at me. "Ah, when you graduate, Jacko. When you graduate."

I shake my head. "Secrets, secrets, secrets. Did you keep this many secrets from your favorite students before me?"

Dr. Thurmond laughs and claps three times. "Oh, you're a funny one, Jack. You know I don't have favorite students."

Classic Dr. Thurmond.

"What about you, old sport? Any girl in your life?"

I try to keep the reddening of my cheeks to a minimum. Unfortunately, I still feel them burning.

"Ah, there is one!"

"No, not really. I mean, there is. But there isn't." I sit down in the chair he gestured to. "I met her at work and we've been texting a bit and seeing each other after work sometimes, but she's got a boyfriend."

"I see. That is unfortunate."

I shrug. "It is what it is."

"Admitting defeat so easily?"

I nod my head. "It wasn't easy, but yes. It's better if I just move on. Odds aren't exactly in my favor."

Dr. Thurmond looks at me in a long moment of silence with one of his classic, everything-is-a-teachable-moment looks. I brace myself, preparing my brain for one of his analogies.

"England. 1940."

I think for a moment. "World War II. First half of the year or second?"

"Second."

I think again. "My guess you're referring to September 1940. France has surrendered to Hitler and his Nazis. The Soviet Union has a truce with Germany, so they aren't fighting back yet. The US won't be pulled in for another year."

"So, England stands alone?"

"Yes," I reply, trying to recall as much information as I can. "Hitler has his eyes set on a European empire. England is the only real threat left at the time."

"So, what does he do?"

"He launches a massive offensive campaign of bombing England into submission. Millions of tons of explosives were dropped across England in the attempt to force surrender."

"Does it work?"

"No. The sheer force of will of the British people basically endures over Hitler's attempt to entice fear. They hold on for another year until America gets dragged into the war by Japan and they are able to open fronts in North Africa, Italy, and eventually France."

Dr. Thurmond smiles. "Very good. It's an oversimplified answer, but still good. Do you remember who leads them?"

I'll be honest, history isn't my strong suit. Mathematics and science? Oh, hell yeah. I only really like the social studies because of Dr. Thurmond. And he can tell if I don't know something even before I realize I don't know it.

"You don't remember?"

"No, sir."

Dr. Thurmond shrugs. "Your intelligence lies in other subjects. Winston Churchill led England through and out of World War II. One of his most famous speeches was given during The Blitz. This ring a bell? Remember what he said?"

I do this time. "Never surrender."

"'Never give in. Never give in. Never, never, never, never—in nothing, great or small, large, or petty—never give in, except to convictions of honor and good sense.'"

I nod.

"Do you understand what I'm trying to say?"

"I shouldn't give up on this girl. But isn't that forceful? Isn't that, like, the opposite of what Churchill was trying to get at?"

Dr. Thurmond nods. "Indeed. What you need to do is listen to what your heart thinks and what your convictions are. I have rarely seen you infatuated enough with a girl to visibly turn red. This one must be special. And if she is that special to you, I wouldn't give up. You shouldn't give up."

I nod. "But her boyfriend?"

He thinks for a moment. "Be patient. Only time will tell."

I shrug. "I suppose."

Dr. Thurmond smiles. "Only time will tell, old sport. Now, what I meant to talk to you about was my expectations for being my TA this year."

I talk with him for about another half an hour, forty-five minutes until he feels like I sufficiently understand what he wants me to do for him. It's pretty basic stuff – making copies, grading multiple choice, true-or-false, and matching sections on tests, helping him with explaining things to students, and other things similar to that. I get copies of his teaching materials so I can freshen up and become more familiar with the content so I can actually help the younger students. It's going to be a lot of work, but I know a recommendation letter from him will really help me get into MIT. His sister is a professor in the engineering program there, which would also be a huge plus.

As I'm leaving school, my phone vibrates.

A text from Z.

Z: Busy?

Me: Just got done meeting up with the teacher I'm TA-ing for this year.

Z: Fun! Work tomorrow?

I smile unintentionally.

Me: Yeah, until 9.

Z: Beach?

Me: Sure!

Z: Cool.

Something's wrong. She's never this blunt.

Me: You good?

Z: Not really.

Me: Boyfriend?

Z: Yeah… I don't really want to talk about it though. I'll see you tomorrow.

Shit, I think to myself. *Something must have happened.*

Me: I'm here to talk if you need to, Z.

Z: Thanks, piano man. I'll tell you about it tomorrow.

With the promise of seeing Z after work, the rest of my Thursday and Friday morning fly by. When I get to work, it's already busy. The last Friday before school starts is always really chaotic with families coming out for final hurrahs and friend groups making the best of their final weekend of freedom. And I make bank since everyone is feeling pretty generous. It's a win-win situation for everyone. Even Farrow is happy about it as he makes his rounds around his establishment, wishing kids good luck on their upcoming year of education and taking the opportunity to flirt with the single moms.

By 9:00, I've made close to $400 and feeling pretty good about it. As I'm walking out, the bartender slides me my virgin Estirinian Specials – a drink of Farrow's own concoction of special fruits and spices. I'm not sure what fruits are in here or where he gets them, but it's one of the tastiest things he's added to the menu in a long time. I jog out to the beach with drinks in hand to where I see Z, sitting with her back to me and her face to the cold ocean air. I slow down, hoping she's not crying.

"Hey, Jack," Z says, her voice flat and unexcited. She must have heard me coming.

"Hey," I casually reply, lowering myself down to sit next to her. "I got a different drink tonight." I hand her the cup.

"Thanks," she takes a sip, then looks at the cup. "Fuck, that's good."

I nod. "New drink Farrow added just last week. A little late in the season, but it's selling fast."

Z nods, her eyes sad and avoiding making contact with mine.

"Z?"

"I think Pete's cheating on me."

I don't say anything for a long moment. I'm not even sure what to say. That's some heavy shit, what am I supposed to do with that?

"Why do you think that?"

Z lets out a long sigh. "While we were hanging out today, he kept getting Snaps from someone. Pretty sure I saw a girl's name. Pretty sure I saw Shelly."

I shake my head in disbelief. "She's one of your closest friends though, right? She wouldn't do that to you."

She shrugs. "Pete's a popular guy. I don't doubt he's got his eye on whoever is available to him. And I'm sure Shelly is interested. She's attracted to popularity."

I slowly nod my head. "I don't think Pete would do that though."

Why am I supporting this guy?

Putting her cup down in the sand, Z brings her knees back into her chest and puts her chin on them. "I didn't think Pete would do a lot things that he's done. But I was wrong before."

Something bothers me in the way she's said that phrase. Alarm bells go off in my head as my mind wanders to the worst possible meaning behind the words.

"Z, has he… ya know… abused you?"

Z turns her head so her ear is resting on her knee and gives me a light smile. "No, Jack. He hasn't abused me. That's not what I meant. But I appreciate the concern. It's cute."

Part of me thinks I need to start wearing make up around her due to the number of times I blush. "Just making sure."

Z relaxes her legs and lets them stretch out. She moves closer to me and rests her head on my shoulder. I force my body to not freeze and tense up, trying to be as relaxed as she is. I slowly tilt my head so that it is resting on hers. I wait a moment to see if she moves. She doesn't and we stay like this for a bit, listening to the crashing waves and the faint hint of assorted music coming from the tiki bars and restaurants.

This is wrong. I shouldn't be doing this with her. She has a boyfriend. I don't want to be the 'other guy.' I mean, I was just defending the guy and now I have his girlfriend's head resting on my shoulder? That's absurd. My parents taught me better than this. They always say honesty, integrity, and intentionally positive behavior are better than any feeling another person can give you. This feels wrong.

Yet, it feels right. It feels natural. It's Z. I can't stop thinking about her. I can't stop wanting her to break up with Pete and be with me. I want to be her boyfriend so, so badly. It weighs on my mind like an anchor in the surf.

But I suppress it. I shove it away and try to forget about it. I'll pour myself into piano again. I'll work on that piece for the performance coming up. I'm getting close to getting it, I think. It's complex so it should suffice.

"This is probably going to be our last rendezvous for a while, isn't it?" Z asks in a whispered tone.

"What do you mean?"

"School starts soon. You start Tuesday, right?"

I sigh. "Yeah. I suppose this is our last one. I don't work Fridays during the school year. Just Saturdays and Sundays."

She sighs as well. "I have some other obligations on the weekends. It'll be hard to get away."

"I'll still text you."

I can feel her cheek muscle tense as she smiles.

"I'll still text you, too."

"Where are you going to school?"

I feel her shrug. "Right now, I'm enrolled in two different schools. Just trying to figure out which one fits best with what I want."

"What do you want, Z?"

I feel her head shift and I raise my head up so I can see her. Her eyes are sad. She looks like she's lost in the wilderness with no compass, almost pleading to me for answers that I do not have.

"I don't know, Jack. I don't know."

We don't say anything after that. I eventually put my head back on hers since she hadn't moved, but something about that look she gave me haunts me. Something about that last 'I don't know' haunts me. I don't bring it up, though. I don't want to sour this last late evening escapade. I want to tell her that I'm going to miss her. To not forget about me. But I don't. I don't want to sound desperate.

I'll keep being here for her when she needs me. I'll hold fast and be patient. And maybe, just maybe, something will happen.

Maybe.

CHAPTER 4

The first day of school is always a super weird time. On the one hand, I don't want summer to end. I enjoy making more money on a consistent basis and the freedom of being able to go wherever, whenever, with whomever I want. But school also means I get to consistently see my friend group rather than intermittently throughout the summer. We are fortunate to have lunch together every single day and, since we are seniors and all rather intelligent, means that we have almost all our classes together. Sure, there are some exceptions here and there – I'm not in choir with Lisa and Nick; Mona, Nick, Khalan, and I don't have advisory together; and I am certainly not in the crazy ass, advanced gym class Khalan and Mona decided to 'conquer' their senior year. Nonetheless, I think this final year at H&H will be like none other.

I pick up Nick and Khalan before school and we roll in with ten minutes to spare before the first bell. First class is AP Government, a class that all of us are taking together. We listen to some new pop music Nick has found and Khalan and I simply deal with it – Nick really likes making sure the only music played in any car is up to his 'high standards.' Not really sure I agree with any of his systems of measurement, but I don't try to fight him on this. It's really not worth it.

"Okay, but, like what if she wants to be friends? I'll have to say yes and show her everything there is to know about H&H," Nick proclaims, getting out of the car and shutting the door. He won't shut up about this new girl coming to school.

"Dude, she's a famous actress. There is no way, *no way* she's going to even notice you," Khalan replies, shutting the front passenger door and tossing their apple core at Nick.

"I will reject your realistic assumption and substitute it with my own fantastical expectations!"

I lock the car and start walking towards the main entrance. "How about we just keep our status quo for the next nine months and get the hell out of here?"

Khalan points at me. "Now that, *that* is something I can get behind."

We fist bump as Nick throws his hands dramatically in the air. "I quit! I. Quit!"

"First day of school and you have him quitting already?!" A familiar voice calls from a few cars away.

I turn and see Mona and Lisa getting out of Mona's car.

"We've truly broken him!" I shout back.

Mona and Lisa come running over and we all exchange hugs. Mona Balaskas is the star basketball player here at H&H. Standing at over six foot three, she can dunk on just about anyone. She shaves the sides of her head and keeps the top brown hair at around six inches and flips it to the side. She's built like a train and can wrestle Khalan to the ground. In fact, she has on multiple different occasions. She never wears skirts or dresses, just pants and hates uniforms with every fiber of her being. Today, she's protesting the dress code by wearing a bright pink tie with no blazer and has apparently cut off the sleeves of her button up. Will she get dress-coded? Probably. Will she care? Nope.

Lisa is very different. Lisa Johnson is one of H&H's many theatre divas. She is probably the most dramatic person south of the Mason Dixon. She has long blonde hair that she is constantly putting in crazy ass hair dos and accessorizes to the max. She's incredibly witty and hates dim-witted people. Whenever her and Nick are around, it is an overdramatic, crazy, hilarious affair. She also enjoys wearing crazy make up. Today, her outfit is accentuated by red wings around her eyes and black lipstick.

Which is very obvious on Mona's lips and neck.

"Darling, here, you're still a little dirty," Lisa says, handing Mona a wet wipe.

"Thanks, babe." Mona takes the wipe and tries her best to get rid of the black lipstick marks on her neck. She succeeds with her neck, but not so much with her lips. Khalan and I bump one another and start snickering.

Mona looks at us with a dead stare. "Something funny, gents?"

Khalan squares up. "Absolutely hysterical."

Mona and Khalan start play fighting in the parking lot, trying to grapple one another to the ground.

"Lisa, my beautiful angel, how are you?!" Nick says throwing his arms around Lisa.

"Oh, Nicky, just fine and dandy, my dear. So ready for this year to be over!"

They do the whole European, kiss on both cheeks thing. Like I said, they are incredibly extra.

"Love, it's not even first period on the first day!" Nick exclaims, stepping back. "How will you survive?!"

"Ugh, I will simply have to pour all my efforts and energy into the fall play and spring musical." Khalan grunts as Mona has out maneuvered them and pinned them against the Subaru. "And I suppose my brute of a girlfriend."

"You know you love me, Lisa," Mona says, picking Khalan up off the car.

"Guys, does it have to be on my car?"

Mona punches me in the shoulder. "Only car that works for the job, Jacko."

I roll my shoulder and my eyes at the same time. "Dude, come on."

Lisa takes my arm and I bend it so she can delicately place her hand on the crook, one of her favorite ways to walk with just about anyone since it makes her feel like she's from a 'better time.' "Jack, my dearest pianist, Nick has told me all about this mysterious lady you have been flirting with and fawning over all summer long."

I roll my eyes. "Milady Lisa, it has been but a month." We talk to each like this often since she wants me to become 'more dramatic.' "I will have to give that Nicholas a good licking after school."

"Oh, don't hit him too hard, chap. He's such a gentle soul." Her and I laugh together as Mona throws Nick in a head lock. We make our way inside and greet others around us. Mona fist bumps the other basketball players as Lisa rolls her eyes at 'the savages.'

I forgot to mention – Lisa hates athletes. Except for Mona. Mona is her kryptonite and they have a lot of... *fun* together.

Our lockers aren't anywhere close to one another, but I manage to miss my combination three times and Nick is by my side once I finally do get the stubborn thing open.

"Planner?"

"Nick, I don't need you to micromanage me at school. Yes, I have my planner."

"Laptop?"

"Dude, seriously. Of course, I have my laptop."

"I'm just trying to make sure you..." Nick unexpectedly stops talking.

I look at him. He's staring with his mouth open at something on the other side of my locker door. "Nick? You good?"

He just nods at whatever he's looking at.

I close my locker door to see what it is.

And it's a who.

"Z! What the hell! Hi!"

"Jack! Hi!" Z is standing there in a H&H uniform and skirt. She throws her arms around me in a huge hug. I return the embrace and start laughing.

"What are you doing here?! I didn't know that H&H was one of the two schools you were in enrolled in."

She jumps back half a step, her hands on my shoulders with a big smile on her face. "Well, piano man, you never did ask."

I shake my head. "I'm sorry, I totally forgot to ask! But hi! Welcome! It's so good to see you!"

"And you! Can I see your schedule?"

I pass her the sheet of paper with my eight class periods listed on it. She grabs it and looks it over, lifting her own schedule to compare. I feel something poking my arm and I look over to Nick.

"Oh, yeah, sorry. Z, this is Nick, my best friend. The one I've told you about. Nick, this is…"

"Zendaya Thompson. Star of *A Pirate's Heart* and several other TV shows and an upcoming Netflix original movie."

I snap my head back to Z, who is simply smiling. She sticks her hand out to Nick. "Hi, it's nice to meet you. Jack has told me a lot about you!"

Nick pushes me against the locker. "What the actual hell, Jack! First, you tell Zendaya Thompson 'all about me' – all good things, right?" Z nods and tries to get a response out, but Nick's not done. "Second, and by God man, you don't tell me the girl you have been talking about for the last *month* is THE Zendaya Thompson!"

I look back at Z. "Wait, hold on, seriously?"

Z nods. "Yeah, Jack, I'm surprised you didn't know. I thought you were just being nice about it."

Mom has always told me I'm a bit clueless. I've always denied it. But now I look dually stupid. First, for telling my mom she's been wrong all the time. Second, for not realizing that Z is Zendaya Thompson.

"I don't really watch TV."

Z laughs. "Yes, so you've said. Is this going to change our little thing we've got going on?"

I shake my head. "No, it won't. Only if you make it weird."

She hits my arm and turns back to Nick. "Yes, Nick, all the things Jack has said about you have been overwhelmingly positive. He's spoken very highly of you."

Nick sighs. "Oh, thank God."

"Nick, don't make it weird," I say.

"Yeah, Nick, if I can't make it weird, *you* can't make it weird," Z teases.

"Babe! Who you talking to?!"

I know that voice. I hate that voice. And he just called someone babe. And it wasn't me. For sure, it wasn't me. And it wasn't Nick. Which meant it was Z.

"Just a friend, Pete!"

"Son of a bitch," I mutter under my breath as I watch Pete come over to Z and wrap his arm around her shoulder.

Pete is none other than Pietro Dimitrov, my long-time rival here at H&H. Pietro is H&H's prodigy boy. 1589 on the SAT. 36 on the ACT. Running back for the football team with more rushing yards than any previous player in school's history. His whole story is pretty much rags to riches kind of thing. See, his grandparents defected to the United States during the Cold War. The money they received from the defection was then well invested in Xerox and Johnson & Johnson. His grandfather was also a super important scientist for something or other, so the accumulated wealth made his family quite rich here in the states. His parents moved to Florida around the same time I moved here and have basically given him everything he needs. And he knows it. He knows he is smart and rich. One of *those* kids. He flaunts it.

Which makes him the biggest jackass I have ever met.

"Well, well, well," Pietro says, shaking his head at me. "Look who it is. Little Jackie C. How are you, man?"

"Just fine, Pietro."

Z smiles wide. "Oh my gosh, how great! You guys know each other?"

Pietro smirks. "Oh, yeah. Jackie and I go way back."

I don't say anything but my fists are clenched to the point where my knuckles are stark white.

See, Pietro has made it his point to make my life miserable. Humiliation tactics. Throwing shit at me – not actual shit but I'm sure he will get there someday. Recently, he showed up at Lucy's with eight or so of his friends, stayed for the maximum amount of time, took up half of my section, and left exactly three cents for the tip. Missed out seating multiple groups of people who left the other waiters more than three hundred dollars. Between the two of them. And Pietro knew it.

"I didn't know this was Pete, Z," I say as calmly as I can.

"Yeah, I would've said something if I knew you knew each other!"

Nick shakes his head. "No, probably better you didn't."

"Shut it, Nicole," Pietro says, menacingly.

Nick glares at him. "That's not my name, you fucking cu…"

"Nick, stop. Not on the first day."

Pietro shoves me. "Why not on the first day? Come on, Jack, it's senior year."

"Pete, stop, don't be a dick," Z says, trying to pull him back.

"Babe, no, it's okay, we're just having fun!"

"Can I jump in on this fun, Pietro? Or is one more too much?"

Khalan. Thank God.

Pietro eyes them and I can see his mind changing. "No, I think we're good, Khal. See you in gym." He looks back at me. "See you around, Jackie C."

He tries to turn Z away, but she stands her ground.

"Babe. Let's go. You don't need to spend time with these… people."

Z laughs. "Oh, Pete, go to math. I've got first period AP gov with Jack. I'll see you after school."

"But, babe, what about…"

"After school!"

She grabs my arm, twists me around, and begins to walk away, still arm in arm with me. I look at her and see her face getting redder and redder. Whether it's out of embarrassment, anger, or a combination of the two, I can't tell.

"Z…"

"I didn't know."

"Z…"

"Jack, I didn't know."

"Yeah, how could you have known? We didn't really talk much about school."

She nods and I can see her bottom lip tremble. I take her by the shoulders and stop her on the landing between the first and second floors. "Z. It's okay. I've dealt with Pietro for four years now. You didn't know."

"I just don't want you to stop being my friend, Jack…"

"That's not going to happen." I say, guiding her back towards the stairs. I want to make a joke about how I will just have to live with the fact she has a terrible taste in men, but something tells me that is not the thing to say at the moment.

We enter Dr. Thurmond's room where Mona and Lisa have already saved us some seats. When Z enters the room on my arm, Lisa's mouth drops.

"Jack, do you know who this is?"

"Yeah, it's Z," I say, trying to play it cool.

"Yeah, as in Zendaya Thompson! Oh my gosh! HI!" Lisa says, basically yelling at Z. "My name is…"

"No, wait. Let me guess. Elaborate eye makeup – which is beautiful, by the way – and a boisterous personality… You're Lisa… Lisa Johnson? Right?" Z asks, extending a hand.

Lisa takes Z's hand and shakes it but turns to Mona. "Babe, did you hear that? She said my eye makeup is beautiful!"

Mona shakes her head, stands, and offers her hand to Z. "I heard. Mona Balaskas, Lisa's girlfriend."

Z shakes Mona's hand. "Yeah, and you're a star basketball player here in the Orlando area, right? My Uncle Simon loves high school basketball and is a big fan of yours. Not in a weird way."

Mona raises an eyebrow. "How is that not weird?"

"Well," Z says, rubbing the back of her neck. "He's, uh, not interested in women."

"Oh, so a fellow gay. Love that! I'd love to meet him, then."

Something clicks in my mind. "Hang on, hang on. Did you just say you have a gay uncle named Simon?"

Z nods. "Yeah, I'm living with him while my parents are still out in Cali."

"He wouldn't happen to be Gay Simon, would he?"

Gay Simon – his insistence on the nickname, not mine – is my next-door neighbor. He and my parents get along really well and he's been over a bunch this past summer for barbeques. He's been talking about his niece that's been living with him, but she was always gone for cook out days.

"That's what he tells the neighbors to call him, yeah?" Z's eyes go wide. "Are you in my neighborhood?!"

I start laughing. "Yeah, apparently! In fact, I'm literally right next door."

Z joins in my laughter as my friend group shakes their heads.

I now accept that I am incredibly clueless.

Z turns her attention back towards Lisa. "Okay, but seriously, I need you to teach me how to do that makeup. I *love* it. How long did that take?"

Lisa's smile is now the widest I have ever seen. She takes Z away from me and guides her to a seat next to her, describing her morning routine and eye makeup adventures. I catch Z's eye and she winks at me. I smile and shake my head, turning to Nick, Khalan, and Mona, who all have their eyebrows raised in the 'I can't believe you didn't put that stuff together' kind of looks.

"Okay, yeah, I know…"

"Dude, you're so incredibly naïve," Mona says, laughing harder than I've ever heard her laugh.

"Ms. Balaskas. Care to share the humor?"

I jump as Dr. Thurmond's voice is way closer than I thought.

"Just Jack, sir."

"I didn't believe he had a comedic bone in his body." He nudges me and chuckles.

"He doesn't, sir," Khalan says. "He's just very clueless."

Dr. Thurmond shakes his head. "And I chose him as my TA. Pity."

My friends all laugh with Dr. Thurmond as he heads to the front of the room to start class. Everything goes pretty normally throughout the day – lots of syllabi, rules, expectations, and all that first day mumbo-jumbo. Z and I have a couple classes together, but after first period she gets whisked away by Pete. She had said after school, but I'm sure Pete said some sort of charming thing about whatever to get her to not be mad at him anymore. I see them kissing in the hall before lunch and my jealousy could never be higher. I try to shrug it off, but the image replays in my mind throughout the day when my brain isn't engaged with something academic. Luckily, I have piano after school today so that will help distract me from… that.

For how first days go, it was pretty decent. On the way back to our cars, Khalan and Mona are discussing the gym class they are in while Nick and Lisa talk about choir. I just want to get going to piano. Clear my head.

"Jack!" Z's voice rings out from a few lanes away. "Bye! I'll see you tomorrow!"

"Bye! Yeah, tomorrow!" I call back and wave, but slowly put my hand down when I see Pete open the door to his Honda Civic Type R.

"See you tomorrow, Conners."

"Alright, *Pete*."

Khalan gives me a look as Pietro gets in his car and drives off.

"Dude. If you can't win that fight, don't pick it. I can't always be there like I was this morning," Khalan says, shaking his head.

"Sorry, I'm just…"

"Jealous he's with Z. Yeah, I caught that." Khalan stops by the Subaru and stops me from opening the door. "Jack. Don't try and push it, man."

I nod and slowly open the car door. "This is going to be one hell of year."

"Only if you keep that attitude, Jack."

I sit down and turn my car on. My phone vibrates and I unlock it to find a text from Z.

Z: I'm sorry…

Me: About what? You have nothing to apologize for.

Z: I know… but still… I didn't realize you two didn't get along.

Me: You had no reason to suspect anything. Please don't apologize. It's all good.

Z: I guess, I'll see you around…

Senior year is going to be a bitch.

CHAPTER 5

There is something about the sound of many keyboards being typed on and mice being clicked that brings me great happiness. It's truly one of the purest forms of ASMR. It's a Sunday afternoon and school only started about a week ago, but my friends and I are applying for our first round of colleges. My checklist is printed and lying flat on the carpet next to me - I didn't want to sit on the couch because my legs are stiff from sitting all week. I worked last night as well so that doesn't help things much either, but luckily Lisa's pool house is an insanely comfortable location to hang out in. It's not one of those grungy pool houses that has just a hard floor and some walls where people can change and adjust the pool's pumps. It's got vinyl floors on one half for those who are drying off and whatever, but it also has a full kitchen, carpeted living space, TV, internet, and a spare bedroom. It's more like a small guest house than a pool house, but Lisa insists we call it a pool house since it has the pumps and stuff for the pool and what it is primarily used for is changing and getting supplies for pool parties.

But today, we all are sitting on our computers, eating popcorn, chips, and other junk food, sipping sodas, and applying for colleges. There is the occasional conversation or joke, but most of the time we are all focused. This is our time to shine and figure out what we are going to do with our lives.

I'm applying to MIT, Stanford, UC-Berkeley, Carnegie-Mellon, and University of Michigan – Ann Arbor – to start with that is. Like I've said before, I'm looking to get into an engineering program where I can develop the skills to create a new, energy-efficient, eco-friendly, emission free (if possible) mode of transportation. I've got some ideas already and I'll need to start somewhere. I've always had really high ambitions for myself and my parents support me in this endeavor. Mom really wants me to stay here in Florida and try to get into UF or FSU, but I really just want out of Florida at this point in my life.

Surprisingly, Nick is the most focused out of all of us. He's applying for stuff on the West Coast, primarily UCLA or the University of Portland. He's not sure what he wants to do yet, but he wants to be in a more 'free-thinking society of like-minded people.' We all thought he was going to be the loudest of us all, but he's laser-focused today. I've even thrown popcorn at him a few times and the only reaction I received is a quick, icy glare.

We all jump when the intercom sounds in the living room.

"Ms. Lisa," the voice of Lisa's butler, Jesper, sounds out over the speaker.

"Yes, Jesper?" Lisa answers.

I should have mentioned this – Lisa's family is stupid rich. She can trace her genealogy back to some of the original settlers of Florida who got big into cattle ranching, then real estate, then basically running a ton of different entities down here to the point where most of her family's money is decades old. Luckily, Lisa isn't super snobby – don't get me wrong, she can be – and her parents actually provide four scholarships for students at H&H.

"A Ms. Thompson is here. She says you invited her. May I send her your way, ma'am?"

I look at Lisa, my eyes wide. "You invited Z?!"

I'm in no condition to be seen. I thought it was just going to be the five of us so I'm wearing grubby clothes – a pair of gray basketball shorts with a bunch of little holes and a t-shirt that really should be rags. Not exactly the outfit I want the biggest crush of my life to see me in.

"Of course, I did, she has to apply for colleges as well. That is her plan - go to college and get a degree, I thought you knew that!" Lisa scolds, before turning her attention back to the intercom. "Yes, please, Jesper, that would be lovely, thank you."

"Are you in need of any further refreshments?"

Lisa scans the room. "No, Jesper, thank you, dear. You don't have to worry about us, we can get things ourselves if we run out."

"Only doing my job, ma'am."

"I know, and I appreciate it so much. If it suits you, I bought you a tea earlier and it's in the fridge."

"You are too kind, Ms. Lisa."

"Anything for my favorite butler!"

He's their only butler.

A few moments pass and the door to the pool house opens. In walks Z, laptop bag hanging off her right shoulder and a forty-ounce Wawa cup in her hand.

"Zendaya, darling!" Lisa gets up from the couch and gives Z a hug and they exchange a European greeting. She's wearing black biker shorts and the same style crop top that she was wearing at Lucy's the first time I met her, but this time it's red. She's chosen to wear some Hey Dudes and easily slips out of them once Lisa gives her enough space to do so.

"Lisa, thanks for inviting me!" Z says, scanning the room and resting her eyes on me. I can see and feel her scan me as I sit stretched out on the floor. "Jack, what in the name of everything that is good and holy are you wearing?"

I can feel my cheeks begin to burn. "It's a Sunday afternoon and I don't have to work. I wanted to maximize my comfort."

Z laughs, shakes her head, then makes her way in my direction. "You look ridiculous. Those shorts must be ancient."

I'm fairly certain she's going to take the loveseat that I'm leaning against, but she decides instead to sit down next to me, taking out her computer and booting it up.

"I admit, they're a little old. But they have that really comfortable, used feel, ya know?"

She nods. "I do, actually. I was wearing an older pair of short shorts that I just love earlier, but thought they would have been a little too embarrassing to wear in front of other people."

I look up from my computer and see that she is holding in a laugh. I drop my jaw with a smile. "Excuse me, are you bullying me for my outfit?"

She can only nod before bursting into a fit of laughter. I bump her with my shoulder and she shoves me playfully, but just hard enough where I almost lose my computer off my lap and I need to catch myself with one hand. More laughter peels when I notice that I have spilled my drink. I'm lucky that the edge of the carpeted area was close and fluid has only spilled out over the vinyl floor. I quickly get up and run to get some paper towels and slide across the smooth floor in my socks. Z is finally calming down by the time that I've come back and cleaned up the spill.

"I'm so sorry," she says, wiping her eyes and letting out a couple of more chuckles. "I shouldn't be laughing."

"It's okay," I reply, shaking my head as I walk back to the kitchen to throw away the used paper towels. "While I'm up, does anyone want any more snacks? Any refills on soda?"

"It's pop, dude," Khalan remarks, not looking up from his computer.

"I disagree," Z says. "This is a pop." She makes a popping noise with her mouth by curling her lips in, pressing them together, then quickly shooting them forward and slightly opening her mouth. "Soda is something you drink."

"Ugh, not you too!" Mona cries, arcing her neck so it rests in Lisa's lap.

"Not me too?" Z repeats.

"Yes, Jack says the same damn thing."

I smile while grabbing a thing of popcorn. "I only say the same thing because it's right."

"Hey! Something we agree on that's not something we hate!" Z exclaims.

We've both joked with one another that we found friendship not in the things we enjoy, but in the things we both hate. Chick-Fil-A. Tourists. Country music. Los Angeles. Miami. Teslas. And, of course, Florida summers. We are trying to find more similarities in what we enjoy in our lives and we have found a few things. We'll get there.

"Can you grab me some of those chips, Jack? Please?" Z asks as I'm about to leave the kitchen area. Setting down my popcorn, I quickly dump a bunch of corn chips into a larger bowl so we can share. When I sit down next to her, she takes the bowl and pops a few into her mouth, smiling her thanks. I smile back, feeling the warmth in my heart start to emulate into my chest.

"Where are you applying, Z?" Khalan asks, still not looking up from their screen.

"Oh, here and there. A few places out in California. A couple on the East Coast. And a few in the Midwest."

"What are you wanting to study?" I ask, taking a few sips of my new soda.

"Oh, I'm not sure. My mom wants me to keep going with the whole acting thing - wants me to go to Juilliard or California Institute of Arts."

"Okay, but what do you want?" I find myself asking aloud. I thought I had simply thought of the question but it is now out there in the open.

Z looks at me and smiles. "Not many people ask me that. Everyone assumes I want to be an actress once I'm done with high school. I mean, I still have directors and producers asking me to audition for roles in both movies and TV shows. But... I don't know... I don't really want to do that for the rest of my life."

I instinctually close my computer to pay more attention to her. "What do you mean?"

She shuts her computer as well and shifts so she is sitting more on her side and her arm is resting on the cushion of the couch, the supported arm now propping up her head. "Well, it's really time consuming. I mean, even for cameos in films and shows can take several days. Filming as a lead role feels like it never ends. It leaves very little time for me to be... well... me. And I really only became an actress because my parents wanted me to. I mean, when Zendaya - the one in *Spider-Man* and *Dune* - when she got big, my parents were like 'Oh my gosh, our daughter's name is Zendaya too! Maybe she can become an actress!' So, they auditioned me in a number of things at a young age and I started getting attention. A few years ago, I landed my role on *APL* and felt like I was obligated to my parents to keep going."

"But you've never really wanted it?"

"No, I wouldn't say that," Z says, shaking her head. "There were times that I loved what I was doing. I had a lot of fun. I've made some really good friends. I met Pete when he was an extra on *APL*. But the number of times when I wanted to be done far outweigh those good things."

I nod. "What would you want to be doing?"

Z looks off into the distance for a moment, running a hand through her hair as she thinks. "I want to help people."

"How?"

She shrugs. "Nursing? Therapy? Maybe?"

"All good things."

"I also have thought about talent-seeking or talent-requisition. I like helping people discover their talents and gifts."

"I think that's very cool," I say with a smile.

She touches my arm. "Thanks. And you're still thinking about engineering? Where have you applied so far?"

I show her my list - so far MIT and Stanford are crossed out.

She takes the list and scans the colleges. "Would you really want to go to Stanford? That's on the West Coast - not really sure if you would like it much better than here."

I shrug. "It's a top-rated school in engineering. I mean, my goal is MIT. But Stanford is a good back up."

Z nods. "I think you'd make a cute engineer."

My cheeks burn again as she laughs and shifts back to a normal sitting position. She bumps me with her shoulder, but doesn't really shift her body weight back so she's half leaning on me. She reopens her computer again and I can see a few tabs open including Harvard, University of Minnesota, University of Michigan - Ann Arbor, and New York University. I open my computer again and resume my application to Carnegie-Mellon.

But my brain isn't focused on the applications anymore. I can feel the bare skin of her side resting against my arm. I feel creepy focusing on the sensation, but don't have the nerve or desire to move my arm. The feeling that overwhelms my brain is intoxicating and mind numbing. The only conceivable way I can distract myself now is through conversation. But I only want to talk to her.

What should I ask her? Favorite food? French fries, I already know that. Favorite comfort? Funny gifs, damn it. There has to be something to talk about before my heart explodes.

"What's your favorite TV show?" I blurt out. This isn't a great conversation for me. I really only know one TV show and it's one of the most popular ones out there. I'm screwed if she asks me anything regarding her own.

Z tilts her head back and thinks for a moment.

"*Gilmore Girls*. I love how quick and witty Lorelai and Rory are. The banter is so fast paced and so cunning that I just love it. Have you seen it?"

Before I get a chance to respond, all four of my friends do it for me. "Jack doesn't watch TV shows."

Z joins them in laughing as I throw some chips at Nick, the closest individual for my wrath.

"Oh my gosh," Lisa exclaims. "Is that why you always call Pete 'boyfriend?' Like Lucy from Yale?"

Z smiles and nods. "Yes, she's one of my favorites."

I keep the smile on my face as my friends talk about the show, but my insides are boiling with jealousy. It's really hard for me to hear her talk about Pietro like she does. For years, this guy has been a pain in my ass for no apparent reason other than we were the new kids in school at the same time. He happened to be the all-star running back. I was the piano playing nerd. To gain face, he picked on me. To save face, I tried not to care. High schoolers, especially us males, are one of the most ridiculous groups of people on the face of this earth. Mona and Lisa often say that men suck. I often feel obliged to agree.

But Pietro is the worst of us all. I may be biased, but he's genuinely a dick. He might be the football captain this year, but he is also the one to organize the hazing rituals for the new kids on the team. The level of disrespect he gets away with towards teachers simply because he's *Pietro* is beyond comprehension. Even Mom, the most patient, loving, and accepting person I know, despises him. And she doesn't even know the history between him and I. But Pietro is with Z. For some reason, she refuses to leave him and stays with him through all of the crap he pulls and says and does. I don't understand it.

I could be a better boyfriend to her… right?

"Jack, what are you thinking about?"

Z snaps me back to reality – I have let my mind wander too long and it must have been noticeable.

"Oh, nothing really," I lie. "Just trying to remember something my piano teacher taught me this week."

It's not a terrible lie. I often will space out thinking about piano. It's very much a large distraction for me.

"Oh, play us a song, Piano Man!" Z says, poking my side and pointing at the keyboard plugged into the far wall.

I try to attempt an excuse. "I really should…"

Z grabs my hand. "Please? For me?"

It's all over now.

"Alright. Alright. What do you want me to play?"

"Do you know any Phil Collins?"

I stand up. "Yeah, my dad would have thrown me out if I didn't."

Z laughs. "Help me up!"

I take her hand and pull her to her feet. She jumps a little and pats my chest, pushing me towards the keyboard.

"Do you know *Against All Odds*?"

"Jack can play anything from the album *…Hits*," Nick replies for me.

"Oh, perfect!" Z says, grabbing a stool from the kitchen. "You play, I sing?"

My heart starts to beat faster. Z can sing. And I mean really sing. Her voice is angelic and she's so confident about her vocal talent. She's truly incredible.

"If that is what you want," I reply as coolly and calmly as I can.

"Is that okay, everyone?" Z asks, turning to the four still working on their applications.

Mona closes her computer and Lisa's. "Absolutely. It's definitely time for a break."

Z smiles and nods to me. I situate myself on the small bench that accompanies the keyboard and I start playing the introduction. Z closes her eyes and I can see her let the music flow over her. She comes in with perfect pitch and perfect timing and her voice is gold. As she keeps singing, I dive deeper into the music, letting it fill me. Z must feel it too as her intensity grows and swells in synchronization with my playing. Soon, we are like one musician. I can almost feel what she is wanting to do with the piece and we move as one in every aspect of the music. About three quarters of the way through, I look up at her and she looks back. We lock eyes. I can't look away and I don't think she can either. The music is overwhelming and I can't help but smile. When the final measures are played, we let the music ring out and then fade, still smiling at one another.

"Oh. My. God," Lisa says, her mouth wide open. "That was incredible!"

The four clap for us and Z takes a goofy bow.

I just nod.

I can only nod.

I'm completely crazy for Z and it's tearing my heart to pieces. I hear about Pietro all the time. I know he's in the picture.

But all I want, all I can even think about, is tearing that picture apart and then making one with just her and I.

I can't keep doing this. I can't keep doing this whole dance around the feelings for her – tell myself that I can just be a good friend. Tell myself that I can be content like this. But in my heart, I know I can't be. That I will probably never be. There is too much connection. Too much passion. Too much… everything.

"Jack?"

I shake my head, prying myself out of my own head. "Sorry, what?"

Z was smiling at me, but I could see the question in her eyes.

Before she could ask, I quickly divert her train of thought.

"Do you know *Don't You?*"

"*Forget About Me?*" Z replies. "Yeah, absolutely."

I immediately start playing and this time everyone joins in and we're all singing, even Khalan. I play a few more big hits before I declare I need to actually submit some applications. We sit down and are all pretty focused on the task at hand. Z sits as close as she can to me, but I try to not let it affect me.

Keyword: try. I can barely focus on the answers to basic questions. What is my middle name? What do I want to study again? Where do I live currently?

Finally, I stand up.

"Alright, I told my mom I would be home for dinner and it's about that time, friends."

Everyone looks at their watches.

"Shit, I was supposed to be home an hour ago!" Khalan almost shouts, vaulting to their feet.

Everyone packs up, but Khalan is out the door, in their car, and on their way home well before any of us get to the driveway.

When we get to the driveway, I don't see Z's car.

"Jack, can I get a ride?" Z asks and my heart falls.

She's trying to kill me, I swear.

"Yeah, absolutely, no problem."

Yes, there is a problem, dude! How long can you keep this up?!

Z hops into the passenger seat and shuts the door. I start heading to the driver's side door when Mona stops me.

"Jack. Are you good?"

I nod. "Yeah, totally fine."

"Bullshit."

I give her a weak smile. Not very convincing.

"Be careful, man," she says, shaking her head. "You're falling. And you're falling hard."

I slowly nod. "I know, Mona. Don't tell her though, okay?"

Mona laughs, shaking her head. "Dude, if she doesn't know by now, she's just as clueless as you."

I sit down in the Sub and start the car. "What are we listening to?"

Zendaya grabs my phone. "Passcode?"

"2382."

"Significance?"

"It's my lunch code from Alaska."

She smiles. "Very nice. Well, I was thinking we should listen to some Phil Collins."

I laugh. "Sounds good to me."

"But this time…"

"Oh, no, what now?"

"You're singing with me!"

We sing through the first few songs of his *…Hits* album on the way back to the neighborhood before we start talking. She's so easy to talk and laugh with. I get swept in by her beauty and she keeps me there with her wit, charm, intelligence, and grace.

"What are you thinking about?" She asks after I'm quiet for a smidge too long.

"Oh, nothing really."

Z smiles and my heart hurts again. "Jack, the human brain is capable of thinking of hundreds of different things in a matter of minutes. You physically can't be thinking of nothing."

I chuckle. "I was just thinking of us and *Against All Odds.*"

Z clasps her hands together. "Ugh, that was so fun! I didn't know you knew so much music by heart."

"Once you know music theory and understand chords and keys and all that kind of stuff, it's really easy to pick out a tune and play it. And my dad gave me Phil Collins sheet music on my birthday when I was like ten. It's nothing, really."

"Well, I think it is far from nothing. I think you're incredible."

My heart soars. "I think you're incredible."

I can see the slightest hint of blush on her cheeks before she looks away.

"Thank you, Jack."

It's quiet for a moment, giving my heart the time, it needed to come crashing back down into the pit of despair.

"Pietro… Sorry, is Pete busy today?"

Z doesn't say anything.

"Z?"

"I don't really want to talk about him."

What did he do this time?

"Okay, that's fine. What were you thinking about before I asked?"

Z opens her mouth like she's going to say something, then closes it again.

"Come on, Z, you can tell me."

"Promise you won't say anything to anyone?" I nod and she sighs. "I was thinking about what it would be like to be dating… someone that isn't Pete."

My heart stops. "What?"

Z nods. "Yeah. I've been dating Pete for over a year now and… I don't know… I feel like I don't know him anymore. Or he's not even worth knowing anymore. I feel like he's changed so much since I first knew him and is so much fuller of himself than before. I don't know, Jack. Am I wasting my time?"

Yes. You're wasting your time. But you wouldn't be wasting your time with me.

I force a laugh. "I'm not sure I'm the person you should be talking to about Pietro and wasting your time, Z."

She sighs again, this time deeper and more exasperated. "Ugh, then there's that."

I look at her briefly with an arched brow. "There's what?"

"Okay, you can't get mad."

We're talking about Pietro. A little late for that.

"Okay."

"Pete doesn't like that I spend so much time with you and talk to you."

I laugh. "I kind of figured that."

"It's so dumb! You've been one of the greatest friends I've ever had and he can't just be happy for me that I have someone like you in my life. He's so… he's so… he's so fucking blockheaded!"

She's mad now. Her face is turning red. I need to change the subject before she starts crying.

"Z, I can't give you any advice about your relationship. I've never been in one and I'm certainly biased when it comes to you and Pete because… well… Pete."

Z nods. "I know…"

"But I will say this: no matter what you decide, whoever you end up with is going to be the luckiest guy alive. Anyone who captures your heart and your love will be richer than anyone else in the world. And Pete's a dumbass for not realizing that and treating you the same way."

I see a tear trickle down her cheek while we're stopped at a red light. "That's really sweet, Jack." She quickly wipes the tear away. "How on earth are you still single?"

I give her a half smile. "The right girl has never been available."

I'm sorry. What did I just say?! I thought I was just thinking! This is the second time today!

Her mouth drops a little and I can see a small smile on the corner of her lips.

"What do you…"

Phil Collins comes to my rescue with one of his most iconic songs.

I dramatically gasp and point to the stereo display, the words *In the Air Tonight* prominently glowing on the screen. She smiles, returns my gasp, cranks the volume, and we sing the song at the top of our lungs. When the legendary drumline hits, we mime our own over-the-top hits on our fantastical drums and laugh before resuming our singing.

When we finally get home, she gives me a big hug.

"Thank you for today. I appreciate it."

I hug her back.

"Anything for you."

This heartbreak is going to hurt like a bitch…

CHAPTER 6

I may hate a lot of things about Florida, but homecoming at H&H is always a blast. The student council always picks fun themes for the dress up days. Every year, the football game seems to bring everyone together, despite all the differences. The football team is seen as a bunch of legends and even I get caught up in the celebration and uplifting. It's fun and my friends and I usually have a good time. They drag me to the dance – not really my thing – every year, but this year I'm actually looking forward to it. We decided to go as a friend group and not with significant others, except, of course, for Mona and Lisa.

Today is Friday and everyone is dressed with school pride. Most students participate in the dress up days because it's one of the only times we are allowed not to be in uniform. Jeans, hoodies, t-shirts, shorts, flip flops, and many other articles of relaxed clothing make their appearance and Nick *finally* gets to show off his sense of style to the world. He and Lisa make sure that all of us participate in the themes of the day and have at least half way decent apparel. I hate to admit it, but Lisa has shopped for clothes for me multiple times and every time she does, the clothes fit me better than when I shop for myself. Do I always like the style? No. Do I always feel super comfortable? Absolutely.

I'm wearing my favorite jeans and a H&H t-shirt, sitting at lunch talking with the group. Nick is talking about some elaborate dance he wants to do tonight while Mona argues with Lisa about having to put make up on for only a couple hours (Mona hates make up). I'm laughing and listening when I feel a tap on my shoulder.

"Can I sit by you?"

I look up and it's Z. We haven't talked in about a week and I'm not sure why. But the second I see her my heart doesn't fail to speed up and cause me to feel all warm inside.

"I'm sorry, this seat is taken."

I can see her disappointment and I almost feel bad. "By who?"

"By you," I reply with a sly smile.

She hits me with her free hand. "You're such a jerk sometimes! I thought you would be happy to see me."

"I am! I just thought it would be fun to mess with you."

Nick immediately stops talking about whatever crazy move he was talking about when he realizes Z has sat down.

"Madam Thompson, I presume you have plans for this evening's festivities?"

Nick has pulled Z into his fancier way of talking alongside him and Lisa. I think she enjoys it just as much, if not more, than he does.

"My darling Nick, yes, I do have an engagement for the frolicking festival, but as my date has to play in that barbaric disgrace of a sport, I do not have a soul to sit with to observe."

A pang of jealousy hits me when I hear her say the word 'date.' Her and Pietro are still going strong. And it hurts.

"Oh, sweet angel!" Lisa exclaims, butting into the conversation. "You must recline with us in the viewing gallery. In fact, I insist on it. No arguments."

Z looks at me. "Is that okay?"

I don't know why she's asking me if it's okay. I don't have a say in the matter now that Lisa has invited her – one does not simply say no or object to Lisa. And I want her to sit by us. I haven't spent any time with her outside of school since the application session. And the last summer beach session was the time before that.

But I know this can only hurt me at the end of the night. Win or lose, she'll end the evening with Pietro. I will end the evening with my piano, trying vigorously to drown out the jealousy with Vivaldi, Mozart, Rachmaninoff, and Grimaud.

My friends and my heart overpower my logic. "Yes, why wouldn't it be?"

Z shrugs. "I don't know. Just checking."

Why is she acting weird?

The interaction bugs me for the rest of the day, but as the game gets closer, the memory of the conversation gets equally further away. The school is buzzing with energy. There are the exceptions – students who normally don't buy into this school stuff – but for the most part, everyone is looking forward to the game. Teachers start having a hard time trying to keep everyone focused – especially Mrs. Halverson, our Literature teacher, since she decided to schedule a test today which seemed pretty silly when she announced it last week. When the final bell of the day rings, chattering and cheering can be heard throughout the halls as the student body surges out into the parking lot. Most of the parking lot has to be cleared since there is a big homecoming/fall festival thing that happens every year and the vendors and games need to be set up as fast as possible, so most of the students have to move their cars somewhere else and walk a couple blocks to come back. Not us though. We thought ahead. Nick, Khalan, Lisa, and I all parked our cars closer to the football field, away from the allotted area of the carnival. Mona drove her mom's minivan to school and we all hop in and head to her house for a while. There, we talk about the test we took for Halverson and the rest of the days antics, including the tech club 'Rick Rolling' the entire school by hotwiring an audio jack into the PA system, pressing play and infinite repeat, then hiding the entire contraption in the ceiling. The song played at least four times before the school finally figured out how to just turn the whole thing off, which gave them time to find the phone and dismantle everything. They never did find the culprit, but I'm sure there is an ongoing investigation. Mrs. Halverson swore up and down the halls that the 'perpetrator shall face justice,' whether by the hand of the principal or by her own. We also get the opportunity to laugh while Lisa tries to get Mona to cooperate while attempting to apply makeup. Mona eventually caved and let Lisa put on half, promising to let her do the more detailed pencil work closer to the actual dance.

Around five we head back to school for the homecoming fair. We walk around for about an hour and a half or so, getting food and playing games. There was plenty to eat – walking tacos, burnt ends, pork chops on a stick, cheese curds/bites (buyer's preference), cotton candy, popcorn, mini-donuts, fries, and much more – and even Lisa manages to find a vegetarian option at the far end of the food stands. The games are pretty standard and, of course, incredibly rigged, but Mona manages to win a stuffed bear which had caught Lisa's eye pretty early on. We make our way up to the top of the student section in the metal stands a half hour before the game – ensuring we have a good seat for the spectacle.

Just before kickoff, I wave down Z. She gives me a brief smile, but it fades faster than it appeared. As she makes her way over to us, Khalan nudges me with their elbow.

"You going to be okay?"

I nod. "Yeah. We're friends."

Khalan just nods as Z sits down next to me. Lisa and Nick exchange their flourishing greetings with Z, who responds in kind. However, as soon as they end, her smile fades and she stares flatly at the football field as the football soars through the air at first kick off.

I bump her gently. "You okay?"

She bumps me back, but doesn't move her body away from mine. "I wish we were at the beach."

This is the first time she's mentioned anything about the beach since we last went.

"Why do you say that?" I have to almost yell the question as the student section is erupting with cheers and chants.

She leans in so that she doesn't have to yell, pressing tight against me. "Got a text from him before the game. Says that if they win, he wants us to go to a big party on Lake Lancaster. He promised he would take me to the dance. I…" She pauses her sentence as we realize H&H just scored off an interception. She doesn't cheer, but waits till everyone else is done. "I've never been to a high school dance before…"

I look at her. "Seriously?"

She nods. "I couldn't in California. Between shooting *APL* and all the other shit that comes with the industry, I never got the chance."

I give her a side smile, trying to figure out what to say. "I'm sorry, Z. That sucks."

She shrugs like it isn't a big deal. But I know it is.

"He promised he would take me."

There it is. She might be sad about not being able to make it to her only and last homecoming dance, but that's not the main thing. It's the possibility of him breaking yet another promise. Disappointing her yet again. I can see the pain in her eyes. All I want to do is hold her. Tell her it will be okay. Tell her that she's better off without him. But she's heard all that before. Not from me, but from others. I know Gay Simon has told her that much. What I can do right now is be a good friend.

"You know what would cheer you up?"

She looks at me, trying to put on a brave face. "What?"

"A bag of popcorn. Extra butter. Slight on the salt."

The attempted courage is rapidly replaced with a genuine, warm smile. "You remember how I like my popcorn."

I stand up, deciding to go with a bolder approach to make her feel better. "Indeed, I do, milady. And I shall fetch you some along with a refreshing beverage."

Her smile brightens as she puts a hand daintily above her heart. "Has the Lord Nicholas and Lady Lisa finally brought you into our fold? You are true gentleman, my good sir. I would be ever in your debt if you did this errand for me."

I bow clumsily. "It shall be done, Lady Z."

She laughs as I head down the stands and is still smiling by the time I come back with a large bag of popcorn – I have a hook up in the concession stand who gets me the biggest bags – and two Cokes. Z bumps me when I sit down, taking a sip of her drink and snatching the popcorn bag from my hands. We then turn our attention back to the game. At halftime, we are down by twenty points and things aren't looking good for us. I'm almost relieved. If we don't win, Z will get her high school homecoming dance promise. Yeah, it might not be with me, but at least it will make her happy.

By the end of the third quarter, we're only down by ten and the bag of popcorn is gone. The whole student section watches in anticipation as the ball soars through the air and through the uprights for a field goal. Now, it's a one touchdown game. We manage to stop the opposing side, but we only have a few seconds left in the game and we are down at our own sixteen-yard line as the punter absolutely sent that ball down field. The student section is silent as our offense takes the field, nobody wanting to break the silence created by excessive nervousness. I watch as Pietro gestures all of us on our feet and to make some noise. We all get up – yes, even me – and start cheering. The ball is hiked and the fake handoff to the fullback is so convincing that I follow him down the opposite side of the field from Pietro, along with more than half of the defense. It's only when the crowd roars in excitement that I realize the ball is actually passed to Pietro, who takes off down the field with the home fans' cheers pushing him forward. He manages to outrun the safeties and into the end zone for a touchdown. The crowd goes crazy. Popcorn is thrown into the air as well as people's drinks and discarded cotton candy sticks.

Then, our coach calls a gutsy play – he wants to go for the two-point conversion to win the game instead of tie it all up and go into overtime.

"What is he thinking!" Khalan yells – who apparently is very much into football. Or, at least, this game.

The team lines up on the field and I recall this is the same set up as the last play that just scored. The defense sees this and shift their position, the safeties and other down field positions ready to cover the pass instead of being fooled by the handoff.

"Dude, it's the same play!" I yell to Khalan.

"No, it's not! Look!" Z shouts, pointing. "Pete is where John was."

Sure enough. John – the fullback – and Pietro had switched positions. The ball is hiked and everyone expects the fake. But it's not a fake. Pietro manages to hurdle a number of linemen into the end zone for the two-point conversion.

H&H wins by a single point.

The stands begin to shake as both students and parents alike are jumping up and down. The student section spills from their seats onto the field where Pietro is being hoisted up on the shoulders of his teammates as the opponents leave the field, kicking the dirt and no doubt themselves for blowing such a lead. Z takes off running down to the field and I can feel my heart sink to my stomach.

We sat together the whole game. At least I was lucky enough to get that.

My friends and I begin to make our way off the field, high-fiving other students who we consider friends or at least acquaintances and agreeing with everyone on how crazy a game that was.

"Well, ladies and gentlemen," Khalan says as we are heading to the school's gym for the dance. "I shall see you all on the dance floor. Even you, Jack!"

I nod. I don't really want to go to the dance anymore. I really just want this night to end and go home and play piano.

"I don't know, guys. I think I'm going to go," I say, diverting my course to my car.

"Oh, hell no, dude," Khalan says, steering me back towards the school. "You said you were going to be okay. You also promised you would go to this dance. It's our last one. You don't get to get out of it."

"Fine, but I need to grab my suit and stuff from the Sub anyways."

Nick grabs my phone from my hand. "This is my hostage. You will get it back once you meet us on the dance floor."

I roll my eyes and head to the car. As I hit the unlock button, I see an illuminated overhead lamp of a car relatively close to mine. I take a look at the car's details and realize that it's a friend of Z's car. I hadn't seen her or her friend leave the field and my anxiety spikes. I make my way over to the car, clenching my fists like I am going to be able to stop a carjacker. As I get closer, I recognize Z's hair as she's hunched over the steering wheel, shoulders shaking.

Despite the fact we won the game, Z lost a promised night of fun.

"Z?"

I hear her sniffle and see her wipe her eyes. She turns to see who it is and, when we lock eyes, she starts crying again.

"Hi, Jack."

I quickly run to her and squat by her open car door. "He really bailed on you?"

She can only nod.

"Oh, Z, I'm sorry." I rub her knee for some reason, thinking that will help. She falls forward and hugs me. I hug her as well, rubbing her back in my best attempt to comfort her.

After a few minutes, she sits back up in her car. "I'm going to go home, I think. Uncle Simon will be happy to play games with me, right?" She forces a laugh.

I can only nod. I can't imagine how disappointed she must be. Her last and only chance to go to a homecoming chance is being ruined by the biggest asshole I know.

But it doesn't have to.

"No," I say, the confidence in my voice surprising me.

"What? What do you mean 'no?'"

I stand, taking her hand in mine. "Milady Thompson. I humbly request you accompany me to the frolicking festivity this fine fall... night?"

My attempted alliteration failed, but I'm not sure it matters because Z's smile slowly overtakes her tears and brightens the very night around us.

"Really?"

"Oh, yes, absolutely. What say you?"

She quickly gets to her feet, smile still shining. "Oh my gosh, yes! Oh, I need to call Lisa. Only she can fix... this." She gestures to her tear-stained face.

"I don't have my phone as Nick is holding it hostage, but I also need to grab my change of clothes."

"He has your phone?"

"He didn't want me to abandon the group. I guess I'm a flight risk."

She laughs and I can see her sadness and disappointment wash away.

"Okay, so," I say pointing to her phone. "You call Lisa and tell her you need her help. I'll grab my clothes and we'll walk back in together."

Z is basically bouncing with glee. "I'm so excited!" She lets out a little squeal before getting her phone open and calling Lisa. As we walk back to the group, we run into Z's friend and give her the keys to her car back as Z proclaims she isn't going to let the broken promise ruin her evening with friends.

Within the next half hour, the entire gang is dressed up and heading to the dance. I do my best to keep my mouth from dropping when I see her in a dazzling red dress with black heels and braided hair. Lisa had done one of her elaborate makeup specials around her eyes, the red and black flaring beautifully out to a point near her temple. She laughs and pushes me, commenting on my black suit and tie combination, which Nick quickly remedies by giving me his red tie to match Z.

Z takes my arm as we enter and her jaw drops at the transformation our gym has taken. The student council goes overboard on decorating every year, but they make it look like a dream. Music pulses as we pay the fee, go in, and claim our table. Z immediately drags me out to the dance floor and starts dancing with the music. She makes it look so easy and fun and carefree that I try to join in. She laughs at my attempts, takes my hands, and guides me through the choreography with ease. The rest of the friend groups joins and we dance and laugh the night away.

With about an hour or so left in the night, Z and I finally sit down at our table after grabbing some of the punch at the refreshment table.

"Ugh, this is so fun!" Z exclaims, smiling wide. "I can't believe this is my first. I've missed so much!"

"And to think, you almost went home," I reply, poking her arm that is resting on the table.

"Thank you for saving me from the mistake, I really appreciate it."

Her smile is so disarmingly sweet that I don't say anything and just stare.

The introduction measures of *I Don't Want to Miss a Thing* by Aerosmith starts playing from the speakers and Z straightens up.

"Oh, I love this song." She looks at me and stands. "May I have this dance, Sir Jack?"

I look at the rest of the people heading to the floor. They're slow dancing. My heart races.

"Please?"

I look back at her and her face is light, but serious. I nod and take her hand and she leads me close to the center of the dance floor. Instinctually, I move my hands to her waist as she interlaces her fingers behind my neck and we sway to the flow of the music.

We don't say anything. I'm not sure what to say either. My heart is beating fast and my brain can't seem to focus on what to say. Her smile is light, but her eyes speak a different intensity that I have never seen in them before. I try my best to smile, but my facial muscles aren't cooperating and it's more of a twitchy kind of semi-smile, semi-wince. Z lets out a laugh, undoes her laced hands, and moves her right hand to my shoulder and down my arm. Something tells me to lift my hand and, as I do, she takes it and holds it out so we have more a traditional waltzing pose rather than a modern slow dance. I feel her thumb rub a light circle on my thumb and she lowers her head to my shoulder so her forehead is pressed against my neck. I lower my head lightly on top of hers. We stay like that until the song ends and for a brief moment after.

We didn't say anything the entire dance. I'm not sure we had to.

The evening winds down with a few more dances and Khalan and Nick both ask Z to dance with them. I pass her off to them each time. Granted, it was begrudgingly so, but I don't have a monopoly on her time. When it is announced that everyone needs to go home, Z comes over to me and takes my arm once more.

"Drive me home?"

"Absolutely."

We walk out to my car and say good night to the rest of the crew before heading back to our neighborhood. I make a surprise stop at McDonald's to grab some fries and Sprite. Z claps when she realizes what I've done and thanks me profusely, claiming the Sprite was 'hitting different' after such a fun night. I take the longer way home so we have more time to talk and she doesn't object. We laugh and even sing together to some music she puts on. When we finally pull into my driveway, I reluctantly get out of the car and open her door.

"Thank you, good sir."

"Of course, my lady. May I walk you home?"

The side door to her uncle's house is maybe thirty yards from where we parked. She laughs and nods, taking my arm as we walk over to the door.

"Jack, I just want to say thank you again for tonight. This is the most fun I've had in a long, long time," Z admits, squeezing my arm.

"It was my genuine pleasure, Z."

We reach the door and Z turns to me.

"Well. This is me."

I nod. "Thank you for letting me be your substitute tonight."

She smiles, goes on her tip toes and whispers. "You're so much more than that."

I feel her lips press against my cheek. She's close enough to my lips that I can feel the corner of her lips touching the very corner of mine. She holds herself there for a long moment, before opening the door and going quickly inside, leaving me with a racing heart and a lipstick-stained cheek.

When I finally crawl into bed, I can't help but smile and touch the cheek she had graced with a kiss.

CHAPTER 7

Z isn't at school on Monday. I thought about her all weekend and was hoping to catch her going out to her car or sitting in the backyard. But I never do. In fact, I don't see a sign of her at all. It's almost like she disappeared from existence for the entire weekend. Part of me thinks that I had something to do with it. Like, maybe I pushed things a little too far with the popcorn, the dance, the McDonald's on the ride home, and the whole walking her to her door thing. Maybe she felt ashamed that she let herself have that much fun with someone who isn't Pietro. Maybe she felt ashamed because that kiss on the cheek – that kiss that has been the only thing I have thought about for the past 60 hours – was too close to my lips and she knew it and did it anyways despite having a boyfriend.

During third period, while Dr. Thurmond is lecturing about the Ancient Greek and Roman philosophers, I try to text Z and see if she's okay.

Me: Hey, I'm missing you at school today. Everything okay?

Z is typically really good at responding. I wait for ten minutes before checking to see if my message has actually gone through. It has. But she hasn't responded. Concern begins to grow in my chest. I definitely have something to do with this, right? I can't unsend this text now. I've gone and ruined everything.

Breathe, Jack. Just breathe. I'm sure she's just sick. No doubt some of the food between the game, the dance, and McDonald's was just bad and she's got food poisoning.

She would text if she had food poisoning…

I shrug off this mentality the best I can, focusing instead on the stack of quizzes Dr. Thurmond has handed me to grade. I force myself to trudge through English with Mrs. Halverson, despite the fact she has the uncanny ability to make Shakespeare the most boring thing I've ever heard in my damn life. I mean, she's an English teacher. Being able to read a text with some sort of intonation and varying vocal tones should be a prerequisite for the job.

"Mr. Connors," her shrill voices rings through my frustration. "Are you paying attention?"

I nod. "Yes, ma'am."

"Then you would not mind picking up where I left off and read to the class."

Shit. I have no idea where we are.

"I'm sorry, ma'am, I can't seem to find the spot."

"Lying to me again, I see? I'll have to write you up for that. Ms. Johnson, please resume where we left off so Mr. Connors can find where we are again."

"Yes, ma'am," Lisa replies, looking at me with wide, angry eyes. "I'm guessing you want me to start on page forty-six, line twenty-seven, or should I go back a few lines so Mr. Connors can have a little refresher?"

It might sound like Lisa is being the absolute worst friend right now, but she's actually helping, telling me exactly where we are.

Mrs. Halverson narrows her eyes at Lisa, seemingly discovering her little trick. "You know where to begin, Ms. Johnson."

Lisa picks up at the line she indicated and I again have to force myself to focus on the tasks at hand.

At lunch, Nick is really quiet.

"Hey, Nick. You good, man?" I ask, nudging him with my elbow.

He only nods.

"Nick?"

"I'm fine, Jack."

Lisa puts her hand on Nick's arm. "Darling, you're not fine. What's going on?"

Nick looks up from his food for the first time. "I just heard some gossip that is hard to believe. And I'm not going to repeat it until I can confirm or deny it being true."

"Oh, so this shit is serious," Mona whispers in a shocked tone.

I have to agree with her. It's not like Nick to keep gossip to himself.

All he does is nod and goes back to his food.

The rest of the day slowly crawls to a close and I rush home after school. Despite having sent Z a couple more texts and some funny gifs – one of her favorite things if she is upset – I still haven't heard back from her. So, when I park the car in the driveway, I walk up to the front door of Gay Simon's house with the bag of fries and a Coke I grabbed on the way home. She was probably really upset and I know this will help. I knock on the door and wait patiently.

Gay Simon opens the door. "Jackie! How are you? It's good to see you." He points to the bag in my hand. "Oh, honey, you know I can't eat those. Why do you bring me such a temptation!" He laughs and flicks his wrist.

I let out a few chuckles, trying to hide my concern. "I actually didn't grab these for you, Simon…"

"It's Gay Simon, sweetheart, please."

"Sorry. I was wondering if Z is feeling okay? These are for her."

He touches his chest the same way Z did Friday night at the game before I bought her popcorn. "Oh, that's so kind of you, Jack. You know, I'll go talk to her. Adrianna stopped by earlier and Z didn't want to see her. Gotta respect the lady's privacy, you know what I mean?"

"Yes, sir, I understand. I'll wait here."

Gay Simon ducks back inside, closing the door behind him. I think I can hear a Disney animated movie in the background before the door closes, but I can't be sure. A few moments later, he comes back with his lips drawn tight to one side. "You know what, Jack, Z isn't feeling up to visitors today. She says she appreciates the gesture and is wondering if she can still have the fries and Coke even if she doesn't want to be seen right now?"

I nod and hand him the bag and cup. "Oh, yeah, absolutely. Just tell her I say hi and that I'm worried about her – I've sent her a couple of texts and didn't hear back. I got a little concerned, that's all."

He pats my shoulder daintily. "You're a good kid, Jackie. I'll tell her to maybe turn on her phone for a little bit just to text you. She's had it off most of the day."

That's odd. She almost never turns her phone off.

"Oh, I didn't realize she had turned it off. It's not a big deal, then. Tell her I hope she feels better and that I'm just a text away if she needs anything."

Damn, I sound desperate. Gay Simon nods and closes the door. I turn on my heel and head back to my house and go inside to sit at my desk and work on my math homework. After dinner, I dedicate some time at the piano bench to play some pieces for fun – Don Headley's *The Boys of Summer*, Guns 'n' Roses *Sweet Child of Mine*, Aviator's *Find Me*, Billy Joel's *Piano Man*, and Elton John's *Tiny Dancer*. Most of them my dad recommended to me, but *Find Me* was one of mine. As I warm up with a few scales and fun little ditties my teacher taught me, my phone vibrates. It's Gay Simon.

"Simon?"

"Hi, Jack."

It's Z.

"Z, hi, it's good to hear your voice."

She sighs. "It's good to hear yours, too."

"Z, are you…"

"I don't really want to talk about me, right now, if that's okay."

"Yeah, no, that's totally fine. What would you like to talk about?"

"You're at your piano right now, right?"

I smile. She seems to know my evening routine pretty well. "Yeah, just finished warming up."

"Can you… I don't know… Can you… Never mind, I'll just leave you alone."

"No, Z, wait." I dial back my tone – I sound very desperate to talk to her. "Were you going to ask if I can play for you? Just put the phone down in front of me so you can listen?"

Nothing for a moment. When she does speak, I can tell she's trying to desperately keep herself together. "Yes please."

I don't say anything and just set my phone down. I start with *Sweet Child of Mine*, then move on to *Tiny Dancer, Find Me,* and *Piano Man* and end with *Boys of Summer*. I don't sing *Sweet Child of Mine*, but my gut tells me I should sing the others. I don't have a particularly amazing voice, but my mom tells me I have a decent enough voice to sing now and then. I don't stop and talk between songs. I don't think that's what she needs. And I don't hear much from the phone other than the occasional post-sob breath or a shaky exhale. When I let the outro of *Boys of Summer* ring out, I pick up my phone and put it to my ear.

Z doesn't say anything and we sit there for a while, just listening to the light breathing in the background. Part of me thinks she fell asleep and I think I should hang up. Just before I do, I hear Z let out another sigh.

"Thank you. That was nice."

"Of course. Anytime. I will say, it's a little better live."

She chuckles. "I'll keep that in mind for next time.

"You're always welcome. I'll get a comfy chair and everything."

I hear her laugh and it's the sweetest thing I've heard all day.

"Thanks for the snack earlier. I would've texted you, but…"

"You have your phone off. It's all good, Z. I was just worried about you. Wanted to do something nice."

She doesn't say anything, but I can hear her breath shaking over the phone.

"Z, do you need to go?"

"Yes," she whispers.

"No school again tomorrow?"

"Yeah," she whispers.

"That's okay. Take care of yourself, milady. Would you like me to fetch anything for you tomorrow on my way home?"

"A Frosty?"

I smile. "The biggest I can find."

"Thanks, Jack." Her voice is breaking faster.

"I'll talk to you tomorrow?"

"Yes, okay."

"Okay. Try to get some sleep, Z."

"I'll try."

"Okay."

"Good night, Jack."

"Good night, Z."

I hear the line disconnect and slowly put the phone down on my lap. She had been crying. Like, hard crying. My concern only grows, but I don't call her back. I mean, I'd be calling Gay Simon. Not even her.

I wrap up my homework for the night and head to bed.

The next day, at lunch, Nick sits down at lunch but hasn't grabbed any food.

"Nick? You good, man?" I ask, the concern very obvious in my voice. Nick likes to make sure he eats a balance of food evenly throughout the day. It's something in his life that he keeps very controlled and is very strict about it. So, arriving to the lunch table without any form of sustenance is an extremely concerning thing.

"I got confirmation on the gossip from yesterday," he says, drumming his hands against his lap – his classic nervous tick. "And it's not good."

All four of us stop chewing to listen.

"So, apparently there was a big party over at Lake Lancaster after the football game."

"Yeah," I interject. "Z told me that the football guys were going to go over there if they won."

Nick just nods, not even bothering to chastise me for interrupting him. Meaning this is very, very serious.

"It was your classic high school, rich kid party. Lots of booze. Loud music. Splashing around in the pool and the like. And, of course, people hooking up all over the house."

Khalan shakes their head. "I don't understand you sexually charged people sometimes."

Nick nods again, ignoring yet another disruption to his story. "I guess Adrianna was trying to find the bathroom when she found…"

Nick hesitates, looking at each of us in turn. "She found Shelly and… Pietro in one of the bedrooms."

I can feel the anger rising in my chest.

"How did you confirm…" Mona begins to ask.

"Adrianna had her phone with. I guess she was suspicious of Shelly and Pietro for a while and had tried to talk to Z about it, but Z didn't believe her or didn't want to. I'm not sure."

"Wait, wait, wait," Mona interrupts. "Adrianna took a pic of them… doing… it?"

Nick shook his head. "No, she started a recording and put the phone in her pocket, then confronted the two of them. The recording caught both of them admitting to what they were doing and that they had been doing it for months now."

"Holy fuck…" Khalan whispers.

"I don't feel comfortable talking about this," I say abruptly. "Z is our friend. We shouldn't be gossiping like this."

Khalan nods. "Jack has a point."

Lisa drums her phone. "I've tried texting Z. Even calling her. No answer."

I nod. "She's got her phone off."

"How do you know?" Nick asks.

"She called me on her uncle's phone last night."

The other four nod.

"At least she called someone," Khalan remarks.

I nod at them, thanking them for backing me up.

"Can we agree to be here for her when she gets back to school?" I ask.

"Yeah, at the very least," Lisa answers immediately.

The rest quickly agree, wanting to solely support our new friend.

I try to get through the day as fast as I can and speed my way to Wendy's after school, then to my neighborhood so fast the Frosty doesn't have time to melt. I sprint to Simon's front door and knock. I fully expect Simon to open the door and take the Frosty. He surely would know I am coming to drop off the ice cream. When the door opens, my heart breaks at what I see.

Z is dressed in a completely gray outfit with her hood up. She isn't wearing any make up and her eyes are so puffy from crying and slightly bloodshot. She doesn't look like her strong, confident self. Instead, she looks weak and hollow. Bags droop under her eyes and the cuffs of her sleeves are stained with tears and snot. She offers me a weak smile.

"Hi."

"Z, hi."

"Do you want to come in?"

I nod and step inside once she swings the door open. She leads me to the kitchen where I offer her the large Frosty I had picked up for her. She takes it, eats a few bites, smiles, and sets the ice cream on the counter. We both lean against whatever is behind us and say nothing, her eyes not really leaving the tile on the floor. I know this has to incredibly difficult for her and I realize that I can't really know to what extent the difficulty actually is. She's hurting. It's obvious.

"Jack, something happened..." Z starts explaining.

"Z, you don't have to say anything."

She looks up at me for the first time since we got into the kitchen. "You know?"

I nod. "Nick heard from Adrianna."

Z looks back down and slowly nods.

I'm not sure what to say. I hate being like this. I know she's hurting. I know she wants to have some sort of comfort in her life right now, but I can't come up with anything to say. I don't have the words. I don't know the phrases. All I know is that I'm so incredibly sorry for what happened, yet I feel like she doesn't want anyone else's pity.

"Z, I'm so sorry..."

Z hurls her body into mine and breaks down sobbing again, her fists in tight balls against my chest with her head resting between them. I quickly wrap my arms around her, knowing not to say another word and just hold her while she cries. And she cries. Hard. It gets to the point where I'm afraid she'll start hyperventilating and pass out, so I try my best to calm her breathing by rubbing her back with slow, but strong movements. I remember a trick an old teacher taught us in Psychology and I breathe deeply as if I'm demonstrating what she should do and how she should do it. It's a neat little trick that subliminally influences the target individual to copy whatever the initiator is doing and has a fairly high success rate. Sure enough, after a couple of minutes, Z is taking deep breaths and letting them out slowly in sync and rhythm with my own. After another five or so minutes, her sobbing is to a minimum and all that is left is shaky, tired breathing. Her fists relax and she grabs my damp button up lightly, clinging onto whatever support she can find.

"You had nothing to do with this, Jack. Please know that."

I nod. I hadn't even considered it. In my mind, I was just trying to be a good friend. I've never told her about how I feel. I never even forced the idea of a break up in her head. I only ever questioned their relationship once and that was only after she admitted she wasn't sure what she was doing.

"I know. Thanks for the reassurance, though."

She nods and a few more sobs appear before she speaks again. "I feel so stupid."

"You're not stupid."

"But I had my suspicions. I even saw texts and pictures. I still denied it."

"You're not stupid."

"Adrianna even told me about what she thought and saw before she called me on Saturday. Even after hearing the recording, I didn't want to believe it."

"You're not stupid."

"Jack, come on…"

"No, Z, listen. You're not stupid. You wanted to see the best in Pietro. I mean, you two have such a long history together that you wanted to see him as the boy you… I don't know, the boy you fell in love with."

She grips my shirt tighter.

"You're not stupid, Z. You have a good, kind heart. It's very different."

She nods, but still doesn't move away from me. We keep standing there and I can feel her breath evening out into a more steady and consistent rhythm.

"Do you think he went to Shelly because I refused to have sex with him?"

I don't even spend a second thinking about my answer. "No, he did that because Pietro is a fucking asshole and a complete idiot."

She laughs this time, then maneuvers her arms so they are wrapped around my back and under my armpits.

"Thank you, Jack."

"Always."

There's a knock at the door. Gay Simon appears from his study and smiles at me before heading to the front door.

"Good afternoon, how can I help you?" He asks whoever is at the door.

"Yeah, hi, is Zendaya here?"

Z recognizes the voice and her fingers quickly turn back to fists, scratching my back with her fingernails in the sudden motion.

I recognize the voice, too.

It's Shelly.

Z pushes off of me and storms to the door.

"Wait, Z," I say, trying to stop her. "Don't…"

Too late. Z explodes into a tirade, her voice shrill and high and angry. I watch as she shoves Shelly out of the doorway and back onto the driveway, yelling obscenities and curses down upon her so-called friend. Shelly tries to defend herself, but Z refuses to give her the time of day. I step into the doorway, ready to jump into action if I need to pull Z away from Shelly – I honestly don't know what Z is capable of at this point, she's never been this angry. Shelly catches my eye and stares, asking Z something that I can't hear. Z, again, is not interested in what Shelly has to say. She shoves Shelly into her car, slams the car door, and marches back inside. I watch as Shelly starts to cry, start her car, and then drive away.

Note to self: Never piss off Z.

Z grabs her Frosty from the counter and eats three giant spoonfuls of the chocolatey mixture. She starts laughing, then crying, then laughing again before eating more of the ice cream.

Between bites, she looks up at me and smiles genuinely.

"You're staying here."

I pull out my phone and text my mom, telling her of my change of dinner plans.

"I'll order some pizza and you can watch some movies with me."

"Sounds good."

"Are you sure? Don't you have homework?"

I shrug. "I'll get it done tomorrow. The only thing due tomorrow is some math homework and I can do that later."

She takes my hand and brings me to the living room and plops down, patting the cushion next to her. I sit down and she rests her head on my shoulder.

"What sounds good?" she asks.

"*Tarzan* or *Robin Hood*."

"Haven't watched either of them yet."

She selects *Tarzan* in the streaming service and we sit through the whole movie. Simon is gracious enough to grab the pizza when it comes and bring it to us while we watch. We watch both movies back-to-back before I discover she has fallen asleep on my shoulder. I wake her up her up after *Robin Hood* ends.

"Oh, shit, I'm so sorry," she says, rubbing her eyes. "I didn't mean to."

"Don't apologize. No need."

She nods. "Can you drive me to school tomorrow? If I drive myself, I'll just convince myself to turn around."

"Are you sure?"

"Yes, positive."

"Okay, I'll be in the car by 7:00."

"Perfect. I should turn my phone on."

I laugh and nod. "Yes, you definitely should. And please call Lisa. She's worried sick."

Z sighs. "Oh, you're right, she probably is. Damn it, I meant to call her last night after I talked to you."

"I'm sure she didn't take any offense."

Z walks me to the front door and hugs me before I leave.

"Thank you again, Jack. Unimaginably grateful to have met you once again."

"Anytime, Z."

The next day, we drive to school to find Lisa, Mona, Nick, and Khalan waiting by my parking spot. Lisa ensnares Z in a tight embrace and won't let her go, so we end up laughing and walking into the building with Lisa basically dragging Z with her. Lisa and Mona walk Z to her locker, Mona using her sheer size and indomitable stature to put a stop to anyone who tried to get even relatively close to Z.

I fist bump Nick, thanking him for helping get everyone here on time to help Z, before heading to my locker to grab my stuff for the day.

"Connors!"

The audacity of this kid.

"What do you want, Pietro?"

"You fucking Z?"

I look at him with an eyebrow raised. "You serious, man? I'm not that shitty of a person. No, I'm not doing anything with Z, much less that."

Pietro is fuming mad, his cheeks red and ruddy. "Not what I heard. Shelly says you were over there yesterday."

"Yeah, I was at her uncle's house. I had brought her a Frosty. We were talking when Shelly showed up."

"Oh, yeah? Just talking?"

"Yep, just talking. A lot less than what I'm sure you and Shelly did when you saw her last night."

I've never been punched in the face before, so I didn't even see it coming. Pietro's fist connects hard to my left cheek, sending me crashing against the locker, and then into a heap onto the floor. His foot comes next, smashing into my ribs and sending the air whooshing out of my lungs. I feel his hand grab my shirt like he is going to lift me up off the ground, but then he lets go quickly and I feel an air current pass over me.

"Back off, Khalan!" Pietro yells.

I don't see anybody at this point, the pain is basically blinding me, but I can feel who I assume to be Khalan plant their feet a few inches away from me, in-between my helpless self and my assaulter.

"I'd love to see you make me, Pete."

I hear two solid thuds and I think it's Khalan going down. I roll over and finally get my vision to focus just in time to see Pietro hit Khalan's raised defenses with a similar third thud. I can't see Khalan's face, but their defense drops fast and they connect a hard right hook to Pietro's jaw. I watch as Pietro crumbles to the ground, looking very dazed and confused. Two sets of hands grab my shoulders and lift me upright and I come face to face Z.

"Jack! Jack, are you okay?!"

I give one of her three figures a thumbs up.

"BACK UP!" Our liaison officer yells, pushing Khalan back against the locker. Khalan doesn't resist – instead, they just put their hands up and behind their head.

"Sir, Pietro hit them three times before Khalan reacted!" Mona yells over the din of voices.

"I'll take a look at the cameras once we get things figured out. In the meantime, someone help these two boys to the nurse. Khalan, come with me, I'm taking you to the principal's office," the officer says, grabbing Khalan by the arm.

"Khalan…" I weakly say, trying to reach out to them.

"Don't worry about me, Jack. I'll be fine. I didn't start anything."

I nod as Nick helps me to my feet, Z covering her mouth behind him.

"Shit, you're bleeding on my uniform, man," Nick says, grabbing some tissues from Z and draping them on his shoulder as I lean against him.

"Sorry…"

Getting punched in the face sucks.

I spend the next half hour or so in the nurse's office – separate from Pietro, of course. The inside of my cheek is busted a bit and has started to externally bruise. Every time the door to my little isolated room opens, I see Z pacing outside, trying to catch a glimpse of me. I wave to her when I'm a little more cognitive, and she tries to enter my room. However, she is instantly stopped by the nurse. After another ten minutes, my mom shows up and is absolutely furious. I don't even need to see her – I hear her from inside the nurse's office on the other side of the closed door. I hear the low voice of the officer outside explain the details of what happened. The nurse opens my door and I see my mom hugging both Z and Khalan, who has been apparently let out of the principal's office.

But I don't get to see either of them as Khalan is escorted by the officer out of the room and Z is told she needs to go back to class. I hear her protest for a little bit, but she is immediately shot down by Mr. Balaban. My mom is let in and she hugs me to the point of suffocation. I reassure her that I am okay, just feeling the pain of the punch still and a little drowsy. The nurse recommends I go see a doctor to see if I have a concussion – I guess I hit the locker and the floor pretty hard. My mom helps me up and we move to the door. Dr. Thurmond is standing outside, tapping his arm impatiently with worry. I smile at him as he shakes his head at me.

"My boy, what did you get yourself into?"

"Nothing that would get me into Valhalla, I promise."

He chuckles and smiles. "I believe you."

I dig the keys to my Subaru out of my pocket and hand them to him. "Z doesn't have her car here. And I can't drive, so, she might as well."

He nods. "I'll make sure she gets these."

After seeing my doctor, she reassures me that I'm not severely concussed. Maybe a little bit, but nothing serious. She instructs my mother to take me home immediately so I can get some rest. No electronics for a few hours and I shouldn't do anything physical – including playing piano. When we get home, I go right for the couch and lay down. My mom brings me a blanket along with a cup of water and some ibuprofen. I down the latter and wrap myself in the blanket and promptly fall asleep.

I wake up to the slamming of the front door and hurried feet rushing toward me. The big clock on the wall reads 3:34pm. As my sight focuses, a blur of a person rushes into the living room and falls to their knees in front of me before throwing their arms around me and accidentally bumping my now very bruised, very swollen cheek.

"Jack! Oh my god, Jack!"

It's Z. She's crying again.

"Ow, Z, ow," I grunt as her head is pressed against my bruise.

"Oh my god, I'm so sorry!" She immediately pulls away, but keeps one arm draped on my side. "Are you... well of course you're not okay... but are you okay?"

I give her the best smile I can without hurting or straining my cheek. "Yeah, I'm okay. Never been punched in the face before. Definitely can cross that off my bucket list."

She slaps my arm. "That isn't funny!"

I start to laugh. "No, I think it's terribly humorous."

I can see she's a little mad, but that soon disappears as she slaps my arm again and laughs with me. She rests her head on the couch's armrest and slides so that she is sitting down.

"What were you thinking, Jack?"

I shrug. "I think that may have been the problem – I wasn't."

She shakes her head. "No, you probably weren't." She gingerly touches my bruised cheek.

"I'm okay. I promised. Not even a little concussed."

She nods and I can see her bottom lip trembling.

"What happened with Khalan? Are they expelled?"

She sighs and looks me in the eye again. "No, they've just been suspended for a few days. The school was going to let them go with a warning since it was technically self-defense, but they had an issue with them supposedly egging Pe... Pietro on."

I nod. "Khalan did say they would love to see him try."

Z smiles lightly. "I appreciate that about them. Khalan. They are very loyal to their friends."

"Yeah, I'm glad they were there and did what they did."

"Me too."

I can still see her fighting off tears, so I take her hand and squeeze. "I'm fine, Z. I promise."

She nods.

I look at the coffee table and see a bag and a cup. "Fries and a Coke?"

Z smiles. "Yeah, thought I would return the favor."

I look at her with squinted, inquisitive eyes. "Pretty sure I would have preferred the Frosty."

Her mouth drops like she is offended, but I can tell she's smiling at the same time. "Well, maybe I'll just eat them all myself."

"Can we share?"

Z smile grows wider. "Yeah, we can share. *Inside Out*?"

I shake my head. "I really don't feel like crying right now."

She laughs. "Okay, what about *Moana*?"

I nod. "I can get behind that one."

Z stays for the duration of the movie, but doesn't move from her spot on the floor in front of me. She stays there almost like she has to protect me from whatever might come through the door. We laugh and chat during the movie as well, and more than once her hand is on my side or she rests her head on my shoulder. I can feel the connection between us growing, but I don't hope for much. She's been through a terrible break up. And I'm me. There's no chance.

But when I walk her to the door after the movie, she turns and kisses me on my unbruised cheek again, the corner of her lips touching mine. With a final smile, she walks across the yard.

Maybe… maybe there is a chance after all.

CHAPTER 8

It's been an interesting past few weeks. The swelling on my face dies down within a day or so and the bruise is gone in about a week. I'm glad, too, because I have a recital coming up in about a month that is going to be in front of roughly two thousand people and I definitely didn't want to have to wear makeup to that.

Z and I have been spending a lot of time together these past few weeks as well. I drive her to school most days and she's even driven me to work a couple Saturdays. We spend most of the time laughing and singing different songs and we have sat out on the beach most nights after my shifts. One weekend, she invites me to come with her to Universal and we explore the different parts of the park. Our favorite was the Harry Potter World parks. We took the King's Cross between the two sections, drank butterbeer (it was way too sweet for me, but Z loved it), and even bought wands at Ollivander's. I got Dumbledore's first wand, but Z bought one of the wands that has the sensor at the end where if she flicks her hand in the right motion and says a word at a spell spot, something would happen. We laughed so hard as we took turns trying each spell. And we even had one of those cheesy moments where one of us stood behind the other and tried to show them how it worked. But, unlike the movies with the guy showing the girl, it was Z who was behind me. My heart raced and I could barely move my arm in the right motion.

It's been a dream to be able to do all of this with her, but it's probably not going to last. I saw her talking with Pietro on his last day at H&H. Despite his parents' best efforts, he was expelled. The cops had asked me and my parents if we wanted to press assault charges against Pietro. I made the argument that my comments and behaviors weren't exactly of the most peacemaking variety, but I guess due to some sort of brutality clause or something, we had a pretty big case. Khalan was safe too - Pietro's parents wanted to press charges but because of video evidence and the school's lawyer, it was ruled Khalan acted in self-defense. But that left Pietro's fate in my parents' hands. Mom wanted to press charges - she was irate. Dad, however, is a much gentler soul and 'didn't want to ruin the boy's future.' He said that they wouldn't press charges if the school's punishment fit the crime. Therefore, the school decided expulsion was the best course of action. Mom still wanted to press charges - probably still wants to - but I told her it's really not a big deal. I'm fine. No harm, no foul. I mean, I was harmed but I'm not going to try and argue with my dad. Remember, he's super stubborn.

I have this feeling Z will end up with Pietro again. And I'll be left wherever I am with her now - friends who confide in one another, who rely on one another. I'll just always care for her far more than she cares for me.

We're all hanging out at Lisa's pool house again, playing games and messing around. Mona, Khalan, Lisa, and I are playing Call of Duty on the big TV while Nick and Z are talking about something. Z is sitting next to me so I should be able to hear what they are saying, but I am far too focused on trying to beat Khalan and Mona. They've won the last few matches and Lisa and I are getting irritated.

We all jump when Nick leaps to his feet. "My friends, I have a proposition!"

"Can it wait till after the game?" Khalan asks. They're quite serious when it comes to competitive gaming.

Nick grabs the remote. "I will turn this off, young person."

Khalan pauses the game. "Fine. You have five minutes. What's the proposition?"

"My parents recently purchased a beach house in Clearwater. It's fall break next weekend and it's like, what, 5 days?"

I nod. "Yeah, pretty sure."

"I thought it was four?" Mona asks.

"Teachers have four since they have a professional development day on Monday. At least, that's what Dr. Thurmond said on Friday. So, we have five since we're back on Tuesday," I reply.

"Yes, thank you, Teacher's Pet! We have 5 days!" Nick exclaims in an almost annoyed tone. "My moms want to go that weekend and have a little vacation. I say, you all come with - they already said I could invite some people."

Mona looks up at Lisa. "Could be fun."

Lisa nods. "Sounds good to me."

Z thinks for a moment before answering. "Yeah, I think I can make that work."

Khalan eyes Nick suspiciously. "What's the catch?"

"What do you mean?"

"You tend to have ulterior motives with these kinds of things."

"I just want to have a fun, long weekend!"

Khalan nods slowly, obviously still not believing Nick.

"What about you, Jack?" Z asks, nudging me with her foot.

I think for a moment about my week. I don't have a piano lesson as my teacher will be gone with her boyfriend somewhere. My parents haven't mentioned anything, but that doesn't mean there isn't something. "I'd have to ask. My parents like having me home."

"So, ask!" Z urges.

I take my phone out, get to my mom's contact, and hit the call icon. The line starts ringing - she's probably painting so it might take a second.

I hear her pick up. "Hey, Jack, you okay?"

Before I have a chance to answer, Z takes my phone from me.

"No, it's Z, Mrs. Connors… Oh my gosh it's good to hear from you too!... Oh, you know, been a little busy but keeping up with things. You?... Ugh, Jack sent me a picture of that painting and it's *amazing*… Oh don't blame him, Mrs. Connors, I asked him after he absolutely raved about your skill and how beautiful the painting is… Yes, he's *such* a good boy…" Z winks at me as my friends laugh hysterically. "Why am I calling? To talk to you! … I know, I'll come over for dinner one of these nights… There is another reason too if you have a second… Yeah, Nick invited us to go out to Clearwater… Yes, his moms' new place! … Oh, Diana told you about that? … Yeah, it sounds *super* nice… Can Jack come with? … Only if I promise to look after him?" More laughter as Z pushes me with her shoulder. She stays leaning against me after I regain my posture. "Oh, I can definitely keep him out of trouble… Thank you so much, Mrs. Connors! … Okay, thank you so much, *Lydia*… Yes… tomorrow night for dinner… absolutely, I'll let Uncle Simon know… You too! … Bye!"

Z hangs up and hands me my phone back with a coy smile. "I knew your mom wouldn't say no to me."

I roll my eyes. "She would have probably said yes if I asked her too, you know."

"There is a huge difference between probably and definitely," Z states. "And your mom was *definitely* going to say yes if *I* asked."

I smile as she sticks her tongue out at me playfully.

"Then it's settled! We shall have a grand adventure out in Clearwater this weekend!" Nick shouts, striking a courageous pose.

"Sunsets on the beach!" Lisa exclaims, matching Nick's enthusiasm.

"Some really good food and some much-needed relaxation," Mona comments, smiling.

I smile at my friends. No matter what, it'll be a fun weekend.

"We might have to double up on rooms," Nick says, doing some math in his head. "Yeah, we definitely will need to double up on rooms. We might even need to have someone on the couch."

"That's fine," I say. "I can sleep on the couch. I'm usually awake before any one of you as it is."

It is settled – a five-day weekend in Clearwater to relax and recuperate. We talk a little more about the details and it's decided that I'll drive down with Z and Khalan after Khalan's boxing practice while Nick, Lisa, and Mona head out with Nick's moms. We all volunteer to bring snacks and drinks so that we wouldn't have to go out every night. It sums up to be a very promising weekend of fun and friendship.

But of course, the three days of school before the trip are the slowest we've ever had. Mrs. Halverson has us write a massive essay on Shakespeare as homework while also lecturing each day for the entire class period. Mr. Montez gives us this colossal math test that takes literally all three days. Dr. Naboline has us do a lab in human bio that she claims is the greatest lab of all time but all it does is take massive amounts of both concentration and patience - it feels like watching grass grow. Even Dr. Thurmond's class wasn't exciting as we had to go over different impacts of the Constitution Era when it came to foreign relations, inalienable rights, and the perception of the common folk on a national government system. On both Tuesday and Wednesday during lunch, Z gently slams her head on the table in a protest of boredom. On Wednesday, both of us get written up in Mrs. Halverson's class for making faces at each other across the room during her lecture on the intricate weaving of love, death, power, and ambition in *Macbeth*. We had a good laugh when we left class, despite our lovely English teacher's grumbles.

When Wednesday afternoon finally comes around, I can feel the excitement growing amongst our friend group. Around 5pm, Nick sends a picture of the beach from the house on our group chat and it looks amazing. The three of us left behind finally get on the road around 6, grabbing some food prior to getting on I4 to Clearwater. Khalan promptly falls asleep in the back - a very typical thing for them to do on long car rides. Z wants to be polite and we whisper to one another as we drive. At one point she talks about how she's been studying palm reading and insists on giving my hand a look. She takes it in hers and traces her finger along the lines of my palm. With each gentle brush, every fiber of my body stands on end, feeling the current of emotion surge like electricity through my body, warming my heart, and renewing my hope that something might become of whatever this was between her and I. She keeps my hand in both of hers for a while, tracing different lines and giving me some bullshit on what they mean or what my life will be like. That something inside of me - that hope of a more intimate relationship with Z - burns brighter as I realize she's not tracing different lines. She's tracing the same few over and over again. Is she looking for an excuse to simply hold my hand? Is she wanting something between us just as much as me?

Or am I just reading into this more than I ought to? Like always?

When we finally get to Clearwater, it's around 8:30 since traffic was an absolute nightmare. We quickly unload the car and head inside, warmly greeted by both our friends and Nick's moms, Diana and Winona. They are both incredible people and super accepting of anyone and everyone.

"Alright, who's going on a beach run with me in the morning?" Diana, who is definitely the more athletically inclined one of Nick's moms, asks after everyone is settled in the living room. "Me and Nickie are hitting the beach at 0600!"

I look over at Nick. "Bro. Are you for real? This is vacation."

Nick shrugs. "Got to keep in shape, dude. Can't slack off just because you guys are."

Khalan narrows their eyes. "You're on. I'll run in the morning."

"Me too!" Z exclaims. "It'll be good to get a breath of that cool morning air and get those endorphins pumping."

"Shit, she makes a good point," Mona says. "I'll go, too."

Lisa takes my arm and looks at me very seriously. "You will stay here with me, won't you, Jack? You wouldn't abandon me."

I smile and dramatically take her hand. "I would never dream of it, milady Lisa."

"Exquisite. Good man."

I laugh and shake my head. "Lisa, you're not even going to be awake until, like, 11!"

She throws her hand up and presses it against her forehead and falls back against me, pretending to faint. "But I would not sleep well if I knew that all those who loved me had vanished to the beach and abandoned me to the perils of my nightmares!"

All eight of us laugh at her tragicomic gesture. We end up playing a few board games before we turn in for the evening.

I don't wake up with the runners like I imagined I was going to.

Instead, I wake up to several pokes in the side of my head. I groggily open my eyes to find Z smiling down at me.

"Good morning, Jackie."

With her hair put in a tight ponytail, she's wearing her running shorts and a very tight crop-top-style running shirt that resembles more of a sports bra than a shirt. She must have had a good run because she's still glistening with sweat. Z laughs as I groan.

"Don't call me Jackie. Please."

I squirm as she tickles my sides. "Oh, why not, Jackie? Where's the fun in that, Jackie?"

I can't help but start to laugh as she's tickling me more and more. Finally, I throw off the blanket and grab her sides to reciprocate the flirtatious play.

Wrong move. She's super sweaty.

Z laughs and pushes me down on the bed again and tries to dart away. I recover quickly and cut her off before she gets through the entryway into the kitchen. She drops into a defensive pose, protecting her sides and laughing heartily. I follow suit, closing the distance between us. But by the time I get close she jumps at me and throws her arms around me in a giant hug.

My first reaction is to get out of her grip. I mean, she's *really* sweaty.

But I don't. I wrap my arms around her, ignoring the dampness of her perspiration, and laugh with her.

"Good morning, Z."

"Good morning, Jack."

She pulls out of the hug and kisses me on the cheek. "I'm going to go shower. Take me exploring after breakfast?"

"If that's okay with everyone else, sure!"

She winks at me. "I was going to ask everyone else to come, too."

I blush. "Oh, right, since, it's a… you know… group vacation… thing."

Z laughs as she goes down the hall and into the bathroom. Shortly after, I can hear the shower running and her singing to whoever listens. I smile and run my hands through my hair.

What am I doing? There's something there, right? I just got to… I don't know… man up? No, that's a stupid ass phrase. I just need to be courageous. That's too dorky. Damn it, this is weird and exciting and frustrating all at the same time.

"What. The actual hell. was that?"

Khalan's voice makes me jump. They are standing in the dining room about thirty feet away from me, a glass of water touching their lips. My cheeks are burning hotter than before.

"Shit, Khalan, you scared me!"

They shake their head. "Dude, what was that?"

I shrug. "I don't…"

"Don't give me that 'I don't know' crap, man. It's so obvious she likes you and it's always been hella obvious you're into her. Do something or, so help me, I will vomit next time."

"What the hell, dude? Are you mad at me?"

Khalan laughs. "No, Jack. I'm just in awe of how long you can keep up this charade of cluelessness."

They walk into the kitchen and I sit down on the couch. Am I really this clueless? Is there something… No, I can't think about this.

She's recently single.

I want to be her boyfriend, not her rebound.

After breakfast, we head into the main area of Clearwater and look through the shops. Z has us all try on obnoxious hats, but seems to single me out more than the others.

I, of course, more than happily oblige.

There's got to be something here. Right?

The next few days are pretty much the same. Runners get up and do their thing. Z wakes me up when she gets back and our interactions are similar to the first. There's the exploring, the time on the beach, games, talking, walking in the surf, dolphin spotting, napping, and anything else anyone could ever ask to do on a beach vacation. We all stay out and watch the sunsets together.

And every time Z puts her head on my shoulder.

It's now Sunday morning and none of us really want to go home. It's been a really fun weekend and we have no desire to go back to school on Tuesday.

"What do we want to do tonight?" I ask.

"I would like to take Lisa out for a romantic dinner, if that is okay with everyone?" Mona responds. "I know it's the last night and everything, but I haven't got the chance to take her out."

"Fine with me," Z replies. We all quickly follow suit.

"Sounds like my parents came to Clearwater to get dinner, too," Khalan says, putting down their phone. "Just got a text."

"Totally fine, Khal, you definitely should go," Nick replies. "My moms are going out on a date tonight and I just got one."

"That girl from the beach?!" Z exclaims.

While Z and Nick talk about his upcoming activities, I do some math in my head.

There are eight of us total.

Diane and Winona are going out. Down to six.

Mona and Lisa are going on a date. Down to four.

Khalan will be out with their parents. Three.

Nick has a date now. Two.

Those two are Z and I.

Oh shit, those two are Z and I?!

"What do you say, Jack?" Z asks, taking my arm. "Take me out on the town?"

I smile, trying to hide its nervous nature. "Be happy to."

I can see Khalan give me a look from across the porch, but I refuse to meet their gaze.

"Then, it's settled! We'll rendezvous back here after sunset, unless I have, uh, other accommodations," Nick says, a sly smile now setting in on his face. We all throw popcorn at him.

"Where do you want to go?" I quickly ask Z.

"Um, I'm not sure. I'd rather not do some tiki bar, if that's okay?"

"Yeah, no, that's fine." I try to think of different restaurants I know in the area. I won't bring her to a chain, that's tacky. No tiki bar. Nothing too American either, she would want something a little more exquisite, a little more ethnic. One restaurant rises to the occasion for tonight in my mind.

"Let me make a call and see if I can make a reservation," I continue, getting up from my chair.

"A reservation?! What are you thinking?!" Z calls after me. I don't respond. "Jack?!"

Turning to walk backwards, I smile at her and waggle my eyebrows. "Trust me?"

She returns my smile with a touch of curiosity in her eyes. "Absolutely?"

"Good." I pull out my phone and look up the restaurant I have in mind – Cesare's at the Beach - and call them.

After a few rings, a female voice answers the phone. "Hello, Cesare's at the Beach. How can I help you?"

"Yes, hi, my name is Jack and I was wondering if you have any availability tonight?"

"How many guests?"

"Two. Both of us are under twenty-one."

"Hmmm… Let me see… I don't have much… But I have a spot at 5:30? Gives you plenty of time to eat and then go see the sunset? Otherwise, you'd have to wait until closer to 7."

"No, the 5:30 spot would be great."

"Excellent. Name was Jack, correct?"

"Yes, Connors."

"Okay, Jack Connors, I have you down for a table for two at 5:30 tonight. If you could give us a call when you're close, that would be appreciated."

"Will do, thank you."

"Thank you. See you tonight."

I hang up the phone and tap it twice on my other hand. Z loves Italian. This will be good. I return back to the group and see Z eyeing me suspiciously.

"What?"

She smiles a little. "What are you planning?"

"Nothing, just wanted to make our last night here special, I guess."

"You guess?"

"Yeah, I guess."

She shoulders me when I sit down next to her and I playfully return the nudge.

"Did you bring something a little nicer to wear?" I ask.

"I tend to have a habit of bringing something a little nicer along on vacations, but how fancy are we talking about?"

I shrug. "Something nicer than your average street clothes but not like red carpet fancy."

She pushes me. "Where on earth are we going?!"

I smile ruefully. "It's a surprise."

Z gives me a jaw drop smile. "Well, my outfit is purple for tonight. Are you going to try and match?"

"I've got a gray button up?"

"Light or dark."

"Light."

Z smiles. "Then that will work."

The rest of the day we spend all together, playing games and swimming in the ocean. We see another group of dolphins around noon and then, unfortunately, a number of rather large shark fins closer than the authorities and many vacationers were comfortable with. Shortly thereafter, a notification went out that we needed to stay out of the water for a few hours.

Around 4:30, I tell Z to change and we meet back out by the car. I force my jaw not to rendezvous with my toes when I see her. She's wearing a purple evening beach dress, strapless with a chiffon finish that drifts down to her ankles. The innermost layer clings to her body and overtop flows a sheer fabric which drifts when she moves towards me. I thought I looked good with my black pants and gray shirt. I even managed to find a black sport coat that matched well and a tie at a nearby shop that was a good shade of purple, but I can't compare to her. She's radiant. It's a simple dress, but she makes it look like the most elegant piece of fabric in Clearwater.

"Wow, you look… You look amazing."

Z blushes and brushes her hair behind one ear. "Thank you." She walks up to me and adjusts my tie - unsurprisingly it sits more comfortably once she's done. "You look handsome as well."

Before I can even think of blushing, I open her car door. "Your chariot, milady."

Z curtsies whimsically. "Why, thank you, milord."

After she sits and makes sure none of her dress is hanging out of the car, I shut the door and look up at the house. Khalan stands at the top of the steps, leaning against the railing.

"Tell her, Jack."

I nod.

"I want to hear you say it."

"Say what?"

"That you'll tell her."

"Khalan, I…"

"No. Stop giving me excuses. Remember that boxing analogy before school started?" I nod. "It's your shot now, dude. If you wait too long, you'll blow it and never get another chance again."

I nod again - seems to be my thing when I'm nervous. "Okay. I'll tell her."

"Good. Now, you kids have fun. But not too much fun."

I give them the middle finger as they laugh at me. Getting in the car, Z has an eyebrow raised. "What was that all about?"

"Oh, they were just reminding me of something stupid," I reply. Before she can ask any more questions, I grab her hand which I think startles her a little.

"Are you ready?"

She nods enthusiastically.

"Okay. Here we go."

When we get to the restaurant, Z almost skips ahead of me with happiness. "Oh, I wanted to go here all week! How did you know?! I didn't say anything to anyone about it!"

I smile. "I just know you, Z. I know you like Italian food."

She takes my arm, smiling up at me. "I do."

Our table is ready almost as soon as we enter and we are seated relatively quickly. We order our drinks and start sipping the waters they brought out earlier. When the bread is served, we dip it into the olive oil. Z takes a big bite and, after a moment, closes her eyes and smiles while she chews.

"Oh my god," she says after swallowing. "That is so good!"

I nod and take another bite. "It's quite good, indeed."

"Did you know both of the founders were from Italy? This place raves about their authentic experience and a lot of people have supported their claim. I'm *so* excited."

All I can do is smile at her enthusiasm as she looks down at her menu.

"What are you going to get?" I ask.

She starts to twirl some of her hair around her finger. "Can we get an appetizer?"

"Whatever you want."

Cool it, man.

She looks up at me, joy flooding her eyes. "I like that."

I blush and look down at the menu.

"Let's start with the burrata, then. Then I think I'm going to get the Linguine ai Frutti di Mare," Z states, her finger tapping the menu on her selected items.

"Sounds delicious."

"And you? Is the burrata okay?"

"Yeah, absolutely. I think I'm going to get the Veal Frank Sinatra."

We order shortly after and enjoy the burrata along with great conversation and a side of laughter. When the food is served, it's like we were actually in Italy. The food was beyond description and tasted like it was prepared for Jupiter and Juno. I pay the tab before Z can see it or object to it and we leave around 6:55 to make sure we catch the maximum color as the sun sets. I quickly drive down the road to Sand Key Beach and we walk, arm in arm, into the warm sand and sit down to watch the sun set.

"This evening has been so much fun, Jack. More fun than I've had in a long time," Z says, leaning against me and resting her head on my shoulder.

"I'm glad," I reply, gently resting my head on hers.

She shakes. "Ugh, I'm starting to get chilly."

Without thinking, I move away from her so I can take off my new sport coat and drape it over her shoulders.

"Thank you." She smiles at me with a new, soft, gentle smile.

If I didn't know any better, I would almost say the proper way to describe it would be to call it a loving smile.

But I know better.

"Jack?"

"Yeah?"

"Can… can you…"

"What is it?"

"Can you hold me?"

My heart races. "Yeah, absolutely."

I put my arm around her and she nestles under it, pressing herself against me. I feel her take my hand and interlace her fingers.

"Thank you. I figured this would keep me warmer."

Just for warmth then.

That's okay.

I'll take it.

We watch the night sky shift from the light sky blue to magnificent reds, oranges, purples, and yellows. Clouds dot the sky, adding the shadows to the glorious sunset.

"It's so beautiful," Z remarks.

"Probably the most beautiful sunset I've ever seen."

"Better than that one at Sunset Glacier? Back in Alaska?"

I nod. "Absolutely."

She lets out a deep sigh. "I can't believe this was just a couple hours away."

"I should have taken you out here sooner."

We don't say anything for at least fifteen minutes as we watch the beautiful colors fade to a dark blue.

"Jack, can I tell you something about Pietro?"

No.

"Yes."

Damn it.

"I… I blocked him on everything…"

I look down at her. "What?"

She nods, not looking up at me quite yet. "Yeah. He tried to explain everything to me on the last day he was at school. I'm pretty sure you saw us talking. But I finally saw him for who he is. A jackass. A terrible boyfriend. An absolute dick."

"Hence blocking him?"

She nods again. "Jack, I want to say… I want to say I'm sorry."

"For what, Z?"

"For not listening to you that night on the beach before school started."

I try to think back to that conversation. "I don't follow."

"I don't really know how to explain it."

"I'm just confused. You didn't say anything that needs an apology. And I don't remember saying anything regarding breaking up with him or whatever."

She nods and doesn't say anything back. I wait for a few moments, giving her a chance to say something. She's still quiet and I'm pretty sure I upset her.

"Z, you don't…"

"You didn't have to say anything, Jack. You just knew. You always just know. You know me so well. You knew I was hurting. You didn't even know who was hurting me and yet you were there and you cared. You're… you're a much better guy than Pietro and I should have listened to the silent advice you were giving me. I'm sorry."

"Z. Please. You don't have to apologize for anything. I can't even imagine what that feels like - to have someone you've been friends with for years and then dating for over a year betray you and hurt you like that."

"But you always knew Pietro was an asshole."

We both chuckle as I nod in agreement. She finally looks up at me.

"Thank you for being there for me, Jack."

We stare at each other. Her eyes are so hypnotizing.

I should tell her now. Let her know how insanely crazy I am about her. Tell her how much I admire her and want to be with her. Tell her how much I think about her and… and…

No.

I should kiss her.

She's only a couple of inches away. I can smell her perfume and her breath - an odd combination of raspberry, pear, grapefruit, and garlic.

She's not moving away, either.

Is she silently telling me it's okay? Does she want me to?

No. She probably doesn't. There's no way. I'm nothing special. She's everything special. I can't compare myself to Pietro. I'm not a star football player. I'm not a rippling specimen of muscle and masculinity. My hands are barely calloused.

But she might want me to, right? I mean, what about all those playful mornings these past few days? She kissed me on the cheek every time. We've been together constantly for almost the entire vacation. Sure, we spent time with our other friends too, but when that wasn't happening we were side by side. Basically inseparable.

And there is nothing I want more than to kiss her.

But I won't.

I can't.

She doesn't want me.

She never will.

She's her. I'm me. A beloved actress and a lowly pianist.

Our relationship is a stuff of whimsical fantasy and fairytale.

Not reality.

My emotions get too high and I do something stupid - I kiss her forehead. I feel her press her head against my lips and I close my eyes, trying not to let myself break. I finally pull back and she smiles up at me.

"Do you want to head back?" She asks.

No.

"Sure."

Idiot.

We drive back in relative silence - only some soft music playing in the background. When we get back, I open her car door and she takes my arm.

"Can I keep the jacket on? I'm still a little chilled."

"You can have it for as long as you want."

She smiles, goes on her tiptoes, and kisses my cheek. I can feel the corner of her lips against mine.

Kiss her, Jack. Just do it.

She pulls away and for a split second and I think I'm going to do it.

But I don't.

I chicken out and offer her my arm instead.

"Cribbage?"

She nods. "I believe we are tied in wins, good sir."

"I believe you are correct, milady."

We go inside and everyone is back already from their nights out, even Nick. He says it went well and the night even ended with 'a sweet, longing kiss' but no more than that. Khalan raises an eyebrow when I finally look at them. I purse my lips and shake my head. They nod, looking down at their cards.

I chickened out.

CHAPTER 9

I have been playing piano since I was about six. My mom, an avid piano player and lover of fine music, insisted that I take lessons starting so young. My father, citing studies that say learning piano makes children smarter and more successful later in life, was more than happy to pay out the nose for a private teacher. And I, wanting to please my parents, put on a fake smile and went to practice every Tuesday and Friday for the past twelve years. I should say, the smile was fake until I moved to Florida.

Not all things in Florida are awful, despite my strong hatred for Florida summers. When we moved, I thought that I was going to be finally free of the ivory keys. I mean, there was no way that my seventy-year-old teacher, Mrs. Chan, was going to move to Florida when all her kids were in either Alaska or Hawaii (talk about dichotomy). But my mother, bless her, decided to find another teacher. To be honest, I was quite pissed off but I hid that from her as a dutiful son would and should. So, I went to my first Tuesday lesson with the mentality of hating it all over again. However, I was surprised when the lady sitting on the chair by the piano in her private studio was only in her mid-thirties with a light smile and big, wide-rimmed glasses. She already had gray hair, which I thought she had dyed until she told me her hair had grayed in high school. She was and still is one of the kindest people I have ever met in my life. Her name is Ms. Genevieve Pillard and she brought the best out of my piano skills. I went from being good to qualifying for national and international competitions. Ms. Pillard said that I was already this good, I just needed the proper encouragement to create passion for the art. My mom agrees and loves that I play for hours on end on the weekends and holidays when I don't work.

Ms. Pillard taught me to the point where I won a competition about six months ago. The prize: a $10,000 scholarship from the foundation running it – The Annotator Foundation – and a spotlight performance at an event held at *the* Steinmetz Hall, one of the premiere orchestra halls in Orlando. I poured my heart and soul into this competition. Not for the money, to be honest, but for the chance to perform at the Steinmetz. Orchestras from around the world have played there. I kept telling myself of the honor and privilege that it would be to perform there. I was so excited the day of the competition and absolutely thrilled and over the moon when we got the letter saying that I had won.

But not now. Now, I'm incredibly nervous sitting in the wings of the hall, waiting for my time to perform.

I had mastered the piece I competed with. I mean, I knew that piece like the back of my hand. I could play the entire thing with my eyes closed. When I got the details for the concert, it said that I had to pick a new piece. One that "redefined how I looked at piano." My original piece, I guess, was too moody. Ms. Pillard, even though I constantly told her that it wasn't her fault, blamed herself for the comment. When we were selecting a piece, she said that I needed to delve into my emotions. At that time, I was focused on the idea that I hated much of Florida with the exception of only a few things. She had smiled and snapped her fingers, rummaged through a few drawers, and pulled out a piece that starts with these minor key flourishes and heavy, oppressive notes, but then changes into something hopeful and meaningful at the end. I loved the piece. I worked on it constantly for hours and just fell in love with it, heart and soul. So, when I read that letter telling me to pick a new piece, my heart sank and my anger rose. But Ms. Pillard tapped my shoulder and reassured me that I will have the capability of learning something as good, if not better, than that original piece.

We started looking the following Tuesday. I had listened to a few that she had recommended over the weekend, but I didn't really feel the same about the pieces compared to the one that I had played before. I stood at her music shelf and started to let my mind wander – a very typical thing for me to do when I'm upset. I had no idea she was talking to me until she appeared by my side and nudged me with her elbow.

"Where were you, my young pupil?" She had asked.

"Just daydreaming, ma'am, my apologies."

"OH! OH OH OH!" She had exclaimed, almost jumping out of her shoes. She then ran over to a drawer, whipped it open, and immediately pulled out a piece. "I was saving this for the summer competition next year, but I feel like this is the perfect time."

She handed me *Jeux D'eau* by Maurice Ravel. Fifteen pages. Five and a half minutes in standard counting – four/four. I didn't know what to think about it at first when she played it for me. But when I started to play it for myself and progressively got the hang of it, I started to love it. It has so many trills and movements and flows like water from a fountain – which is ironic since it roughly translates to water games or water fountain.

I learned the piece quickly, pouring almost all of my spare time and energy into the piano – even some time and energy that I probably should have dedicated to school or friends. About a month prior to tonight, I had the piece technically mastered. But something still felt off. I tried more dramatic dynamics, lighter trills, more legato smoothness from measure to measure. Nothing seemed to be right and I was getting frustrated which came to a head on a Monday night before my Tuesday practice session. When Ms. Pillard noticed my clunkiness in the piece the next day, she had asked me what was wrong.

"That's just it, Ms. Pillard! I don't know! I've tried everything, *everything*, but nothing seems to work to make *Jeux D'eau* sound the way I want it to!"

"Ah, then there is your first mistake, my young apprentice," Ms. Pillard replied. Ms. Pillard is a big Star Wars fan and often uses lingo like that. "You do not dictate what the music does. You do not command the melody. You must let it flow through you and then out of you."

"I don't get it."

Ms. Pillard shoved me down the bench and she began to play. It was light at first and her fingers gently tickled the ivory. "One master pianist once compared this piece to day dreaming. He said that it reminded him of the times he let his mind wander and be free, letting the music take him to worlds of his own romanticism."

"Okay?"

"Hush, child. Only listen," Ms. Pillard said before closing her eyes. "Let the music flow in, through, and then out. Become one with the piece. Let your mind go. Day dream."

Admittedly, I was hesitant at first. This seemed like some really hippy stuff. But after I let my mind go, the piece transformed in an instant. It washed over the room, filling every nook and cranny with beautiful, lovely music. It was so powerful that I too closed my eyes and allowed my mind to flow with the course of the water in the notes.

Without speaking, she took my hands, my eyes still closed, and placed them on the piano.

"Now, play."

The music I had been searching for was finally there, full and beautiful and bright. I began to sway towards and away from the piano, letting the notes vibrate the center of my being and connect every corner of my mind. I smiled, feeling the magic of Monsieur Ravel course in me, then through me, and then out onto the keys. Once I played the final notes, I opened my eyes, still smiling but much wider than before.

"That was… thrilling and magical and… oh, man, indescribable!" I said, laughing at the same time.

Ms. Pillard smiled back. "Good. Now, take what you have learned here." She poked my head. "And connect it with what you feel here." She poked my chest, right where my heart is. "And then *play*."

The piece only got better from then on. Every time I played it with both my parents home, they would stop in or just outside in the hallway next to the piano room. They claimed it was the most beautiful work of art I have ever done.

All of that seems to account for nothing as I am sitting in the wing of the stage waiting for my turn to go on. I am only a few musicians away from going on and my mind feels like someone is pouring wet cement onto it. It is unable to go anywhere, think anything, other than I am about to go on stage and perform this piece in front of almost two thousand people. My knee starts to bounce as I get more and more anxious.

I knew this was going to happen. I called it on the way here, gripping my Sub's steering wheel so tightly my knuckles turned white. I knew once there were only a handful of musicians before the enormous Steinway concert grand piano was rolled out to indicate it was my time to go up that I would start feeling like I am right now.

My phone buzzes in my pocket. I move my hands from my pant legs and notice for the first time they are quite clammy. I wipe them on a towel I had asked for upon coming in – something Ms. Pillard instructs me to do every time I perform at larger venues – and pull my phone out. I have a text message from Ms. Pillard. I tap the message notification and my face is successfully detected. The light from the phone glows softly in the dark and I have no doubts the other performers can see me now.

Ms. Pillard: Jack, my young apprentice. I know you well enough by now to know that your hands are clammy and you are feeling nervous. Don't be. You know this piece. You have felt its magic and seen its beauty. Let your mind go. Day dream.

I'm about to reply when I see the typing bubble in the conversation window. I wait to see what she says.

Ms. Pillard: And put your phone in the bin, you nitwit. The last thing you want is your piece being ruined by some vibration or ringtone.

I laugh as I set the phone in the bin of my personal items that rests by the foot of my chair.

"Mr. Connors, you're next. Are you ready to go on?" The all-black-clad stage hand asks me.

I stand and nod to him, straightening my tuxedo. "How do I look?"

"Oh, absolutely marvelous, sir," the stage hand replies smiling. "May I?"

"Please, I can't see myself in this light."

He chuckles lightly as he readjusts my tuxedo and bow tie. "Much better."

I hear the audience applaud the cellist who finishes her bow. I know her from other smaller venues – Carmen something or other – and she smiles at me as she comes off stage.

"Good luck, Jack!" She quickly whispers.

"Thanks, Carmen! You sounded great by the way!"

She winks her thanks as I chastise myself for lying through my teeth.

I hadn't heard a damn note.

"Ladies and gentlemen, our next performer of the evening," the host says from the stage, "Is a young man that is well known in the piano community. He's won several state and regional competitions and has even competed in Germany and England. His teacher describes him as tenacious, talented, and downright tailored for the piece he is about to perform. This year's Annotator's Award Winner, Jack Connors performing *Jeux D'eau* by French composer Maurice Ravel."

The audience's polite applause fills my ears as I walk out on the stage, shake the hand of the host, and situate myself at the Steinway. I start my routine. I gently run a finger down the keys, not hard enough that any sound comes out but only light enough where I can feel the cool ivory pieces under my skin. I flick my tuxedo tails out, feeling the expensive wool on my fingertips. I place my fingers on the starting notes and close my eyes.

Let my mind go. Day dream.

I wait a moment longer then begin to play. I feel my mind begin its drifting, the memorized notes appearing in the clouds of my day dreams. I smile lightly as I recognize the location my imagining has chosen to drift to for the piece. Glacier. Montana. My dad had insisted on a road trip to visit the national park. It was an almost forty-hour drive from our home to the park, but it was so worth it. The sky seemed to be endless and the mountains' natural beauty inspired my mom to paint one of the most beautiful landscapes she had ever done. Sitting by the campfire, eating s'mores, seeing bears, and reading quietly.

This is where my mind wanders to as the notes ring from the piano.

Then she appears.

Z.

The girl that I can't help myself from thinking of. I have never thought about her when I play before. I try not to. She's too distracting as it is. I can't seem to ever get away from the thought of her. Our late-night conversations, our texts, our chats at school, our bickering, our inside jokes.

I can't pull my mind away from her. She is a constant.

As I'm trying to stop, the music begins to build as Z dominates my headspace and turns into something more amazing than anything I have ever played before. I give in and let my mind take me to the beach where we first met. The drives to and from Cocoa Beach. The weekend we spent in Harry Potter World, trying to cast spells with her wand. Our night at Cesare's at the Beach and that beautiful sunset where I almost kissed her.

I begin to sway towards the piano as I lean into the music, retreating when I feel as if my head will touch the housing case. I continue both my day dream and my playing.

I drift to the times where she kissed me on the cheek. My smile grows more as the memory of getting punched in the face led to a moment I have begun to cherish deeply.

She is there. She is in the music. She is in the intonations and artistry of the piece. She is the music.

As I come to the end of the piece, my heart soars higher than ever before. I bring *Jeux D'eau* to her finale – a long procession of intricately quick scale progressions – down into her final fade to *piano* and lightly brush the last notes. I let the note sing and fade out before I lower my hands to my sides.

I barely hear the audience as they applaud until the host comes over and claps my shoulder. I shake myself and stand next to him, taking his outstretched hand.

"Take a bow, son!" He says to me without using the microphone. I approach the edge of the stage and take a light bow, making eye contact with my three biggest fans – mom, dad, and Ms. Pillard – sitting just a few rows away from the front. Mom is in tears and my dad is elbowing the guy next to him surely just to say 'that's my boy!' I clasp my hands together and bow lightly to Ms. Pillard, who simply mouths *incredible, simply incredible.*

"What a piece, ladies and gentlemen!" The host says. "Give it up one more time for our Annotator Award Winner, Jack Connors!"

I bow one last time before leaving the stage and into the claps and handshakes of the fellow musicians in the back. I smile and nod the best I can to the compliments flooding my ears as the adrenaline normalizes its run through my body. I start feeling more and more relaxed as I sit down in my spot once again, graciously accepting a glass of water offered to me by the stage hand who had fixed my bow tie.

"Thank you," I carefully whisper.

"You were outstanding, Mr. Connors! Absolutely riveting."

I smile back, feeling the weight of my performance relieving its tension on my shoulders.

The rest of the event was relatively short – only a few adult artists playing such amazing music that it put mine to shame. But that didn't matter to me. I can say that I've played at the Steinmetz and I played superbly.

A dream come true.

I quickly exit the hall after we performers have been dismissed to try and find my parents and Ms. Pillard in the parking lot. The cool air of a Florida November night greets my body with a loving embrace. I look around and find my trio standing not too far from where I had parked the Subaru.

"My boy!" Dad exclaims as he picks me up off the ground in a bear hug. "That was brilliant! Absolutely phenomenal. I was just blown away!"

"It was undoubtedly the best playing I have ever heard from your fingertips, dear," Mom says, her tears resuming as I give her a big hug.

"Thank you, both, so much. I felt really good about that tonight." I turn to Ms. Pillard, who stands as calm as ever after any performance. "Ma'am, how did I do?"

She gives me her best stern look, trying to hide the fact it was fake. "You let your mind really go this time, didn't you?"

I nod.

Her look breaks and she smiles, opening her arms. "I'm very proud of you, my young apprentice. Truly a masterful performance."

"Thank you, Ms. Pillard," I reply, returning her smile and stepping into her embrace.

"Are you hungry, son?" Dad asks.

"No, I'm good. They served us a small meal prior to the event. I'm still running off adrenaline, so I can't tell if I'm hungry or not as it is."

We laugh as my dad claps me on the back. He pulls a twenty out of his wallet. "For McDonald's if you need it on your drive home. I believe there is someone else who wants to congratulate you."

I lift an eyebrow at him in curiosity. Dad just winks, smiles, takes my mom's arm, and guides her to the Land Rover.

"Don't be out too late, honey!" My mom calls back to me.

"I won't, I promise!"

Ms. Pillard hugs me one last time and begins to head to her car. She turns back after a few steps and, still walking backwards, says, "So, spring festival competition?"

"Oh, most definitely. I'll see you Tuesday for the new piece."

"Good man!" She waves and continues to sojourn to her vehicle.

I turn to meet my last congratulator, who was standing by my car waiting patiently. I couldn't believe I didn't see another person there, but my adrenaline is still pretty high.

I realize who it is and my heart flutters.

"Z?"

Z stands by my car wearing a strapless black dress with opera gloves to match. She carries a small clutch and her hair is lightly curled and combed to one side. Her necklace and earrings sparkle in the light of the street lamps and her white teeth glistened as they are framed by lips colored deep red.

"Wow… you look… wow… um… you look absolutely beautiful," I stammer as she takes a few steps toward me. I run my hand through my hair, feeling nervousness quickly replace any adrenaline left in my system. Her smile grows and I can see her start to blush a little in the lamplight. "I didn't know you were going to be here tonight. When did you get your ticket?"

"A few days ago. I heard a rumor you would be playing. I wanted to hear what you sound like when you don't know your friends are listening," She coyly replies.

"A few days ago? I thought this was sold out?"

"It was, but my agent always buys tickets to these kinds of things and offers it to those of us interested or in town. So, I got to sit with a couple of my friends from a previous show. It was a nice evening."

"Well, I'm glad you enjoyed yourself." I smile at her and lock eyes with her, the enchanting blue ever so mesmerizing. I quickly notice it looks like her makeup is recently redone and a slight puffiness to her eyes. "Oh my gosh, Z, are you okay? Have you been crying?"

She smiles and touches my arm, electricity pulsing to my brain. "Yes, I'm fine. But yes, I had some tears earlier."

"Did Pietro text you again?"

She laughs hard at that. "No, no, I blocked him, remember? Um, actually…" She grabs her hair and plays with the ends. "Jack, it was your piece. That was amazing. Some of the most beautiful piano I have ever heard."

I can feel myself blushing. "Oh… um thanks Z… that's… Uh sorry I'm just a little caught off guard. I wish you would have told me you were going to be here!"

Z shakes her head. "Now, where would the fun be in that?!"

We laugh for a moment and awkwardly stand there in the parking lot for a time.

"Jack, can I ask you something?" Z asks after a long spell of silence.

"Yeah, of course."

"And you promise you won't laugh because it feels like a weird question?"

"Is that your question?" I ask with cheeky grin.

She smiles again and hits my arm with her clutch. "No, of course not. Promise you won't laugh?"

"Yes, of course, I promise I won't laugh."

Her smile fades slightly and I can tell whatever her question is, it's hard for her to articulate.

After another long pause she finally speaks again. "What did you think about when you played tonight?"

My heart sinks in my chest.

"I know that's a weird thing to ask but I have a few friends that play instruments and they say whenever they play their most powerful and stirring music, they are thinking about a specific something or someone. Tonight, you became an entirely different person. And not in a bad way. It's almost like you became the perfect version of yourself. I was in awe of you, Jack. I was watching you and this wave of emotion flooded over me. It was like the music you were playing was speaking directly to me. I couldn't help the tears absolutely streaming down my cheeks."

I feel my heart flutter in my stomach.

"I guess what I'm really asking is what were you thinking about when you played tonight? Was it me, Jack? Or is this just me reading into things unnecessarily?"

My first instinct is to lie. I can't admit to her that it was her. There's no way she would remotely reciprocate those emotions. I mean, she's a damn movie star! I'm just some guy that can play piano fairly well who works at a tiki bar and wants to be an engineer. That's it. Nothing special. Nothing for her to latch on to.

When I open my mouth, it's not my first instinct that prevails, but the second.

Tell the truth.

"Yes."

She blinks twice. "Yes what? Yes, it was me or yes, it's just me reading into things unnecessarily?"

"Yes, it was you."

"Oh."

"Z, I'm crazy about you." The words are just pouring out now and I can't seem to stop them. "I think you're one of the most talented people in the world and I genuinely don't watch TV shows. I've only seen clips of your acting. But I've read the things you've written. Heard the songs you've composed. Watched you present on one of the most boring topics in Gov and yet I was enthralled. You're funny and witty and intelligent."

She is starting to blush again, but I keep talking so I can get all of this out before she shoots me down.

"I can't stop thinking about you. I try to focus on anything else, but you pop up. I poured myself into *Jeux D'eau* in the hopes that it would distract me from you. And it did for a while. I obsessed over the technical aspects of the piece and I didn't think about you. But tonight, when I performed, I leaned into what my piano teacher taught me – she told me that I needed to day dream and let the music take me wherever it wanted. And I did. And it took me to you."

"Jack…"

"And I know! I know you don't feel the same way about me. Why would you? I'm just some guy and you're *the* Zendaya Thompson. You've won a bunch of awards and you're being chased by movie directors and executives across the industry. You've said so yourself.

And I'm just me – a guy who was lucky enough to stumble across you sitting on the beach."

"Jack…"

"I just hope that you still want to be friends now that you know this. You're one of the best things about Florida and you know how much I hate this blasted state. Please, don't hold this against me. I just had to tell you."

"Jack…"

"Z, please just…"

"Jack, please stop talking."

She steps into my space and kisses me.

I don't feel it at first. I mean, I'm not exactly experienced in this sort of thing. I've kissed maybe two girls in my life – a crush back in Alaska and Mona kissed me once when she was drunk and she's gay so I don't think it counts.

I feel her arms wrap around my shoulders and back, one hand pressing against the side of my face as she pulls me closer to her. Though I didn't think I am actually doing it, I feel my arms pull her closer to me by the small of her back. She separates only for a moment to simply kiss me again and again and again, her hand running through my hair. Her scent overwhelms my nostrils – lavender, I think. She feels so slender in my hands, yet not fragile in the slightest.

When we finally separate, she doesn't move away from me. Her nose still touches mine. Her hand is still in my hair.

"Jack, I'm crazy about you, too. And I would rather not be friends when we both want to be so much more to one another."

I can only nod and hold her tighter.

"Good, that's what I was hoping you would say."

She kisses me again and this time I try to participate more.

Z steps back from me after a few moments and smiles at me. "I think your dad said something about McDonald's?"

I sheepishly hold up the twenty. "My treat?"

"You're damn right. I'm starving! Kelly is on some stupid ass diet and guilts everyone she goes out with into not ordering normal food." Z walks over to the passenger door of the Baja and I quickly hit the unlock button.

"Sounds like she's just the life of the party."

"She normally is!" Z exclaims, watching me get into the car as she takes off her opera gloves.

I look at my tuxedo. "We're a little overdressed for McDonald's, don't you think?"

She leans over the console to get closer to me. "Maybe. But you look really good so I don't want you to change."

I kiss her this time. Somehow, she remains as sweet as the first kiss. "Same goes for you."

Z smiles at me. "I'm glad. Now, let's go. Large fry. Chicken Nuggets. Large Coke. And make sure it's regular because, I swear, I will die if I don't have any sugar. Just don't tell Kelly, okay?"

I smile wide again. "Of course not. Wouldn't dream of it."

I turn the key in the ignition and we drive to the Golden Arches, fingers interlaced the whole way.

CHAPTER 10

My mind is still spinning from last night. Z and I had a great time simply going to McDonald's and sitting in the parking lot talking about anything and everything. I don't think I've ever laughed so hard in my life. Once the food was gone, we realized it was almost midnight. When we got back to our neighborhood and I parked the car, I got out and almost went inside. She grabbed my hand and pulled me to her, kissing me good night.

It was, in a word, magical. Phenomenal. Indescribable.

It had taken me hours to fall asleep and now, at 8:00 in the morning, I'm wide awake.

And incredibly nervous?

What if last night was just a fluke? A music induced moment of romance? A congratulatory thing for my accomplishment?

No, no, it couldn't be. Last night was too real for that. There was too much connection. Too much fun.

Right?

Or am I making this up?

My mind starts to race. This changes everything. What if it changes things for the worse? What if she realizes that I'm nowhere even close to her league? What if she still has feelings for Pietro and he wins her back?

Wins her back? Come on, she's not some sort of game to play. She's her own woman with her own thoughts. She would never go back to him.

Right?

I'll just call her and ask her on a date. I'll make reservations at some fancy restaurant and we can talk about what this all means. Or is that too soon? Is it too corny? I've never done this before, how am I supposed to know any of this!

My phone starts buzzing and brings me out of the chaos. I quickly roll over, thinking it's probably Nick since I had texted him at one in the morning telling him what happened. I am positive he'll call.

It's not Nick.

It's Z.

I quickly slide the phone icon over. "Hey."

"Oh, good, you're awake."

"Were you just going to keep calling me if I wasn't and wait for my phone's buzzing to wake me up?"

I can almost feel her smile from the other side of the line. "Maybe."

"You're crazy."

"Hey, that's no way to talk to the girl you just made out with last night."

"Was that making out?"

"I mean, not really, but we could fix that today."

My body feels tingly all over. "I wouldn't object."

She laughs. "How about you buy me dinner first?"

I shake my head. "Did you just ask me out on a date?"

"Yes, I did. It's a new era, Jack. Women can ask men out, too."

"No, I didn't..."

She's laughing again. God, I love that laugh. "I'm messing with you, Jack."

"Oh, good, okay." I scratch my head - I need to shower. "How about I make reservations at Kadence for, like, 7:00?"

"Oh, fancy man today."

"I just know you like sushi."

"I appreciate the offer. I really do. And no, I don't like sushi, I love sushi."

My heart sinks. 'I appreciate the offer.' Did I do something wrong?

"But I think we should go to Disney Springs instead."

"Disney Springs? Won't people recognize you?"

"Maybe. I'll wear my University of Michigan hat and my big sunglasses."

"But I like seeing your eyes."

But I like seeing your eyes? What the fuck, Jack? What was that?

"Ah, that's so sweet, Jackie-Poo! Aren't you just a little fawn!" She erupts in laughter as I groan into the phone.

"Please. Don't call me Jackie-Poo. I just got my mom to stop calling me that. It does not need a resurgence."

"Fine, but I will have to come up with a pet name for you, I hope you realize that."

"Only if I can call you one."

"Well, yeah, obviously! So, what do you say? Day at Disney Springs?"

I smile wide. "Absolutely. It doesn't open for another couple of hours though. Do you want to get breakfast?"

"I would love to! I still need to get dressed and get ready. Give me, like, half an hour?"

"Absolutely. I need to shower."

"Okay, good. I'll come over once I'm ready."

"Sounds good."

"Okay, bye, boyfriend."

Before I can say anything, she hangs up.

Did she just call me boyfriend? The tingly sensation is back in full force this time.

I get up and select my outfit for the day - a pair of khaki shorts, a blue t-shirt, and a slightly darker blue sweatshirt to go over top. It's November and sometimes the mornings are uncomfortable. Like, the temperature is between being too hot and being too cold, but it's not a good thing. It's hard to explain. I jump in the shower and I can't help singing a little bit. I'm in a really good mood.

"Jack? Are you singing?" Mom asks from the hallway.

"Oh, yeah, sorry, did I wake you?"

She cracks the door a little without stepping in so I can hear her better. "No, no, we were already up. But you rarely sing in the shower. What's going on?"

I smile as the water rinses off the body wash. "I, uh, have a date today."

Nothing from Mom.

"Mom?"

"You have a date? Today?"

"Yeah? Is that such a surprise?"

"No. I mean, yes, you've never been on a date before and been this happy about it."

"Well, this girl is different."

"It's Z, isn't it?"

Again, smiling. "Yes, yes it is."

"Oh, how fun! What are you two doing?"

"Mom, I'm in the shower. Not exactly the best place to be having this conversation. I'll tell you all about what we're doing when I get out."

"Sorry! Sorry! I'm just *very* excited for you!"

I laugh and hear the door click shut. I dry off as fast as I can and throw my clothes on. As soon as I get my socks on, I hear the doorbell ring. With a much faster pace than I should be doing with socks on hardwood, I race to the stairs and rapidly head down.

"Oh, Z, hello! What a lovely Sunday surprise!"

Damnit, Mom.

"Hi, Mrs. Connors. Is…"

"Jack is on his way downstairs. Why don't you come in for a little bit?!"

I turn the corner and see her. She's wearing black leggings and a long sleeve crop top, hat and sunglasses in hand.

"Hey!" I basically shout at her.

She jumps at the suddenness and loudness of my voice. "Well, hi, jeez, you scared me!"

"Sorry," I say as I make my way to her. "Are you ready to go?"

"No, I'm gonna talk with your mom for a couple minutes. She invited me in!"

Damnit, Mom.

Mom is all too pleased with her little trick. "How polite and thoughtful of you! Can I get you some orange juice? Maybe a cup of coffee? Simon bought me one of those fancy espresso machines that you just put those little pods in and it makes a great cup of whatever you like!"

Z smiles and grabs my hand as we walk down the hall to the kitchen. "A cup of coffee would be great. Caramel latte if you have the pod!"

"Coming right up!"

Before Z and I make it into the kitchen, she quickly spins me around and kisses me. Her arms go around my neck and her hand is back in my hair. I wrap my arms around her lower back and lift her off the ground. We stay like that for a couple seconds before I set her down and she lets me go.

"Hi," Z says, her bright smile shining up at me.

"Hi," I reply, holding her hand.

"I'm glad last night happened."

"I agree. I was scared that it wasn't real when I woke up this morning or it was just some music induced romantic moment."

She touches the side of my face. "No, this is very real. The music may have helped us get there, but this is very, very real."

I pull her back in for a quick kiss before she drags me into the kitchen to retrieve her cup of coffee.

After Mom hands her the mug, Z takes a sip. "Oh, this is so good! Thank you, Mrs. Connors."

"You're very welcome, my dear. Anything for you, Jackie-Poo?"

My face reddens as Z almost spews coffee out of her nose.

"Mom!"

"Oh, that's right, you don't want to be called that."

Z winks at me. "I don't know, Mrs. Connors. Jackie-Poo has a nice ring to it."

I give Z a look before Mom turns around and she just laughs at me.

"Oh, sweetheart, don't be such a spoil-sport," Mom says. "But I can respect your wishes. Do you want anything, *Jack*?"

"No, mom, I'm good."

"What are you two doing today?" Mom asks before I have a chance to grab Z and go.

"I think we're going to get breakfast and then go to Disney Springs. And then we'll probably come back here or to Uncle Simon's," Z replies after another sip of coffee.

"Feel free to come back here anytime. Have you decided where you want to take Z for breakfast, Jack?" Mom looks at me with one of her have-you-even-thought-about-this looks.

"I have some ideas."

No, I don't.

Mom shakes her head - she's seen right through me. "Have you considered taking her up to Shakers?"

"Shakers?" Z asks, looking at me.

"Yeah, it's a family favorite of ours. It's about a half hour north from here, which means it'll be another half hour back down to Disney Springs."

"That's totally fine with me. More time with you," Z replies, winking.

My cheeks are burning.

Mom takes Z's cup and dumps the rest of it in one of our travel mugs. "I won't keep you any longer. Have fun, you two!"

Z thanks my mom for the coffee and begins heading out the door. As usual, I go and hug my mom good-bye. "Thanks, Mom."

"For what?"

"Suggesting the diner."

"Oh," Mom laughs at me. "You mean saving your ass?"

I laugh with her. "Yes, that. Thanks."

I join Z in the hallway who immediately takes my hand as we walk out to the car. Something about how I feel when she touches me is so foreign and yet so natural, it makes me feel like I'm walking on air. I honestly still can't believe it.

"She's so nice," Z says, taking a big gulp of coffee.

"She's the best," I reply, opening the car door for her.

"What a gentleman - thank you," she remarks, kissing me on the cheek before sitting down.

I go over to the driver side and plop myself down, handing her my phone. "What are we listening to today?"

Z opens my phone - she knows the passcode, doesn't even have to ask - and opens the music app. "Well, I am really into this newish artist lately. He's from New England and has really blown up recently. I'm sure you've probably seen his videos on TikTok or at least heard his music used."

I shake my head. "I doubt it. My TikTok is mostly nerdy stuff and engineering stuff."

"That's redundant, Jack."

I laugh as she pokes me in the side, making me squirm a little.

"I'm sure you'll like his stuff," Z says as she taps a playlist of the artist's top songs. His sound is pretty cool – it's definitely pop but it's also infused with folk. But that's not really what I care about. Z took my hand shortly after getting on 417 and is using it as her personal microphone, belting out the lyrics in perfect tune and sync.

She really is absolutely incredible.

We get to Shaker's around 9:15 and get seated a few minutes later – we must have just beat the brunch rush. Z takes immediate interest in the little figurines that are actually salt and pepper shakers that are on all of the tables, on the counter, and on the shelves. We are seated at a table with a Popeye and Olive Oyl duo, Olive Oyl doing her classic "my hero" pose with Popeye giving her a kiss on the cheek.

"Hey," Z says with a deadpan look and tone. "It's us."

I try my best to not laugh, but the second she even remotely breaks I'm gone. It really wasn't that funny, but I can't help it. She sits down across from me, a big smile on her face as she accepts the menu from our waitress.

"I'm sorry, miss," the waitress, Connie, says. "But you look familiar. Do I know you from somewhere?"

Z gives her a light smile. "No, I'm not from around here. I've been told I have 'one of those faces.'"

"Oh, I suppose so," Connie remarks and I can't tell if she buys Z's classic lie or not. "What can I get you to drink?"

"I'll have a Coke," I reply.

"Same," Z says.

"Two Cokes, coming right up."

Connie walks away and Z looks at her menu. I know what I'm going to get – the Brioche French Toast 2x4. It's the perfect kind of French toast matched with great eggs, bacon, and sausage. Two of each, of course.

Z eyes me not touching my menu. "Not hungry?"

I shake my head. "Oh no, I'm always hungry when I come here. I just know exactly what I'm going to get."

"What?"

I tell her my usual order and she nods. "Definitely going to be my back up."

"What are you looking at?"

"I'm eyeing the Southwestern omelet, but the only thing that's not really appealing to me is the…"

"Black beans."

She looks up from her menu, her beautiful smile sending tingles down my spine. "Yes, the black beans. You really do know me."

She reaches out with one hand and I take it without hesitation. She rubs my hand with her thumb as I watch her mill over her decision. She's adorable when she thinks. The menu lays flat on the table as her free hand twirls her black hair. I can tell she's really pondering her decision as she begins to chew the corner of her bottom lip. I can feel my smile growing.

I try to stop it.

But I can't.

She's just… her. Amazing. Beautiful. Incredible.

She squeezes my hand. "Jack," she sings out warmly, "I can feel you staring at me."

"Sorry," I reply, my cheeks burning. "I just can't get enough of you."

Pull it together, man.

Z looks up from the menu. "I didn't realize you were such a fawner!"

My cheeks are blazing now. "Sorry."

She squeezes my hand again, harder this time. "Babe, don't apologize. It feels good to be... doted on? I'm not sure if that's the right word."

"What do you mean?"

She traces a circle with her thumb on my hand. "I've just... never had a boyfriend that knows me the way you do. Or notices the things about me that you do. You just seem so much more attentive to me. And I hope you feel the same way how I've been with you, because I've really been trying, I promise."

It's my turn to squeeze her hand. "I have. I mean, you came to my performance last night. Even Nick didn't show any interest in it, much less plot a surprise for after."

She smiles again as Connie comes back.

"What can I get you two lovebirds this morning?"

I nod at Z, giving her the first go.

"I'll have..." Z starts. "Can I have the... Can you not put the beans in the omelet?"

"Which one, hon?"

"Oh, right, sorry. The... uh... Southwestern?"

"Absolutely, we can. Do you want them on the side?"

"Oh, um... no, not at all, if that's okay?"

"Perfectly fine, dearie. And you?"

"Brioche French Toast 2x4. Scrambled eggs. And can you bring a plate of hashbrowns for us to split too? She's got to have them."

Connie chuckled. "You must be a regular."

"I'm one of the Connors that comes in."

"Oh, Simon's boy?!"

"Yes, that's me."

"Oh, that Simon. Always leaving tips bigger than he should. I'll get those hashbrowns on there for you, but it'll be on the house, okay?"

I almost begin to object, but Connie wasn't going to have it as she turned on her heel and went back to the kitchen, yelling out the order to the cooks in the back.

"Your family must come here often?" Z says in such a way that it felt like she was making a statement and asking a question all at once.

"We try to come up here every weekend. My dad has always been a huge fan of small, 'ma and pa' places like this. He likes to avoid chains at all costs. And it has some of the best food in Orlando."

"Well, I hope that it tastes as good as you hype it up to be," Z reassures me with a smile.

Neither of us say anything for a little bit. To be honest, I'm okay with that. It's nice just to hold her hand in silence. I love the way her hand feels in mine. Her skin is smooth and soft, fingernails neatly trimmed. But two things are eating away at my trains of thought, and I feel like I need to address them.

"Hey, Z?" I ask, timidly.

"Yeah?"

"I've got a couple of things I want to talk about. Is that okay or do you just want to sit and relax for a while?"

She nods. "I love talking with you. Not to mention this is our first date, so we should probably talk about stuff."

I chuckle before bringing up the first conversation. "Fair enough. And I guess that is what I wanted to talk to you about. At least to start with. You called me boyfriend this morning and then implied it when saying how you like how much I know you. Is that what I am? Am I your boyfriend?"

She smiles sweetly. "If you want to be."

"More than anything."

"Okay, good, because I've been calling myself your girlfriend since last night."

I laugh. "Were you talking to anyone in particular?"

"Mona and Lisa. I called them almost the second I got home."

"And they both answered?"

"Oh, yeah. They knew I was going to the concert last night and they at least wanted to hear my reaction to your playing."

I have a feeling that isn't it.

"What are you hiding?" I ask with a coy smile.

She rubs my hand with her thumb again. "I was planning on confessing how I feel about you after the concert, hoping you would feel the same way. I didn't plan on you saying what you did first, nor did I plan on kissing you, but I am *so* glad I did."

Again, cheeks are burning.

"Which I guess brings me to the next thing on my mind," I continue. "Are you worried that we're moving too fast? I mean, we kissed before our first date. I feel like that's not a typical thing?"

Z laughs for a second and then sighs. "I appreciate your concern in the matter, but that's not how I see it. Jack, think about the last, like, two months. We've been flirting and playing this weird 'you like me, I like you, but we both aren't doing anything about it' kind of game. I mean, think about the beach just three weeks ago. We watched the sunset together, basically cuddling the whole time. Kissing you last night didn't feel like rushing anything. It felt like a 'oh my God, this is finally happening.' Do you know how long I've wanted to kiss you? Do you have any idea how long I've wanted this?" She raises our hands.

"No, I honestly didn't have any idea. But I'm more than happy this is happening."

Z raises an eyebrow. "Why didn't you have any idea?"

Whatever you do, don't say she's out of your league.

"You're so far out of my league that it makes my head hurt."

Damn it, man, pull yourself together!

Her face grows serious. "Why do you say that?"

I hesitate for a moment. "I mean, think about what I said last night. You've been in TV shows and a movie. You're not just incredibly talented, you're very versatile, too. I'm just some guy who plays piano and is lucky enough to even know you."

A light, kind smile appears on her face. "Jack, you're so much more than that. You make me feel safe. You make me feel seen and heard. You make me feel like I am the only girl in the world when I'm around you. Do you know how rare that is? Especially in my line of work? Actresses get replaced all the time. Once we age out of whatever genre we're in, we're lucky to move on to the next. But around you, it's like nothing else matters to you. And I want that in my life. I want you in my life."

I return her smile. "I feel like an idiot for not telling you sooner."

"So do I! But that doesn't matter now. What does is that we are here now."

Our food comes shortly after our little conversation and we talk about school and different opportunities. She asks me about the time I went to Berlin for a piano competition and I ask her about the different places she's been – the most intriguing being her visit to New Zealand to film part of a movie. And times flies. Our conversations are so unbelievably natural and the laughter is infectious and so constant that my sides hurt by the time I've paid the check and we're back in the car, heading to Disney Springs.

She decides she wants to listen to some classical piano and asks me about the different pieces that play in the shuffle. I know a couple of them and start talking about how I play them or would play them. The entire time she's looking at me, smiling and nodding. She says she is committing everything I say to memory so she can better understand my passion for piano.

We eventually reach Disney Springs – traffic is always bad midday on a Sunday. Z puts on her Wolverines hat and heavy tinted sunglasses, and I get a little sad. Her deep, gorgeous blue eyes are one of the many things I really like about her and I hate to see her cover them. But I totally get it. There's no way in hell that she would go unrecognized. I mean, there's still a chance that she'll be recognized even with the guise on. She immediately grabs my hand and begins dragging me through the park. We walk through The Art of Disney and she tells me all the different drawings and sketches and pieces of art in the room that she wants to buy and I find out that anything related to the classic Disney movies are her favorite things. We meander through the shops and find some things we like, but don't buy – everything is pretty pricey at Disney Springs.

When we walk towards the marketplace, Z almost jumps out of her shoes and looks at me with the sweetest smile she has.

"Jack?" She asks in sing song voice. "How much do you like me?"

I chuckle at the persisting melodic musing. "Quite a bit, why?"

She pulls me closer to her and wraps her arms around me. "Can you do something with me, *please*?"

I eye her suspiciously. "What is it?"

She sways her body so that I bend with her and she dramatically rolls her head at one of the store fronts. It's a simple design with an old styled wooden sign above the brown awning door. It reads 'Disney PhotoPass.'

"Oh, Z, I don't…"

"No, please Jack!" She dramatically whines. "I've always wanted to do this but everyone who has come with me here has always said no."

"Z, I'm not…"

She kisses me. "Please." Another kiss. "Please." Again, kiss. "Please."

I have a feeling this is going to be her tactic until I cave in.

And the sad thing? It's working.

"Fine! Fine, I'll do it with you."

"Yay! And you're going to let me dress you up!"

"What! That wasn't part of the agreement."

"Do I need to kiss you again to convince you?" She asks, bringing her lips closer to mine.

"Oh, I guess it wouldn't hurt," I say before taking the opportunity to kiss her first. "Fine. I'll wear whatever you want me to wear."

She giggles cheerfully before pulling me into the studio. Inside is an arraignment of different outfits and props that Z immediately starts to rifle through. She ends up giving me outfits of a few different Disney princes as she dresses up as the corresponding Disney Princess, ranging from Tangled to Star Wars.

Despite my earlier apprehension, I have the best time. We humorously pose with different special effects backdrops and settings. I feel myself starting to loosen up as I let Z take me into a realm of silliness, both our sides hurting from laughter by the time the photographer tells us that we need to get going since we're holding up the line. Once we change back into our own clothes, we go to Blaze Pizza and get some lunch. I get a classic Pepperoni, she gets a Meat Eaters, and we split a simple salad. Instead of sitting across from me, Z sits next to me and pulls up the pictures we took at the marquee on her phone with her My Disney Experience profile. We eat and we laugh, picking and buying the ones we love the most. She laughs so hard that she wheezes and snorts, which causes me to laugh even harder.

We explore for a few more hours and check out the different Disney exclusive boutiques before we head back home. After stopping for coffee, we pull into my driveway and get out of the car.

"Wait, so you mean moose just roam the side of the highways?!" Z exclaims.

I have been telling her about different parts of Alaska that people normally don't believe. "Oh, yeah. I mean, the bulls are bigger than some trucks I've seen down here. They rule the road. If you hit one, you're lucky to leave the accident unharmed."

"That's so absurd. And I thought California was weird."

We stand in front of my car as our laughter fades. She's looking at me with this longing look. I draw her close and kiss her. She wraps her arms around my shoulders and neck, kissing me again and again.

She pulls only a few centimeters away. "Uncle Simon isn't home."

My heart starts racing. "Oh, yeah?"

"And I did say we could fix the whole make out situation."

My heart is now going Mach 5. "Are you sure?"

She kisses me deeply. "Yes, very much so."

Z brings me into the house and guides me to the couch. She gently pushes me onto the soft cushions and straddles my lap.

"Z?" I say, trying but failing to hide the sheepishness in my voice. "I've never done this before."

Z kisses me again. "Are you intimidated that I have?"

"A little."

"Do you hold it against me?"

"No. Never."

She kisses me again, this time as deeply as before but with more passion and fervor. She tastes like coffee and caramel and everything sweet in life.

"Good. Because I already am enjoying it far more than I ever have."

I run my hands up her thighs and then around the small of her back, pulling her close.

"Just follow my lead. Tell me if you ever get uncomfortable."

"I will."

She kisses me again, much like the last time but with even more intensity.

It is easy to say that I was never uncomfortable. Not even for a moment.

CHAPTER 11

Z and I are officially dating and we're coming up on our one month anniversary. I mean, we were together already, but now all of our friends and our parents know. And it's been amazing. We're probably just in this honeymoon phase of our relationship, but I thought I had imagined what it would be like being with her. To be hers. To be able to say she's my girlfriend. To know that I wasn't just texting her while she was with some other guy. To know what it would feel like to be *that* guy.

I couldn't have been more wrong in such a good way. It is nothing like I have dreamt about because that fantastical feeling is nowhere near the feeling that is now my reality. It's honestly overwhelming sometimes. We have so much fun together. Just the other weekend we went to Disney's Hollywood Studios and built lightsabers together (her treat despite my objections) and explored the park, then the next day went to Magic Kingdom to explore everything there, then Monday - the teachers had a professional development day - we went to EPCOT and tried all the different foods and treats it had to offer.

But none of it comes close to the feeling of simply being with her. She makes me laugh harder than ever before every time we meet. I feel full when I'm with her. Holding her hand and kissing her is such a different sensation than anything I've felt before. I mean, she's my first real girlfriend - unless you count Laura back in 7th grade when we dated for, like, a week - and I've been having an incredible time getting to know her. I've learned all of her favorites. She loves the color blue - specifically light, pastel blues. Purple is a close second. Her favorite drink is Coca-Cola Cherry and hates that many restaurants don't have it and won't even make it for her using grenadine. We were at a burger joint not too far from my house and they were out of Coke Cherry, so when our waitress went back to the check to put in our order, Z pulled out a small bottle of grenadine and mixed it into her cup. My own Coke came out of my nose as she poured it in since she looked like a kid trying to sneak a candy bar past their parents, which then caused her to laugh as I reacted to the burning sensation in my nose. She enjoys playing board and card games and has never really got the hang of video games. She's fascinated by ancient cultures and their fashion, specifically looking at Roman and Egyptian cultures. She likes to cuddle during movies, but not make out - she says that if she turns on a movie, her intent is to watch. However, she loves making out as well and has told me that I'm getting better at it, which has boosted my self-confidence a lot.

We talk for hours on end, even on days when we don't get to see each other. One weekend she had to go to California and film a cameo in some new TV show. The texting was sporadic, but we still found time. I kept my ringer on so that when she was done filming for the day and video-called me, I would be able to answer since it would end up being pretty late by the time she wrapped. It was good to see her and hear her voice. I was able to pick her up at the airport and I did the cheesiest thing - I showed up in my suit with flowers and a sign with her name on it (like she didn't know who I was). Z had burst out laughing when she saw me and then ran to me to throw her arms around me in a hug.

This girl is amazing and I grow more and more crazy for her every day.

Today, however, we promised our friends we would hang out with them and it's a rather chilly day in December. Gathering at my house, we had started the day off with studying for finals coming up this week, but now we aren't sure what to do.

"Do we need to study more?" Khalan asks. "I don't really think I do, but it wouldn't hurt?"

Lisa slams her math book closed. "I'm so, *so* sick of studying! Please, let us do literally anything else."

I look at the clock. It's about three in the afternoon.

"What about Lucy's?" I ask.

Z curls up under my arm and rests her head on my shoulder. "Ugh, yes, please! Some of those cheese bites with sriracha ranch and an Eastbound and Down sound absolutely scrummy."

I shake my head and laugh - we've been watching the Great British Baking Show together and she likes to throw the different words and phrases they use 'across the pond.'

"I wouldn't mind," Khalan says, finally closing their computer. "But we would all have to drive separately and I'm not sure I trust Jack and Z to actually make it there."

Z and I blush as our friends laugh - they had caught us making out in the car a couple of days into our relationship and now it's their little inside joke.

Yes, we make out a lot in the first week of our relationship and in a few random areas, including the Baja. Don't judge us.

"I can ask Mom if I can borrow her new Tahoe," I volunteer. "Not sure if it'll work, but I'll ask."

"Take Z with you! The last time she asked your mom something, you got to go to Clearwater for the weekend," Mona teases.

Z laughs. "No, he's got this. I don't want to abuse my powers."

Everyone joins in with Z's laughter as I leave the room to find Mom. I eventually find her out on the enclosed porch, working on a painting of a group of anhinga on the shoreline.

"May I enter your creative space?" I ask. This is a routine she has set up with Dad and I. She doesn't like interruptions to her work, which is understandable. It can take her a long time to get into the headspace she needs to work on a particular painting. Each painting requires a different headspace - at least, that's what she claims - and she gets frustrated if she falls out of it. So, whenever Dad or I want to get her attention, we ask her if we may enter her space. Once she is in a place where she can either step out of her headspace easily or she is finished with a particular stroke or section, she will allow us to enter. I watch as she finishes the bright orange beak of one of the birds, then turns to me with a smile.

"Yes, sweetheart, you may."

I smile back at her and walk over to look at the painting.

"I love what you've done with the blacks and whites on the birds," I say, pointing at the different brush strokes and color tones. I try to engage my mom in conversation about her art as much as I can since it is her favorite thing in the world to do. She appreciates it as well so it is a double win.

"Thank you, Jack. I'm not really happy with the water behind them, but it will get there."

I nod. "You could try that thing you did with the waves in the… oh shoot, the… the painting of St. Lawrence Island?"

Looking back at her painting, Mom nods slowly. "Yes… that… *might* work… it would have to be on a much less grandiose scale." She looks at me and smiles. "Thank you, Jack."

"Of course, Mom," I say, wrapping an arm around her shoulders and squeezing.

"Did you need something?"

"Only if you feel like you can get back into the creative space for this painting."

She smiles again. "I can manage. What do you need?"

"I was wondering if I could drive your Tahoe to Cocoa? We were thinking about hitting up Lucy's and wanted to drive all together rather than separate."

"Let me see," Mom says, pulling out her phone. She opens the app for our insurance and clicks on the drivers list. "Just looking to see if you are insured on the vehicle."

"I figured."

"May I enter your creative space, Mrs. Connors?"

Both Mom and I turn to see Z standing in the doorway of Mom's studio. Without fail, I smile when I see her.

Still can't believe I'm dating her.

Mom also smiles. "Yes, dear, you may but only if you call me Lydia. I insist, again."

"Okay, I will, Lydia," Z says, walking over and kissing me on the cheek. She turns her attention to Mom's painting. "Oh, my gosh, Lydia, that's amazing!"

Mom's smile grows. "Thank you, Zendaya."

Z points at the water behind the anhinga. "I'm no expert at painting, but what if you did that thing with the water like you had done with the waves in your painting of St. Lawrence Island? The…" Z flourishes her hand, wielding an imaginary paintbrush.

"Oh, yes, the infamous…" Mom mimics Z and they both laugh. "You have a good memory. And good intuition. Jack gave me the same recommendation."

Z smiles at me. "Well, one more reason for us to be together, babe."

Mom laughs. "You two do make quite the couple. Is there something I can help you with, Zendaya?"

Z shakes her head. "No, I just came to check on Jack. The others were getting kind of antsy and I wasn't sure if you two were talking or if Jack was waiting on your permission to enter."

Mom shakes her head. "Those children. Always in such a rush." Mom looks back at her phone. "Jack, yes, you may take the Tahoe, but you need to be careful. Promise me you won't do anything stupid."

I nod reassuringly. "Of course, Mom. Wouldn't dream of driving otherwise."

Mom gives me a 'really-you're-going-to-pull-that-crap' kind of look - the one where her lips are pursed and left eyebrow up - and then looks at Z. "Hold him accountable, will you?"

Z grabs my hand, interlacing her fingers, and squeezes tightly. "Yes, ma'am. I'll sit shotgun the whole way."

Mom nods and looks back to me. "Good. Finally, someone I can entrust you with." Both of the women laugh as I just roll my eyes. "Keys are hanging up. Full tank of gas. Please fill it up when you get back."

"Yes, Mom! Thanks, Mom!" I say, leading Z out of the studio. Before we leave the threshold, Z stops and turns around to look at Mom.

"Lydia, before we go, can I ask you something?"

"Of course, dear, what is it?"

"Would… Would you…" Z runs a hand through her hair and plays with the ends - her telltale sign she's nervous about asking or talking about something she's not 100% confident with. "Would it be okay if… if I painted with you sometime? I'm not the best at it, but I just thought it would be nice to do something with you… you know… my boyfriend's mom?"

I've never seen mom smile as big as she does at this moment. "Zendaya, it would be my genuine pleasure to paint with you. Who knows?" Mom shoots me a wink. "Maybe Jack will play some background music for us."

Z's face lights up. "Oh my gosh, would you?!"

I shrug. "I'm sure we can work something out."

Z shoves me, then grabs the front of my shirt to pull me swiftly back to her so she can kiss me. "Ugh, you're so ridiculous."

I laugh. "Yes, I will pull out some calmer classical movements for the occasion."

"Next weekend?" Mom asks. "Friday before we leave for the Keys?"

"Sounds great!" Z exclaims. "Thank you so much!"

"Anytime, sweetheart. Now, you two go have fun with your friends."

I smile, dragging Z out of the studio. "Thanks, Mom! Ladies, gentleman, and noble person! Let's go! To Lucy's!"

"To Lucy's!" They all call back and I hear the clamoring of bodies getting up and ready for the adventure. We get in the car - not before grabbing some sodas from the garage fridge, of course - and begin our hour or so journey out towards Cocoa. Z immediately handles the music, accepting requests from everyone in turn so there is a nice balance of music that each person likes. After establishing a satisfactory and lengthy queue, Z takes my right hand in both of hers - one of her favorite things to do when I drive. We all talk about school and how excited we are for winter break. Z expresses how thrilled she is to be spending the holiday with my family and her Uncle Simon down in the Keys, though I know she is sad that her parents aren't able to make the trip out. I had asked her why she didn't want to fly out to California and she said that if she went back, the doorbell to their house would just ring and ring with reps from different directors or agencies or companies trying to get her to work over the break - something she didn't want to do.

We reach Lucy's around 4:30pm and make our way inside. Nick and I say hi to our co-workers and Nicole, the hostess, seats us at Nick and I's favorite spot - the front far corner from the door that has what we call alternative seating. It's made to look like a backyard patio complete with the appropriate furniture and fake turf.

"Oi! Lads! What's with ya not saying hello?!"

Nick and I turn to look at Farrow, who comes out wearing an apron which is very messy.

"Farrow, you old bastard, what are you doing in that outfit? Aren't you the owner of this establishment?" Nick asks, a rueful smile on his face.

"Oh, Nicky, you cheeky twit. Aye, I'm the owner of this here bar but one of me cooks is out for the night and I couldn't get someone to cover. So, I'm back at it again, after all these years."

Z looks at me, left eyebrow raised. "Should we go somewhere else?"

If it were anyone else, I would have been upset. Farrow is a great cook, he's just kind of old and slow at what he does sometimes. But since I've brought Z here a few times and she's picked me up from work before, so her and Farrow are acquainted and have been keeping up this light banter of jokes between the two of them for a while.

Farrow smiles at her and shoves me. "She's a feisty one, ain't she? Got a little spirit in her, eh boy?"

I nod. "Indeed, she does."

Farrow laughs. "Ah, she reminds me of a lass I once knew. Her name was Lyla, but she had the nickname of The Masked Queen. She, oh, she was a fiery one. Died far before her time. It was a tragedy. Her husband almost lost himself. It's a very sad tale. I'll tell you about it sometime, if ya want."

We all agree that it's a story for another time. Katie, our waitress for the evening and one of the few waitresses I actually call a friend at work and Z's personal favorite (other than me, obviously), takes our drink orders as well as the appetizers for those who want them. We have a great time laughing and chatting about random conversations and joking around. After we pay, Z drags us all out onto the beach for a brief walk around in the cool sand. She convinces me to take some pictures with her, using a ring light Lisa tends to bring with her for photo opportunities. Mona and Lisa take some photos as well while Nick, Khalan, and I try our best not to burst out laughing - sometimes I forget that Mona is almost a foot and a half taller than Lisa and it makes for a comical image when they do a session of couple's photos. Do we ever say that to Mona? Absolutely not. She's just as likely to kick my ass as Khalan and just as capable.

Finally, around 8:00, we make our way home. Everyone falls asleep but Z - the car is very smooth and has great noise reduction technology - so her and I whisper to one another about the day.

"I had a lot of fun," Z says.

"So did I," I reply. "Are you going to hang out with Katie tomorrow?"

Z nods. "I think it will be fun to get to know her outside of Lucy's. And it'll be nice to expand my friend group to someone outside of school, ya know? Like, no offense to anyone at H&H or in this car even - I'm just..."

"Extremely extroverted," I say, finishing her sentence with a wink.

She pokes my side. "Yes, extremely extroverted. I was going to say fairly social, but that works."

I laugh as quietly as possible. "You two will have fun."

Z nods. "I'm also really excited to paint with your mom."

"I've been meaning to ask you about that. Where did that come from?"

Z's quiet for a long moment, then sighs. "I miss my mom."

Z doesn't talk about her mom a whole lot. She has some hard feelings towards her regarding her acting career. It was primarily her mom that shoved her into the business and was very ruthless in the more recent years, heavily critiquing her body and her voice and her hair. Anything external. Not really caring about the internal. It was actually her that pushed Z to want to come to Florida and live with

Gay Simon for her senior year. It was a subject that was really touchy and emotionally charged.

"I'm sorry, Z," I say, squeezing her hand tightly. "Aren't you still mad at her, though?"

Z nods. "Yeah, I am. But she's my mom, Jack, you know? And, yeah, what she did and said to me before I made the decision to come here to Florida still guts me when I think about it. But I keep coming back to the fact that she's my mom. And I love her. I'm grateful for how much she believes in me, despite how harsh she can be."

"So, you want to spend time with my mom to try and counter that?"

"I wouldn't say counter. Maybe pacify? I don't know. I love your mom, though, babe. She's so much fun and she's so caring and so loving."

I smile. "I love her too. Best mom I've got."

Z laughs a little and lays her head down on my arm draped across the console.

"Change of subject?" Z asks.

"Sure! Have something in mind?"

Z nods. "I want to come up with more unique pet names."

I chuckle. "What do you mean?"

"I don't know, babe and honey and sweetheart and whatever are just so basic."

"Okay, so what do you have in mind?"

"I'm going to call you askim."

"Ask him?"

"No, askim. Bright 'i' almost an 'e'."

"What does that mean?"

Z doesn't say anything.

"Z?"

"It's a Turkish word - my dad's part Turk. And it means…" She sits up. "It means… my love."

Did she just say 'my love?'

I look over at her briefly before looking back at the road and she's staring intently at me.

"Z… what are you saying?"

"I'm saying… I'm saying I love you, Jack."

My heart flies to the moon and back. She just said 'I love you' to me. She loves me.

Isn't that too soon? Like we've been dating for a month. Don't couples wait longer? Shouldn't we?

No.

No. We shouldn't.

I waited way too long to tell her how I feel. I waited far too long to actually share with her how much I think about her and how much I care about her. I waited way, *way* too long to kiss her. I should have told her how I felt about her at the end of the summer. I should have told her how much I think about her and how much I care about her at homecoming. I should have kissed her that night on the beach in Clearwater.

I won't let this be another one of those moments. I will not deny myself of the fact that I am in love with her and that I have been since we connected on the beach.

"I love you, too, Zendaya."

I can see tears in her eyes when I look at her again. "You only call me Zendaya when you're being really serious."

I nod. "I waited too long for everything else leading up to this moment. That trend stops now."

She giggles as tears stream down her face and she kisses my hand.

"You picked one hell of a time to tell me that. I can't even kiss you!"

Z laughs and rests her head back on the seat, staring down the road. "Just wait till we get home."

"I think I know what I'll call you, if you approve."

She looks back at me. "What are you thinking?"

My mind goes back to something I heard Dr. Thurmond call his girlfriend over the phone. "Hjartat."

"Scandinavian?" Z asks, then smiles. "You got it from Dr. Thurmond, didn't you? What does it mean?"

"It means 'my heart.'"

Z's smile grows. "I love it."

We drive the last twenty or so minutes in silence and I think I hear Z breathing deeply as if she is sleeping. Once we get back to my house, the rest of my friends take off as I walk Z back to her house. She takes my hand and looks me dead in the eye.

"Come inside for... a bit?" Z asks, her smile light but her eyes intense.

I don't say anything, just nod. I get too excited when she looks at me like that. I know what she's getting at - Gay Simon is working his weekend shift at the hospital. I let her lead me to the couch where pushes me lightly onto the cushions. This time, I lay down when she straddles me.

"I love you, Z."

Her lips gently brush mine once. Twice. Three times.

"I love you, Jack."

Our lips collide with passion unknown to me and I pull her as close to me as possible.

I finally go back home after an hour or so. I lie down in bed and smile, watching my ceiling fan spin gently to move the air in my room like nothing else could. It reminds me of Z who stirs my heart like no one else can.

My phone goes off and I open the text from Z.

Z: Well, that was fun.

Me: Yeah, you can say that again.

Z: Are you okay with not seeing me until Monday?

Me: Of course, have fun with Katie.

Z: I will. But I might sneak in through your window tomorrow night. Keep it unlocked.

I shake my head and laugh

Me: Alright. I will.

Z: Good night, askim.

Me: Good night, hjartat.

Z: I love you.

Me: I love you, too.

CHAPTER 12

Finals week is one hell of a week. Every class is required to have a final - even the arts. Most finals are just tests with well over a hundred questions or projects that require presenting, stuff like that. The best part - each final is worth 20% of our overall grades for the semester. Here's how it works: the Friday before is a big review day in all of our classes. Each class gets 35 minutes for review and then students are allowed to study in school till the end of the day, having access to all the teachers if they need help. On Monday, first and second period finals take up the entire day. First period runs from 8:00am to 11:00am. We have lunch from 11:00am to 12:00pm, then second period runs from 12:00pm to 3:00pm. This repeats itself each day until Thursday when seventh and eighth wrap it all up. If someone is lucky enough, which I happen to be this year, they have a study hall on one of these days and can either come to school late or leave early. We are also able to come to or stay at school and study in the commons, but many students don't.

This year, however, I don't have that luxury.

I have study hall fourth period, but Z has it sixth period. And her habit now is still to ride with me to school every day rather than drive herself. I tried to get her to drive herself to school on Tuesday and Wednesday this week so I could leave early on Tuesday and she could leave early on Wednesday, but I quickly abandoned that attempt as she put on her best performance of pleading with me to 'not make it so.'

I caved so fast.

The kicker? I forgot I had third period TA-ing for Dr. Thurmond and TAs aren't allowed to grade finals. So, Tuesday was a day that I didn't even have to come into school. But I did anyway, Z in tow.

It's Tuesday today and I would be lying if I said I am not bored out of my mind. I spent the majority of third period studying for my English final tomorrow, but as 10:30 creeps toward me, I want to slam my head against my computer. Or a wall. Possibly both. I'm about to give up and leave the school and just come back to pick up Z, when her arms wrap around my neck and I feel her press her lips against my cheek.

"Hi, babe," I say, smiling and closing my laptop.

"Hey, you."

"Were you dismissed early or something?" I ask as I see other seniors from the same class she was just in. Z hops over the couch I'm sitting on - we have a lot of alternative seating here at H&H - and kicks off her shoes. She swings her legs up onto the couch and maneuvers her way under my arm so she's resting more on my shoulder and holding my hand.

"Yeah, everyone was finished and Ms. Polanski didn't want to keep us any longer than she had to, apparently."

I chuckle. "Classic."

"Thanks for being here today. I know you didn't have to be."

I smile and kiss the crown of her head. "Anything for you."

She twists so she is looking up at me. "Anything?"

I arch an eyebrow. "What are you thinking?"

"Practice room?"

We both laugh at our little inside joke. We had been sitting near the practice rooms for band and choir when we started hearing noises coming from one of them. I thought I recognized the sounds, but couldn't really place them. But it all clicked when two freshmen, both red faced and breathing heavily, walked out of the practice room. The look of sheer terror in their eyes when they locked eyes with us and sprinted away was one of the funniest things I've ever seen. We had a good laugh and now it has been our favorite joke between the two of us. However, we agreed that we would never do that in school. Just seems a little excessive and unnecessary.

"I mean…"

She pokes my sides. "No, we agreed. Besides, I doubt that was comfortable for either of them."

I smile. "Later."

She looks up at me again. "Oh really? Later? I think you're forgetting something."

I think for a moment. "Shit, I have my piano lesson then Christmas dinner with Ms. Pillard."

My parents, as a "thank you" for teaching me so enthusiastically, always invite Ms. Pillard out for a fancy meal at Christner's every Christmas season. She tries to turn it down every year since Dad gives her a holiday check as well, but Mom insists upon it with equal tenacity. I had introduced Ms. Pillard and Z a week or two after we started dating since Z drove me to a piano lesson one day 'for fun.'

Ms. Pillard looked at me and immediately guessed she was the reason behind *Jeux D'eau*. They got along really well and talked quite a bit at the lesson - which I only played for about ten minutes out of the hour and a half session.

"Yes, and I'm invited this year so you need to be on your best behavior," Z says with a smirk and an elbow to my side.

"Yeah, it sounds like it's like a triple date without actually being a date."

Z shoots up so she's sitting up and facing me. "Oh, my god. Ms. Pillard is bringing her boyfriend?!"

Ms. Pillard, while very forthcoming about her experiences with music and emotions about different pieces, is quite secretive about her mystery boyfriend. At least, I'm pretty sure her significant other is a man. She uses he/him when talking about their time and trips together, but with a best friend who is trans and another best friend who is non-binary, I try my best to avoid assuming too much.

"Yeah! Mom knew she was seeing someone and told her to bring her boyfriend along. Dad confirmed the reservation is indeed for six, so he must be coming."

Z eyes grow wide with excitement. "Oh, my god, I can't believe it!"

"Me neither! I hope he's cool."

"Oh, I'm sure he is," Z remarks, returning to her prior relaxed position.

"Aren't you hungry?" I ask.

"A little."

I reach into my bag and pull out a bag of kettle chips. "Interested?"

I don't get a verbal response - she just smiles and snatches the bag out of my hands.

"I thought so."

The loud crunching of the salty snack fills my ears for a few minutes while Z polishes off the bag. Once she's done, I reach back into the bag and pull out a bottle of Coke, an apple, and a stick of beef jerky for her.

"God, you really are the best boyfriend."

I laugh. "I do try my hardest, hjartat."

Z twists her head so she can kiss me. "I love you."

I smile. "I love you, too."

"Oh, for the love of St. Peter, get a room!" Lisa yells as she collapses on the couch across from us in the most dramatic fashion.

"My sweet lady Lisa, pray tell what happened to thy spirits? Thou were in such high estates when we departed?" Z asks with her best English accent and dramatic flair.

Lisa pressed the back of her left hand on her forehead. "Halverson's test. 'Twill be the death of me. When I die, place a single white rose on my coffin so that she may see the devastation she has rained upon her victimized students."

I shake my head. "It can't be that bad, Lisa. Besides, it's your fault for taking the test early."

Lisa bolts to her feet, pointing menacingly at me with a shaky index finger. "Thou shall not doubt me, boy! Thou doth not know the wrath and ruin she hurls. Her fire and sulfur shall scorch thine fields of creativity and her cascading rain shall drown thy joys into the depths of sorrow."

Z laughs. "Oh, Lisa, how dreadful!"

Lisa collapses back on the couch. "I shall only be saved by my truest love, but, lo, she is not here. If I perish before she arrives, tell her my heart was always hers and I will wait for her eagerly at the pearly gates."

We all look at each other with the straightest faces possible before bursting into fits of laughter.

"So, you aced it?" I ask.

She does this every year.

"Oh, yeah, totally. No problem. Shakespeare is my shit."

"No kidding."

Z takes another bite of her apple. "Where is Mona, by the way?"

Lisa looks toward the gym. "Doing her crazy fitness final with Khalan, I'm sure."

"Oh, so she'll be really sweaty when she returns."

Lisa smiles. "You know what they say…"

"Please don't quote *House of Cards* again," I beg.

Lisa shakes her head. "When she's hot and sweaty, then she's hot and ready."

I make a vomiting sound while Z's eyes go wide and lets out a bewildered laugh.

"Babe," Z nudges me. "They both have fourth hour study hall with you, don't they?"

Lisa's eyes go wide. "I didn't even think of that!"

As the three of us laugh heartily, we see Khalan and Mona coming from the locker rooms. Lisa immediately gets up, runs over to Mona, and pulls her down so she can whisper in her ear. Mona immediately smiles wide, looks at Khalan, Z, and me, and bows.

"We take our leave."

The DaVinci pair takes off toward the student parking lot.

"I don't want to know," Khalan remarks, sitting down on one of the non-leather, non-upholstery seats in our little area. They are still dripping sweat.

"Brutal final?"

Khalan nods. "Yep. My hardest fights didn't compare to that. A few of the others didn't even finish it."

I let out a low whistle. "Did you shower?"

Khalan shakes their head. "No, not yet. I got to cool down first. But," they slowly get to their feet, groaning slightly. "I forgot I need to talk to Dr. Thurmond about the World History IV final."

They walk off towards the stairs going up to the second floor.

I look down at Z and her demeanor has changed. She's picking at one of the corners of the Coca-Cola plastic label that's wrapped around the bottle. I move my head so I can see her eyes and they are off in a thousand-yard stare.

"Z?"

"Hmm?"

"What's on your mind, hjartat?"

She nestles her head closer to mine. "Our future, askim."

"What do you mean?"

She points off towards the student parking lot. "DaVinci just got me thinking about dating in college."

I nod. "Yeah?"

"They're both dead set on going to the same university. Living together starting freshman year. I mean, I hope they make it and everything works out, don't get me wrong. I'm just... I'm just... a little... jealous, I guess."

I nod again. I've thought about this too. I've applied to a number of colleges on the east coast and in the Midwest, but only three - Stanford, Berkeley, and CalTech - on the west coast. Z is the opposite. A majority of her applications went to the west coast colleges and only three - Harvard, Yale, and University of Minnesota - in both of the regions where mine landed. We've avoided this conversation for a while and I'm not sure if I am ready to tackle this.

"We'll figure it out."

Z smiles at me. "You're always so optimistic."

I smile back. "I was head over heels for you for so long without being your boyfriend. Now that I am, I won't let you go."

She nestles back against my shoulder. "I know you won't. I won't let you go, either. But I just want to be ready."

I nod. "Do you want to plan a little now?"

Z nods back. "Please."

I draw in a deep breath and let it out slowly. "Communication will be key. And, at the same time, we'll need to create a social life."

"Oh, I'm not worried about my social life, it's you I'm worried about."

I laugh. "I'll just find the other pianists. We'll be fast friends."

Z giggles. "So, texting whenever we can."

"Phone calls if we get a chance."

"Video calls?"

"Absolutely."

"I'll fly out and see you whenever I can," Z says.

"Same here. Might not be easy, but I'll figure it out."

"We can make this work. Right?"

"Absolutely."

Z settles back into my shoulder and closes her eyes. "Okay. I'm going to try and nap for a little bit before my next final. Wake me up at 11:55."

"Yes, ma'am."

It doesn't take long for her breathing to become deep and even, her hand in mine. I gently rub her hand with my thumb as my mind races.

I didn't realize how hard this could potentially be. College isn't an easy time. It's phenomenally busy. We'll both have full loads of classes. We'll both have extracurriculars. Will we have time for each other? Will we be okay?

What if I go to one of the schools in California? Her number one spot is UCLA. CalTech is number… Well, it's on my list. But I could go there! CalTech is a great school with a great engineering program that boasts leading innovations into the field. And I would only be an hour away from Z. It's actually a lot closer than that, but LA traffic… oh shit, LA traffic… I didn't think of that. But I can drive an hour! I do it right now for work and Z would obviously be a much better motivator while waiting in the car.

But my dream is MIT. It's the top engineering school in the nation. Basically, a guaranteed job anywhere right after graduation. I've been dreaming about going there since I was little. I even have a flag up in my room.

This is what it has come to. Or, at least, this is what it feels like it has come to. Deciding between a dream I have had for nearly a decade or the dream that I'm currently living in. Being with Z has been better than I could have ever imagined. She's been the greatest thing to happen to me since I started lessons with Ms. Pillard. She's made Florida feel more like home and so much less shitty. But MIT has been my goal since seventh grade. I'm torn. And I feel stupid for it. But at the same time, I feel justified in this emotion.

Nick sneaks over after he's eaten and we talk quietly while Z sleeps. I wake her up at 11:57 - I know she was up late last night (not my fault this time) and needed more sleep than she admits - and I watch her run to her next class. Before she enters the door, she turns and blows me a kiss, then dips in. I'm left sitting on the couch while Nick reads and my thoughts of the future consume me, no matter how hard I try to shift my thinking.

I'm finally saved when Z gets out of her final and I whisk her away to Wendy's to celebrate her surviving her math final with Frosties and fries before heading to my piano lesson. We make it home around 5:00 and she runs to her house, shouting something about needing to get ready. I go in and shower, letting the warm water soothe my racing mind into submission. Mom tells me that I need to wear my best suit to dinner tonight and I get a confirmation from Z on the color of tie I need to wear to match her – purple and I pick the tie I bought and wore to take her out in Clearwater. Dad insists that we all ride together in the Land Rover, so Z and I hop in the back while my parents take the front. Mom and Z immediately discuss what they are wanting to paint on Friday and Mom promises to get things set up for inspiration on Thursday. We eventually arrive at Christner's where we see not one, but two familiar faces waiting for us in the lobby. I half smile and feel both my eyebrows rise as I see who Ms. Pillard's arm is in his own.

"Dr. Thurmond?"

Dr. Thurmond looks like he's coming from the set of a spy movie. He is wearing a black suit with a dark gray button up and black tie. His beard is neatly combed and the runes are polished. His head looks like it was waxed clean. He offers me his hand and I shake it firmly.

"Jack Connors. I didn't realize you were the student I was meeting tonight."

Ms. Pillard looks up at Dr. Thurmond. "Ryan, you know Jack?"

"Know him?" Dr. Thurmond laughs. "Genevieve, he's my TA."

Her eyes go wide and she looks at me. "Our worlds collide!"

Dad shakes his head. "Gen, you know my son goes to H&H - how did you not put two and two together?"

I put a hand up in Ms. Pillard's defense. "We don't really talk about school when we're at practice, Dad. I'm sure she had an inkling I knew her boyfriend but would never guess I was his TA."

"And I don't tend to share my romantic life with my students, Simon," Ms. Pillard says, smiling. "But I'm glad you both know each other already. I was wondering how I was going to introduce him."

The host comes over to us and tells us to follow him to our table. I manage to sit between Ms. Pillard and Z, but our table is luckily a circle so everyone is able to talk to one another. Dad and Dr. Thurmond begin talking about economics and seem to be lost in their own universe while Ms. Pillard and Z chat about different music Z has been listening to per Ms. Pillard's request. I smile. My worlds collided and worked out perfectly. Z squeezes my hand every once and a while to make sure I'm still paying relative attention to everyone.

"Oh, I would love to get a picture of this," Mom says, gesturing to Ms. Pillard, Dr. Thurmond, Z, and me. "Is that okay, Ryan? Or are you not allowed to take photos with students outside of school?"

Dr. Thurmond shakes his head. "No, no, it's fine."

He slides his chair so he's sitting closer to Ms. Pillard. Z scoots closer to me and wraps her arms around my left arm. Mom pulls out her phone and takes a few pictures, smiling the entire time.

"Ugh, I love this!" Mom exclaims, showing us the picture.

"Lydia, could you send that to me, please?" Ms. Pillard asks.

"Me as well, please!" Z says.

Soon, we're all laughing together over some amazing food. Dr. Thurmond and I talk about my exploits in piano and he is genuinely fascinated by my work. It's nice to connect with him outside of school and see him more in a relaxed setting. Ms. Pillard also seems very enamored by him, which is nice to see.

By the end of the night, we're all tired and very full. When Dad gives Ms. Pillard her annual Christmas card and bonus, Mom produces a small gift for her as well which she opens to find a silver necklace with two sapphire pendants and one diamond in between.

"Lydia, I can't…"

"You can and you will," Mom says with a coy smile. "You have done so much for Jack. The benefit at the Steinmetz was the best he's ever played. It's simply an additional thank you."

I give Ms. Pillard a big hug. "I couldn't be more grateful for having you as my teacher."

"And I you as my student," she replies, hugging me back.

Dr. Thurmond lets out a low whistle. "Mr. Connors…"

"Please, it's just Simon, Ryan."

"Apologies. Simon, that's one nice necklace. I might be off the hook for Christmas gifts this year."

Ms. Pillard punches Dr. Thurmond playfully. "No, you are not. This has nothing to do with you!"

We all laugh as Dr. Thurmond dodges another punch and steps towards me and Z.

"Jack. Z. Have a wonderful evening. Make sure you get some studying done for your finals tomorrow."

"Yes, sir," We both reply in unison.

We exchange our good nights and head home. I end up inviting Z over to study and we make our way to the entertainment room.

"You two," Mom says, catching us before we enter the space. "Study."

Z gives Mom the most blameless smile and puts on her most innocent voice. "Why, of course, Lydia. What else would we do?"

Mom gives her a look and a smile and Z dips into the room, pulling me with her.

We end up studying, both of us very aware my mom is patrolling the hallway and staying in a relative line of sight. Around 10:00 pm, Mom decides she's too tired to stay up any longer and goes to bed.

Z looks up at me and smiles. "As much as I love the opportunity that has presented itself, I think I should go home. I don't want to break your mom's trust."

I nod. "Good call. Come on, I'll walk you home."

"My gentleman."

I walk her the dozen or so yards to her front door and she puts her arms around my neck and runs her fingers through my hair.

"I love spending time with your family and being part of your life. It feels like I fit."

"You do."

She pulls me in for a kiss and we hold it for a few moments before she takes a step back and opens her front door.

"Good night, Jack."

"Good night, Z."

"I love you."

"I love you, too."

She blows me a kiss and shuts the door. I smile and head to my house and up to my room. I lay down and watch my ceiling fan spin. I'm incredibly happy.

Right up until the idea of being so far from her creeps back into my mind.

CHAPTER 13

Finally, Winter Break. A chance to have no homework, no finals, no school obligations, and no people you don't want to see. It's absolutely fantastic. The teachers, bless them, were very much ready for this break – probably more than we kids were. I know Dr. Thurmond was – he was taking Ms. Pillard to Minnesota over the break. He is originally from Elk River, Minnesota and all of his family still lives up there. Why he moved to Florida is simply beyond me, but I know Dr. Thurmond was looking forward to the trip.

Mom is really excited for this break, too. Her parents are coming all the way down from Alaska to spend the holiday season with us in the Keys. Since they flew in to Miami to avoid the four-and-half-hour drive from here, they are there already at our rental home soaking up the Florida heat to shake the Alaskan cold. We haven't seen them in over a year, so this is really special for Mom. I'm kind of nervous about it. This set of grandparents is super, *super* conservative. I mean, I don't really care about politics or political parties. You believe what you believe, I'll do the same. But I don't approve of prejudice or discrimination in any way, shape, or form. My grandparents, however, don't feel the same way I do. There have been times where I've heard Grandpa use a number of slurs regarding a number of individuals both from the racial spectrum and sexuality spectrum. And now that I have friends from across both of those spectrums, it makes me incredibly uncomfortable. Even angry. Another reason why I'm concerned for this trip is because Dad had the idea of inviting Z. Of course, I was more than willing to say yes to that being that it would be our first Christmas together. But Z said she wasn't sure since it would leave her uncle alone of the holiday. Her parents weren't able to come out and Gay Simon's partner was going to be busy all break with a conference or convention or something. Dad then promptly invited both Z and Gay Simon.

Gay Simon. My grandparents. In my opinion, my apprehension is quite justifiable. It's going to take my grandpa, like, ten seconds to know Gay Simon is... well, gay. And I'm sure that is where the fun will begin. And by fun I mean slurs from Grandpa, witty comebacks from Gay Simon, and then arguments between, well, everyone. Not exactly how I want my grandparents to meet my girlfriend. Or how I want to spend the first Christmas with her. But I'm going to stay on the positive side of things.

Or at least try to.

But before any of that happens, Z gets to paint with Mom. She has been looking forward to it since they planned it. Z is so nervous to paint with 'a master painter,' that she's been secretly painting at home in her free time. I've seen a couple of her paintings and she definitely has some potential. They are by no means perfect, but they aren't terrible either. Kind of what you would expect from an amateur painter who has more interest in the arts than your average person. Z still doesn't know what she wants to paint, but I'm sure my mom has something planned.

Now, it's Friday morning and Mom is setting up the studio for her painting session with Z. Mom is also incredibly excited – none of my friends have ever asked to paint with her. Nor have any of her friends. She has a few down here she spends time with, but most of them aren't interested in painting. Mom says they make for great company 'until they just can't shut up and gossip.' That's when she checks out. She has no doubts that they talk about her behind her back, but I'm not sure she actually cares about that at all.

Dad helps me move the piano to the studio and we set up in the corner of the studio with the back facing the outside wall. It's not exactly an arduous task since it is on wheels, but it's still awkward and clumsy. It takes us the better part of a half hour, but everything is set up by the time Z knocks on the side door. She kisses me as she walks in, but I can tell her excitement is pulling her somewhere else. She quickly makes her way to the studio where Mom is waiting with a wide smile.

"Welcome, Z!"

Z runs up to Mom and hugs her. "Hi, Lydia. Thanks for doing this with me."

"Absolutely, dear!" Mom leads her over to the spare chair and easel, handing her a smock. "Put this on. Did you wear clothes you don't mind getting paint on? The smock should be enough to cover everything, but I would hate to ruin good jeans and whatnot."

Z nods. "I did. What are we painting today?"

Mom points at the array of inspirational materials she has laid out. "Well, I have this basket of fruit and this vase of flowers. If we're lucky, we might see some anhinga or an alligator come up on the beach – hence having us face the outside windows."

"Sounds doable," Z says as she ties the smock laces behind her.

"Jack, what have you prepared for us today?"

I pat the stack of sheet music on top the piano. "I've picked out a lot of calm music. Nothing with a lot of fast tempos or minor keys. I even have some light jazz Ms. Pillard suggested on Tuesday."

Mom smiles. "Wonderful. Shall we begin?"

Z nods and I start to play *Dawn* from *Pride and Prejudice* as the two ladies begin their painting. I don't see what colors they are using, nor the canvases they are painting on. But I can see them moving their brushes against the canvases. It's not long before I see Mom shift into her creative mindset as she flows with her brush and becomes one with the painting. In a way, it's a lot like how I play piano. We meld into the artistry, leaning into our imagination and letting our innate skills lead us into the wonder that is our craft. I lean into my music and close my eyes, listening to the piano quietly fill the corners of the studio. I only open them every once and a while as a solid two hours pass as the two women paint.

When I open my eyes completely and look around the room, I think I can see frustration in Z's eyes.

"Hjartat, what's wrong?" I ask in a half whisper.

"I don't know, askim." Her voice confirms the anger she is feeling. "I can't... I don't... Ugh... I don't know..."

"Z, what is it?" Mom asks this time, only partially leaving her inspired focus.

"I don't like how this looks." She points to the painting and Mom looks.

Mom nods. "How are you feeling?"

Z looks at my mom with a curious look. "I'm fru..."

"Not in regards to painting. How are you feeling emotionally?"

Z's shoulders sag. "I'm... I'm... I'm sad..."

"Sad?"

Z nods and I think I see tears forming in the corners of her eyes. "My parents aren't coming out for Christmas... I won't be able to see them until the summer now. They are going to Hawaii for Spring Break with some of my dad's relatives and it's a twenty-one plus event so... Yeah..."

Mom rubs her back. "I'm sorry, sweetie. Jack said something like that happened."

Z nods, more tears streaking down her face. "It's been so long…"

"I know, honey. I know. Have you called them?"

Z nods. "Sometimes… sometimes I have regrets about coming here."

My heart sinks. I knew she did. But whenever I hear it, it hurts. For me, having her here has made Florida all the better. I think I make Florida better for her, too, but it was her choice to come here. And it was a choice made out of anger.

"I'm sure you do, Zendaya. And I'm sure you wish you could see your parents. I feel the same way quite often. Don't tell Simon this, but sometimes I miss Alaska."

I hit a wrong note out of surprise, but quickly move on and pretend not to notice. Mom has never said something like that. I've never heard her once say she misses Alaska. I mean, a big part of us moving down here was because of her arthritis and other health concerns. Her doctors said a warmer environment would be much better for her. And she always wanted to leave Alaska. I didn't know she actually liked part of it.

"You do?"

"I do," Mom says and I can see her put her brush back to the canvas. "I miss the glaciers and the sunsets. I miss the changing of the seasons. And," Mom chuckles. "I miss the snow sometimes. Not all the time, but there have been days."

"What do you do when you feel like that?"

Mom smiles. "First, I think of everything here that I am grateful for here. Like the warmer weather year-round. Beaches where it's actually comfortable to go and spend a day in the sand. The variety of people and places available to us. The animals that have been my most recent art subjects. And then, of course, the things I am grateful for that have been a constant in my life. Simon. Jack. His lovely piano playing."

I can feel myself blushing brightly now.

"And finally, the things that are new in my life. Primarily, you."

Z lets out a sob and then gasps for air. "Me?"

Mom places a hand on Z's shoulder. "Indeed, you, my dear. I have enjoyed our times together and our conversations. I especially enjoy doing this with you. Not many people ask to paint with me."

I feel very called out, but I just keep playing.

"And I am grateful the happiness you have brought into my son's life. He hasn't been the same since we moved here. The piece he played to compete for the Annotator Award was proof of that. It was dark and moody. Angry, even, at points. I was afraid I wasn't going to see my happy boy again. But then you arrived and *Jeux D'eau* showed me that he was still there."

"That was before we even started dating, though."

"Indeed. It was your mere friendship that created that. Now, I know he has always had a deep crush on you…"

"Mom…" I mutter as I play, causing both of them to laugh.

"Sorry, Jack," Mom replies. "But I knew he did. And then I saw you at the performance at the Steinmetz and I knew you felt the same way. And I was happy. I am happy. So, yes, Zendaya, I'm quite grateful for you and I'm glad I get to spend Christmas with you, sweetheart."

Z smiles as tear trickles down her cheek. "Me too."

"Now, what would help get you into the artistic headspace you need?"

Before Z answers, I already have an idea of what will help. *Jeux D'eau.*

I close my eyes and let myself drift into a daydream of Z. It's not hard. It's become a fairly easy thing to do. I touch the keys and begin to lightly play the piece. Whatever Z was saying has quickly faded away as she stops and listens to the music. I can't see anything, but I can hear Mom whisper something like 'precious' followed shortly by the sound of paintbrush on canvas. I smile as memories of adventures with Z fill my head. Then the times of being alone with her. Where there is only her. The music fills my head and heart, spilling into the room.

"Oh, Z, that's… that's a great idea," Mom remarks in almost a reverent whisper.

I don't stop playing. Whatever I'm doing is working for Z. I feel my body wanting to rise out of the stool, so I stand up a little. It's not comfortable, nor is it easy as I have to still work the damper pedal. But I can feel the music more now than ever. Ms. Pillard said this would happen. She told me the more I lean into the emotion of the piece and explore the fantasies of my daydreams, the more the music would come alive. And it has. My fingers aren't mine anymore as the music takes them from me, transforming the memorized piece into something beyond beauty.

Once *Jeux D'eau* is done, I immediately transition into several arias and sonnets by various composers letting the calm rush over me. Before I realize it, I've been playing for two hours off memory and my fingers begin to hurt from the effort. I finally let the last chords of a classic aria ring through the air and turn to Z and Mom.

"May I take a break?" I ask with the most charming smile I can muster.

"Yes, dear, of course," Mom replies. "But first, you need to see this painting your beautiful girlfriend has done."

"No, Jack, please, it's not…" Z starts to say before Mom cuts her off.

"Z, don't be modest. This is a wonderful piece full of emotion and heart. Jack, come look."

I look at Z. "I'll only look if you say it's okay."

Z nods, though I can tell it's a reluctant one. I walk over to see her work and my heart fills in an instant.

She's painted me.

I mean, it's really an interpretation of me. She's painted it in a very Van Gogh-esque style of painting with unblended brushstrokes and planes of color, the brushstrokes very obvious and evident throughout the painting. I knew this was going to be the style she was going to try, but I think Z must have started painting the lake, but only the shoreline and surface area of the lake are present. But in the forefront of the painting, is my piano and me. My face is very simply detailed with only fine lines and impressions for facial features, but I can tell it is me by the clothing and the very way I sit at the piano. Cheesy musical notes float out of the piano and ducks sit at the edge of the pond, but my heart fills.

"Babe… it's…"

"Hideous. Awful. Disgusting. Corny."

"Amazing."

She looks up at me. "Really?"

I nod. "I'm flattered."

I wrap an arm around Z and she leans her head against me.

"When you started playing *Jeux D'eau*, I felt that wall of emotion come over me again and I knew I needed to capture it. And," she gestures to the painting. "I feel like it works? Right? It translates to water sports?"

I laugh. "Yeah, it works, Z. This is amazing."

Mom touches her knee. "May I have it?"

Z goes wide-eyed out of bewilderment. "What? You want… this?"

Mom nods vigorously. "I think it captures Jack's playing perfectly."

Z thinks for moment, then nods. "Yes. Eventually I think I'll want it back, though."

"Of course, dear. Just let me know."

We all turn to a knock at the door. It's Dad.

"Ladies. Jacko. We all packed and ready to go here in an hour?"

We all look at the clock in unison. We indeed have one hour to when we said we were going to leave. Luckily, I'm a bit of a planner and have everything packed.

I doubt the other two though.

"Crap!" Z exclaims, quickly standing up. "I haven't even started!"

"Me either!" Mom replies. "Simon, I'll need…"

"The big black suitcase. Already in our room."

"What about my…"

"Black leather bathroom bag. In the bathroom."

"And my…"

"Comfy travel shoes? By the door."

Mom kisses Dad quickly before heading down the hall. "You are the best, love!"

Dad winks at me. "Oh, I know, dear."

Z grabs my hand. "Help me pack?"

I nod and she races out of the studio to the front door, dragging me behind her.

"Be quick, kids! I'll need Jack to help load the car!"

"Yes, sir!" Z calls out behind her.

We dart inside Gay Simon's, who is currently cleaning out the fridge.

"Z! Young lady! We need to leave in an hour! I thought you were going to try and be back long ago!"

"Sorry, Uncle Simon! I lost track of time. Jack and I are going to go pack right now."

Simon points at us with a leftover tray of some kind of meat. "Pack. Only pack."

Z rolls her eyes in jest. "Ugh, fine, Uncle! You're no fun though."

Simon shakes his head. "Oh, you know me. An absolute killjoy."

I laugh as Z sprints up the stairs and I follow close behind. Her room is a disaster as always – there is a reason why we tend to make out either on the couch or in my room – but at least she has her suitcase open on the bed packed with a few articles of clothing.

She grabs a couple of sports bras off the side chair and tosses them into the suitcase. "Do you remember where I keep my socks?"

Before I move over to the dresser on the far side of the room, I grab her hand and spin her around. She lets out a surprised 'ooh' before I kiss her. She then slowly wraps her arms around my neck, pulling me closer. When we finally separate, she smiles at me.

"What was that for?" She asks, slowly running a hand through my hair. "I loved it, just curious where it came from?"

"The painting."

"Ah, the painting. What about it?"

"It felt… I'm not sure what the word is… maybe a phrase? … It felt like you see me in a way that I don't think anyone else really does. It's new and it's nice."

Z kisses me three times, then pulls away. "You're adorable."

I'm about to kiss her again when Simon's voice calls up from downstairs. "I don't hear frantic packing!"

"Sorry!" We both yell at the same time.

We quickly rummage through her room, finding the clean clothes she wants to bring from different locations. With only a few minutes to spare, we manage to find everything she'll need for the week and we're out the door. Simon offers to ride with my parents so Z and I can drive his car down together and soon we're off down the Turnpike to Key Largo, singing our favorite songs and talking about a myriad of things. She makes the long drive bearable and, by the time we reach Key Largo, I have almost forgot about Grandpa and Gay Simon.

Almost.

CHAPTER 14

The Keys are an interesting place in Florida. The geography is phenomenally unique in the sense that it's just a long chain of tiny islands off the tip of Florida and has a highway connecting all of them to the mainland. It is also full of one-of-a-kind experiences, so anyone from any background and any demographic can find something to do. For the tourists, there are plenty of places to do some sight-seeing or some fun, recreational activities like the Florida Keys Wild Bird Rehabilitation Center or Theater of the Sea. All the way at the end of The Overseas Highway, there is the infamous Zero Mile Marker, the southernmost point of the continental United States and a hot bed for crappy souvenirs and photo opportunities. There are dozens, if not hundreds, of bars, saloons, clubs, and other places of festive revelry with live music almost every night. Famous celebrities come down to the Keys to do special shows – I once saw that Craig Robinson was doing a show down in the Keys. He plays Darrell in *The Office*, so naturally I desperately wanted to go see him, but it was a school night so my parents naturally said no. There are also plenty of places for outdoorsy-people – hiking, fishing, wading, shell-searching, clamming, reserves, and preserves.

The Keys also has a ton of people who are truly exclusive to the archipelago. My family and I have stayed down here a couple of times before and in the span of one day I saw a myriad of characters. One man was wearing nothing but tight pink short shorts and, I'm not joking around, pink wings to match. Another was wearing a full-on peacock looking backpack thing. One woman was essentially just wearing nipple stickers and underwear with boots that went up to the middle of her thigh. Another woman was wearing leather neck to toe that looked so hot (temperature wise) that I thought she was going to pass out from the heat. I also saw a man wearing leather everything with more zippers than a zipper store. It's truly one of the craziest places on earth that has so much to offer to anyone staying there.

There is something about the Keys that makes me think my grandparents really don't have any idea what they asked for – it's considered a paradise for the LGBTQ+ community. A simple Google search proves it. There are articles on articles regarding how gay-friendly the Keys are or what the best things for LGBTQ+ people to do are when they visit. I know Simon is a big fan of the Keys and he and his partner go down every so often for different events, including Pride Week.

So, when my hyper-conservative, traditional, ultra-religious grandparents from the reddest part of Alaska told us they wanted to spend Christmas down in the Keys, I was genuinely surprised. Apparently, they got a good deal on the rental house and wanted to spend the holiday somewhere warm. Mom suggested the Caribbean, knowing that this visit might not go the way her parents think, but the idea was immediately shot down due to the idea of 'spending the most sacred holiday with the likes of *those* people' – which I'm guessing was in reference to the Caribbean natives. My grandparents insisted that the Keys were where they wanted to spend the holiday. Mom, bless her soul, gave up trying to persuade them otherwise. I think Mom has been incredibly nervous for this trip – she kept going over the itinerary on a daily basis leading up to this trip. I have the damn thing memorized by this point. I know she's a planner, but still. What's making her the most nervous is undoubtedly inviting Simon and Z. Not necessarily Z. But definitely Simon.

Mom isn't like her parents. Mom is very accepting and loves unconditionally. She's actually very soft and is only tough when she needs to be. She doesn't really care for politics, but will discuss them if they come up. She appreciates diversity and often tells my dad about how grateful she is to live in a more diverse area of the nation – despite the fact living in the Lake Nona community basically means we live with mostly white people. But there is plenty of diversity in Orlando and the surrounding areas. Mom will always pick some ethnic restaurant over an American one and appreciates art from most places that aren't Europe. Dad always says she is a gentle soul and has a heart far too big for this world.

Her parents think that's a bad thing. I'm not saying that I don't love my grandparents, because I do. I mean, come on, they're family. But that doesn't mean I have to like them all the time.

And I'm not sure this time will be a time where I like them much. I'm trying to stay positive, but it's hard sometimes.

I think Z can sense my anxious anticipation.

"Askim? What's wrong?"

I squeeze her hand. "I need to tell you about my grandparents."

I share what I can put into words and watch as her eyes go from concerned, to angry, to anxious in a matter of moments.

"My uncle…"

"I know. I don't know what Dad was thinking."

"It's not his fault. But, I'm just concerned… Uncle Simon is a patient person and is understanding to a fault. But this might be too much."

I nod. I know Simon is very confident in who he is. He's strong, capable, and willful. But he has this tendency to make peace with whomever is in his life, even if he has to sacrifice his own ideals or plans. He doesn't change them. He simply doesn't insist upon them.

But he hasn't met my grandparents – specifically Grandpa. Grandpa was born and raised in Talkeetna, a town north of Anchorage on Highway 3 with barely over a thousand people. When he was growing up, it was even less. It's considered to be one of the wilder places in Alaska, more rugged and nature heavy. His parents were 'patriots' to the core – if there was a group of people who had the same vigor for American federalism as Soviets hardliners had for communism, my great-grandparents would have been their poster children. Grandpa keeps that tradition very much alive and makes it obvious.

Painfully obvious.

"Maybe Uncle Simon and I should go back… I don't want to ruin your holiday with your grandparents," Z says, rubbing a circle on the back of my hand with her thumb.

I squeeze her hand again, harder this time. "No. We'll just make sure to avoid… well… everything my grandpa would use to cause mayhem."

"Oh, so your grandpa is the guy in those insurance commercials?"

Those are some of her favorites on TV. "Yes, apparently."

We laugh as we finally pull into the driveway of the house we are staying. It's a little later than we expected – traffic is always worse around the holiday – but there's Grandpa, sitting on the porch, right leg crossed over his lap in front of him, and the glow of a cigar illuminating his face.

"You ready?"

Z nods. "I promise to be on my best behavior."

"Damn, I was hoping for your worst," I say with a wink. She drops her jaw in surprise, but eventually joins in with my laughter as we get out of the car.

"Jack, sonny-boy, make sure you grab your lady's bags. Ain't proper to have a lady carry her own bags."

"Yeah, sonny-boy," Z whispers to me. "I'm so fragile and weak, I need a big strong man to help me with my bags."

I stifle a laugh as Grandpa pops his cigar out of his mouth. Grandpa is a taller guy, standing around six foot five. His hair is still pretty thick for a seventy-year-old and he has a big, bushy mustache. He's not slim, but he's not fat really. He's what a normal grandpa is depicted as in TV shows and movies – not jacked out of his mind but still strong with a bit of a beer gut. Some of his teeth are permanently stained yellow from smoking cigars. He's pretty wrinkled and it makes him look quite a bit older than he is due to his time working as a lineman up in Alaska. The hard work created a hard man. And one that is incredibly stubborn and set in his traditional ways. He's wearing some classic blue jeans and a red flannel.

"What did you say, girly?"

Z looks at me with a flabbergasted look as if she was silently asking me if she heard him right. "Oh, nothing, Mr. Johnson, I just said that I've been waiting all week to meet you!"

I can see my grandpa smile. "Me too, young lady. I've heard so much about you from my Lyds."

Z quickly climbs the stairs and hugs my grandpa, who was waiting with an outstretched arm. "I've heard so much about you, too! Jack is a big fan."

"Oh, is he now?" He says, extending a hand to me. "Sonny-boy. How are you?"

I shake his hand firmly. "I'm doing well, sir. How are you?"

Grandpa laughs as he pulls me into a hug. "Just fine, just fine. Where's that father of yours? Late again I see?"

I shrug. "He was right behind me earlier. You know how traffic is around the holidays, Grandpa."

Grandpa grunts. "Your father was always a bit of a pussy when it came to driving."

I see Z cringe at the word and I know I need to change the subject.

"Where's Grandma?"

"Is that you, Jackie-Poo?"

Damn it, Grandma. I thought that nickname was dead.

Z's eyes go wide and she mouths 'Jackie-Poo!' with a brilliantly bright smile on her face, almost like she forgot.

Like she ever would.

Grandma comes out of the house, her white teeth shining in a wide smile. Grandma is a bit shorter than Grandpa, but not by much – maybe an inch or two. She's very slender and is far less wrinkled – she worked at the bank in town which was pretty low-key as, like I said, there were less than a thousand people in Talkeetna. She's never smoked a day in her life and keeps up a very rigorous dental hygienic routine. Her hair is still fairly black with only whisps of gray flowing throughout. Being as traditional as Grandpa, she's wearing a plaid sundress with her hair up in a messy bun.

I hug her as she flings her arms around me. "Jackie-Poo, you're so big! Look at you!"

I give her my best smile, hiding my annoyance with the exhausted pet-name. "It's good to see you, too, Grandma."

"And who is this?" Grandma looks over at Z and grabs her by the shoulders, turning her this way and that. It's like she's examining some sort of denomination of money for flaws or mistakes.

"Grandma, this is Z, my girlfriend."

"Girlfriend?!" Grandma exclaims. "Why, darling, it's a pleasure!"

Grandma wraps Z in another big hug.

"Same here, Mrs. Johnson! Jack has told me a lot about you – all good things of course."

"Oh, what a sweet boy," Grandma replies, pinching my cheek. "Are you two hungry? I made some cookies fresh this afternoon."

Of course, she did.

A set of headlights illuminate the driveway and the porch as Dad pulls in with the Land Rover. Mom is out of the car before Dad even has the thing in park and runs up to her parents.

"Mom! Dad!"

My grandparents give Mom the biggest hug and I can see tears in Grandma's eyes.

"Oh, Lydia, it's been too long," Grandma says, obviously stifling back tears.

Dad walks to the bottom of the stairs. "George."

Grandpa nods at Dad. "Simon."

Dad and Grandpa have had some beef with one another since we moved to Florida. See, Dad's dad died a year or two before we moved and his mom died when he was really young. So, Dad doesn't have any ties back in Alaska really. His only sister now lives in Maine with her wife and two kids. We see them every once and a while, but I know Dad wishes she lived closer. I think he misses his family sometimes – which is perfectly logical. But when Dad told Mom about the Florida deal and she told her parents, Grandpa was furious. He blamed Dad for 'stealing his little girl' and 'abandoning this family.' Mom had tried to talk Grandpa down, reminding him over and over again that it was really what she wanted. But, of course, Grandpa was a stubborn man and keeps a grudge like nobody else. That was almost five years ago now.

"Oh, dear, stop that," Grandma says, lightly slapping his shoulder. "Simon, it's good to see you."

Dad hugs Grandma. "You too, Norene. Jack, come help me with the bags."

"Yes, and don't forget mine, honey!" Z calls out from inside. I look through the door way and see her holding back peals of laughter. I give her a look and she shoots a wink back at me.

That's when I remember Simon was also here.

Gay Simon.

"Mom, Dad, this is our neighbor, Simon de Garcia. He's the one we told you we were inviting," Mom informs the two elders.

"He's my uncle, too," Z says, leaning in the doorway. I look back again and can see the apprehension on her face.

"Good evening, Mr. and Mrs. Johnson. It's too kind of you to include Zendaya and me on your holiday vacation," Simon says, offering his hand to Grandpa.

Despite Simon putting on a weird, 'macho' accent to his voice, I think Grandpa sees right there it. He only grunts.

Doesn't even take his hand.

"Oh, stop it, George." Grandma ignores the outstretched hand and hugs Simon. "It's good to have you. Especially if Ms. Zendaya has captured my little Jackie's heart."

Somebody kill me. Please.

"Connors, I'll help you with your bags," Grandpa says, moving past Simon to help Dad.

"I will, too," Simon says, turning back to the Land Rover.

Grandpa shoots up a hand. "No need, son. I think the men can handle it."

I can see the shock in Simon's eyes and Z's cheeks are turning red.

"Dad!" Mom says, almost yelling.

Grandpa only grunts.

Simon ignores Grandpa's little gesture and insult and grabs his bag and Z's from the other car. I grab both of my mom's bags and mine and head inside.

"Did he really just fucking say that?" Z whispers to me.

I nod. "I don't want to say I told you so."

"Oh boy…"

Luckily, we turn in for the night. Grandpa, however, makes sure that Z is in the farthest room away from me. I wake up in the middle of the night to go to the bathroom and find that he has moved a twin mattress into the egress of the upstairs hallway, placing himself directly between Z and me.

This is going to be a long week…

To my relief, the first three days aren't so bad. I am successful in steering Simon and Grandpa away from one another on excursions. I make sure that Z and I are between the two of them at the bare minimum. It's not exactly relaxing, but it's better than the alternative. Christmas day goes off without a hitch and gifts are exchanged in a surprising peace. Z cries when she opens the gift I got for her – a Cancer zodiac sign necklace made with sterling silver inlaid with diamonds and a ruby at the center. I'm blown away at her gift to me – box tickets to the London Symphony Orchestra at the Steinmetz next month. We kiss in front of my grandparents – much to Grandpa's disapproval.

It's now Thursday morning and we are trying to decide what to do. We leave the Keys on Monday and we want to maximize our vacation. Z and I still have a few days till we need to go back to school and I personally could go with maximum relaxation before the insanity of senior year comes back.

"I would love to see the Zero Mile Marker!" Grandma exclaims, startling Z and I as we play cribbage with Grandpa.

"Okay," Grandpa says. "How far of a drive is that?"

Always with him and drive times.

"About two hours, Dad," Mom replies.

"Alright then." Grandpa puts his cards down and immediately gets up. "Everyone get in the Suburban. No need to take two cars."

"But Dad, don't you think…" Mom starts saying.

"No arguments. Easier this way. Can't get separated."

Dad touches Mom's arm in a silent apology as we get up and go out to the car. Z and I get into the back with Simon and Mom and Dad take the middle seats. Hopefully, this will be a peaceful endeavor.

An hour into the drive, it takes a turn. We see a number of fabulously dressed men. The rainbow flags and elaborate colors are a clear indication of who they are – remember, the Keys are considered a paradise for the gay community. But I know Grandpa is going to say something.

"Dad, how are things up in Talkeetna?" Mom swiftly asks, knowing full well someone needs to try and deflect the conversation.

"Oh, much better than down here," Grandpa states with a grunt. "None of these damn…"

Z's hand cuts off all circulation to my fingers when the slur comes out of Grandpa's mouth.

"Babe," I whisper. "Ow."

"Sorry," she whispers back. "I have to…"

"Yeah, I know," I reply through gritted teeth.

"George, come on," Dad interjects. "We don't use that language down here."

"Don't you tell me what to do, boy. You're the one who dragged my Lydia down here into this den of sin and debauchery."

I feel my knuckles pop and I stifle a groan.

When Z is mad, she has a death grip.

"Dad, you know he didn't drag me anywhere, now stop," Mom replies, her voice stone cold.

"George, please, not in front of Jackie and our guests," Grandma intercedes.

Grandpa grunts, but I know he wants to say more.

We drive the remaining hour in relative silence, listening to whatever religious music Grandpa has decided to listen to today – sounds like a church choir from the eighties.

The Zero Mile Marker is pretty underwhelming. It looks like an oversized, upside-down bobber with red, yellow, and black paint with white letters stating that we are standing at the furthest southern point of the continental United States. We take a couple of obligatory pictures and make our way back to the house. The car ride is silent again and arguably the most uncomfortable one I have ever been in.

When we get back to the house, my parents take Simon out to the beach and talk with him, no doubt making sure he's okay. Grandma takes Grandpa into the kitchen and I think they think they are quiet but they very much aren't.

"George, that was unnecessary."

"Norene, you know what I'm saying is true. This shithole is full of..." All the obscenities and slurs my grandpa knows come flooding out of his mouth. "...than I care for. I say we just drive to the airport and get on the first flight out of here to Anchorage."

"George, we haven't seen Lydia in an age. Just hang on a little longer. We'll be home soon enough."

"I just hope that Z girl doesn't turn Jack into some pussy, like his father. She's a liberal bitch, I can tell."

Z throws down her cards and storms outside, letting the screen door slam behind her. I quickly chase after her, certainly not wanting to face both my grandparents after that. We catch up with my parents and Simon and I can see Simon is angry.

"Simon, don't go," Mom pleads.

Simon is leaving? Something more must have happened that I don't know about.

"I can't stay, Lydia," Simon says, his voice shaking. "Not after what Norene called me last night. Not after what George said in the car today. I dealt with this in the nineties and the early 2000s because I had to. I don't have to deal with it now."

"Simon..."

"Lydia, it's okay," Dad says. "Simon, I understand if you need to go. I know they aren't the easiest people to get along with."

Mom lets out a huge sigh and I can see her shoulders shake. "I'm so sorry, Simon..."

Simon pulls Mom into a huge hug. "It's not your fault, Lydia. I'm not angry with you."

Z starts to cry. "I want to go, too, Uncle Simon."

"Z..." I quickly wrap her in a hug and look to Simon. "Grandpa... Grandpa said some things just now in the kitchen. We overheard."

"Oh, honey..." Mom takes Z from me and hugs her. They both cry while Dad, Simon and I just stand there, feeling helpless and powerless.

And phenomenally angry.

"I'll go grab your things, Z," Simon says, making his way back to the house.

"I'll help you." Dad follows him inside.

Mom lets Z go and kisses her forehead. "I know this wasn't what you wanted for your break. I hope you don't hold this against me."

"Never."

I follow the two of them back inside where Grandma is making a fuss about the two of them leaving. I don't say anything and neither does Mom or Dad. Simon and Dad carry their things out to Simon's car. I walk Z out, holding her hand as tight as I can.

"Do you want to sit in the back? You can try and sleep?"

Z nods, tears still falling down her cheeks.

"Okay." I open the back and stand there awkwardly for a moment.

"Jack, I'm…"

"Don't say sorry. You have no reason to say sorry. I'm the one who should be saying sorry. I can't… I can't believe my grandparents."

She throws her arms around me and sobs. I hold her as tight as I can, my rage now coursing through me at a million miles an hour.

My grandparents made my girlfriend cry. The girl who has made my life infinitely better down here in Florida. The girl who has made my mother, *their daughter*, smile more in the last few months than I have seen her smile than she has in the last few years here. The girl who even Dad has found a kinship with.

And they made her cry.

Z pulls away and kisses me. I kiss her back with as much love as I can muster, but I know it's not enough.

"I'll see you when you get home."

"Okay. Call me when you get home."

"Okay. I love you, askim."

"I love you, too, hjartat."

I close the door to the car and turn to Simon.

"I'm sorry, Simon…"

Simon shakes his head. "It's not your fault, kid. He's a stubborn old man and there's no changing that."

I nod and start heading back inside.

"Jack."

I turn back to Simon.

"You're a good kid. Don't beat yourself up over this."

"I'll try."

Simon pats his pockets. "Shit. I left my keys inside. They must be in the bedroom."

We both head inside where an eerie quiet dominates the space. I can see Mom doing her best to hold back tears and Dad is doing everything he can do to console her, but I can also see he is holding back a great amount of anger.

Grandpa walks into the room, setting down a tray of lemonades. I casually pick one up and sit down next to Mom, sipping down my anger on the way too sweet drink. Simon heads down the hall, not making eye contact with anyone, especially Grandpa.

Grandpa sits himself down on the recliner across kitty corner from my parents and takes a long pull of the lemonade.

"Good riddance," Grandpa mutters as Simon walks past him.

"Dad…" Mom whispers angrily.

Grandpa ignores Mom and looks at me instead. "It's for the best, Jack my boy. She was a bad influence on you and you're better off without her. Living with her dandy of an uncle and wearing all those slutty outfits. We'll keep you on the straight and narrow, don't you worry."

I've never stood up to Grandpa before. I've wanted to in the past. This isn't the first time he's said offensive stuff in front of me. This probably won't even be the last. It's been more than a decade of this and I wasn't sure how long I could keep going. I'm a pretty patient guy. I endured Pietro on a daily basis for three years of school. I put up with the drunks and horny moms at Lucy's almost every shift. I wouldn't have lasted in the service industry if I wasn't patient. I also play piano and that didn't happen overnight. I practiced and I was patient with myself as I honed my craft and learned everything from the basics to advanced music theory.

Tonight, things are different. Tonight, he told me that I would be better off without Z. Z, the girl who has literally changed my life for the better. Z, who actually makes me enjoy living down here. Z, who has been my closest friend since Nick and the first love of my life – hopefully the only one. And Grandpa just essentially called her a slut.

Something inside me snaps. Something big. And now a fire burns in my chest that I can't seem to put out.

Nor do I want to.

I throw my glass on the ground, causing lemonade to wash over the floor and glass to fly everywhere. "What the actual fuck is wrong with you?"

"Jack!" Mom yells.

"Grandpa, do you not realize how much you've hurt your own daughter?!" It's my turn to yell now. "How dense are you?! Do you know how good of friends Mom and Simon are? Simon comes over for dinner at least once a week. Has for the last five years. Simon brings a smile to Mom's face even in her darkest moments. Simon is ten times the man you will ever be! He's kind and caring and hospitable and understanding. And want to know something about Z? She painted with Mom. That's right, Mom and her set up easels side by side and painted or hours. Do you know how many people have done that before her? None. Nobody has even asked. And Z? Z is the best thing that happened to me moving down here. She makes living in Florida so much better than it has been. Damn it, it's actually been great! Did you know that I love her, Grandpa? Did you know that? No, of course not, you're too busy worrying about those 'other' people out in the world! You don't even take the time to see that Mom is happier down here! Her bones don't hurt and ache as much! The sunshine has been great for her! You don't realize how much happier I am down here! So, I ask again, what the actual FUCK IS WRONG WITH YOU?!"

Grandpa springs to his feet and jabs a finger into my chest. "You watch your mouth, boy! And you best remember your Scripture – thou shall respect thy elders!"

I stand up and hold an unwavering stare. "And that's another thing! You spew Scripture and talk of sin and debauchery to people all while praising and glorifying a Savior that preached love and kindness! You spew hatred despite the fact that the God you claim to serve instructs the people who believe in Him to love everyone, including their enemies! Did you forget that or do you just cherry-pick Bible verses that suit your needs and desires and personal opinions?!"

Grandpa doesn't say anything and slowly lowers his accusing finger.

I turn to my parents. "I'm leaving with Simon."

Mom looks up at me with the saddest look in her eyes. "Jack…"

"Lydia. It's okay," Dad says before looking at me. "I'll bring your stuff back. I think Simon needs to get going, bud."

Startled, I look over at the hall. Simon is standing in the hallway, smiling with tears in his eyes.

"I'm sorry, Mom…" I say before squatting down and hugging her.

"It's okay, Jackie… I'm sor…"

"No. Don't apologize. They aren't your responsibility."

I step back and Mom gives me a light smile. I turn back to Grandpa, but decide not to say anything else. I've said enough. I look to Grandma.

"Sorry you had to see that, Grandma."

She only shakes her head.

I turn and walk out the door, grabbing my wallet and keys before shutting the door behind me. Simon and I don't say anything as we get into his car. Z is startled to see me get in the back seat, but when she sees the tears in her uncle's eyes and the determined look my face is sure to be projecting, she quickly repositions herself so she's leaning against me and resumes crying. Not even fifteen minutes into our drive home, I can tell Simon is also crying. I've never seen him cry before. He's also been this strong pillar of joy in the middle of whatever comes his way. Seeing him cry breaks my heart and solidifies my resolve.

"Do you need me to drive, Simon?"

Simon shakes his head. "No. You be there for Z. I'll get us home."

Ten minutes later, Z is asleep in my arms, her breathing slowly calming down from fluttering shakes to the deep breath of sleep. The rest of the drive is quiet and I refuse to let my mind wander back to the yelling match with Grandpa.

I did the right thing. I love Z with everything I have. I would do anything for her. And if that means standing up to my grandparents, I will.

I just hope Mom will be okay.

When we get home, I carry Z upstairs to her bed and gently lay her down. She only stirs a little so she can kiss me goodnight, but then is immediately back to sleep. I shake Simon's hand and go back to our empty house. I make my way up to my bed and lay down, watching my ceiling fan spin once again.

Then I cry.

It's a bittersweet release, but needed to happen all the same.

Some vacation…

CHAPTER 15

I would love to say that I forgot about what happened with my grandparents in the Keys the minute I got home. I would like to say that Z and I were able to relax and do our own thing after it was just us. I would love to say I didn't think about how Mom was feeling for hours on end when I tried to sleep. I would be thrilled to say every vibration of my phone didn't make me jump, despite it never being my grandparents nor my parents.

But I can't.

I wish I could. I really do. It would have made the times Z was over and the times we did make out more enjoyable. It would have made sleep come in longer stretches than a few hours at a time. I wouldn't be a ball of anxiety and stress, so tight and wound up that even playing piano was difficult and nothing sounded like the way it should have. Nothing relaxed me. Z would take my mind off things, but the second she left, everything flooded back in with ten times more force.

So now, as I'm sitting in the living room anxiously waiting for my parents' return from the vacation that was, my knee is bouncing faster than a hummingbird's wing. Z isn't here – she had a video call with her parents, which I think was great and I encouraged her to do – but I definitely wish she was. I've been rehearsing what I wanted to say to Mom since I woke up seven hours ago. It's only noon, but I should have been sleeping for much later being that it is the last day of my winter break. School looms in the near future and is not helping my anxiety in the slightest.

My phone vibrates and I jump – again.

Z: You okay?

Me: No

Z: :(

Z: I'm sorry babe…

Me: Hun, it's not your fault. My grandparents were… well… my grandparents.

Z: Still… Do you want me to come over?

Me: Aren't you on a video call?

Z: Yes, but they're talking with Uncle Simon right now. I meant after it's done and your parents are home?

Me: Yes. 100% yes.

Z: You're cute. I love you.

Me: I love you too.

I hear the garage door open and I immediately get off the couch and go to the entry way. I can feel my hands start to clam up and I pick at the cuticles on my thumbs. I haven't heard from my parents at all the last few days other than Dad texting me once asking to see if I was okay and made it home safely. I'm sure they had their hands full with trying to put out the fires I unintentionally started. Probably.

Dad is the first one to enter the door. He looks tired, the dark circles under his eyes emphasizing his exhaustion. He gives me a light smile and pulls me in for a hug.

"Son. Good to see you," Dad says, his embrace tightening.

"Good to see you, too, Dad," I reply, returning the hug.

"Your mom is pretty distraught," he whispers in my ear. "She fought with her parents about seventy-five percent of the time, but stayed to enjoy the other twenty-five. Give a hug, but then let her go to her studio. I think she just wants to paint it out."

"Okay," I reply, matching his tone. "I'm sorry, Dad…"

"It's not your fault. And things will be okay in the end. Mom just needs… she needs some quiet."

The garage door opens again, slower this time, and Mom is standing in the doorway. I've seen her weak from sickness before. She got a pretty bad case of influenza a couple years back that got so bad we had to take her to the hospital. She looked like a husk of her normal self. It had worried Dad to the point where he couldn't sleep at night and didn't sleep for three days.

That was nothing to how she looks right now.

Someone looks differently when their emotions are the causation of their sickness. It might not be influenza or even the Coronavirus, but heartache and sadness can drain the life from someone just as quickly. Mom's eyes look sunken into her skull. Her skin is white as paste. Her usually brilliant blue eyes are dulled to a dark blue. She is shivering, despite having a sweatshirt on as well as Dad's old letterman jacket.

She doesn't say anything as she approaches me. I don't want her to. I think if she said anything, her heart would shatter. So, I just put my arms around her and hug her tightly. She tries to hug me back the best she can, but I can tell she's weak from exhaustion and emotional fatigue.

"Why don't we get you to your studio, Mom?" I say, putting my arm around her to make sure she doesn't fall.

She just nods.

"I'll get you some tea, love," Dad states, heading towards the kitchen. He turns back to look at her. "Chamomile?"

Mom only nods again.

"Jack, could you grab the stuff from the car once you have her situated?"

"Sure, Dad, no problem."

I get Mom to her easel and stool. She sits down and stares blankly at the white canvas. I know she's trying to imagine what she wants to paint, but I can tell she's struggling to focus on anything other than her parents.

"Do you want me to shut the door?" I ask, quietly.

Again, only a nod.

"Okay. Dad and I will check in every once and a while."

A nod.

I walk out to the garage and grab the remaining bags and bring them to their respective rooms. I come back to the hall to the studio and see Dad walk out, closing the door behind him. He motions for me to follow him into the kitchen and I can hear Mom sobbing from the other side of the door. I want so badly to go into her studio and tell her everything is okay and that I'm not mad anymore and apologize for leaving. But I know that's not a good idea. I know that's not why she's crying. So, I just follow Dad into the kitchen.

"How are you?" Dad asks as he takes out a package of bacon from the fridge.

That's how I know he's upset. Dad is a pretty simple guy. He enjoys simple things. Black coffee. Original Coca Cola, no flavors added. Old mystery novels. Classic rock. Nothing that contains crazy or weird elements. One of his favorite lines from *The Office* is "Keep it simple, stupid" because that's how he lives. He likes simplicity. He says that his work offers enough crazy solutions and weird gimmicks, so he wants to keep his personal life simple. So, if Dad is ever upset, he turns to something simple that he enjoys. Bacon is one of those things. It's just thin slices of meat that are thrown on to a frying pan or in the oven and cooked until they are crisp. That's all it takes. Delicious. Easy. Simple.

"I'm okay. How are you?"

I watch Dad's shoulders rise as he takes a deep breath. He grabs a cast iron from the wall and sets it on the stove top, ignites the burner and sets it to high so the thick metal can heat up quickly. We stand there quietly for a few moments. I don't want to rush him as he's thinking and preparing what he's going to say. And he doesn't want to rush the cast iron.

"I'm tired, Jack."

I knew that. I could see it when he walked in. I can hear it in his voice.

"I know…"

"No, son, you don't." Dad slaps some of the meat onto the pan, the heat immediately causing it to sizzle. "Before I start, I want to say one thing: I'm proud of you. Not everyone has had the guts to stand up to George. Not to mention to call him out on his religious hypocrisy. But you did. And I understand why. And I'm proud of you."

"Thanks, Dad…"

"However, you should have done it with a little more dignity and a lot more class. Profanity is an indication of poor intelligence. I understand you were angry – trust me, I was angry as well – but you're smarter than that. Be the man I know you to be."

"Yes, sir. I'll do better if there is a next time."

Dad nods, flipping the bacon over and turning down the heat. "Good. And, knowing George, there probably will be a next time."

I move so that I'm across the kitchen from him and lean against the island. "What happened, Dad? What did Grandma call Simon? I know Simon was upset with Grandpa from the very beginning just because of his attitude towards homosexuals and all, but the talk on the beach made it seem like Grandma made it worse."

Dad nods again, but doesn't say anything. He examines the bacon in the pan and takes out the slices and puts them on a plate covered by paper towels before putting more of the package in the pan. He hands me a piece and we crunch down on the crispy snack. I wait patiently, knowing this is a frustrating subject for him.

Dad says the word Grandma used to refer to Simon and I instantly recoil. To me, that word has the same connotations and vulgarity as the n-word. I can't imagine Grandma saying it. She is always the sweeter one of my two grandparents.

Dad shakes his head. "I've never heard Norene use any language like that. I almost expect it from George at this point, but not from her."

"I agree. I mean I've heard Grandpa use rather… colorful language before and Grandma always rebukes him."

I see Dad's knuckles whiten as he grips the edge of the island hard. "I don't know what they were thinking when they booked a vacation there. I don't know what your mom was thinking when she didn't tell them about who lives in the Keys. But I know your mom misses her parents. I know she does. But I know she also prefers living here. She's healthier, she's happier, she's enjoying more and more things down here. I just wish her parents would see that."

"Same."

"I'm also frustrated at myself. I should've thought more about inviting Z and Simon and what that implies when it came to vacationing with George and Norene. But I wanted to make sure they had people to spend time with. Especially Z."

"Dad, you can't blame yourself for that, you were just trying to be a good person."

Dad only nods and moves so he's leaning against the island next to me. There's a long pause before he starts talking again.

"That's why I'm tired, bud. I'm tired of your mom trying to make her parents happy despite the fact the only way to make them happy would be to move back to Alaska. I'm tired of fighting with George constantly."

"What do you mean?" I ask. "Constantly? We never see him."

I watch as Dad unlocks his personal cell phone and he shows me his call log. There are numerous calls from Grandpa – all of which are incoming. Some Dad answered. Some he didn't. He taps the voice message icon, showing me dozens of voicemails left by Grandpa. He switches over to text messages and I see that Grandpa writes him a novel on why he needs to move us back to Alaska at least once a week.

"Holy crap…" I whisper in astonishment. "Does…"

"Your mom know? No. And I don't want her to. She would feel obligated to move back up there. But it would be terrible for her health. So, even if she felt obligated to move back, I wouldn't do it. I can't…" Dad's voice breaks. I turn to look at him and can see tears starting to well in his eyes. "I can't lose her… Jack… which makes this all the more difficult. Her parents don't see what I see. What you see. They only care about what they want. It's always been like that."

I slowly nod.

"Remember this, son. When you get married, you get a wife *and* an additional set of parents. Make sure you establish good relationships *and* appropriate boundaries. That's the best advice I can give to avoid something like this from happening to you."

I nod again. "Thanks, Dad."

There's a knock on the door. Dad jerks his head towards the front of the house and I move to go see who it is. I open the door to see Simon and Z standing there.

I smile. "Hey, guys."

Simon lifts the bouquet of flowers in his hands. "Can we come in? We saw your dad's car pull in."

"Let them in, Jack," Dad calls from the kitchen.

I step aside and gesture them through the door. Z gives me a hug as Simon goes towards the kitchen.

"Are they okay?" Z whispers.

I shrug my shoulders. "Dad is pretty mad at Grandpa still. And he's tired. I don't think either of them slept well. Mom…. Mom looks like she's been to hell and back."

Z kisses my cheek and steps back. "Where is she?"

"In her studio. I doubt she wants to see anyone right now."

Z looks towards the door to the backroom. "I need to try."

We walk to the kitchen and find Simon and Dad hugging. I see tears streaking down Dad's cheeks and a patient, understanding look in Simon's eyes.

Of course, Simon is calm and collected.

Z grabs the flowers from the island and goes to the studio door.

"Z, I'm not sure Lydia wants to be around anyone right now," Dad softly calls after her.

Z turns and gives him a light smile, but I see tears in her eyes as well. "I need to try, Simon."

Dad just nods and she goes to the door and knocks. She cracks it open and sticks her head in.

"Lydia? May I enter your creative space?"

Mom must have nodded because Z steps in, closing the door behind her. I walk back to the kitchen where Dad is washing lettuce and Simon is slicing up a tomato.

"BLTs?" I ask.

"Yep," Dad says. "Toast some bread, will you?"

I grab the loaf from the top of the fridge and stick a few slices into the slots of the toaster.

"Jack, I want to thank you," Simon says, the sincerity quite obvious in his voice.

"For what?"

"For sticking up for Z. For sticking up for me. I didn't realize how much of an impact we have had on your family and I hope you know that you've had an equivalent amount of impact on the two of us."

I nod. "Yeah, it's no problem…"

"Jack, the wounds made on that night between you and your grandpa are nothing but a problem. Which is why I'm being as straight with you as I can when I say thank you. It certainly wasn't easy. And it certainly won't be fixed overnight. So, thank you. It's good to know my niece has someone who loves her like you do."

I smile and run a hand through my hair. "I'm not sure what to say."

"I do," Dad says with a smile. "Simon, I didn't realize you could do anything straight."

The three of us look at one another in a moment of utter silence before laughing heartily at Dad's joke. I feel the tension in the room break and dissipate as our laughter only increases. We eat our BLTs while talking about anything but the holiday break. While we joke, I keep thinking about Z and Mom. I haven't heard anything from the studio since Z went in.

"Do you think they're hungry?" I ask, gesturing towards the studio.

Simon nods. "Z hasn't eaten since breakfast. Probably should check on them."

"I'm not sure how much Lydia has eaten the past couple days. Jack, would you mind?" Dad asks. "I know she wants to spend some time with you."

I nod and make my way over to the studio door. I gently nock and slowly open the door.

"Mom? May I enter your creative space?"

What I see warms and breaks my heart all at once. Mom has Z under one arm and they are both leaning against each other. When they both turn, I can tell each had been crying. In front of them is an eleven by fourteen canvas. It looked like Mom had started painting a dark background with a mix of blacks and grays. It truly looked like an empty void of nothingness.

But then two figures are painted, one blue, the other yellow. Z's favorite color and Mom's favorite color. The two figures are leaning against each other, just as Mom and Z were. From them sparks lines of blue, yellow, and green shooting off into the void. It brings light and life back onto the canvas. I can see and feel the emotion that was being put into this piece. And it emanates what they are feeling. Mom feels this dark void of sadness and shame. It swirls in her soul, clouding and polluting wherever it goes. Her shame is real and valid and poisonous. But then Z came in, offering what life and love she can bring to the situation. Joy returns. The shame and sadness still exist, but they are not as powerful as they could be.

I slowly walk over to them and hug Mom, then put my arm around Z's shoulders.

"What do you think?" Z asks, leaning her head against my side.

"I think it's incredible."

Mom takes my hand. "Jack, I'm…"

"Mom, no. There's no need to apologize. What's done is done. What's won is won. What is lost is lost. I don't hold anything against you and you shouldn't either. I love you, Mom. Nothing is ever going to change that."

Mom smiles at me and squeezes my hand. "Okay. Thank you. I love you, too." She takes in a deep, deep breath and I watch as she straightens her posture. The color returns to her face and she looks more like her normal self now. "Is that bacon I smell?"

I nod. "Yeah, you know Dad."

She laughs and stands up. "Indeed. His 'simple' things.'"

The three of us exit the studio, leaving the painting on its easel.

"Lydia," Simon says, walking over to Mom and wrapping her a big hug. "Darling, thank you for the lovely vacation. I know it may have not been what we wanted, but it was still so nice to spend the holiday with you."

Mom smiles and tightens the hug. "You don't hold it against me?"

Simon steps back and smiles. "Never, darling. Never."

Mom walks over to Dad and kisses him, taking the plate of sandwiches from his hands. "Thank you, dear."

"Anytime, gorgeous. Anytime."

We all talk and laugh for the next few hours until Mom suggests we go to the entertainment room and watch a movie all together. Z and I pop popcorn while Dad orders pizza. We settle on *Shrek* and spend the evening laughing at the jokes and puns that kids don't understand. Dad reminds us that big movie companies do this all the time, saying that the adults need something to laugh at too. We watch the whole movie and decide to turn on *The Hunt for the Red October* on Dad's behest. Between movies, Mom and Simon make plans to paint together, which Mom is simply overjoyed to hear. It's past midnight by the time I kiss Z good night and say bye to Simon. Mom and I stay up for another hour, talking and reconnecting through a variety of different conversations. I think she just needed to reassure herself that we were still okay and that our relationship wasn't permanently damaged. I, of course, kept saying as much, but she's my mom. She needs to know for certain.

It's now 1:15 in the morning and I crawl into bed after saying good night to Mom. School didn't start for another couple of days, for which I am grateful.

Senior year can end better than this break did.

Right?

CHAPTER 16

The New Year. So full of promises and anticipation for a better tomorrow. It's been about a month since the disaster that was Christmas, and I think things are back to normal. Mom had a video chat with my grandparents that lasted for a few hours and she came back out with a look of relief and less stress on her shoulders. School resumed like usual and my group and I had to make deals with one another to watch out for each other as we want to avoid senior slide.

Nick fell off the wagon about three days in.

Classic.

It's the end of January and everyone is over at our house for a college acceptance reveal. Six stacks of envelopes sit precariously on the dining room table where Nick, Mona, Khalan, Lisa, Z, and I look at them with nervous anticipation. Our parents or guardians are hovering behind us, possibly just as nervous as we are. Even Z's parents are present via video chat and they show their nervousness all the same. An assortment of beverages has been laid out for people to select from and Dad smoked a pork butt for pulled pork sandwiches, but no one at the table is really thinking about that. We've been receiving these letters for a few weeks now and it's time to open them.

If anyone knew our group well enough, they would instantly guess this was Nick's idea. And they would be right. Nick, in his never-ending quest for more flair in his life, wanted to put together this dramatic evening where we would put all of our letters on the table and open them, one by one, in front of everyone, to see where we were accepted and where we would decide to go. We had objections, of course. What if we didn't get in to any colleges and then opened disappointment after disappointment to end the evening with heartbreak and devastation? Lisa's words, not mine. What if we don't get into our number one pick? What if our parents don't want to do this? What if this? What if that? We tried our best to detour Nick, but, in the end, we all reluctantly agreed it could be a fun night.

"Alright," Nick says from my left. "Shall we roll a dice and see who opens their letters first?"

Mona shakes her head from across the table. "No. I'll go first. I've waited long enough."

She starts with her number one pick – New York University.

She tears open the envelope and quickly glances over the contents, her parents leaning in with worried looks.

Mona looks up at us and can't help but smile. "Accepted."

The room erupts with applause while Mona quickly hugs her parents and kisses Lisa, the smile never really leaving her face.

She goes through the rest of her envelopes and finds she is accepted to Baylor and Boston, but rejected from Michigan State and UF. Mona, however, doesn't care about the rejections. She got her number one pick.

Lisa goes next and, unsurprisingly, she also got into NYU. She doesn't bother opening the other letters. Instead, she opts for simply tearing them in half in full theatrical form. She doesn't care – Lisa will be going to school with Mona. No questions asked.

When Khalan goes next, they smile awkwardly. "Okay, so, I already know what my letters say."

"What?! You read them?!" Nick exclaims, standing angrily.

Khalan shakes their head. "I got a call from the recruiter at University of Minnesota – Twin Cities. They want me for their new boxing program they want to set up. Pretty big scholarship and opportunity, so I took it."

We all applaud for them and they smile, shaking Dad's hand – he's been a big proponent of Khalan's boxing career.

Z, sitting to my right, is next. She gives me a nervous smile. I look to her stack of envelopes. It's not that big, especially compared to Nick's who applied to almost thirty colleges. It's probably six or seven high with her top choice – UCLA – on the top.

"Let's see what you got, kiddo!" Z's dad says over the call. He's a cool guy – I got to meet him briefly a couple days ago while he was on a business trip. We got along well and he seemed to like me quite a bit.

Z smiles and picks up the letter from UCLA. She slowly and meticulously cuts open the envelope with a letter opener, making sure to not damage the paper more than what was necessary. Her eyes briefly scan over the page – I look at her eyes so I don't come off as nosey. After reading it, she folds the paper, sets it down, looks at me, and then looks at her parents.

"Accepted."

The room explodes with cheers and her parents both jump out of their chairs on the other end of the line. Her dad went to UCLA and is now over the moon, jumping around their living room in LA proudly wearing a UCLA t-shirt.

I smile and clap and cheer with the rest of them, but then quickly look down at my top pick.

MIT.

Thousands of miles away.

Three-hour time difference.

She opens the rest of her envelopes and my chest continues to tighten under the anxiety.

Stanford. Accepted.

Yale. Rejected.

University of Minnesota. Rejected.

UC-Berkley. Accepted.

UC-Irvine. Accepted.

CSU-Long Beach. Accepted.

All schools out west. None in the east.

We would be apart if I kept chasing MIT. Or Carnegie Melon. Or University of Michigan – Ann Arbor.

My dreams, my top 3 colleges. All far away from her. Space and time separating me from this girl that I fought so hard for.

All that. Gone.

I try to force it out of my mind. I force myself to be present and she talks to her parents and the others in the room about how excited she is. I try to focus on her smile and a sly wink she manages to send me, masking my inner emotions.

But I can't. I can't be present. I can't be in the moment. My life has changed immeasurably since I met her. My life has been fuller since we got together. And now, we would have miles and miles and miles between the two of us. What does that mean? Are we going to do long distance? Are we going to be okay? Or are we going to break up? God, I can't do that! We just got here. We're so happy here.

"Okay, Jack, your turn!"

My mom's voice echoes in my head as it yanks me back to reality. I see Z give me a curious look out of the corner of my eye, but I do my best not to acknowledge it.

"Okay, up first," I say, pausing to clear my throat as I notice it's shaky. "MIT."

My finger slips under the flap of the envelope and I slowly and methodically run it down the seam to open it. I pull out the piece of paper and my mind goes blank. This is the accumulation of over six years of dreaming. Years of hard work. Long nights of studying and cramming and working. Everything else, suddenly, does not matter as much as it did. My brain focuses clearly on one, sole thing.

Whether or not I got into MIT.

I open the piece of paper to find the words and my mind goes numb.

Then accelerates.

I got in.

With an acceptance rate of just over 4%, I was certain that MIT would not accept me. They're incredibly picky.

But there it is. Right in front of me. I am accepted into MIT.

"I got in!" I shout, standing up so quickly I almost knock the chair over. My parents cheer and Z gets up as fast as I did and gives me a huge hug. I hug her back, picking her up and spinning. The rest of my friends join my parents' cheering and congratulations are said across the room.

I still can't believe it. It's like I'm living in a fog and my brain can't focus on anything but the realization that I got accepted to one of the top engineering schools not only in the country, but in the world. This means that if I stick with my major currently or end up switching, it doesn't matter because there is a guaranteed job after graduation. The opportunities are endless. Not to mention that getting into a grad school would easier now as well.

I open the remaining envelopes without much care.

CalTech. Accepted.

University of Boston. Rejected.

Stanford. Accepted.

Carnegie-Mellon. Rejected.

University of Michigan – Ann Arbor. Accepted.

It was disappointing to read the rejected letters from Boston and Carnegie-Mellon, but the exhilaration of getting into MIT definitely helped quell the disappointment, if not put it out entirely.

The rest of the evening goes rather well. Nick was accepted at all of the universities he applied to and settled on going to the University of Portland. We all end up raising a glass in a toast to the success of those of us around the table and we thanked our parents for their support in getting us to where we are today. Dad gets emotional during the thanks and cracks a couple of jokes about being skeptical of our future outlooks, which receives a pretty good reaction from the other parents. It's not until Nick leaves and it's just my parents, Gay Simon, Z, and I that I remember the reality that's emerged from the opening – Z didn't get into any school along the east coast.

"Z, I'm going to go home and go to bed," Simon says, stretching as he gets up from the couch. "Are you going to stay here for a little while?"

Z looks up at me from her cuddled up position at my side. "Movie?"

I nod, trying to hide what I'm really feeling – the boundless amount of anxiety and apprehension of being apart.

She smiles and turns back to Simon. "I'll be home after a while. If you could just unlock the sliding glass down in the back, that would be great. I'll lock up once I'm back."

He gives her a casual thumbs up before shaking Dad's hand, hugging Mom, and then exiting through the front door.

"You two," Dad says, his voice stern. "We're going to bed. Can we trust you?"

I blush. "Yes, Dad. We're just going to watch a movie and we'll watch it in here if it makes you more comfortable."

Dad nods. "Good man. Keep the volume down."

"Yes, sir. We like having the subtitles on anyways."

Mom and Dad head upstairs while Z grabs the remote, opening up one of the streaming services on the smart TV and scrolling through the movie selection.

I'm not really paying attention. I am trying. But I can't. I'm far too distracted by the almost 3000 miles that will separate me from Z next year. I looked up the distance the first time we had this discussion. Now, it haunts me.

"Do you want to talk about it?" Z whispers. I can hear in her voice that she is worried too.

"Only if you do."

Z nods slowly, putting down the remote. "Jack…"

"Z, I want to stay together."

"Jack, so do I. That was never in question."

I intertwine my fingers with hers. "Really?"

"Yes, really, you idiot." She says, trying to sound playful.

I reciprocate by attempting a smile, but it doesn't last. "Z, it's 3,000 miles."

"I know."

"44-hour drive."

"I know."

"6-hour flight."

"I know, Jack. I've done as much research as you about this. I've been worried, too."

"You have?"

Z nods. "Ever since that conversation we had during semester one finals, it's been in the back of my mind. If I couldn't sleep, I was looking up things like flights or drives or communication styles for successful long-distance couples or computers with good webcams or good ways to stay intimate while apart. I love you so much, Jack. I don't want to lose you."

"I don't want to lose you either, Z."

"Is there a 'but'?"

"No, there's no 'but.' Only worry for next year."

"We can make it work."

"I know."

"We'll have to find a balance. Obviously our workloads at college will be different and I want to make sure you do well. MIT is a big deal, babe. I'm really proud of you for getting in."

"I got into Stanford and CalTech, too," I say, trying to mask the hesitation in my voice. "We would be a lot closer to one another. It's a good school…"

"No, Jack," Z says, pivoting on the couch so she is facing me. "I won't let you do that."

"Z, I can make my own…"

"I know you can make your own decisions. But I don't want you to make your decisions based around me. Would I love to have you closer? Yes. But what I want more than that is for you to achieve your dreams. MIT has been your dream for so long now. There's no way in hell that I would want you to sacrifice that dream for me."

I don't know what to say, so I just stare at the couch.

Z lifts my face with her hand. "Jack. I love you. You know I do. And I know you love me. I know you would do anything for me. I know you would choose Stanford or CalTech if I asked you to. And I love that about you. But I want what is best for you, even if it means you're far from me."

I nod. She's right. I would do that for her. I would do anything for her. Hell, I'd move heaven and earth for her if she asked. But she's not asking me to do that. She's asking me to go to MIT so that I can fulfill my dream.

"Thank you, hjartat."

Z kisses me. "Of course, askim."

I remember something from the day at Lisa's pool house. "You didn't get a letter from Harvard?"

The smile on Z's face fades. "What?"

"You applied to Harvard at Lisa's that one day, right? You didn't get a letter from them? An email?"

Z looks down.

My heart sinks.

"Z?"

"Jack… I didn't apply to Harvard."

I'm shocked. She had lied to me. I had asked her weeks ago which colleges she applied to and I specifically asked about Harvard. Z had said yes.

"You… you lied to me?"

Z looks back up at me. "Yes… I'm sorry…"

"Why?"

Z rubs her palm with her thumb. "I… I don't…"

"You don't know?"

"No… Jack… I'm… I lied to you because I was hesitant about going to Harvard in the first place."

"Hesitant? But you said that Harvard would be a great choice? You said it would be a great place to get your degree and we would be close?"

"I know I said that… But… I felt like I was applying to Harvard because you would be close…"

"Okay? So?"

"Jack, I don't want to make decisions based off of you or where you're going."

My jaw drops. "But that's what we talked about."

"Yes, I know, babe, but…"

"No, there shouldn't be a 'but,' Z!" I'm getting angry.

"Jack, don't yell at me…" Z says, her chin dropping down so she's looking away from me. I hurt her. I can tell.

"Z, I'm sorry…"

"Jack, you can't be angry. I just told you that I want you to chase your dream. That I want you to make your decision based off of what you want. You can't turn around and tell me to do the exact opposite."

I nod, taking my turn to lower my head out of shame. "You're right. I'm sorry. I just… don't appreciate being lied to…"

She picks her head up and takes my hand. I return the grip the best I can, forcing my mind to not be mad anymore. "I know… And I'm sorry… I shouldn't have lied to you."

I look up at her, giving her a small, weak smile. "It's okay."

She returns the light smile. "Not really, Jack. Lying to one another isn't something that should become a habit. Especially if we are going to make long distance work next year."

I nod. "I know. What I meant is that I forgive you. I don't want to hold it against you."

She kisses me and I pull her closer. Her hand moves through my hair and she repositions herself so she is somewhat on top of me. After a few moments, she pulls herself away.

"We told your parents they could trust us."

I let out a deep sigh. "Yeah, I know."

Z kisses me again. "I love you."

"I love you, too. Do you still want to watch a movie?"

She nods and settles back in as we select a go to movie. Once it's over, we get up and I walk her over to Simon's and say good night. It's close to one in the morning now and I can feel exhaustion begin to set in.

As I crawl into bed, I expect to feel some sort of comfort in the clean sheets. Some release of anxiety under the weighted blanket. But there is none. The anxiety only grows.

3000 miles. 44-hour drive. 6-hour flight.

We'll be fine. We have a strong foundation. We've talked about these things. We clearly love each other. Sure, there will be a bit of a learning curve. It might be hard at times. We might have a fight here and there. But we'll make it work! It'll be okay.

3000 miles. 44-hour drive. 6-hour flight.

What if it's too hard? What if we fight more than just 'here and there?' What if we find out that the love that we share only exists in close proximity to one another? What if she finds another guy? What if the foundation we have is a joke?

3000 miles. 44-hour drive. 6-hour flight.

I could go to Stanford. They have a pretty impressive program. It's a good school. Their engineering program is rated pretty high and they do pretty well when it comes to graduates finding a job. We would only be an hour or so away from one another. I can still do everything that I want to do.

But it's not MIT. It's not this dream I have been chasing, this goal I've been pursuing. It's not where I would like to live for nine months out of the year, especially if I have to come back to Florida every summer. It's not what I want.

3000 miles. 44-hour drive. 6-hour flight.

But Z is who I want. I want Z in my life. Sometimes it even feels like I need Z in my life. She's made living in Florida so much easier. So much better. I'm, for the first time that I can really remember, extremely happy. My parents are happy. My parents love her. Z is who I want in my life and I can't see myself without her. I don't want to be away from her.

But my dream is across the country.

3000 miles. 44-hour drive. 6-hour flight.

Z was a dream, too. It was a dream of mine to be her boyfriend. To be the one in the picture with her instead of whoever else. She was the daydream that brought *Jeux Deux* to its magnificence. Z is my dream.

MIT is my dream.

Z is my dream.

MIT is my dream.

3000 miles. 44-hour drive. 6-hour flight.

What happens… what happens if I can't have both?

3000 miles. 44-hour drive. 6-hour flight.

3000 miles. 44-hour drive. 6-hour flight.

CHAPTER 17

Spring Break. Thank God.

Here's the thing about school and spring break: it's needed far more than winter break despite the fact that the time between summer and winter break is longer than between winter break and spring break. Let me explain. From mid-August to Thanksgiving, everyone is still running off of summer energy. Teachers are more optimistic, students are more orderly, and school is smoother. Thanksgiving break offers a brief, but beloved break for everyone and the holiday does a good job at setting everyone up for a few good weeks before winter break. Admittedly, teachers probably have a harder time than students between the two breaks, but I would argue that those few weeks are still better than January to mid-March. After winter break, it's the dog days of winter – January and February. Granted, up north it's far worse. With temperatures well below freezing (far below zero sometimes even) and snow, it makes for a miserable two months. But even in Florida, those two months aren't a ton of fun. The weather doesn't really know what it is doing and can feel very bipolar. Everyone bundles up right away in the morning since it's cold, but then its shorts and long sleeve shirts in the afternoon. It's odd. This affects morale across the board, putting everyone on edge. Students are far more unruly; teachers are drained from trying to make the dog days less doggish. It's miserable for everyone.

But then spring break comes, letting its majesty ring out across the moody, irritable populous and promising to make for an easier last two months of school.

It is truly a magnificent time.

This year, however, things are a little different. My parents decided they wanted to go on a multi-week cruise, starting with the week of spring break and last for two weeks after. Because I can't miss those two weeks after, I don't get to go. I've known about this cruise for a while – almost a full year - and I wasn't really bummed about it. I figured that I could work or see if I could spend the week with Nick or Khalan. Then I started dating Z and I went from not really bummed to incredibly relieved because now I can just spend it with Z. But about two weeks ago, we discovered that the entire friend group was free over spring break. Nick's mom Diane found out about a seminar in her field of medicine in Nashville and was going to take Winona with her. Khalan's parents wanted to join mine on their cruise and managed to procure a couple last minute tickets. Mona's parents were going up to South Carolina to visit old friends and Lisa's parents were going on their annual trip to Paris. When the realization had been made, we also discovered that Simon's partner, Frederick, owned a large horse ranch up in Ocala – a city about an hour or so north of Orlando – and had plenty of space if we wanted to go up there. Simon was already planning on going up to spend the week with Frederick and told us that we wouldn't be a bother since Frederick's estate was quite large. So, with that in mind, we made plans to travel up to Ocala for Spring Break.

Here's the thing about Ocala – it's kind of the opposite of what people expect to do over spring break. The movies depict beaches and booze and crazy times. TV shows show exotic destinations and palm trees and coconuts. But Ocala? Ocala's not like that. Ocala is the absolute middle of nowhere. Not only an hour north of Orlando, it's about forty-five minutes south of Gainesville, home of the University of Florida. The closest beach is Lake Weir, but that's even a sleepy little lake with tons of people living around it that aren't exactly what someone pictures when they hear spring break. To get to the ocean, vacationers either need to drive an hour and a half east to Ormond Beach, which is just north of Daytona, or two hours to St. Pete. There's Crystal River and Bird Creek Beach, but Crystal River is more known for its manatees and Bird Creek Beach isn't exactly an ideal beach spot. Sure, it's nice, but it's no Ormond or St. Pete.

Going back to Ocala, it's pretty spread out. It can take up to forty-five minutes just to drive from one end to another. That's because there's a ton of horse ranches and fields of cows sprinkled throughout the city limits. Ocala is actually considered to be the Horse Capital of the World – a ton of Triple Crown winners have been bred, born, raised, and trained in Ocala. Other than that, there are a few parks to go to, some shopping centers, lots of hiking trails, and a bunch of different restaurants.

Honestly, I would have been opposed to the idea of going if it weren't for the fact Frederick owns a horse ranch. I enjoy riding horses, but don't really have an opportunity to do it in Orlando. And it's a great time to go riding – like I mentioned before, it's not super-hot during this time of year here, but it's not super-cold either. It's almost perfect.

Mona, Lisa, Khalan, and Nick end up driving with Simon since they were able to get out of the last half of their school day, but I can't leave with them. I still have my piano lesson – I tried to get out of it because I know Ms. Pillard and Dr. Thurmond are going to Costa Rica and I'm sure Ms. Pillard needs to pack. But Dad, the ever so-stubborn one, insists I go to practice so I can work on my new piece for the summer competition. The winners of that competition get to go to Geneva for another competition. Z sided with Dad, so I really ended up with no choice. However, because she did so, I told her she had to wait so we could drive up together.

As I throw the last of her bags in the back of the Baja, I start laughing.

"Babe, we're going to be up there for a week and a day. Do you really…"

She places a finger to my lips, clicking her tongue. "Nope. You don't get to say anything. That's a rule when you're dating someone. The boy doesn't get to ask why the girl has so many bags, even for a short vacation."

I roll my eyes as she kisses my cheek, smirks, and gets into the car.

"As you wish, dearest."

I sit down and start the car. Mom pokes her head out the front door as we drive away and waves. We both wave back, but Z takes it one step further. She rolls down the window and sits in the open window.

"Bye, Lydia! Love you! Have fun in the Caribbean!"

I'm sure Mom tries to yell something back, but her voice doesn't carry well.

"Okay, so," Z starts, grabbing my phone. "What are we listening to?"

"How about the blend of our music?" I ask, pulling onto Nemours Parkway to pick up the 417. "That way it's a good mix, ya know?"

Z takes my hand. "Darling, you know I love you, yes?"

"Yes, and I love you. I don't see what…"

"Jack, half of the music on our blend is yours. That's what the algorithm dictates. And I'm pretty sure you don't want to listen to piano music while we drive an hour or more, am I correct?"

I chuckle and shake my head. "You know me so well."

Z smirks and lifts her shoulders, trying to put on a goofy, cute, innocent kind of face. "I know. I also know you enough to know what non-piano music you like to listen to, so I made our own playlist blend without the piano music."

I give her a questioning glance. "When did you have time to do that?"

Z's smile widens. "Oh, you know. English class when Halverson wasn't looking."

"You got away with that?!"

"Oh, Jack, I'm very sneaky when I want to be. Uncle Simon calls me a ghost at home. He doesn't hear me half the time."

"I'm impressed with that, but even more impressed with fooling Halverson. She's got eyes like a hawk."

"She may, but I have the deftness of a cat."

I roll my eyes. "Okay, babe, whatever you say."

As we get on the 417 to meet up with the Turnpike, Z starts the playlist. The smooth guitar introduction of Rusted Root's *Send Me On My Way* opens our drive up to Ocala. Z sings along and when the song gets to the part of the verse where it sounds like a bunch of gibberish, she goes way over the top with no recognizable words whatsoever.

I laugh and shake my head. "Z, you know there are actual lyrics there, right?"

Z looks at me with a confused look. "No, there's not."

I cock one eyebrow at her very determined answer. "Yes, there is. It's 'you know what they say about the young.' It's online if you look it up."

Z shakes her head. "No, there are no words to that part of the song."

I shrug. "I don't know what to tell you, babe. That's what the internet says."

Z pulls out her phone and begins to type feverishly. After a few moments, she finds what she is looking forward and exclaims loudly. "The lead singer, in an interview, says that there are no words to that portion of the verse! He says that in the process of writing he came up with oombayseeyou and then oombaysee, seemoobadeeyah and didn't change it because it was so fun and could mean whatever it needed to be. He claims it is far better to use these words than try to find other, actual words that would fit the feeling just the same!"

"No way!"

"Yes way!"

I run a hand through my hair. "That's unbelievable. I have been convinced, *convinced* for *years* that the lyrics were 'you know what they say about the young' and have been correcting literally everyone, but apparently, I'm wrong!"

We have a good laugh about that before starting the song over and singing along at the top of our lungs.

The drive is relatively uneventful and easy. We're heading in the opposite direction of the worst traffic as most people are heading to the nicer beaches or the airport for spring break or just a fun weekend. Not many people have the idea of going to Ocala, I guess.

Not a surprise.

We talk about a number of different things as we go up – what we want to do, where we want to go. We revisit our college discussion, but I quickly change the subject. It's not something I want to fight about… again. Not on Spring Break, at least. I want to focus on having fun and being with friends and spending time with her.

While I can. While she's here. In arm's reach.

We get to Ocala around 7:15 and I'm blown away at Frederick's place. I've seen big houses and estates before and I would even say my house is bigger than average. But Frederick's place is huge. It's a gated driveway that's about a quarter mile long back into a wooded area. The house itself is stucco (which is pretty normal for Florida) and is surrounded by gardens. It's two stories tall and, a straight guess, thirty-five hundred to four thousand square feet. The lawn is huge and has tall oaks scattered throughout. I'm pretty sure Frederick hires a lawn crew because the grass is pristine and green. I park the car and get out to stretch when Nick comes running out of the house.

"Dude! I got us the rooms in the Horse Barn!"

"I'm sorry, what?" I say, my eyes wide from shock. "Why are we sleeping in the Horse Barn?! I thought Frederick had enough rooms for all of us!"

Nick laughs. "Grab your shit and I'll show you."

After helping Z bring her things inside, I grab my bag and follow Nick through the house and into the backyard. A few dozen yards from the house is another similar building, but smaller. It honestly looks like a barn, but something tells me it's not since there is another barn down a path off to the right that is more of the traditional wooden red building. Not to mention, there are horses around that barn so what I'm walking to is probably not what it seems.

It's definitely not.

It was probably, at one point, a barn. The entry way leads to a hall that is wide and long with two rooms on either side and I'm instructed to always take my shoes off before leaving the entryway. Nick first leads me down the hall to the farthest rooms. I peer into one and it looks to be outfitted with a pool table and other games. I walk across to the room opposite of the billiards room and look inside. There are a number of bookshelves lining the walls and it smells like burned tobacco. On one of the bookshelves are several boxes standing at an angle, displaying what I can only assume to be expensive cigars.

"Damn! Frederick is classy."

Nick nods. "He's so cool. He and Simon went out for dinner, but I'm sure they'll be back in like an hour. Come on, I'll show you your room!"

Between the two rooms on each side is a bathroom, which I notice has a door connecting them to the rooms. I take a step inside my room for the week and am amazed. A queen bed is pressed up against the middle of the far wall. A mahogany dresser is on the wall to my right with matching side tables on either side of the bed. The light fixture is a gentle yellow and has a ceiling fan that spins lazily overhead. To my left, a window looks out toward the house and has a great view of the gardens and lawn. I sit down on the bed and feel the topper and sheets which are both as smooth as smooth can be. I let out a low whistle as I scan the room again.

"Son of a bitch. These are really nice!"

"Right?! It was dumb luck that we got them. Mona and Lisa wanted them so badly, but Simon said he wants you out here and Z inside."

I shake my head. Despite saying she is a ghost, Simon had caught Z sneaking out late one night and put a quick end to her escapades of sneaking to my room through the upstairs window. He wasn't mad for long, but we both knew we really shouldn't test his good graces again.

"Understandable. But they're okay with Mona and Lisa being in the same area?"

Nick laughs. "Mona asked the same question. Simon said she had a good point, but Frederick told him that it was fine. Said something about the gays sticking together."

I shake my head. "That's ridiculous. Fair, but ridiculous."

Nick nods. "We're in the living room of the house right now trying to plan out some things to do this week. Frederick gave us a list. There's not much, but we can make it work."

I smile. "We always do."

"Holy shit, this is your room?!" Z exclaims. Both Nick and I jump –
neither of us noticed she had come down from the main house.

"Yep, I guess so!"

Z cross her arms and puts on a fake frown. "You get this and I get
stuck with a twin bed and sharing a room with Mona."

Laughing, I walk over to her and give her a hug. "I'm sorry, hjartat.
I can try to switch if you want."

Z hugs me back, then takes my hand and begins walking us back to
the main house. "No, it's okay. I don't want to get on Uncle Simon's
bad side. Come on, we've been waiting for you two."

We stay up for another couple of hours, planning out the week. We
couples ask for times that we can do things individually and promise to
do things with Khalan and Nick as well. Simon and Frederick come
home about an hour and a half after we get there and I introduce
myself to him since Z has already met him. Nick is right – he is super
cool. He used to be a stock broker until he got tired of the New York
lifestyle and moved down to Florida. He shifted gears and started to
breed and train horses, keeping up his lavish lifestyle by catering to the
local wealth as well as foreign investors. His latest champion horse,
Up Around the Bend, recently won the Triple Crown and he is quite
pleased with himself.

After cementing plans, we all head to bed. In the morning, Frederick
and Simon have made a huge breakfast spread for us – bacon, sausage
(both links and patties), a bunch of scrambled eggs, French toast,
pancakes, and some of the best hashbrowns I've ever had in my life.
Even better than Shaker's. Once we're all properly fueled, we head up
to Payne's Prairie near Gainesville. There is a boardwalk which goes
out into this lagoon area where there are typically a bunch of alligators.
It's not in the park, but it is relatively close. We see a few gators and
end up going up to the actual trailhead of Payne's Prairie to hike for a
while. After a couple of hours, we end up driving back after picking up
some food. It starts raining on our way and once we're home, we go
into the living room and turn on a movie. Everyone seems to be pretty
tired – it must be the rain combined with the hike and being quite
relaxed on spring break. Z and I are the only ones awake – and Z is
barely conscious as it is.

An idea sparks in my brain and I shake Z.

"Hey," I whisper.

"Mmmm, what? I'm so comfy, I could fall asleep," Z says,
snuggling closer to me.

"I honestly thought you were. But let's get out of here."

She lifts her head and looks at me. "What?"

"Let's go somewhere. Just you and me. Everyone is asleep. We'll come back when they're all awake again."

Z smiles and my heart flutters. "Okay. Where?"

I waggle my eyebrows. "Trust me?"

She rolls her eyes. "Ugh, one of these again? Yes, askim, I trust you."

We quietly sneak out of the living room and leave a note on the island in the kitchen suggesting we go to Brooklyn's Backyard for dinner since it was rated the best pizza in Ocala for a few years in a row. We get in the Baja and drive out towards Silver Springs.

Silver Springs is a state park that has the world-famous glass-bottom boat rides over a number of springs. Luckily for us, the rain dissipates when we get to the park and the sun starts to shine again. Z puts on a University of Minnesota hat and her sunglasses and we head into the park. A sign greets us saying to be careful for Rhesus monkeys as they are wild animals and can be temperamental. I thought that was kind of obvious, but I never know with some people. After purchasing our glass-bottom boat tickets, we head to the line and climb into the boat when instructed. The pilot takes us around the park, showing us different hot springs, telling us about the different movies and trivia the park has, and lingers around while a couple of gators are swimming near us so tourists can take pictures. Through the glass bottom we can see hundreds of different kinds of fish. Z is enamored by all of it – she has a deep love for nature.

After our boat tour, we get ice cream and French fries at the little shops that are right by the lake and then walk around the park. Just as we are about to leave, a few girls end up realizing who Z is and swarm us, begging for pictures. Z is kind enough to take a few pictures and she insists that I, her boyfriend, take the photos. I oblige happily, but get antsy when they start asking questions about me and how we met and if I'm famous. Z quickly shuts that down, dismisses us, and we take off.

The trip continues like this for a few days. We explore what Ocala has to offer – hiking the paved trail at Santos, visiting different places to eat like Mojo's, Brooklyn's, and El Toreo, getting soft serve at Twisty Treat, wandering through the Historic District, and simply having a good time as friends. Z and I manage to sneak out a few more times and even succeed in going to Eaton's Beach, a really, *really* good restaurant on Lake Weir. But the most memorable food we all got together was the donuts at Tas-T-O's. It's this little donut shop off of Silver Springs Boulevard and, believe me when I say this, they are the best donuts in the entire world. I will be recommending them to everyone until the day I die.

I'm happy. Happier than I've ever been in Florida. And it's not just because of Z – despite the fact she's a really big part of it. But it's my friends, too. Nick keeps us all laughing with his antics and attempted escapades. Khalan shares anecdotes and keeps us on track. Mona and Lisa are… well… Mona and Lisa. I'm really fortunate to have them in my life. I love them a lot.

And I feel like I'm even starting to love Florida, too.

Even if it's just a little.

Very little.

It's now Thursday night and it starts raining around ten at night, which is odd for Florida in Spring. It's not super heavy, but heavy enough that it's not comfortable to be out in. I kiss Z good night, but the kiss feels different. She holds it for longer, the connection and release are slower and her hand is through my hair most of the time. I guess it was passionate enough that all our friends start oohing. Nick even whistles before he and I head out to our rooms in the Horse Barn. He fist-bumps me before heading into his room.

I try to sleep, but it doesn't come which is odd because I usually sleep really well in the rain. Staying in my sleeping shorts and no shirt, I click on the lamp, pick up my book, and sit up in the bed. The book is intriguing, but it's not one of those novels that causes my brain to overwork or pump my adrenaline. When I look over at the clock, it reads 11:44pm and I'm still not tired. I pick up my phone to text Z, but set it back down on the charging pad. She's probably really tired and I don't want to wake her up.

I see the outside motion triggered light turn on and I quickly see if I can't catch Nick sneaking out. As much as Z and I have been sneaking away, Nick has also been sneaking out to see some girl he met the first day here in Ocala. I must have missed him because I don't see anyone. I shake my head, thinking my best friend has become a master of stealth and sneak.

I set my book down now and decide I'm going to try and fall asleep again. As I'm about to lay down, I hear the click of the latch and the creak of my door opening. I sit straight up, my heart pounding. I only relax when I realize it's Z standing in the doorway.

"Hey, hjartat. What are you doing? Are you okay?"

Z steps into the room and closes the door. She's a little damp from running out in the rain and is only wearing her favorite short shorts and a tank top. I reach for my t-shirt and she puts up a hand. "No, no, it's okay. And yeah, I'm okay. I just couldn't sleep."

I pat the bed next to me. "Come here."

She smiles and quickly makes her way over to the bed. She crawls under the covers and I slide down next to her. Z presses herself up against me and I can feel her shivering.

"Babe, you're freezing!"

She nods. "And you're so warm."

My body tenses as I feel her cold hands on my side. "Oh, my god, not for long!"

We laugh and I hold her close and slowly start to feel our heat accumulate under the covers. Soon she is much warmer and tracing circles on my chest. We don't say much, but I don't think either of us are tired. I start gently rubbing her shoulder with the tips of my fingers, hoping maybe this will lull both of us to sleep somehow.

"Jack?"

"Yeah?"

"I've had a lot of fun these past few days."

"Me, too. Wouldn't have traded them for any cruise in the Caribbean. And we still have a few days left."

"Same here."

Z moves so her head is resting on top of my chest rather than alongside. "What do you want to do tomorrow?"

I smile. "Maybe we should do something as a group."

Z nods. "Okay. I still want to do something with just you though."

"Alright, I think we can find a compromise somewhere in there. Oh, I heard about this one diner here that is really good. It's called… shit… um… Ocala Downtown Diner. Really good French Toast."

Z chuckles. "You and your French Toast."

I smile. "Hey. I'm a big fan."

Z kisses my chest lightly and I feel a pulse of electricity course out from the spot of impact. "And me?"

I arch an eyebrow. "You?"

"Are you a big fan of me?"

I let out a deep sigh. "I mean, I guess."

We both laugh as she tickles my sides and I squirm, trying to get away. But she has too good of an advantage on me. After a few moments, she finally stops and we are both breathing heavily and laughing. Somehow, she's shifted so her head is even with mine and only a few inches away from my face.

"I'm not just a big fan of you," I whisper. "I love you, Zendaya. Very much."

Z runs a hand through my hair. "I love you, too, Jack."

She kisses me and a flood of energy washes over me. It seems to wash over her too as she shifts to be top of me and everything becomes phenomenally more passionate. I hold her as close to me as a I can and I can feel her entire body pressing against mine, trying to get closer than ever before.

Z pulls away, put only enough so she can talk. It was like our first kiss outside the Steinmetz – our noses still touching and her lips brushing against mine as she speaks.

"Jack."

"Z."

"I… I want you."

My heart, which was already beating fast, begins to quicken its pace. "You mean?…"

Z nods. "Yes."

I move my hands to the bottom of her shirt. She slides back a little so I can sit up, raising her arms.

"Can I?"

"Please."

I slowly take off her shirt and drop it off the edge of the bed. She takes my hand and guides it over her curves until I figure out how to use my adrenaline pumping arms again. Her skin is phenomenally smooth and she smells amazing – intoxicating even. My mind is racing and spinning and reeling. We have done other stuff before, but this is new and exhilarating and I don't want to mess it up.

"Z, I need to confess something."

She kisses me before answering. "What?"

"I've never done this before."

She shakes her head. "Neither have I."

I kiss her this time before asking her another question. "Won't it be awkward?"

Z laughs and kisses me again. "Definitely. But I don't care. I want you. I want you more than anything."

We reconnect then and soon, there is nothing between us. It is simply her and I intertwined in an embrace that I could never put into words. And yes, it's awkward. Yes, it's not perfect. Yes, it's not exactly the smoothest thing – nothing like they show in the movies or TV shows.

But it doesn't matter. It's her and I. It's the love we share which has us ignore the awkwardness and imperfection. We find a rhythm and move together and breathe together and meld together.

We manage to do it twice – the second time being much better than the first, both satisfying the other before collapsing on the bed. I finally feel tired and the bed feels more comfortable than ever before. Z kisses me and gets up out of the bed.

"Don't go," I say, grabbing her hand while trying to mask the desperation in my voice.

She leans back over to me and kisses me again – it's easy to say the connection we just encountered has now inhibited us from not kissing. "I'm not. I just need to go to the bathroom and grab some water. Then I'll be right back. Would you like some?"

I nod and she smiles before putting her shorts and shirt back and sneaking through the door into the bathroom. A few minutes later she's back with two glasses of water. I drink mine in one go, setting the glass on the nightstand. Z crawls back under the covers and smiles at me.

"How do you want to do this?"

I shrug. "I'm guessing no matter how we start, we'll end up laying differently in the morning."

She nods and smiles. "I want to be little spoon."

I smile back. "As you wish, hjartat."

We reposition ourselves and, much sooner than we both anticipate, we are fast asleep, our fingers interlaced and breathing in sync.

CHAPTER 18

I don't think I'll forget this day for as long as I live.

It's the Wednesday after Spring Break and most of the fun that happened over that week is now the farthest thing from my mind as my knee bounces with anxiety in the waiting room of the hospital. I've always been afraid of something like this happening. I just never thought it would be like this.

I was in the middle of grading quizzes for Dr. Thurmond when my phone started going off. First, it was just a single text from Dad. I simply ignored it – he had been sending me pictures of him and Mom on their cruise. Then came another. Then another. Then a phone call. Then another text. And another. I opened my phone out of sheer curiosity.

Dad: Jack, I need you to call me.

Dad: I know you're in Dr. Thurmond's right now, but this is serious.

Dad: Son.

Dad: Jack, this is an emergency!

Dad: It's Mom…

'It's Mom…'

That text still sends shivers down my spine.

I quickly showed Dr. Thurmond the texts and he gestured me to go outside and hurry. I almost ran into Ms. Presley going down the stairs. I guess she was on her way to come and get me. She tried to say something but my phone was already in hand and Dad's number was dialed. He picked up and I knew things were far worse than I thought – Dad's voice was shaky and full sentences were absent from his usually well-thought out and articulate manner of speaking.

"Jack…"

"Dad, what's going on?!"

"Your mom. Fell. Not sure… What… happened. She was… fine one minute and now… God, Jack, I'm shaking…"

"Where are you, Dad?!"

"Orlando. Emergency flight. Flew from… wherever we were."

"Great, that's great, Dad. What hospital?"

"Health."

"Advent Health?"

"Yeah…"

"Okay, I'll be right there."

I hung up the phone to look up at Ms. Presley, who nodded and told me I could just go, she'll cover the absence until my dad was able to call. I thanked her, quickly sent a text to Z about what was going on, sprinted out to my car, and drove as fast as I dared to the hospital.

Dad was a nervous wreck when I got there. He was pacing so much that I thought he was going to wear a hole right through the hospital floor. When he saw me and finally registered it was me, he wrapped his arms around me and held me in a vice-like bear hug and started to completely break down. All I could do was hold him and, at one point, it started to feel like I was holding him up instead of him holding me up.

Dad explained that Mom had collapsed while at port. They were walking around the different stalls and vendors when Mom had complained about feeling weary and worn out. This hadn't made sense to him since they had just left the boat, she had been sure to drink enough water, and had slept well the night before. There was no way that it could be anything heat related. But the next second she was on the ground and unresponsive, breathing shallow. The local medical personnel weren't sure what was going on. Luckily, Dad had a friend who had a private jet wherever they were and he was able to fly them back to Florida. His friend had radioed ahead to the airport and informed them what was going on, which resulted in a helicopter meeting them on the landing strip to get Mom to Advent Health.

When I had gotten to the hospital, I briefly saw Mom before they wheeled her into the radiology department to do some further screenings.

She looked like she had already died.

I'm not sure how this happened, but she looked like she had aged at least a decade from the last time I saw her. She was whiter than a sheet of paper and looked like she was trying everything in her power to avoid falling asleep. Her lips were bluer than my mental strength could handle and, when she was out of sight, I crumbled into a chair. I was numb. I had no thoughts other than if Mom was going to make it.

Or was I going to lose a parent at the age of eighteen?

I'm still numb. I haven't moved from the chair. I'm ninety percent sure my phone has vibrated at least a dozen or so times, but I also haven't moved to take it out of my pocket.

Nothing on my phone matters. Mom is in radiology getting scanned and screened for cancer.

My brain has recovered enough to let anxiety take over and my mind begins to race.

AP Human Anatomy. I took it last year.

First thing to figure out: what cancer does Mom have? Could be anything. Most deadly cancers in women: Lung or bronchial, breast, colon and rectum, pancreas, ovary.

Second thing: how early or late did we catch the cancer? This is pivotal. If we have caught it early enough, chances of survival increase dramatically. Even with lung cancer, the deadliest one for both genders, the survival rate for lung cancer is fifty-six percent, which is pretty good. Better than half. Still not great nor something I would ever be comfortable with, but still better than half.

It's better than half. Think on the positive side of things. Z has told me that dozens of times in the last few weeks. Always try to find the positive side.

But there's a really bad negative side…

What if it's too late? What if it is lung cancer and it's spread and she has distant tumors – tumors that have spread to other organs? The survival rate for individuals who don't catch lung cancer early on – which, if I remember correctly, is *most* cases – is only five percent.

Five.

Percent.

Not even double digits.

Just five.

One in twenty.

But this can't be lung cancer. Mom doesn't smoke. Nor has she ever smoked. I know her parents well enough. They threatened that if they ever caught her smoking that they would force her to smoke three packs of cigarettes back-to-back and have her light the next cigarette with the butt of the last. Grandpa knew that smoking was bad – he just couldn't quit it. She had told me that she had been terrified of that and never touched a cigarette or even thought about having one.

There could be another reason for getting lung cancer, but that's the most common. So, it's pretty ridiculous to assume that it's lung cancer.

Next deadly: breast.

This one can still kill, but the odds of it doing so is much lower. I mean, if I remember the statistic right, if it's localized and hasn't spread anywhere, five-year survival rate is ninety-nine percent. That's great odds! I mean, that's almost everyone!

Almost…

It still leaves one percent who die.

"Son, are you alright?"

I look up at the nurse who has spoken to me, her blue scrubs neat and her eyes showing concern. I didn't realize that I have been rocking back and forth for whoever knows how long.

I can only shake my head.

"It's okay, ma'am, I'll take care of him."

Z.

"Do you know her, honey?"

I nod.

"Okay," She turns to Z. "If you need something, just holler, sugar."

"Thank you, ma'am."

The nurse leaves and Z immediately rushes to my side, pulling me into a tight hug.

"Jack, I'm so sorry. Are you okay? Wait, no, of course not. What can I do? Babe, what can I do?"

I can't say anything. I start crying. And I don't mean little tears. I mean full on sobbing and hyperventilating.

"Hey, you're okay, you're okay. I got you, askim. I got you."

I fling my arms around her and hold her while I shake and sob.

Z rubs my back and tries to calm me down with reassuring shushes and the occasional kiss on the side of my head. She doesn't say anything for a while and I can only assume that it's to let me cry.

Once I calm down a little, she kisses the side of my head again and breaks her silence.

"Have you seen either your parents, babe?"

I nod. "I saw Mom before she went to radiology. Dad was with her, too. I think he told me to sit down and he would be right out, but I can't be sure."

"Do you know what's going on?"

I shrug. "No, not really. I think I heard a doctor say cancer, but I could be wrong."

Her fingernails gently graze my back. "Oh, askim, I'm sorry."

I don't say or do anything.

"Jack! Z, thank God you're here."

It's Dad.

I bolt out of my seat and collide with him, my tears starting up again.

"Is she going to be okay? Dad, tell me she's going to be okay!"

Dad rubs my back and lets out a deep breath. "Yes, son, she's going to be okay. The doctor said he couldn't explain why she fell and was unresponsive at this moment but he's going to look into it a little more. But he without a doubt knew it was linked to some kind of cancer. After some preliminary screening, he assumes breast cancer in early stages. She'll need surgery and chemotherapy, but she'll undoubtedly make it."

I can feel my shoulders slump and relax as the burden of unknowingness lifts from them. She's going to be okay. There's probably going to be a long road to full recovery, but she's going to be okay.

Dad lets me go and pats me on my shoulder before hugging Z. "Thank you for being here."

"Of course, Simon," Z replies, returning the embrace. "Can I do anything for you guys?"

Dad shakes his head. "I wouldn't want to trouble you."

It's Z's turn to shake her head. "Simon, I want to help."

Dad nods. "Okay. Would you and Jack mind running home and taking care of our bags? My buddy Jim is supposed to swing by with the luggage in about an hour or so."

"He's the pilot friend, right?"

"Yeah, he got us from…" Dad thinks for a moment. "I can't even remember." Dad runs a hand through his hair. He looks older now, much older than I know him to be.

"It's okay, Simon," Z says, hugging him again. "This has been quite the ordeal."

Dad just nods again. "I'm not sure if they are going to want to keep Lydia in the hospital overnight or whatever. Jack, would you mind being willing to bring us some stuff if that does happen?"

I nod. "Of course, Dad. Anything I can do to help, I'll do it."

Dad lets out a long sigh. "I appreciate that, son. More than you know. I'm going to head back in there. Tell Jim I say thanks, I owe him a huge favor, and to leave the receipt for the fuel and flight charges on the island. Don't take no for an answer. Make sure he leaves that receipt."

"Okay, Dad. Are you sure you don't want me to stay?"

Dad shakes his head. "I'm sure. Not that I don't want you here or that your mom doesn't want you here. But I think it's wise to have minimal stress for your mom here as possible."

I nod. I understand what he's trying to say. Mom's stress levels would probably elevate if she knew that I was pacing around the hospital and crying on Z's shoulder. It's what is best for her.

I drive home with Z in relative silence as she rubs my hand with her thumb. She got a ride from her uncle since I had driven us to school that morning. I'm not really sure what to say in the car. Things are firing off so quickly in my brain.

My first thought? I need to stay in Florida for college.

I can't leave now. Mom has probably a year's worth of treatments ahead of her. And it's going to be hard on her and on Dad. She's going to fight off this deadly condition and will go through hell and back with her physical well-being. Losing her hair. Losing weight that she can't afford to lose. Going through numerous rounds of chemo. Not to mention this will take a toll on her mental health. To help with her mental health, she likes to paint. I'm sure she'll start seeing a therapist and everything – she has been seeing one already since Christmas – but painting is her at-home remedy and her professional outlet. It's going to be devastating to lose those. And then there's Dad. He'll have to take care of her. He'll have to do everything around the house – all the cleaning, the laundry, the cooking, the organizing, and the maintenance. I mean, my parents definitely have a good routine of balance between them for doing household chores, but Mom wouldn't be able to help much if at all. Knowing Dad, he probably will make sure she doesn't help, even if she does feel up to it and he needs the help. I'm sure Dad could hire a maid or nurse or aid or whatever, but, as I've said before, he's stubborn as hell and believes in doing things himself rather than asking for help. And, on top off all of that, once Grandpa and Grandma hear about Mom having cancer, I'm sure Grandpa's efforts to get us back to Alaska will double, if not triple. And Dad would be on his own if I was in Massachusetts.

I would be of so much help to Dad. I can clean as well as anyone. I can cook. I can do laundry. And I'm willing to help in any way possible.

But this means giving up my dream of going to MIT. I mean, I was accepted to MIT who has a 4% acceptance rate. That's huge. And I've worked so hard to get where I am now.

But family is more important. Family has always been more important. I need to do this for my family.

Jim drops off the bags on time and we get them all sorted in the house. I manage to find the dirty clothes after texting with Dad and decide to put them in the laundry for them. Now, Z and I are just sitting in the theater room, cuddling with *The Office* playing quietly in the background.

Her breathing is slow and even and I think she's asleep right before she breaks the silence.

"Are you doing okay?"

I nod. "Yeah, I'm okay. It's just… stressful."

"Yeah, I bet, babe. I'm sorry."

"Thanks."

More silence.

"What are you thinking?"

I hold her closer and let out a deep breath. "College with all of this."

She slowly nods. "I understand."

Silence again.

"Jack, you can't give up on your dream."

I don't say anything. To be honest, I'm shocked. I know she wants me to chase my dreams, but she also knows how much family means to me.

"Z, I can't just turn my back on family."

"You're not turning your back on family, Jack. You're going after your dream. Your parents know what they're doing. You need to chase your dream."

"Z, I love my mom. And my dad. I can't just leave them while my mom is going through all this stuff. I need to stay here."

"Jack, that's not what she wants."

I can feel myself getting mad now. "How do you know that, Z?"

She must have heard the edge in my voice because she scoots away from me and sits up. "Because I know your mom, Jack. She wants what is best for you. MIT is best for you."

"MIT is best for me? How do you know that? What if I could get into UF and it changes my life?"

"Jack, that's absurd."

"It's absurd? How is that absurd? You don't know that, Z!"

"Yes, I do! You hate it here! You hate living here! You would love Massachusetts. You would love MIT. It's your niche! It's your thing!"

I shake my head. "Yeah, it might be, Z. But I can't just leave my family."

She recoils in surprise. "What the hell is that supposed to mean?"

I know I shouldn't have said that, but my anger and the stress of the day has gotten to me. "I know you left your family in California and you're perfectly fine, but I can't do that. I love my mom way too much."

Z doesn't say anything. She just looks at me with a blank, flat stare. I clench my jaw, forcing myself to stay resolute in my anger. She waits for a long while before saying anything. We stare at each other in silence, the awkwardness of 'Scott's Tots' the only sound in the room.

Z stands up. "I'm going to assume that this is a result of the stress of the day. I'm going to go home. When you've calmed down, you can come over."

She storms out of the room and I'm left in my own shame.

I shouldn't have said that. Her mom and family are a very sensitive topic. My anger got the better of me and I crossed a line.

I should not have said that.

I can't chase after her – Dad calls. He needs some clothes for him and Mom since they want to keep her for a few nights to monitor her due to the unexpected nature of the fall. I bring the clothes in and find Dad sitting patiently in Mom's room. When I look at Mom, my heart breaks a little. She looks frail and thin and worn out. She's sleeping so she should be relaxed, but I can see her body is tense and her breathing is slightly labored. If I didn't know what was going on, I would think that she was dying or had no chance at surviving whatever is going on.

I sit down next to Dad. "How you holding up?"

He shrugs. "I'm okay. Doctor said that she'll make it. She'll need plenty of rest, but the doctor is confident she'll pull through."

I nod then just stare at Mom as she sleeps, my mind racing over what just happened and what needs to happen next.

"You okay, son? Holding up?"

I shake my head slowly. "Not really. I freaked out at Z earlier."

"What happened?"

I recall the last few hours for him. When I'm finished with my story, he doesn't say much.

"Jack, you're going to MIT."

"Dad, I…"

"No. Jack, you're going to MIT. You know if Mom found out that you turned down MIT and switched to a local school, it would break her spirit? This is what she's wanted for you for a long time. I can't imagine how heartbroken she would be if you decided to stay here."

"But, Dad, what about you?"

Dad laughs. "Jack, I'm not your concern, bud. Mom and I will manage as she fights this thing. I'll let go of some of my stubbornness and pride and most likely end up hiring some help for around the house. That way your mom won't feel bad about me doing everything and she'll not feel so pressured to do stuff. We'll be fine. We want what is best for you and we believe that going to MIT and chasing that dream of yours is the best thing to do. End of discussion."

I give him a light smile. "Thanks, Dad. I appreciate it. I guess Z was right."

Dad laughs again. "Yeah, she definitely was. Get used to saying that. Now, you should go apologize to her. And you're going to school tomorrow."

"Dad, come on…"

"No, son, you're going to school tomorrow. Your mom will be just fine and you can swing by after school. You're not missing anything here and you would miss a bunch at school."

I nod, knowing that this argument is futile. I get up and hug my dad, kiss Mom on the forehead, head back to my car, and drive to Z.

When I knock on the door, she opens it with a flat stare.

"Hey," she says.

"Z, I'm sorry. I was upset and angry, but that's no excuse for the way I treated you nor the things I said. That was super douchey of me and…" I start to cry. I've been fighting tears for the last few hours. "I was just so scared."

Z nods and pulls me to her. "It's okay. You're forgiven, askim."

Hearing my pet name breaks me down even more and I feel like I'm going to fall over. Z pulls me inside and shuts the door, still holding me, and brings me to her room at the end of the hall. She gently lays me down and curls up next to me, rubbing my back and kissing my forehead.

"She's going to be okay, babe."

I nod and hold her close.

Mom is going to be okay.

CHAPTER 19

Ezra Drake.

The first time I heard that name, I wasn't sure who it was. It sounded familiar, but the familiar that feels like it's a celebrity that's in a TV show everyone watches, but I don't watch TV so I don't know it kind of way.

And I was right on.

Ezra Drake is a big shot Hollywood guy. Born and raised in Los Angeles, Ezra was raised and trained into the world of the small screen by his parents and grandparents, either actors or directors in hit shows or box-office busting movies. He can sing, dance, and act through a myriad of characters and personas and even knows quite a bit of stage combat. His stage combat really focuses on swords from the Age of Pirates – cutlasses, scimitars, rapiers, the like – and he's applauded as one of the best in the business. He was in this one show that got really popular and he and his co-star have been the talk of Hollywood since.

That show? *A Pirate's Love.* His co-star? Zendaya Thompson, my girlfriend.

So, when I first heard that he was coming to town and wanted to see Z, my intrusive thoughts won and I did a deep dive on the internet on this guy. To be honest, he's impressive. He's everything I mentioned before and, on top of all that, he's extremely successful. Z left the industry after *APL* was over and moved here, but he did the opposite. He doubled down. He went fully remote when it comes to school and got numerous roles for movies that made millions and, in turn, he made a killing. However, he didn't keep most of his money. Instead, he turned into quite the philanthropist, giving most of his money to the Juvenile Diabetes Research Foundation – he has diabetes – and the Animal Humane Society.

But then I saw some articles that made me… well… uncomfortable. During *APL*, a bunch of magazines and pop culture news outlets wrote article after article on the real-life romance between Z and Ezra, which must have happened before she started dating Pietro. There were photos of them holding hands and walking through LA and

Hollywood, the two of them messing around at the beach, and even a couple of them kissing at red carpet events. There were some reporters that wrote stories speculating that the romance was just a publicity stunt and that it was weird that teenagers were being watched so closely due to a supposed tryst, but this was definitely a minority of thinking. They seemed, to quote one reporter, "genuinely infatuated with one another and their chemistry shines brightly off- and on-screen."

Needless to say, I got very self-conscious about my relationship with Z. And, honestly, about myself too. I'm not fat, I've said this, but I'm not jacked either. I mean, I run occasionally and make sure to do some sort of exercise regularly, but Ezra is, to quote a popular phrase, built different. The dude is chiseled like a Greek god. He clearly pours hours a day into his physical appearance. Which, for his line of work, is probably necessary, especially after he got cast as a superhero in one of the big franchises that's dominating the Hollywood scene. According to one magazine, he is 'redefining male standards.' So, naturally, I got concerned with how I look and dress and feel and all that stuff. It feels quite childish whenever it comes up, but I can't help it. He's a good-looking dude.

Then, on top of all this, we get invited to go out for dinner with him. Correction: Z gets invited to go out for dinner with him. He asked her while we were hanging out one night and her demeanor really changed when she realized who sent the text. She sat up straight – straighter than I have ever seen her sit – and she immediately tidied her hair. It was odd. It had just been us hanging out for the past few hours and suddenly she was acting like he was coming over. And it was just a text message from him. Not even a video call.

She had responded quickly, mentioning that she would love for him to meet me. He agreed and set up a date and time with him that worked for the three of us. We were to meet him at Vito's, a fine dining restaurant downtown, at 6:45pm sharp. He also told us to not worry about bringing our wallets or anything of the sort as he would be footing the bill. This made me grateful at first – it's not a cheap restaurant – but then it made me feel like I was less than, especially with how Z said it in a chipper, sing-song tone like she was bragging about him.

She should be bragging about me, right?

I didn't make a big fuss about it. I didn't want to. Recently, I've noticed that tension has sort of grown between us. I asked her once if it was because we were having sex – some studies suggest that having sexual intercourse with a partner can bring in tension due to the natural shift in the relationship. The sex isn't regular, but it also isn't rare – and she reassured me that it wasn't changing anything. She also didn't elaborate on what it could be, so I just decided to let it go. Now, I wish I hadn't.

And by now, I mean in the car driving to Vito's. She asked me to dress up so I decided to wear a pretty standard get up of mine – black pants with matching suit coat, tie, and button up – and she chose one of her black dining gowns she really liked.

I watch her for the millionth time adjust her hair and examine her make up in the small mirror of the visor.

"Z, you look beautiful, there's no need to be so nitpicky."

She sighs and takes my hand, giving it a squeeze. "Thanks, askim. I don't know why I'm so nervous!"

"Well, you haven't seen him for, what, two years?"

"More like a year, but the last time I saw him it was super brief and for a function. So, the last time we spent any real time together was probably two years ago."

"Maybe you're just excited to see your friend again, hjartat. I would be too if I saw Marcus again."

"Your friend from Alaska?"

"Yeah. I mean, I'm not sure if friend is the right classification anymore regarding the relationship that we have, but we still talk every once and a while."

"I understand. And I suppose you're right. Maybe I am just excited."

I squeeze her hand. "It's going to be fun, Z. I promise."

Z smiles, but I can feel that she wants to pull down the visor and look into the mirror.

After the valet takes our car, we head inside. A hostess comes up to us and gives a light smile as we close the distance.

"Good evening. Zendaya Thompson and guest, I presume?"

'And guest?' Seriously?

"Yes, that's us."

"Wonderful. Mr. Drake has one of our more private tables and is waiting for you there. If you would follow me, please."

Z takes my arm and we follow the hostess to the back of the restaurant. She draws back the curtain and there sits Ezra Drake. He's sitting casually, sipping a glass of water, and straightening his cutlery, despite not having used any of the pieces. He's wearing a fashionable turtle neck that highlights his defined muscular features. His brown hair is neatly trimmed as well as his facial hair – even at eighteen, he has a pretty solid beard. It's not super long or full, but it definitely isn't patchy. His piercing green eyes move from his fork to me and then Z before he smiles wide, revealing perfect straight and white teeth. He stands up, showing his full six foot four height and stretches his arm out wide.

"Zendaya." The way he says her name gives me the creeps – it sounds smooth, but cold like syrup out of the bottle on a winter morning in Alaska.

"Ezra, it's so good to see you," Z replies before giving him a hug. His hands rub her back and go a little too close to her butt for my taste before pulling away and looking her up and down.

"You've put on a little weight, my dear."

Hold the fuck up.

First off, he can't call her that.

Second, who in their right goddamn mind tells a woman they've put on a little weight?!

Before I can say anything, Z brushes her hair behind her ear and gives him a light smile. "Well, I'm not acting anymore so it's hard to stay in shape all the time."

Wait, I know that tone. Is she… embarrassed? What the fuck is happening?!

"That's no excuse, Zendaya. I know you still have access to your fitness routine from *APL*. I would encourage you to take a look at that again."

"I will, I promise. Thank you."

Holy shit. This guy really wants to get his teeth kicked in. And what's with Zendaya being so submissive? She's never like this, even with people who are in actual authority over her.

"Well, are you going to introduce me to your gentleman here?" Ezra asks, looking at me.

"Yes, sorry. Ezra, this is my boyfriend, Jack Connors. Jack, this is Ezra Drake."

"Nice to meet you, Jack," Ezra says, sticking out his hand and giving me a light smile.

I take his hand in mine, making sure that my grip is firm. He returns the grip and I swear he gets a little smugger.

"Likewise, Ezra," I reply, making my voice as chipper as possible to hide the searing anger billowing in my chest.

Ezra gestures to the table and chairs. "Sit, sit, please. I took the liberty to order us some appetizers that I figured you both would enjoy."

"Thank you, Ezra. That is very kind of you," Z says as I pull out her chair for her to sit down. I try to catch her eye to give her my look of 'babe-what-is-going-on-right-now,' but her eyes are locked on him as he sits.

"So, Jack, Z has told me a little about you in our infrequent texts."

"I hope all good things."

"Indeed, I wouldn't have mentioned it if they weren't. But, I will say, I'm intrigued. You aren't famous nor do you run with our typical circle of people. So, needless to say, I'm fascinated with the man that has stolen Zendaya's heart. Come, tell me about yourself."

Why the hell is this guy so damn proper?

"What would you like to know?"

"Do you have any talents?"

"I'm quite the pianist."

"Zendaya mentioned that. Where have you played?"

"A number of venues. I competed in Germany and the UK. A lot of regional things. Most recently I won the Annotator Award and played at the Steinmetz."

"The Annotator Award? Very prestigious. Do you plan on using this talent in the future? A career, perhaps?"

I shake my head. "No, I wasn't planning on it."

Ezra lifts an eyebrow. "Oh? What then?"

"Engineering. My plan is to develop an engine that runs on alternative fuel and leaves a smaller carbon footprint, if any at all."

"How noble. A liberated mind truly at work."

It's my turn to lift an eyebrow. "Do I sense some sarcasm?"

Ezra gives me a light smile. "I thought it would go unnoticed, but yes, sarcasm indeed."

"Why?"

He shrugs. "I don't see why you would choose to pursue engineering when you have such a marketable talent. Especially after winning the Annotator. You surely have had offers to go to music college. Full rides, perhaps? Or even job offers?"

I nod. "One or two. But that's not the direction I want to go."

"But it must be a place of passion of yours if you have dedicated enough time to receive such a prestigious reward?"

"It is a passion of mine, certainly." If this guy wants to talk all proper, I'll go toe-to-toe. "But it's not my calling. Be assured, I will continue to play piano for as long as I can. But I do not foresee it being my main source of financial gain."

I'm not sure whether Ezra can tell I'm making fun of him or not because his face is completely unchanged. He simply nods and ponders his next thoughts for a moment.

"Are you employed?"

"I am."

"Where?"

"I work as a waiter at Lucy's in Cocoa Beach."

"What kind of establishment is that?"

"A Tiki bar."

"Ah, a salt-of-the-earth kind of man, eh?"

"It's good money and good experience if that's what you mean."

"Something of the sort."

The waitress – I didn't catch her name – places the appetizers on the table and asks what we want to eat.

I gesture to Z to have her start the ordering. "I think I'll have the…"

"She'll take the chopped salad with a chicken breast on the side. And I'll have the bone-in ribeye, medium-well, with a side salad."

Did he just order for Z?

Did he just *fucking order* for Z?!

"Z, is that what you…" I begin to ask before getting cut off.

"Yes, that's fine, thank you for asking Jack," she replies. I try to catch her eye. But now she's looking down at her plate. Not even at Ezra. Just down at the plain, white plate that's been in front of her the whole time. I see a look in her eye that I've never seen before. A look that devastates me to my core.

Shame. It's a look of shame.

What on earth does she have to be ashamed about? She's a beautiful woman who normally exudes confidence and grace and beauty and awesomeness? But now, in front of this jackass, she's ashamed? I can feel my blood starting to boil with rage and I want to reach across this damn table and knock some sense into this guy.

"Sir? What would you like?"

I blink a couple of times, trying to remember what I was doing. Ezra is looking at me with a calm, but irritated look.

"Order whatever you would like, Jack. I insist."

I nod and look at the menu again. "I'll do the Wagyu filet mignon."

I wasn't going to be cheap with this guy.

"How many ounces?"

"Ten?"

"Excellent choice, sir."

"Yes, excellent choice, Jack," Ezra says, with a cold, hard tone in his voice.

I didn't care. This guy was really pissing me off.

"How would you like that done?"

"Medium-rare, please."

"Another excellent choice."

The waitress finished writing down our orders and turned to walk away.

We have some more conversations while we wait for our food and every time Ezra speaks, he makes my skin crawl. He talks to Z like she's his possession or something and tells her what to think and feel. And the worst part? She lets him. For as long as I have known her – granted it hasn't been long, but still – she has exuded confidence. She has never, ever let anyone take control of her life. But now, he's just walking all over her. Eventually the food comes and it gives me a respite from the cringy-ness of his essence as the food is absolutely phenomenal. Once we finish our food and Ezra declines dessert for Zendaya (I wish I was kidding), we sit in a moment of silence.

"If you two would excuse me, I need to use the facilities. I'll be back momentarily," Ezra says, finally breaking the silence, rising to his feet and walking out.

I wait until he is out of earshot before I turn to Z, unable to mask the concern and the touch of anger in my voice. "Z, what's going on? Why are you acting like this?"

Z shrugs, not looking up at me. "I'm fine, Jack."

"Z, come on."

"Jack, please stop."

"But this isn't like you."

"You don't know anything, Jack."

I back up a little to that remark. "I don't know anything? Z, we've been dating for almost six months and we talked for hours on end prior to that. You even said that I know you better than anyone else. Now, it's either true or you're lying."

She doesn't say anything back and I feel like I hurt her.

"Z, I didn't…"

"You're right," Z whispers. "I'm not acting like myself. But I need to keep it together. At least until after we've left."

I solemnly nod. I'm about to say more, but Ezra throws back the curtain and takes his seats once again. "So, where were we?"

"What have you been up to Ezra? Any new leads?" Z says, quickly taking over the conversation.

He nods. "Yes, I actually just got done working with some other A-listers on a project and that has led to a TV series spin-off."

"Oh really? That's exciting!"

"Yes, indeed it is. It's about time I got the recognition and roles worthy of talents and abilities."

Could this guy be any fuller of himself?

"Absolutely."

"That's actually why I wanted to invite you out for dinner, Zendaya. Jack, you don't mind if we talk shop, do you?" Before I can say anything, he continues. "The director of the series asked me if we were still in contact. I told him of course we were and he said he would love to have you come cameo a few episodes, maybe even get picked up if you did such a good job. I told him you were interested. First read-through is next Friday at nine."

"Oh, Ezra, I don't know…"

"Of course, you know. You're an actor. You'll be at the reading."

"Ezra, I'm not…"

"No, Zendaya, you'll be there. This will be good for you. To be back in your element with the people that push you to be better."

"Ezra, please, listen…"

"No, Zendaya, you listen. You need to hear what I'm saying."

Something inside me just snaps.

"Dude, shut the fuck up."

Both of them look at me in stunned silence.

"I beg your pardon."

"Yeah, well, tough shit. I'm not giving you a pardon. Do you want to know why?" Before he can answer, it's my turn to interrupt. "Of course, you do, what am I thinking? You're an ass, Ezra. You come here tonight and, after not seeing Z for almost two years outside of a business setting, you criticize her weight, boss her around, order her fucking food for her, and demand that she take this series? Have you ever asked her if she even wanted to go back and do this cameo? No, you just assumed! You don't even care what she thinks. You just want whatever it is best for you and what will make you money. God, if your fans could see you right now and understand how much of a misogynistic twat you are!"

This time, I know I got him riled up. I can see the anger start burning in his eyes. "How dare you speak to me like that?"

"Because you're just another eighteen-year-old, dumb ass." I stand up. "Z, let's go."

"I'm not finished…" Ezra manages to say before I interrupt him again.

"You might not be, but I am. Thank you so much for dinner, Ezra. Z will let you know about that cameo. I won't speak for her though because, ya know, she can speak for herself."

Z stands up, completely aghast. "Yeah, I'll text you if I want to."

Ezra remains seated, but throws his arms out in frustrated. "What am I supposed to tell the director? That you flaked?"

"No, you can just tell him the truth. Tell him you didn't ask me. Give him my agent's number and she can handle things from there."

"Zendaya, come on, you're being ridiculous!"

"No," Z laughs and, for the first time since we got here, I see her true self come back out. "You're being ridiculous. And shitty. And an asshole. I'll see you later, Ezra. Thanks for dinner."

Z takes my arm and we quickly leave, despite Ezra's insistent protests. We get in the car and Z starts laughing, then crying, then sobbing.

"Z, hey, it's okay," I say, trying to reassure her.

She just shakes her head and continues to sob. I decide that maybe the parking lot of Vito's isn't the best place to try and have this conversation, especially since Ezra could come out at any minute. I start the car and make my way out of the parking lot. I stop to go through the Wendy's drive through, ordering two chocolate Frosties – it's one her base comfort foods. When we get back to the neighborhood, she's still crying and we make our way into Simon's place so she can lay down. She immediately goes to her room, not even greeting Simon who is sitting in the living room, and lies down while I follow close behind with the Frosties. I let her eat hers in its entirety so she gets a chance to calm down and regulate her breathing.

"He's been doing stuff like that for years," Z finally says, almost in a whisper.

I take her hand and nod. If she is going to tell me this, I want it to be on her own terms.

"It was a few months into filming the first season of *Pirate's*." She sniffles. "I was really stressed out and I was only fourteen. School was different. Home life was different. Everything was just different. So… I developed a bad habit of overeating. I start to gain weight and that made the producers angry because my body 'didn't fit the period.'"

"That's really stupid."

"I know now that it was really stupid, but back then, it was awful. So, I flipped. I developed an eating disorder and starved myself. Ezra started to notice. He came to my trailer after a day of filming and talked to me about what he had been seeing. He kept asking so eventually my guard came down and I told him what was going on. He took pity on me and said he would help. So, for the next three or so years, he ordered my food and held me accountable to eat it. Even after the eating disorder was… I don't know… resolved?"

"Sure, I get what you're saying."

"Okay, yeah, after that, he continued to do so. And he made me work out with him and all this stuff. And I became infatuated. Here was this guy who I saw as really nice and helpful. So, we got together and 'dated' for a while. But shortly after we wrapped the show, I broke up with him for Pietro. He didn't take that great. It's been a really weird back-and-forth between us. And tonight kind of proved that it hasn't gotten any better."

"I'm sorry, hjartat. That's really tough. I'm glad you're not with him anymore."

She chuckles. "Me too. You're a lot better."

I smile, lean in, and kiss her.

"What are you going to do about the TV show? Have your agent turn it down?"

The light smile for my kiss fades quickly from Z's lips. "I don't know."

"You don't know?"

"Yeah, I don't know. There's a lot of heavy hitters on that cast. And the director is unbelievable. Not to mention, it would pay a ton of money."

"How do you know that?"

She shows me her phone. Ezra must have called the director who called Z's agent who sent Z an email regarding the show and everything. And yeah, it was a ton of money.

I give a low whistle. "Yeah, that's a nice chunk of change. And only six episodes?"

"Yeah, with the potential of them signing me on for more."

"But you don't want to do it."

She raises an eyebrow. "I don't?"

I nod. "Yeah. You said in the past you don't want to keep doing this, so don't do it."

She shook her head. "No, Jack, I didn't say that. I said I don't want to do it in California. But this is being filmed here in Florida."

"I don't remember you being specific about location."

"Jack, come on."

"Z, you hate the industry. You've said that multiple times."

"Yeah, I have, but this is different. This looks like a great thing."

"Z, come on, you're being ridiculous."

She doesn't say anything. She sits up in bed and looks me dead in the eye.

"You sound like Ezra."

I open my mouth to reply, but nothing comes out because I realize, yeah, I do sound like Ezra.

"I'm sorry…"

"I want to be alone."

"Z, come on…"

"Good night, Jack."

I'm about to protest, but my brain shuts down. I only nod.

"Good night, Z."

She rolls over and turns off her lamp.

I walk out of the house, bidding Simon a good night before making my way home and to my room. I lay down on my bed and only one thought races through my mind.

What's going on between Z and me? Our relationship feels more strained. Things feel different. And I don't like it.

I think about it all night until, finally around two in the morning, I fall asleep.

CHAPTER 20

I'm not sure why, but Z and I have been fighting.

It's not like we are considering breaking up. Or, at least, I haven't been. I don't think she has either. She would tell me otherwise – I know that much.

But still, we have been fighting.

It's been a wide range of things. Stupid, silly, small things like where we are going to go for date night or what movie we should watch. These things didn't matter and, after the fight, we agree that it wasn't worth fighting about, but we've fought about them all the same. Bigger things have come up, too. There's the whole thing with Ezra Drake. The new opportunity she has to go and guest star in a TV show for at least half of a season, but it meant missing the rest of the school year. It's all a mess.

Then, of course, there is the whole college argument. It's been a rollercoaster of conversation and argument and emotion. I've talked with my parents about it and they agreed with Z – I should go to MIT and continue to pursue that dream and passion. But there is still a part of me that's fighting that decision. Whether MIT, CalTech, or a more local college, I can't seem to make up my mind. There are pros and cons to all of them and I can't make a decision. Which has led to more conversations, more arguments, and even more emotions.

Despite everything going on, there is still one big thing coming up that I'm actually really excited for: Prom.

I went to Prom last year and, I'll be honest, I wasn't a big fan. I'm not fond of that many people in a confined space and the bass was way too high last year. It felt like someone was inside my chest trying to punch their way out, pounding heavily against my rib cage. I understand that's how a lot of people like their music, especially dance music, but it's just not my thing. But I went because Lisa and Nick wanted us to all go together and have a good time. And we did for the most part. We had dinner at Highball & Harvest and then went to Lisa's pool house after the dance and hung out until almost three in the morning.

But this year is going to be so different and, not to mention, so much better. And it's all because of Z. A few weeks ago, the theme – A Night in the Enchanted Forest – was announced and the senior class was buzzing. It seemed like it was going to be a really fun, super unique theme for our senior year. While traditional tuxedoes and dresses were allowed, attendees were being encouraged to find extravagant outfits centered around fantasy – think elves and mythical creatures dressed like they were going to prom and that's what the prom committee was going for. Lisa, as expected, was the most excited out of all of us. And I don't mean with just our friend group, but the entire senior class. This meant that her sumptuous make up skills would be the norm and everyone would seek her advice and help. We had laughed at her at first – remember, Lisa is insanely dramatic and that repels a lot of people – but after a couple of days, our table at lunch would be regularly swarmed by students who wanted to replicate Lisa's styles so they can best fit the theme the night of prom. Lisa *relished* this kind of attention and gave out her advice left and right. Soon, the school was filled with students wearing fanciful flares and whimsical winged eyes as almost all the students who wore make up began practicing.

Shortly after the theme was announced, I was going to simply ask Z to go with me. I mean, we've been dating for six months and I didn't see the point in an elaborate ask.

I should have known better.

Before I could even ask the question, Z stopped me. She said that she would like me to ask her in a creative way. She explained how, just like homecoming, she was never able to go to Prom before and would like to experience it how a 'normal' student would.

So, I agreed and began to formulate a plan on how I was going to ask her. I knew that I wanted to do something related to piano because that's kind of my thing. At first, I was thinking I could play *Jeux Deux* for her again, daydreaming what it could be like to go with her to prom. After a lot of thought about it, I decided that wasn't the direction I wanted to go. Though that song is really important to our relationship, I don't want to overuse it. Once nixing that idea, I started to struggle with coming up with an idea, resulting in soliciting advice from none other than the resident make-up queen, Lisa.

She was more than willing to help and we quickly came up with an idea. Lisa had been impressed how much I've been singing around the group ever since I started dating Z, so she suggested we make a prom-parody thing to a song. Post-deliberation, we settled on remaking "I Think I Wanna Marry You" by Bruno Mars. I'm not the biggest fan of the song – I feel like saying getting married is something dumb to do is a bit problematic – but when we made it so I sang "I wanna go to prom with you" and changed dumb to fun since it made more sense. So, we rewrote the whole thing, made it a fun little song, and scheduled a day to surprise her with it.

Under the guise of a make-up tutorial, Z came over to Lisa's pool house where she had rigged some LEDs to do a kind of lightshow in the main living space. I told Lisa she didn't have to do all the additional stuff, but she said she was practicing her skills as an event coordinator and designer so it wasn't a big deal – I just thought that was a good excuse for her to be a little extra. But when Z walked in the door, the lights changed, and I started playing. Z was immediately crying and dancing out of excitement to the song, which made me have way more fun with it than I was expecting. When I finished the song, she ran over to me, saying yes on repeat, and kissing me dozens of times.

I'm pretty sure I nailed that.

Definitely nailed it.

From then on, I don't think I've ever seen Z as excited as she was and has been for prom. We went shopping for our outfits and decided on green to be our color. It's not really a light green, but more of a darker, fantasy-esque dream. Well, enchanting green I guess. She ended up buying some earrings with elaborate swirls and designs that go over most of her ears and make her look almost elfish. Now, I'm a pretty nerdy guy so seeing her try on her dress with those ear pieces made my heart race and I couldn't stop thinking about it all day. Later that night, she ended up sneaking into my room wearing the jewelry and similar color tank top.

The tank top didn't stay on long.

Once Nick got confirmation from Riley, the girl he met and snuck out to constantly in Ocala and now steady girlfriend, that she could come to our prom, we started making plans on what we wanted to do. Lisa ended up telling us she had rented a limo for the night and wanted the night to be one of grandeur and extravagance. We made reservations at Christner's – the same place where my parents took Ms. Pillard, Dr. Thurmond, Z, and I for Christmas dinner – and made plans for after prom as well at Lisa's pool house once again. When making these plans, I can honestly say that I was far more excited than last year and actually looking forward to such a fun night with friends and with Z.

It's now the day of and Z and I are heading over to Lisa's to get ready. Nick, Khalan – who is taking a friend whose date dumped her literally a week before prom – and I are planning on waiting in the pool house while the girls get ready in the main house. Z had spent the night in my room last night – unbeknownst to my parents and Gay Simon – and wants to stop for coffee before we get there.

"Jack, I'm so excited for tonight!" Z says, gripping my hand, talking quickly, and poking me in the side. I've never seen her this giddy before.

"Me too, Z," I say smiling.

Her behavior shifts to something calmer, almost concerned. "That's not very convincing. Is everything okay?"

I look over at her and smile again. "Yes, love, everything is fine. I'm just tired. I need this coffee."

She laughs and kisses my hand. "Yeah, we were up kind of late. Do you think your parents heard us?"

I shake my head. "I doubt it. Mom would have sent Dad upstairs if they did."

Z nods and laughs. "That's true. She doing okay?"

I shrug and nod, not sure which one is the more truthful answer. "She's doing okay, I think. I mean, you know my mom. Even if she weren't okay, we wouldn't know. She would force a smile and wage her fight quietly."

Truthfully, Mom is doing as well as anyone could be. The doctor diagnosed her with Stage 3 lobular carcinoma – breast cancer. She's started treatment and we have all been very conscientious about upholding the doctor's instructions on how Mom should eat, sleep, rest, and focus on beating this thing. And she will. She's had hard days – especially her first few days of treatment – but she keeps her smile going and reassures her that she's going to come out the other side of this thing an absolute champion.

Z shakes her head. "Oh, Lydia. I'll have to come over and paint with her again soon."

I squeeze her hand. "She would like that."

As we pull into the parking lot of the coffee shop, I look down the row of cars to find a parking spot and see something that makes my heart drop. A 2022 Honda Civic Type R. Black. White rim tires. Red pinstripes. There's only one person I know that has that car.

Pietro Dimitrov.

"Jack…" Z says, her grip on my hand tightening.

"I know…"

"He's right there."

I look to the door of the coffee shop and, sure enough, there's Pietro in the doorway, looking at the two of us in the car. Coming out of the shop as he holds the door open is Shelly, talking to him about something. But from the way he is just staring at the two of us, I don't think he is listening to her at all.

"Do you want to go somewhere else?" I ask, trying not to move my lips for him to see.

"No. We're already running late," Z says, shifting in her seat. "I will not have him ruin this day for me. Just park the car and ignore him."

I nod and pulled into a spot not too far from the door. As we get out of the car, I can already tell that Pietro is still looking at us and, by this point, Shelly is too. I can feel her eyes boring into the back of my skull. I walk to the other side of the car and open Z's door, helping her out of the car.

"Z."

Shelly. The absolute nerve of this girl is astounding. They haven't talked in months – for good reason, obviously.

"Shelly."

"Are you and Jack going to prom tonight?"

"Yes."

"Oh."

I look at Shelly, eyebrow arched with confusion. "Oh? What do you mean, 'oh?'"

Pietro takes a step towards me and I'm surprised I don't react at all. He's not within striking distance, but the gap of maneuverability between me and the door is getting smaller than I want. "We just thought you two weren't going to go. Figured that you and your friend group would just go and do something by yourselves."

"Where did you get that idea?"

"You guys weren't at Winterfest."

Winterfest. Northern schools call it snow days – a week of ridiculous stuff and shenanigans just like homecoming, just later in the year. Our group decided not to go because it was also the night of Khalan's birthday so we prioritized doing what they wanted rather than go to the dance.

"We had something else come up, but we wouldn't miss prom. Why is it a big deal that we're going?"

"Pete is coming tonight with me," Shelly says.

I can feel anger boiling up inside of me. How could the school let him back in after what he did to me? There's got to be some kind of rule against that, right? I look at Z. She's stoic and I can't even read what she's thinking. She does this sometimes – turns on her acting ability and no one can ever tell what she's thinking or feeling. It's really good from a theatrical sense, but when it's situations like this, I wish I could see past it.

"Well, I hope you two have a wonderful time," Z says, not changing her tone or her facial expression as she moves past both of them.

"Thanks, you too," Shelly replies before walking to Pietro's car. I look at Pietro, not sure what he's thinking. I'm sure as hell not going to say anything.

"See you around, Connors," he says, his voice slow and cold.

"Sure thing, Pietro."

I move past him and head into the coffee shop, joining Z in line to order. She's standing with her arms crossed, her toe tapping madly as she stares daggers into the menu.

"Z…"

"Jack, I don't want to talk about it."

I put my hands up in surrender. "Okay, okay."

She shakes her head. "I can't believe her…"

I wrap an arm around her shoulders in the attempt to comfort her. "I know. Neither can I."

Z looks up at me. "He shouldn't even be allowed in school, right?!" I nod. "Then why the fuck is he coming?!"

I shrug my shoulders. "His parents are pretty influential people. I know they still donate to the school despite what happened. Maybe that's what got him in."

Z shakes her head again. "Money pisses me off."

I laugh. "Same."

I can tell she wants to say more, but I know that if she dwells on this that our evening is going to be strained. I step in front of her and grab her shoulders firmly, but gently. "Z. It doesn't matter. It's just going to be us tonight. Nothing else matters."

I can see her anger start to diminish and she gives me a light smile. "Yeah. Just us. At prom."

I smile back. "Absolutely."

We order our coffees to go and quickly make our way over to Lisa's. I help Z carry all of her stuff down to the pool house and meet the non-pool house people in the main house. Nick and Khalan are hanging out in the billiards room and are already changed. I quickly change and mess with my hair to make it look the way Z asked, then join them at the table to play a game of pool before pictures.

When I finally see Z after she gets ready, I feel my heartbeat in my ears and I go numb all over. She's absolutely gorgeous. Beautiful beyond words. More radiant than any song could ever hope to capture. She is, without a doubt, perfect. Despite my best efforts, my jaw drops when I see her. She laughs and comes closer to me, taking my hands and kissing me. One of Lisa's dads snaps a photo of us right before the kiss and it might possibly be my favorite picture of the two of us. I have him send it to me immediately.

After taking a few hundred photos, we drive to Christner's and have one hell of a dinner. The food was amazing and laughter was abundant. We got a lot of compliments on our outfits and Lisa got quite a bit more attention for her makeup – which was far more extravagant than it ever is. She really went all out.

Grand march came and went way faster than expected, though when Shelly and Pietro were announced, I felt Z grip my arm tightly. Her anger is still very real and I don't blame her. I just hope it doesn't affect the rest of our night. Once the entire procession gets through the gym, we are ushered to our vehicles of choice with little tickets that have our name and student ID on them. Most schools have busses that take the students to the dance area if its somewhere other than the school, but H&H wanted students to be able to choose their mode of transportation. To keep us accountable, we had a window of arrival time at the dance venue and had to turn in our tickets to none other than Mrs. Halverson, who threatened not only punishment from the principal but also punishment in her class if any of us should detour or come late or submit someone else's ticket. Halverson might not be the most liked teacher at H&H, but she can be the scariest when she wants to be.

Once we arrive and hand our tickets to Halverson, we go immediately to the tables, claim our own, and then hit the dance floor. I surprisingly have a really, really good time and the laughter continues. But every so often, I can see Pietro and my blood boils because he is staring directly at Z. Z notices too and I can tell she's getting more uncomfortable and more self-conscious by the minute. I do my best to be a wall between her and her creepy ex, but he seems to be able to shift around the room. I tell Khalan what's going on and they step in between Z and Pietro, giving Pietro a very cocky, very instigating smile that makes Pietro finally stop.

He and Shelly leave a few minutes later.

It comes down to the end of the night and slow dances become more and more common. *Baby, I Love Your Way* by Peter Frampton comes on and Z takes me to the dance floor and we dance much like the way we did when we danced at homecoming all those months ago. We hold each other close and I can feel both our hearts beating faster and faster. The connection between us is so real. So powerful. I don't see how anything could possibly get between us.

"I love you," I whisper.

She pulls back and smiles up at me. "I love you, too."

"You know I would do anything for you, right?"

"I do."

I kiss her gently and hold her close again. A moment or two passes between us as we sway to the music.

"Jack?"

"Yeah?"

"Come with me to California."

"What?"

"Come with me to California."

I couldn't believe what I was hearing. How many hours have we fought about this? How many times has she told me that I need to chase my dream? How many times has she pushed back on every excuse or reason I make to not go to MIT? And now she's telling me that she wants me to come to California with her?

"Z, what do you mean?"

"I don't want you to be so far away. I love you and I want you to be close."

"But, Z, what about MIT?"

"I know… but the more I think about it, the more I want you to come to California."

I can't believe this.

Something inside me snaps. I feel it deep in my core. All the pent-up anger over all the fights we've been having begins to just flood my system. She told me to go to MIT when I first got accepted. She told me to go to MIT when Mom got diagnosed with cancer. She's been telling me to go to MIT for weeks. But when she decides *she* wants me to go to California, she tells me not to go?

The song ends and I pull away from her.

"Jack?"

I shake my head and walk – all too briskly – out the door into the cool Florida night.

"Jack!"

I don't turn around until we're in the parking lot.

"Jack, talk to me!"

"I can't fucking believe this!" I say far louder than I expected or wanted. "Z, we've been fighting about MIT for months! It's always been me telling you different reasons to not go, reasons to pick a different college. And it's always been you telling me to chase my dream and go! But now you're telling me that you want me to go to California with you!"

"Jack, don't yell at me."

My anger only rises. "Z, what the hell?!"

"Jack! I just want what's best for us!"

"What's best for us or best for you?"

Her mouth drops. "You did not just say that."

"I did! Z, I've put my deposit down already for MIT. What am I supposed to do? I'm pretty sure it's non-refundable!"

"I'll pay you back for it."

"You'll pay me back for it? What am I, some sort of escort you can just pay off?"

"I think that's a little ridiculous, Jack."

"I'm being ridiculous? Z, we've been arguing for weeks!"

She doesn't say anything to that.

But I'm not done, apparently.

"Is it really about me going to California or is it about you going back and having to face your parents? Alone?"

She glares at me. "That is not fair."

"But is it right?"

"No!"

"Are you sure?"

"What you don't trust me now?!"

"I never said that!"

We're both yelling now.

"Jack, I just want you close!"

"But, Z, I want to follow my dream! You inspired me to do that!"

"I know, but you just said you would do anything for me!"

"I know I did but this seems completely unfair!"

"Life isn't fair!"

"Seriously?! What a lame excuse for all of this!"

"At least I've accepted that!"

"What the hell!"

We both stop talking, both breathing heavily and our tempers clearly flaring.

"Maybe this isn't working."

I couldn't believe that just came out of my mouth. Did it? She isn't reacting.

"Maybe it's not," she finally says.

"So, what are we done?"

She only nods.

"What about the rest of the night?"

Is this really happening?

"We'll act like nothing happened. We'll go to Lisa's and hang out for a while. Then I'll come up with an excuse to leave and you'll take me home."

It's actually happening.

"Z, I..."

"No, Jack. You're right. We've been fighting for weeks. We have different expectations for one another. It's not working. We're not working."

"But, Z..."

"No, Jack. You were right. This isn't working."

I stand dumbfounded. That just happened. She's just looking at me. I can't tell if she's sad or not. It's that whole acting thing she's got going for her. I can't tell. I just nod. She nods back then turns to walk back inside.

The rest of the night means nothing. I don't care to try and remember. We get to Lisa's and stay for a while – no more than an hour. Z makes the excuse she doesn't feel well. I take her home. When I pull into the drive way, I open the door for her. She stands and looks at me and I can see the briefest look of sadness creep across her eyes.

She goes on her tip toes and kisses me softly for the last time.

"Good bye, Jack."

She turns, not waiting from my response.

"Bye, Z."

Z opens the door, looks back at me for a split second and a tear rolls down her cheek. I desperately want to run to her. I desperately want to apologize. But my legs aren't working. Z closes the door and I'm left in the dark of night.

I slowly go up to my room, close the door, and lay down on my bed. I instinctively grab my phone and go to text Z.

But I can't.

She's not my girlfriend anymore.

There isn't a point.

I close the message app I use and look at the background.

It's the photo Lisa's dad took of us right before we kissed at the pool house.

We are so happy in that photo.

We were… so happy in that photo.

I begin to cry and there's nothing and no one to stop the tears from flowing.

I am alone.

Single.

Heartbroken.

CHAPTER 21

Alone.

Single.

Heartbroken.

I'm not sure I could pick three better words to describe how the last few weeks have been. Or worse words, depending how I look at it.

Things have been miserable. I hate feeling like this. I mean, Z was my girlfriend, not my savior or wife or whatever. We dated for a while and then we split. End of story. No more to it than that. Break ups happen. Break ups suck, sure, but they happen. I'll find another girl. I'll be happy. I'll find love again.

At least, that's what I keep telling myself.

It's a cycle, see. I think those things. I write them down. I say them out loud. I say them to myself in the mirror. I type them in my phone. I play them on the piano. I try to convince myself that these words have meaning and depth and truth in them.

But it's a cycle. And those words are not the end. They are only a few spokes in the wheel that never stops turning.

But with all wheels, it needs all its spokes.

There will never be a girl like Z. She is truly the epitome of one-of-a-kind. She is amazing. And I loved her. In fact, I still love her. Sure, I'll find another girl, but not one like Z. I'll never run away from her memory. I'll never want to let it go. I'll not find love like that again.

Pretty lame, right? I mean, I'm a teenager. Technically, I'm an adult but barely one at that. I have, what, another 70 years left? So, I don't need those thoughts in my head.

But maybe I end up alone.

Single.

Heartbroken.

The cycle repeats over and over, despite it being a month since we broke up. I wish I could break the cycle. I really do. But no matter what I think about or what I do, my mind always, *always* wanders back to her.

I haven't actually seen her since we broke up. She ended up taking that job that Ezra told her about. She told Lisa that it was all about the money they were offering and getting to work with a bunch of A-listers on a potentially Golden Globe worthy show. At first, I wasn't a big fan of this decision. I mean, she hates acting – at least, that's what I've gathered from the conversations we have.

Had. Conversations we had.

Based on those conversations, I'm pretty sure she hates acting. The demands of the directors, the pressure from her parents, the expectations of the other cast members, the physical demand on her body, and the emotional strain of stress and long working hours. She said that in the past. I want to text her and tell her that it would have been okay to say no. It would have been okay to just move on to the next thing.

But that's not my place anymore. I mean, truthfully, it was never my place to start with. I never tried to control her life – intentionally, of course, but I'm sure I may have not come off that way. Z is an independent person. She doesn't need anyone telling her what to do or what to think or what to say. She hates people controlling her. I never could nor did I ever want to. But now, especially now, it certainly isn't my place anymore. Not as her ex. Not even as her friend.

Are we still even friends? She never tells me when she's going to be at my house – she still paints with my mom sometimes. Yeah, Mom knows we broke up, but Z has been a close companion to her as she goes through her cancer treatments and I wouldn't want to deprive my mother of that friendship. But Z always comes over whenever I have work or when I'm gone. I'm not sure if that was her idea or Mom's idea. Whoever came up with it, I'm grateful. I'm not sure how I would feel if I saw her painting again. Not after playing *Jeux Deux* at their first session.

It would just remind me that I am alone.

Single.

Heartbroken.

School hasn't been the same. The school allowed Z to finish up the year virtually and she has apparently been keeping up with her studies since she is currently our valedictorian. Whether or not she'll make it back for graduation is a different topic entirely, but I doubt she would miss it.

Lisa was the first to know what happened between Z and I. Z must have called her that night. We had the senior skip day the following

Monday after prom and Z took off that evening for her shoot. On Tuesday, Lisa had walked up to me and gently hugged me, telling me how sorry she was things between Z and I didn't work out and that she was there if I needed to talk. Shortly after, I told Mona, Khalan, and Nick about the break up. All three had sympathy, but I could tell I was putting them in a tight spot. Z had melded with our friend group so perfectly. She was truly one of us. There wasn't another person who could have fit in with us more than she did. And all of my friends had become insanely close to her, even before her and I started dating. I quickly told them that I don't want them to take sides. If they did, I wanted it to be hers. I had been irrational and irked; it was my fault. Lisa told me to stop talking because that wasn't true. Z had really told her everything I guess. Each of them assured me in turn that they weren't just going to abandon their friendship with me. In return, I made them individually promise me to do the same with their friendship with Z. I don't want her to feel how I'm feeling.

Alone.

Single.

Heartbroken.

School feels empty without her. I go to class, stay in my assigned seat, take the notes, participate when necessary, keep my phone in my pocket, study when needed, and leave when the bell rings. Eight times a day my routine is the same. Eight times a day, I go out into the hallway and there is no one to walk with to my next class. No one to kiss before going to fifth period. No one to hold hands with at lunch. No one to ride home with after school. It's empty and lonely and gut wrenching.

Because I am alone.

Single.

Heartbroken.

Why am I so hung up on her? I'm eighteen! I'm supposed to be in, or at least getting into, the best years of my life. I'm not an unattractive guy. If I really tried, I could probably get into the hook up culture and casually flirt and do stuff with other girls. I don't need to have a long-term relationship. College is supposed to be all about fun, right? I can do fun. I can be fun.

But will it be the same with a girl other than Z? Ever since Ocala, we had really melded together. She knew my body. I knew hers. We knew what the other liked, both sexually and non. Our connection was so deep. So pure. So overwhelming. I loved her like I have never loved someone before. Prom night repeats over and over in my head and I keep beating myself up over it. Would it have been that hard to say yes? I could have just gone to CalTech or Stanford, both very respectable schools in the engineering realm of study. Sure, it's not MIT, but it would have been just fine.

Just fine. Just fine. Just fine.

That scene with Holly in *The Office* comes into my head every turn of the wheel. She's not happy with her current boyfriend and Michael is right there. But that isn't the point. The point is that she questions why that phrase – just fine – keeps sounding more and more wrong the more she says it. Would CalTech or Stanford really have been *just fine*? Or am I just fooling myself in this never-ending cycle of retrospection? MIT had been my dream. Fuck, it still *IS* my dream. I want nothing more to go to MIT and get my engineering degree and change with world, one engine at a time. Sure, CalTech and Stanford would be good, but MIT is the best option.

So maybe I'll just be alone.

Single.

Heartbroken.

It's a Friday and I work the rest of the weekend. Work is always a good distraction. Farrow always assigns me the busiest section. It keeps my mind off Z and makes good money. I appreciate that about Farrow. Recently, we've been talking more. He's been allowing me to help close on Saturdays with the older workers as well. He tells me these fantastical stories of heroes of some long-lost nation and mythical beasts like dragons in dungeons and giants in the mountains. One story he has been sharing with me is this story of a man who lost his wife and Farrow says it almost killed him. He was stricken with grief and thought he would not overcome it. But he had responsibilities that he had to attend to. A son, the only child he and his late wife had together. A people threatened by oppression of another empire. A destiny to fulfill. Sure enough, this man achieved his responsibilities and found a new woman to call his wife. In the end, it was happily ever after, until some king did something and another war started.

I don't know, Farrow's stories always are pretty farfetched and I'm almost one hundred percent certain this one was made up. But I liked it and I'm pretty sure he told it to me so that I would have faith in my future – he says I would have faith in my destiny but I don't know about that.

But before I work this weekend, I have my piano lesson with Ms. Pillard. We have been working on my piece for the summer contests – *Liebestraum No. 3 (Love Dream)* by Liszt. I picked the song a few months ago, just before Spring Break, because of the name. Love Dream. Something that I live in.

Lived in.

My heart isn't in it today. I feel myself drifting away from the piece and into a sulking, blubbering, self-pitying mess of a person.

"Jack?"

I look at Ms. Pillard, but don't say anything.

"Drifting into the negative headspace again?"

I nod.

"There is only twenty minutes left in our lesson. Do you want to be done?"

Again, only a nod.

"That's fine. We got through the piece a few times and it sounds good. I'm not worried about you. At least, not in regards to your piano abilities."

I give her a light chuckle as she nudges me.

"Jack, you're going to be okay."

I look down at the keys. "How do you know that?"

"Because before I found Ryan, I had a pretty serious relationship with another person."

She's never talked about her love life before, so it is only natural that I get more curious.

"Who?"

"Well, her name was Violet."

"Her?"

Ms. Pillard laughs. "Yes. I'm not sure how appropriate this is to talk about with a student, but since we've come so far, I supposed I can tell you. I'm bisexual and dated Violet for almost seven years."

"Seven years?! What happened?"

Ms. Pillard lets out a long sigh before she continues. "Well, we were high school sweethearts that went to the same college. We had similar majors – I studied piano and she studied the cello. We would play these beautiful pieces together in the concert hall of the university and we would draw hundreds of people just to hear us play two or three songs. Soon, the president had to ask us to make a regular thing out of our little concerts and we did really well. Soon, we attracted a number of talent scouts for orchestras and groups like that around the world. It was really something. One person even tried to get us to sign a label with their company and put together some albums.”

“That’s incredible! What stopped you?”

“Both of us didn’t want to get into that scene. We had agreed that we were going to help the young people of the world to learn beautiful music. We had a whole plan of opening a studio after graduation and we even had everything planned out.”

“What happened?”

“Well, I was wrong. I guess I was assuming we were on the same page. But just a few weeks prior to our grand opening, Violet came to me and told me that she couldn’t do the studio anymore and that she was taking a job with the London Symphony Orchestra. We argued, which turned into a fight, which turned into days of fighting, which finished with us breaking up. I was alone and heartbroken. Not to mention that I had taken out a loan with her to set up this studio. She was able to buy her way out of the contract we had and I scrounged out what money I could to get out of it too and then had to borrow the rest from my parents. It was a painful time. I was incredibly depressed and devastated not only with the loss of my plans for the studio, but also with the loss of the person who I had thought was my soul mate. My parents, ever so concerned, found me a job down here at a music lessons academy. I took it because, well, I needed the money and I needed to pay them back somehow. So, I packed my belongings, said goodbye to New York, and moved down here to Orlando.”

“And that’s when you met Dr. Thurmond?”

She shook her head. “No. I struggled for a while. It was hard, Jack. I had even purchased an engagement ring for her. I focused on my students and getting better. When I was finally ready to date again, I went out for a drink with some of my friends for the first time in three years. While we were sitting at this bar, up walks…”

“Dr. Thurmond?”

“No, his friend. He was almost black out drunk and really feeling the alcohol. He sauntered up to me and my friends, slurring his words and trying to hit on me before promptly passing out and falling to the floor.”

I laugh. The sound is foreign to me, but it feels really good.

“It was funny! Then came Ryan. All calm and cool and collected. His head freshly shaved and beard groomed and braided. He gave me this most awkwardly adorable smile as he scooped up his friend. I didn’t want him to go just from that smile.”

"What did he say?"

"Oh, he didn't say anything, Jack. I did."

"Look at you, badass boss bitch!"

Ms. Pillard laughs. "I suppose so. I asked him if he was going to come back. He turned to me and nodded, saying if I can wait an hour, he would be back. My friends thought that I was crazy for wanting to wait. But I did. I waited for an hour, unsure of why I was waiting or if he was even going to show up again. I didn't have his number, so there was no way I could check. But, almost an hour later, he was back. He had changed his sweatshirt to what I know now as his favorite – the gray Harvard sweatshirt – since his buddy had thrown up on him. And we closed out the bar that night. We talked and talked and talked until the bartender finally told us we needed to leave. We exchanged numbers in the parking lot and, well, the rest is history."

I smile at her. "That's such a cool story."

She smiles back at me and nods. "Yes, I certainly think so. But I want you to take from this story what I learned – sometimes our plans just don't work out and we need to be open to what the future holds. I never thought I was going to love again after Violet. But I love Ryan more than I think I could have ever loved Violet."

I look back to the keys and nod, knowing full well what she was implying. It was just hard to wrap my head around. If Ms. Pillard could find love again after a seven-year relationship with someone she thought was her soul mate, I could certainly find it again after just seven months.

Right?

"Which brings me to our final piece of conversation before I officially let you go on your way, my young apprentice."

I look back at her. "Yeah?"

"I want to show you something." Ms. Millard reaches out to a small box that I must have missed on the table on her side of the piano. She slowly opens it and shows me the contents.

A marquise cut diamond ring with emeralds surrounding the diamond sat amongst black velvet.

I look up from the ring and feel my eyes grow wider with excitement.

"He proposed?!"

She nodded. "Just a few nights ago."

I fling my arms around her and hug her. "Oh, my god! I'm so happy for you – congratulations!"

She returns the embrace and laughs. "Thank you, Jack. Ryan! Could you come here please?"

I quickly swivel on the bench as the door opens and Dr. Thurmond steps in, smiling wide.

"Jack, my boy."

I quickly stand and stick out my hand. "Congratulations, sir!"

He claps my arm in a classic Thurmond titan shake. "Thank you, Jack, I appreciate it!"

Ms. Pillard takes Dr. Thurmond's hand. "Do you want to ask him or shall I?"

"If you don't mind?"

"Please, do."

Dr. Thurmond turns to me. "Jack, ever since I found out you were Genevieve's star pupil, I've taken a great interest in your talent and artistry. You are truly an astonishing pianist, my young friend."

"Thank you, sir, that means a lot coming from you!"

"So, I'm inclined to ask this of you – would you be willing to play at our wedding? We would pay you and everything, as you are an Annotator winner after all, but we both would love for you to be the pianist at the wedding."

I look at Ms. Pillard in disbelief. "Are you for real?"

She smiles. "Yes, Jack, of course. It would be an honor to have you play for us."

For the first time in a month, I feel excitement jolt through my body. "Absolutely! I would love to! Don't worry about paying me though…"

Dr. Thurmond raises a hand to stop me. "Ah, I won't hear any of that, my boy. You're basically a professional and I will treat you as such."

I smile wide. "As you wish. Then, as a professional, I would like to have the assorted music you wish to hear at your wedding sooner rather than later so I can prepare my best for your momentous day."

They both laugh at my theatrical professionalism.

"It's not until next summer, but we will get it to you as soon as we know the music," Ms. Pillard says.

"Perfect. I promise, I won't let you down!"

I hug Ms. Pillard again and, this time, Dr. Thurmond swats away my hand and gives me a hug as well. I drive home, finally having something worthwhile to think about and distract me from Z. Will they want classical? Neo-classical? Moderna? Smooth Jazz? All of the above and more? None of them and something completely random?

Piano covers of famous songs? It doesn't matter! I'll play whatever they want me to play!

I'm so jazzed up on the way home that I swing through the Wendy's drive through and pick up a Frosty and fries, knowing full well that it will ruin my appetite for dinner. But I don't care. Two of my favorite people in the world are getting married.

My heart, high off the sugar of the dessert and excitement, crashes when I get home.

Z's car is in the driveway and she's stepping out of the driver seat.

She looks tired. Worn out. But still more beautiful than the rising sun. More radiant than all the stars in the sky. And she takes my breath away yet again.

I slowly roll up the driveway and park my car in front of the garage. I step out carefully and we make eye contact. We both freeze. I gently raise my hand and slowly wave at her. She gives me a half-smile, waves back, turns, and then goes into Gay Simon's. My heart shatters and I make my way inside, throwing the leftover fries and remaining ice cream in the trash.

I have no appetite.

Not anymore.

Now, the only thing I have is knowing that I am alone.

Single.

Heartbroken.

CHAPTER 22

It's a bittersweet day today. The last day of school at H&H. It's been a long four years, but there are plenty of good memories that I'm sure I will cherish for the rest of my life. Homecomings, dances, friends, and teachers will be what I cling to as I go off to MIT. I'm excited – my high school journey has come to an end. Tonight, we graduate and I'll never have to endure another one of Mrs. Halverson's lectures or Dr. Naboline's labs or Mr. Montez's tests again. Instead, I'll be learning, working, and testing in subjects that I actually want to learn about in classes that I selected, not ones that were dictated by the state. It's honestly a great feeling and I'm looking forward to not having anything to do with H&H for the foreseeable future. Maybe one day, if I become wealthy and can afford to, I will set up a scholarship or two at the school, but as of right now, the only thing I can think about is getting through the day today and walking across the stage tonight to receive my diploma and be finished with high school once and for all.

The one class period that I'm not excited to see over is that of third hour – my TA period with Dr. Thurmond. I've had a lot of fun with him this year and I've learned a lot not only in terms of history but also what it would be like to be a teacher. I'm not saying I'm going to switch my career paths, but I definitely have an ever-growing respect for teachers and what they do. And Dr. Thurmond has really turned into a friend as well as a mentor this year. He's kind and patient, always making sure that I'm doing well and taking the time to catch up with me whenever he can. Sure, there are days that he is too busy to talk, I get that, but still he will make time when there is time to be made. He's also funny and witty, making not just me but the whole class laugh at his successful attempts to make his classroom a comfortable, chill, and caring environment. He works hard, but if you asked him, it may seem like he doesn't work at all – he simply loves what he does. At least, that's how I see it anyway.

When I walk into the classroom, I'm shocked. A sub is standing at the whiteboard writing down the prompt for the final essay the students will have to write in the duration of the period. I don't see Dr. Thurmond.

"Excuse me," I say, entering the room more. "Where is Dr. Thurmond today?"

The sub turns to me, a smile across her face. "You must be the TA. He's here, he's just downstairs by the event entrance. He told me to send you his way when you got here."

Relief floods my system like a bucket of water into a fire pit. "Okay, I will, thank you, ma'am."

I turn out the door as she starts verbally giving instructions to the class. I make my way to the event entrance – it faces the football field and track – and see Dr. Thurmond waiting patiently by the door.

"Jack, my boy!" He says as I get closer. "I figured since it was our last day together, we could spend it in a more comfortable fashion. Fancy a walk?"

I smile and nod. "Sure thing, Dr. Thurmond."

It's a nice May morning in Florida. Not too hot. Not too cool. A nice gentle breeze providing a balancing effect to the heat of the sun. The rhythmic pattern of our shoes hitting the pavement are in relative sync and I take a deep breath in through my nose. It smells like summer now. The waiting and the drag of the school year is finally coming to a close.

"How are you doing, Jack?"

I shrug. "I'm doing alright, I guess. I'm glad school is over. Sad I won't be your TA anymore though."

Dr. Thurmond laughs. "Oh, young man, as am I. You've been the best I've had, that's for sure."

I smile at him. "Thanks, I've really put my best effort into it this year."

"You would make a remarkable teacher; I hope you know."

I shake my head while chuckling. "I appreciate that, but I don't think my heart is in it. The students would drive me crazy."

"Oh, trust me, I know the feeling."

"Really? You make it look so easy!"

"That is only after years of hard work and developing the skills to be an effective teacher, Jack. My first couple of years were rough, especially since I wasn't working at such a prestigious school like Hurston and Hemingway. It's very different at a public school. But, I worked my way through it. Persisted despite every setback."

I nod. "It's evident sir."

He chuckles. "Good. I do love what I do. I love my students like they were my own kids."

I look at him, noting a distinct shift in his voice. His eyes are focused on the middle distance, despite him keeping a steady pace down the path towards the football field.

"Is there a 'but?'"

Dr. Thurmond lets out a long sigh. "There could be. I'm not sure if I would use such a conjunction in this manner though. You see, using 'but' negates everything before it. It's like someone saying 'I don't mean for this to be hurtful, but' and then they say something completely off putting or hurtful. And I don't want to negate what I said about me loving my students."

"So, what are you saying, Dr. Thurmond?"

"I'm leaving H&H, Jack."

I stop on the path. "What?"

"I'm leaving this school. Not on bad terms, mind you. I was offered a position at a university."

"Well, congratulations, sir. Which one?"

"Harvard."

I burst out laughing. "Of course, Harvard! Dr. Thurmond, that's great!" I stick out my hand which he firmly shakes.

"Thank you, Jack, I appreciate it. I haven't told any of my other students, so if you could keep this between you and I, I would appreciate it."

"Of course, sir. Why tell me, though? I mean, I'm graduating. It doesn't affect me a whole lot."

"Ah, but it does. Genevieve is coming with me. She accepted a position to teach piano at Berklee."

My jaw drops. "No way!"

"Yes, indeed she did, she found out yesterday. She wanted to tell you in person, but won't be able to make your practice tomorrow since she has to fly up to Boston to make the final arrangements today."

"That's incredible! You two are really moving up in the world. Marriage, new jobs, new location. I bet your family is excited, too! Living a little closer to home."

"Only a little closer – maybe three hours, pushing four? But yes, they are glad we will be even that much closer."

We resume our walk down the path and reach the football field. We shift off the paved path and walk across the turf, the grass still moist from the morning's dew. I'm happy for Ms. Pillard and Dr. Thurmond.

They've both worked really hard to get where they are. They are both incredible people and have phenomenal skills that will no doubt be appreciated at both of their new places of employment. Hurt is still there though. I won't be able to come and visit them during breaks or the summer. It'll be a big disconnect – two of the most impactful people in my life gone.

"Dr. Thurmond?"

"Yes, Jack?"

"I'm going to miss you. Miss you both. I can't even put into words how much you both have been so nurturing to me."

Dr. Thurmond puts a hand on my shoulder and I look at him. His eyes are misty and his bottom life quivers ever so slightly. "Ah, Jack, I'm going to miss you too. But, you know what, I don't think we will have to."

"What do you mean?"

"Well, after tonight, you will no longer be my student. You will have permission to call me Ryan and I'm sure Gen will let you call her by her first name too. We'll be more friends than anything – not to mention you'll still play at our wedding. Now this is a little unorthodox, but would you be interested in picking up a new hobby with me in Boston?"

I look at him with an eyebrow raised. "A new hobby? Like what?"

He smiles. "There's a fencing club between Harvard and MIT. I thought we could learn and spar together."

I smile back at him. "Absolutely! I'm in. Thank you, Dr. Thurmond."

He pats my back. "Good lad. Now, I have a gift for you." He pulls a long box out of his suit pocket and hands it to me. "Every year, I get my TA a gift as a thank you for helping me throughout the year. This year, I made this one specifically for you."

"You made it?"

"Yes, a friend of mine taught me how to forge this year and I took the time to make you something. Open it."

I take the box from him and open the lid. Inside is a small dagger with a leather sheath. The handle seems to be inlay with silver and has a sapphire in the pommel. I slowly take it out of the box and draw it, noting the edges are not sharp but definitely have the potential of being sharpened.

"I had to take you out of the building to give this to you. For obvious reasons."

I nod as I look at the blade. Weird etchings are marked on either side of the line going down the middle of the dagger on both sides of the blade. "It's beautiful. You made this?"

"I am a man of many talents, my friend. Yes, I made it."

"What are these designs?"

"They are words, actually. Written in a language that many have forgotten."

"The old Norse language?"

"No, no, this language was used by a single family someplace far away. Even those who live now have forgotten how to speak it. They only know how to read and write it."

"What do they say?"

"'Courage,' 'Grit,' 'Strength,' and 'Forgiveness.' Thought they would be fitting for you as you go off to college." He begins to point at the words. "May you have courage to step into the unknown and try new things, even when you are feeling at your most timid. May you have grit in every endeavor you choose, even when you are feeling at your lowest." He turns the blade over in my hand. "May you have the strength to endure, even when you feel you are at your weakest. And may you have forgiveness for not only others, but for yourself, even when you feel you are at your most foolish."

I can feel that I'm fighting back tears. "Wow, that's… that's powerful, Dr. Thurmond. Thank you."

"You're very welcome, Jack."

I quickly wipe my eyes. "Shoot, all I got you was a 12-pack of Diet Dr. Pepper and a bag of 100 Grand for your end of the year gift."

Dr. Thurmond laughs and I'm quick to join him. "Don't worry about it, Jack, I usually don't go this extravagant for TAs. But since you know Genevieve as well, I thought one with more sentimentality would be more sufficient in this manner."

"Thank you so much."

"Of course. I also want to leave you with a word of advice."

"Oh?"

"Gen told me about what you're going through and I've seen a shift in your mood as well since the weekend of prom."

I can only nod.

"Those four words, Jack? Those four words apply to the situation you're in right now. Find the courage to step forward. Find the grit to keep going despite how down you might be feeling. Find the strength to recover and be better than before. And find the forgiveness that is needed not only for her, but also for you."

I nod and smile lightly. He's right. I need those four things. I need to find them in order to make the next part of my life better than it was before.

I look at him and my smile becomes a little bigger. "I will. This might be the push I needed."

"I'm glad, Jack. I'm glad."

We turn back around and head back inside but not before I quickly run to my car and put the gift in the glovebox. We return to his classroom where I give him his gift and we proctor the test until the bell rings. We shake hands, but it quickly shifts to a hug as both of us are feeling more emotional about it. I leave the room before I have a complete emotional break down and promptly recover from the near crying experience when entering Halverson's for my final test in her classroom. God, she's the worst. Hence, taking the test a day early.

When the final bell rings, the seniors have their infamous walkout to their cars. Teachers, administration, and other staff members line the pathway to the parking lot, applauding us on our final walk out of H&H and reminding us to be back at school by 6:30 so graduation can start on time. I hug my friends in turn as we laugh with relief at the end of the year. We quickly go home and I lay down on my bed, feeling the stress of doing homework leave my shoulders as I won't have any to do from now until late August. Dinner tonight is steak on the grill and Mom, despite having started her treatments and Dad insisting that she doesn't, makes her famously amazing cheesy potatoes with broccoli on the side. It's my favorite dinner that my parents make and I couldn't be happier with it. I'm full by the time I change into my dress pants and shirt, disregarding the suit coat for the evening as the gown that we were forced to purchased is pretty hot with the suit coat underneath. I make my final drive to H&H and meet the rest of the graduating class in the music room outside of the auditorium. Lisa comes over and straightens my tie and we're all laughing right up until the moment Mrs. Halverson storms in and tells us to be quiet and to take our places. We take our places in all seriousness and make our way into the auditorium to the sound of *Pomp & Circumstance*. Once seated, I look up at the stage.

Z is sitting next to Vice Principal Balaban, a small, black folder laying neatly on her lap. I had forgotten Mona told me she was going to give a speech. I brace myself for the emotions to come.

I am alone.

Single.

Heartbroken.

She's as beautiful as ever. She doesn't look tired this time I see her. It could be the distance or it could be make-up, but she looks more like herself than she did the other day I saw her in front of Gay Simon's. Her hair is curled lightly and brushed to one side, just like it was when we kissed after the Annotator Benefit. My heart flutters at her radiance, but I quickly remind it that I am alone.

Single.

Heartbroken.

Maybe I should just leave. Maybe I should just fake an illness of some kind and not walk tonight. Lots of kids do it every year. Whether they are actually sick or their parents wanted to leave on a Thursday night for their summer vacation since it's cheaper to fly on Thursday than Friday, there are about twelve students missing. No one would miss a thirteenth. A thirteenth that is alone.

Single.

Heartbroken.

These words in my head, the ones that have been racing through my mind for more than a month now, come to a screeching halt as four new words come to mind.

Courage.

Grit.

Strength.

Forgiveness.

I need to find the courage to move on, despite missing Z so deeply. I need to find the grit to persist in finding the new, despite wanting the old. I need to find the strength to keep going, despite not wanting to. I need to find the forgiveness for myself since I was the one that messed things up, despite wanting to torture myself for ruining things.

I can't be like this anymore. I can't keep pushing for something that won't happen ever again. My relationship with Z is over. It's time to move on. It's time to try entertaining the idea of friendship.

It's time to find courage.

Grit.

Strength.

Forgiveness.

"And now, a word from one of our illustrious students, Ms. Zendaya Thompson," Principal Julkowski says and I quickly realize that I had just tuned out a majority of the first half of the ceremony. A polite applause ripples through the audience as Z takes the podium and gently places her folder – which now I can assume contains her speech – on the wooden pulpit.

"Good evening everyone and a special welcome to this year's graduating seniors. My esteemed peers, we made it!"

All the seniors, including me, cheer.

"Long have we awaited this day. As I only joined you this past year, I needed to ask a few of you what are some things that have been endured over the four years here at our esteemed school and the answers were pretty similar." She lists out a number of teachers and events at the school, all of which can some sort of reaction from us – laughter, booing, clapping, or cheering. "And all of these things were endured because we had each other. We relied on our friends and relationships here to help us get from being lowly ninth graders to the college and career ready seniors we are today."

Z pauses and I can tell it's a pause where she is holding back tears. I want to go up there and comfort her, but quickly remind myself that it's not the time nor is it my place to do such a thing.

She looks up and smiles at all again. "For me, my senior year here at H&H has been one of the greatest of my life. Being active in the Hollywood scene, most of my high school career was spent in front of a computer, completing virtual classes, and corresponding with teachers solely through email, not once connecting with other students. I didn't have time. But when I made the decision to come out here and live with my uncle and attend school in these hallowed halls, I was apprehensive to go to school. It wasn't my fame that had preceded me here that gave me such anxiety, but the fact I would be interacting with others my age outside of a movie set for the first time since middle school that scared me. You all had three years to create such strong bonds that I was worried I would be an outsider. An outcast. A loner. But that was not the case. I quickly made friends with five of the most incredible people I have ever met in my life. Mona and Lisa, thank you for opening up your hearts and arms to me and welcoming another girl into your little community, And Lisa, thank you so much for the make-up tips and tutorials, they are absolutely fabulous." Lisa stands up to cheers around her and snaps her fingers in the air while thrusting out her left hip, resulting in chuckles from the audience and a louder applause from the seniors. "Khalan, you are undoubtedly one of the wisest and most patient people I know and I will always cherish your loyalty to your friends and your convictions. Nick, I've learned to be my most genuine self from you in the most fearless ways possible. You are truly an inspiration not just for me, but every young member of the LGBT+ community. And Jack…"

All eyes turn to me, but I can only make eye contact with Z on stage. "Jack, you showed me what it is like to care about people, regardless of knowing them or not. Your friendship changed my life for the better, and for that, I'm eternally grateful."

She smiles at me. I smile back. Not like a romantic, gushy smile, but one of those smiles that you share with someone when a genuine thank you can't be said. It's different, but I like it. It's the first time she's said anything directed towards me since we broke up and I'm sad I can't say anything back.

Something new stirs my chest as she continues her speech. I try my best to come up with words to describe what I'm feeling, but only one comes to mind. Only one wraps around the idea of what this feeling is.

Healing.

Unadulterated.

Pure.

Wonderful.

Healing.

CHAPTER 23

Another sleepless night. I have been having these a lot lately. I just can't seem to fall asleep. And when I do, it's often too late – I only get a couple of hours. People think that if someone can't sleep, they just need to lay there until they finally drift off. That's actually not true. The individual should actually get out of bed and leave their room to do something else for like half an hour that isn't anything with a screen – reading is the best.

I'm not the biggest fan of reading. I try to read at least ten books a year, but it's not my favorite late night, can't sleep activity. Admittedly, I was doing well at the beginning of the year, but have fallen off the steady pace recently.

At the beginning of the summer, I bought myself an electric keyboard with an audio jack as well as some really nice, noise-cancelling headphones. That's what I do – I sit at the keyboard that's in the piano room, plug my headphones in and put them on, then play calm, melodic music. I've been tinkering at doing some of my own music, mostly in the LoFi realm of things.

That's what I'm playing – a piece I call "With You on the Beach." It is inspired by my first real conversation with Z. Not at Lucy's, but that night on Cocoa. It is smooth and quiet and elegant, full of happy scales and sounds.

Happier than how I feel.

It's been almost three months since we broke up. She feels so far away, despite living right next door. But we don't talk anymore. I haven't deleted our message thread on my phone, but it's closer to the bottom of my threads now. I've only talked to my friends on the phone for longer periods of time, otherwise it's been simple calls to my parents to tell them I'm on my way home or to see if Nick or Khalan is ready to hangout or go or whatever.

But not her.

My heart hurts thinking about her. People say first loves are hard to forget. I hate how right they are. I told myself that I will get over her. That I have to. But I can't.

When I had started healing, I thought that I would be okay right away. I had thought that healing would be immediate since it had already been a month since we broke up. But that isn't the case. It still hurts. I still cry. I still miss her sometimes. It's not as bad as it used to be. But it still hurts.

I stop playing, feeling a tear trickle down my cheek. I quickly rub it away, angry at myself for crying over her yet again.

As my hand moves away from my face, I see my phone light up with a call.

It's Z.

She never calls anymore.

I quickly pick up.

"Z?"

She's crying on the other end.

"Z? Hey, Z, what's wrong? Are you okay?"

"Yeah, I'm okay." More sobs. "But Nick isn't."

Fuck.

"What do you mean?"

More sobs and a longer pause. "He's in the hospital. He's in critical condition. I just got the call from Winona."

"The hospital?! Where?!"

"Advent…" More sobs. "Health. He's at Advent Health."

I rapidly stand up, not caring to unplug my headphones or turning off the keyboard. I manage to catch it before it falls to the ground, then quickly head to my room.

"Jack?"

"I'm still here, Z."

"Can you drive me?" More sobbing – she's sobbing hard now. "I… I can't… I'm not…"

"Of course, Z. I need to put some actual clothes on and then I'll be right out."

"Thank… Thank you…"

"Absolutely. Meet me at the end of your driveway in like 5 minutes."

"I'm already by your car… if that's okay?"

She's by my car. That's the closest she's been in months.

"Yeah, of course. Totally okay. Can I get you some water?"

"Ugh, damn it, yes please. I forgot my bottle in the sink." She starts sobbing again.

"Hey, hey, it's okay. This is very stressful," I try to reassure her as I'm stumbling around the room trying to put on my jeans. "I got you."

Her sobs are at the hardest I've ever heard them.

"I'll be right down."

"Please don't hang up."

"I won't."

It takes me a couple of more minutes to put on some clean clothes, fill two water bottles, and leave a note for my parents on the kitchen island. True to my word, I didn't hang up the phone despite neither of us saying anything. Z couldn't stop crying and I try my best to get her to calm down to no avail. I don't even bother to tie my shoes as I bolt out the door. Z is standing by the passenger door, no makeup on and tears streaming down her face. I quickly unlock the car and we both hurriedly hop in and buckle up. I turn the car on, my phone instantly connecting and playing the last thing I was listening to – some Vivaldi.

Z laughs a little bit through her tears. "Of course, you were listening to Vivaldi."

Her voice sounds sweeter in person than over the phone, but I can't focus on that right now. I simply smile and nod, pulling out of the drive way and towards the neighborhood exit.

The seven-minute drive is long and quiet. It feels like we are driving so slowly, despite the fact that I'm speeding. A lot. We don't speak and Z's tears resumed shortly after our brief positive interaction. When we make it to the hospital, Z tries to hurriedly open the door but the door isn't working. She slams her head against window, sobbing even harder.

"Z, it's okay, hang on," I quickly get out of the car. That's the problem with owning a 2006 vehicle is that the lock mechanism stops working properly after a while. Well, no, that's not entirely true. It just seems to be happening to my car recently and I keep putting it off. Luckily, all I have to is unlock it from the outside.

Jack. Focus. Nick is in the ER.

I quickly get out of the car and run around to her door. I unlock it and open the door. I help her up out of the car and we run inside. The ER isn't super full, but it's still kind of busy. Nurses are running around and keeping people calm the best they can. I run up to the front desk with Z close behind.

"Excuse me, ma'am?"

The nurse looks up. "You alright, kids?"

"Our friend was brought in earlier. She got a call," I say, pointing at
Z.

"Well, it wasn't from the hospital. It was from one of his moms," Z
says.

"Name?"

"Ostman, Nick."

"Nicole?"

I cringe – his dead name always gives me that reaction. "Yeah."

"Okay, so, she's in the OR. She got roughed up pretty bad. Her
moms are in the waiting room. I'll ask if you can join them. What's
your names?"

"Just say its Jack and Z. They'll know who we are."

"Will do, baby. Just hang tight." She gives us a warm smile and gets
up. "And she's going to be okay. She's got some good people working
on her."

I nod and hear Z sob again. I turn to her, wanting so desperately to
give her a hug.

"You hear that? She said he's going to be okay," I say, trying to
keep my voice calm as my inside mentality is at an all-time anxiety
high and keeps screaming red alert.

"Jack, they always say that," she says.

I touch her shoulder. "He'll be okay, Z. He's a fighter. Always has
been."

I see her trying to stay strong, but she breaks again.

Then she steps closer to me and throws her arms around me. I
instinctually embrace her, holding her as tight as I can while she sobs.
It's the first time we've touched since prom, and an even longer time
since we've hugged. I don't let go. I never want to let go, but I know
I'll have to.

"He's going to be okay, Z. He's going to be okay."

"I can't bear the thought of losing him, askim."

Askim. My pet-name from when we were dating.

I tighten my hug around her. "You're not going to, hjartat. We're
not going to."

"Excuse me, Jack and Z?"

We separate to look over at the nurse. "The moms said you can
come on back."

We hurriedly go into the room and straight into the arms of Winona
and Diane, who were understandably weeping and more than happy to
finally have company. They fill us in on what exactly happened that

caused this emergency visit to the hospital. Nick had been on a date with Riley, the girl he had met in Ocala during Spring Break. They have been going pretty steady since then and would often meet up here in or near Orlando since there is a lot more to do. They were out to dinner when a group of, I'm not sure how to put this but I'll try, unsavory young men came into the restaurant. It was obvious they were drunk and were being absurdly loud. Nick and Riley tried to ignore them the best that they could, but it didn't help any when one of the guys saw Nick and Riley and started making fun of 'the lesbian couple.' Riley stayed calm – she was used to this kind of treatment in northern Florida – but Nick wasn't. I mean, that's classic Nick, he's not one to put up with anyone else's bullshit and has no issue with putting someone in their place. He stood and said that he wasn't a girl, but a guy and there was nothing wrong with the relationship he and Riley had. Some more profanities and slurs were slung at Nick then, degrading his transgender identity and relationship status similar to that my grandpa used in the Keys. It got so loud that the manager of the restaurant came out and had to break up the verbal confrontation. After hearing what happened from other customers around them, the manager deemed it necessary for the group of guys to be removed from the restaurant. They put up a big fuss, apparently, but eventually left when they were threatened with the police. Nick and Riley finished their date, then Nick, ever the gentleman, went to go get the car. On his way to the car, the guys, who must not have left, jumped him and beat him within an inch of his life before they left. When Nick failed to return with the car, Riley went out looking for him and found him, battered and bloody, about ten feet away from his car. She quickly dialed 911 and both paramedics and police officers arrived at the scene. The paramedics took care of Nick while the officers first called Nick's moms to inform them of the circumstance then questioned Riley, the restaurant staff, and some of the other customers.

To be honest, I was shocked when I heard Winona recall the story for us. It seemed like something out of a movie or a book that just didn't feel real. But here I am, living this fantastical story in real time. Nick was in the hospital because he was transgender. Nothing more, nothing less than that. I'm sure he had some witty comebacks to the drunken lot, but witty comebacks are not something that would typically invoke violence, even when the intended party is drunk. No, this was, in my point of view and the point of view of the police on the scene, a hate crime against Nick. I never thought this would happen.

The community we live in is very accepting and loving towards any member of the LGBT+ community and Nick only surrounds himself with people who feel the same way. But this happened right here in Orlando. I know there are people with dissenting opinions towards Nick and others like him, but violence? I never thought it would be here.

A doctor comes in and informs us of Nick's condition. They were able to stabilize him and stitch up the open wounds. There was, thankfully, no internal bleeding, but they had managed to break four ribs on Nick's right side. With the severity of the break and the continued escalation of the beating, the doctors found it miraculous that one of the ribs didn't pierce Nick's lung. Two officers entered shortly after the doctor, who then retold the prognosis to the uniformed officials. They told us that Riley was at the police station with her parents and that they had just arrested a group of men that were driving drunk on the road. Riley would be identifying them shortly after their processing to see if they were the right ones, but the bruising on their knuckles and blood on their clothes indicates they are more than likely the group that beat Nick. They then asked if they could speak with Winona and Diana privately and discuss their options when it came to pressing charges. Winona and Diana happily oblige and go with them to a more private room.

Nick is wheeled in shortly after, still asleep but breathing soundly. Both Z and I break down crying seeing him like this. His face is swollen and bruised. His skin is pale and remnants of caked blood were still visible on different parts of his body. Z collapses into a chair next to his bed and immediately takes his hand, sobbing harder than before. I start to cry, but I don't sit down. I go over to the sink and grab some paper towels, wet them, and begin to clean Nick up, getting as much of the dried blood off him as possible. I look at his knuckles and they are unbruised.

"He didn't even fight back…" I whisper.

Z shakes her head, her sobs becoming more and more labored. "Of course… he… didn't… oh god, Jack, they could've killed him!"

Anger rises in my chest at the thought of this being done in the basement of a police station with a coroner rather than in the hospital with a doctor. I do my best to keep my emotions in check, but my crying becomes more fervent the more I clean blood off of Nick. There was so much of it. I keep thinking about how Nick is still alive or what was he thinking or what were those drunken assholes thinking. Again, I can't believe this is happening.

We wait around a while more before Mona, Lisa, and Khalan show up. They had been dead asleep when we had tried to call them or text them and they were feeling bad about not being here sooner. Neither of us are mad – Z sleeps with her ringer on for emergencies just like this and I couldn't sleep. We commandeer more chairs and bring them into the room and I finally sit down. My body thanks me profusely as I feel exhaustion finally wash over me. I put my head back and close my eyes. I'm about to fall asleep when I feel someone sit down in the chair next to me. I open one eye and look over and see that it is Z.

"Hey," I whisper, seeing that Lisa has fallen asleep in Mona's arms and not wanting to be loud.

"Hey," she whispers back.

"You okay?"

She shakes her head. "This scares the hell out of me, Jack."

I sit up slowly, my body groaning against the movement. "Yeah. Me too."

"People suck."

I chuckle. It's something we used to say all the time while we were dating. "Yep. I hate people."

She smiles lightly at me. "Still glad we have the same hatreds."

I smile back after chuckling a little more. "Me too."

"How have you been?"

I shrug, trying to mask my excitement that we are having this much conversation. "I've been okay. Busy. I've been putting in a good number of shifts so that I've got some money saved up for when I move to MIT and the money has been good so I can't complain really. Just tired and busy."

"How are the tourists this summer?"

"Same old shit, different day, you know?"

She laughs a little and my spirit soars.

"What about you?"

Z shakes her head. "I'm doing better than I have been. I'm back at Simon's, if you couldn't tell. Prepping for going to school and making sure that my agent isn't freaking out anymore."

"What do you mean? I thought you were still doing that TV show with Ezra?"

She scoffs. "Yeah, fuck that show and fuck Ezra."

I raise an eyebrow. "Oh, shit, really? I thought you guys were back together? That's what all the magazines are saying anyways."

She rolls her eyes and puts her head back. "Yeah, I thought we were headed that direction too, but Jack, he's a fucking asshole. He tried controlling my life again and the TV show turned into something that I just couldn't do anymore. It was so forceful and moronic and I felt like my acting was completely thrown off by Ezra and the rest of the cast. I did my cameo for the few episodes that they wanted me in initially, but when they offered to make my character a permanent character for all five seasons they were cleared for, I refused. I packed my shit and got the hell out of there. My agent was less than pleased."

"Oh, shit, I'm sorry, Z, that's awful!"

"Yeah, well, your voice kept ringing in my ears when I was thinking about getting back together with him."

"God, that must have been really annoying. Even I can't stand hearing myself."

She turns to me, her face still laced with anger regarding the show and Ezra and for a second I thought the anger was going to unleash itself on me. But just as I am about to apologize, she bursts out laughing, startling the now sleeping Da Vinci couple awake. Z and I both say sorry and they resume their sleeping positions. I look over to Khalan and it looks like they are fast asleep – they always have been such a heavy sleeper.

"God, Jack, I've missed you."

She's missed me. My heart races.

"I've missed you too. Can I ask you something?"

"Absolutely."

I hesitate but know that this is going to be the next phase of healing. "Can we be friends again?"

Z lets out a deep sigh. "Yes, please, let's be friends again."

We spend the next thirty minutes talking quietly about life and college before my body demands that I sleep. I apologize to her about being tired and she just shakes her head and agrees that we need to sleep. I put my head back against the wall and I'm asleep in a matter of seconds.

I wake up to a heavy pressure on my shoulder and groggily pick my head up. Z must have fallen asleep and slouched down onto my shoulder, because it's her hair that tickled me on my neck to wake me up. I look around the room and see that everyone was still asleep, including Winona and Diana who must have returned after we all fell asleep. I look at Nick and see his eyes open. He catches my glance and gently waves a hand at me.

"Hey, man, what's up?" He asks, almost nonchalantly.

I quickly but slowly shift Z so her head is against the back of my chair to make sure I don't wake her, then rapidly head over to the bed, nudging Winona and Diana awake before getting to the bed.

"Holy shit, Nick, you're insane," I say, chuckling at him.

"Nick, are you okay, dear?" Diana asks, tears resuming down her cheeks.

"I'm hungry as fuck and a little sore, but other than that I think I'm okay. As long as I don't move a whole lot that is." He laughs at his own joke for a split second before wincing. "Ope, can't do that, ouch, shit, fuck, that hurts!"

Winona places a gentle hand on her son's knee. "I'll go get the doctor. She was just in here a little bit ago, but you must have woken up right after she left."

"Thanks, Mama," Nick says, putting his hand on top Winona's before she leaves to find the attending.

Nick looks to Diane. "What a fucking night. Is Riley okay?"

She nods. "I think she and her parents got a hotel not too far from here. She was pretty shaken up last night, Nicky. She was at the police station until three with her statement and identifying your assaulters."

"Oh, so they caught the bastards, eh?" Nick says, pride evident in his voice. "Good for the boys in blue. Glad they did something about it."

"Nick, man," I say, my anger boiling at this point at his almost carefree attitude about what just happened. "You've got to be more careful."

Nick looks at me. "What the hell does that mean?"

"Nick, come on. You were almost killed out there last night! Doctors say you were lucky to only sustain the injuries you have, dude! You can't... You can't put yourself in situations like that."

"What do you mean, Jack? That I can't be who I am in public? That I need to hide my identity because of what other people might think?"

"No, of course not, that's not what I mean..."

"No, I'm pretty sure that is what you are alluding to. But you know what, Jack? I'm not going to. I know you're just looking out for me and you don't want to see me get hurt again, but, dude, I'm not going to deny myself of being who I am just because some people are just too close minded to understand."

I lower my head.

"Jack, my life is mine. I'm going to live it to the fullest by being the truest self I can be."

"I know, man, I'm just…"

"Scared. You're just scared. Come here."

I take a couple steps towards him and he takes my hand. "Buddy. I'm scared too. I'm only acting like this is no big deal because… fuck, dude, I can't remember a time where I was as terrified as I was while getting my ass beat. And, if I wasn't who I am, I would most likely be exactly where you are right now. But I'm not that person. I'm me. I know who I am. I know what I'm about. I won't let some drunk bastards dictate who I am or when I get to be me. I won't let others dictate my future."

I nod and smile lightly at him, a tear streaking down my cheek.

"Jack, I hope we both learn something after this."

"Yeah?"

"Yeah. I hope you learn that it's time to start being who you are. You constantly hide behind something or other and deny yourself of who you really are. It's time that you start moving forward with your life. Try new things. Be spontaneous. Who knows what you might find. What were those words Thurmond told you?"

"Courage, grit, strength, and forgiveness."

"Right. It's time you start using those, dude. To their fullest. Stop apologizing for other people. Start living for yourself."

He's right. I've still been so afraid to move on with my life that I have been more concerned about what others might think or what may happen. It's time that I start being unapologetically me.

"What are you hoping you learn, Nick?" Diana asks as I am still contemplating what he said.

"Oh, you know, that it's time to start taking boxing lessons with Khalan's trainer."

The three of us laugh – Nick not for long due to the pain in his ribs – and the rest of the group wakes up. All are happy to see Nick smile and joke, but I'm still stuck on his words.

I want to be different. I want to be me. But how does that work?

Dedication to spontaneity. Dedication to trying new things.

Having courage.

Grit.

Strength.

Forgiveness.

It's time to start living my life. Not someone else's. Mine.

CHAPTER 24

To say I took Nick's advice to heart would be an understatement. I've really dove into trying new things. For example, I ended up signing up at a local jazz club for a time slot to provide ambience on the piano. It was nothing crazy – a slow, mid-afternoon on a Thursday. Little did I know that the owner was there enjoying some coffee when I started playing. I wouldn't say jazz is my best genre to play, but I'm no slouch at it. I really get into the creative, mistimed, wonkiness of jazz and had an absolute riot playing, despite only playing for about a dozen people. But the owner really liked my stuff and she invited to come back on Friday night and play for a full house. I happily obliged and made a killing off of tips people left me in my jazz hat I put out by the piano. It felt weird and even a little tacky, but it was so much fun. I've been doing that for the last few Fridays – Farrow has been kind enough to let me take Fridays to do that. I've made some new friends – most of them in their early twenties – and I've even got a couple of phone numbers from girls that flirted with me while I was between songs or sets. And one guy, which Gay Simon laughed about when I told him that it had happened.

Another thing I've been doing is putting music onto public music platforms for people to enjoy. I don't have a huge following – maybe a hundred people – but I've gotten some really good feedback on some of my original pieces. It's been a lot of fun and I've even made some contacts on the main platform I use about taking my music to the next level. I'm honestly not interested in it, but it has been fun to toss around the idea of it anyways.

But one of the best things about this month – this last month before moving out to the college – is that Z and I have really rekindled our friendship. We hang out every other day and often take little excursions together. We even managed to go back to Universal Studios together for a day and it wasn't awkward. We laugh and talk and I realize how much I missed her, even if the rekindling is that of our friendship and not our relationship. What's weird is that I'm okay with that. I've healed. I've moved on. I still love her and I'm pretty sure I always will, but the friendship she and I share is something that has really helped me get to a new place in life. Would I be open to getting back together with her? I think so. But it's not necessary nor is it something I actively think on. Instead, it's a beautiful friendship that I will always hold dear to my heart.

Today is Monday and it's the first day of our last week all together. Nick and Khalan move out in a week, Z and I move out on Tuesday next week, and Mona and Lisa head to New York on that Wednesday. It's bittersweet and none of us are really ready to acknowledge that things are about to drastically change. We won't be able to see each other consistently. Our spring breaks don't line up. We'll be in different time zones spanning across the country. We're figuring on trying to do video calls as much as we can, but we also understand that we'll be making new circles of friends and that life is going to get exponentially busier. We'll remain friends, no matter what, but it's just hard to accept it will be different than it was in high school.

We're all sitting in Lisa's pool house, playing Call of Duty and chatting about life. It feels eerily similar to the weekend before fall break and it's nice to reminisce about simpler times.

As I just get a solid headshot on Khalan's character in the game, Nick jumps up into the air.

"My friends, I have an idea!"

Lisa gently guides Nick back down to a sitting position. "Nick, darling, you need to be careful. You still have another four weeks until your ribs are fully healed."

"Yes, right, of course. But this idea is grand so please, stop playing that frivolous game."

Khalan pauses the game and looks at Nick. "Here we go again."

"Yes, again, but this time, a twist!"

"Okay, what are you thinking?" I ask, eyebrow raised.

"I say we have a Final Hurrah!"

"Oh?" Lisa asks, her curiosity visibly peaking.

"My parents said that we can go to their beach house in St. Pete if we wanted to. I was thinking we could leave today, in like two hours, and stay until Friday afternoon. Then we would be back for the weekend with our families before setting off on our grand collegiate adventure."

I smile wide. "That actually sounds like a hell of a lot of fun. I don't work at all this week and I'm sure my parents would be okay with it!"

"How sure are you?" Nick asks, a cheeky grin crossing his face. "Should you call your mom or should Z?"

We all laugh, remembering the last time I got permission to go to the beach house.

"No, I'm positive she'll say yes if I ask."

"I'm down too!" Z says. "I need to get away one last time I think."

Khalan nods. "One last time. All of us together."

Mona smiles. "One final hurrah."

Lisa grabs Mona's hand. "I'm so down."

We all call our parents and, to no one's surprise, all of our parents say yes and encourage us to take this time to ourselves. Dad even offers up the Tahoe for us to use so we can drive together. We go home and pack, going as fast as we can so we can beat the traffic on I4. After everyone is dropped off at my house, we jump in the car and start off on one last adventure all together. Like I had mentioned before, it's bittersweet. We laugh and reminisce, but there is a trace of sadness in the car that no one wants to address.

And it's on the car ride to the beach house that I realize something that I've been fighting for months now. I want to tell everyone in the car, but quickly decide against it – this isn't about me. This trip is about all of us. Together.

One last time.

We get to the house just before dinner and Nick had managed to get us a reservation at Cesare's on the Beach. Luckily we had decided to go there before we left Lisa's and we all packed some nicer clothes. We change at the beach house and make our way to the restaurant where we are seated only feet away from the table Z and I shared all those months ago. I look up at her and smile, indicating where we sat with a nod. She smiles back and winks as we both reminisce about the fun we had eating here. The food is, as always, impeccable and delicious.

We end up spending time in St. Pete much like we did during Fall break – whimsical trips through the tourist shops, playing plenty of games with one another, and Nick even manages to find where his moms keep their expensive alcohol and we make shitty drinks and get a little buzzed a couple nights. I don't normally do this – and maybe we shouldn't have done it in the first place – but what's a final hurrah without some alcohol?

At least, that was Nick's excuse.

Now, it's our last night here and a sadness hangs in between all of us. We don't want to go. None of us do. We have so much fun together and have had an absolute blast on this trip that we don't want to go. MIT feels like it's not worth my dream. I'm going to miss these guys. So, so much.

"I have an idea," Khalan says, standing up from the kitchen table.

"Oh, it's your turn with the ideas, eh?" Nick jests.

Khalan nods. "Let's go have a bonfire on the beach. Watch the sun go down. Share some stuff with one another."

Lisa smiles wide. "Ugh, Khalan, I love that."

We quickly change into jeans and sweatshirts and Khalan and I grab firewood and build the fire. Soon, we have it crackling away with beach chairs in a semi-circle around the fire while we all face the slowly sinking sun. The colors are beautiful, even more beautiful than they were when Z and I snuggled for warmth on the beach during fall break. We don't say anything for a long time. I'm not sure any of us knows what to say at this point. Between being tired from the fun of the trip and the emotional stress we are feeling about leaving, I'm not sure if it is right to say anything at all. I keep feeding the fire, knowing that we weren't going to go inside any time soon. I don't want to. I want to stay like this forever. My five best friends on a beautiful night. It's incredible. I quickly rub my eyes, staining my sleeves the tears that welled in them, and look over at my friends.

Khalan, my loyal buddy through and through.

Nick, my best friend since moving down here.

Mona, my immovable rock of support.

Lisa, my entertainer and fashion diva.

Z, my first love and my greatest friend.

Z catches me looking at her. "What?"

I shake my head, clearing my throat. "Nothing. I just love you guys, that's all."

"I love you too, man," Nick says, smacking my back harder than expected. The rest say similar things and it's nice to feel the warmth of the words. Silence soon takes over again.

"Why don't we go around the circle-esque shape we've got going on here," Lisa says, finally breaking the silence, "and share something that we've never told anyone before?"

"Why don't you start since it was your idea?" Khalan says, chuckling.

"Fine by me!" Lisa pauses for a moment, thinking about what to say. "I'm switching my major."

It's almost comical on how all of us recoil when we hear it, jolting back in our chairs out of pure shock.

"You're not going to major in theatre?!" Nick exclaims.

"No, I'm not," Lisa says. "I'm still going to participate in the productions, don't get me wrong. I mean, I still have that scholarship and everything. But I've felt this pull in another direction for some time now to go into the medical field."

"The medical field? Like, what exactly?" Z asks.

"I want to become a nurse and work with kids with cancer actually."

"That's great!" I say, almost shouting. "I think that's really cool, Lisa."

The rest of the group says their affirmations and Lisa smiles. "Thanks, guys. I've only really told Mona, does that count?"

"Being that you two probably don't hide things from each other, yeah, I feel like that's logical," Khalan states.

"Alright, so, then I guess it's my turn," Mona says, sighing and leaning back in her chair. "Well, I guess if Lisa told you her big college thing, I should tell you mine. I've dropped my basketball scholarship and won't be playing at NYU."

My jaw drops. Mona led H&H to the state championship this year and they won. She scored her 1,000th point in the second game of the season. She's had recruiters from all over the country coming and trying to recruit her for their school. She's a phenomenal basketball player.

"Why?" I ask.

Mona shrugs. "I just think it's time. I played my heart out in high school and had a lot of fun doing it. I've worked hard to be where I'm at, but I feel like it's time to be done. There's more to life than basketball. I'll still play recreationally, but its college! I want to focus on my studies and do well and really start planning a future, ya know?"

We affirm her decision and she smiles wide. I can tell she's at peace with her decision as she just relaxes back into her chair, smiling and holding Lisa's hand.

"Khalan, you're up," Nick says, looking over at them.

"Indeed." Khalan leans forward in their chair, twiddling their thumbs. "Sometimes… Sometimes I feel sad about being asexual."

A stillness surrounds us as we take in what Khalan said. I've always had this notion that when someone talks about their sexual orientation, it's better to let them progress at their own speed rather than pushing an answer. And since I know Khalan to be a confident individual, I know that this subject is hard for them to talk about.

"Take your time, dear," Lisa says in her most reassuring voice. "If you don't want to talk about it anymore, that's okay. Just know that we are here for you."

Khalan nods. "Thanks, Lisa. Part of me really doesn't want to talk about it…"

"Then that's okay, Khalan," I say.

"But we are taking the time to vulnerable with one another. So, here goes." Khalan hesitates briefly before starting again. "Sometimes I see my sister with her girlfriend and I just wish that it could be me. That I could feel some kind of sexual attraction to somebody, regardless of gender. I'll never have my first kiss, which feels like a huge milestone in someone's life. I watch you guys and see your relationships and hear about them and constantly think 'Am I missing out on something?' It's frustrating because I know there is nothing wrong with me. And at the same time, I feel like there is."

Nick immediately gets up from his chair and squats next to Khalan. "Khal, there's nothing wrong with you, comrade. I think everyone who is different than hetero or cis has these thoughts sometimes. Some rarer or more frequent than others. But that's okay. That's life. It's who we are. It's messy and sometimes uncomfortable and complicated. But that doesn't mean there's anything wrong with us."

"If anything," I comment, "it means there is something wrong with society. To be locked into a singular mode of thinking limits the human experience."

"Dr. Thurmond said that, didn't he?" Khalan says, chuckling.

"Yeah, which means it's one hundred percent true."

We all laugh and let Khalan talk again.

"I appreciate you guys and the reassurance you give," they say after a minute. "I figured I could share this with you and not be judged."

"Always, my dear person, always," Lisa says.

Khalan jerks their head over at Z. "What about you, Z?"

Z nods and looks at us all quickly before starting. "Well, I've been meaning to share this with you all at some point on this trip and this feels like a better time than on the drive back. I have officially retired from acting."

"What?" I ask, dumbfounded.

"Yep, I'm done with acting. It's been fun while it lasted, but this last show really killed it for me. I told my agent that I would do select cameos, but I want to be done for the most part. I still get residual checks from APL and I'll get them for the different things that I have been doing since, but it's time to be done. It's way too demanding on me and it negates my self-confidence and self-worth too much to keep going. Instead, I'm going to become an agent for young, aspiring actors and help them break into the industry while also making sure they are taking care of themselves and not overstretching themselves like I did."

Mona smiles. "That is so fucking cool."

Z smiles back. "Thanks. I feel like this is a good switch for me. And a big change of pace. Which is so, so, so welcome right now."

"That's awesome, Z. I'm proud of you," I say, not really thinking about what I'm saying.

She looks over at me and that warm, genuine smile – like the one at graduation – comes to her face. "Thanks, Jack. That means a lot." Z turns to Nick. "You ready?"

Nick nods and thinks for a moment. "I'm scared of moving to Portland."

I raise an eyebrow. "Dude, it's gonna be so great for you! Why are you scared?"

Nick shrugs. "I've been who I am for a long time now. I know who I am and I'm confident that this," he gestures to his whole person, "is who I am meant to be. Transmale. And I've been incredibly fortunate that I've had such great and supportive friends like you all to help me be who I am to the fullest. I mean, it helps that two of you are gay and one of you is asexual and non-binary, but still, you guys have been such pillars of support for me." Nick stops for a moment, his bottom lip quivering. "And now I won't have you guys there. What if I can't find a new group of people? What if my support system is just gone? What if I am pressured to living a lie again? What if… What if… there are more… guys… like…" Nick stops, tears coming down his cheeks.

Lisa reaches over and takes his hands. "What if there are more guys like the ones that jumped you? Is that what you're trying to say?"

Nick only nods.

"Oh, darling." Lisa gets up and hugs Nick tightly.

"Nick, you got this, man," I say before I really comprehend what I'm saying. "You're an incredible individual who is fiercely stubborn. Remember what you told me after you got jumped? You told me it's time for me to live unapologetically and be me. That's what you need to do, man. Be who you are. Don't change to fit in someplace new. You're going to find people that love you for you and you'll all new friends who can relate to you on such a deeper level than anyone has before. I know it. I feel it in my gut."

"But doesn't that bother you? That you aren't my direct support anymore?"

I nod a little. "Yeah, I'm sad about it. You've been my best friend since I moved here. You pushed me out of my comfort zone and I've grown so much, thanks to you. I'll always be here to support you, no matter what. Which means that I need to support you making new connections and finding more direct support when I'm not there."

Nick smiles and sobs. "Thanks, Jack."

I stand up and make my way over to him. "Come here."

He quickly stands and we wrap our arms around each other, laughing and crying all at once.

"I love you, Nick."

"I love you too, Jack. I couldn't ask for a better friend."

Nick and I sit back down, making sniffles and grunts to act more 'masculine,' which gets a good laugh from the rest of the gang. Once we're situated again, everyone looks to me.

"Well, that's my cue." I lean back in my chair, then forward as I'm trying to formulate the words I want to say. "I actually had this thought while I was in the car on the way here and it's been reoccurring this whole trip. It's really weird for me to admit, but I have come to love Florida."

No one says anything. I'm sure they're shocked. I've done nothing but complain about how shitty this hellhole is since the day I've moved here. The hurricanes, the tourists, the corporate greed, the backwards politics, and, of course, the summers have all contributed to a deep hatred. But now… now, things are different.

"I know. It's a lot to take in. But it's true. I love this place. And it's not because of what Florida is. I think I'll always have some sort of disdain for the physical features of Florida. The hurricanes. The ridiculous weather patterns. The swamps and humidity."

"The summers," Z comments with a smile.

"Yes, the fucking summers too," I reply with a smirk. "But those things don't bug me as much as they used to. And it's because…" I feel myself choking up. "It's because of all of you. I couldn't ask for better friends. I sincerely love all of you so, so much that it hurts me to think about moving away in a few days." Tears are coming down my cheeks now. "I hate that we'll be so far away from each other. I know that we'll make new lives and meet new people and have the time of our lives, but losing immediate and frequent contact with you all is going to suck so much. So, before our lives change, I just want to say thank you. Thank you for being the greatest friend an Alaskan transplant could have in this place."

There's not a dry eye around the circle and we all stand up and hug. There's no bitter feeling anymore. Just sweetness. Six friends who love each other dearly embracing in the cool night of a Florida evening.

Eventually we do separate and Khalan looks at their watch. "Shit, you guys, it's one in the morning."

"Damn!" Nick exclaims. "Well, let's hit the sack. I'm sure we all want to stay up, but we need to drive back tomorrow and I've got family stuff going on."

"Yeah, I need to help my parents and Gay Simon set up for our big cookout Saturday night," I say, turning to head inside.

We make our way up the beach back towards the house, laughing and joking in the short walk back. There's some playful shoving and I find myself in the back of the procession with Z. Once we reach the back door of the house on the porch, Z grabs my arm.

"Jack, can we talk for a second?"

I nod. "Yeah, sure, what's up?"

Z starts to fiddle with the ends of her hair. Her nervous tick. Wait, what is she nervous about? What's happening?

"Z, it's okay. You can tell me anything."

"I know I can," she replies, looking into my eyes. I am once again enchanted at how beautiful that shade of blue is. "Jack, I'm still in love with you."

CHAPTER 25

What did she say? Did she just say she's still in love with me? "What?" I ask, my brain not really comprehending what just happened.

"Jack, I am still so incredibly in love with you. I know this sounds so stupid and ridiculous but I can't stop thinking about you. I have scrolled through our text messages dozens of times in the past few weeks, just wanting to have you back like I used to. I haven't said anything because you've told me about those girls at the jazz club, but I can't keep this to myself anymore. Jack, I'm crazy about you. I don't know how else to put it. You are one of the most caring, loving, and compassionate people I know. You're so talented and I'm in awe of you. You make playing the piano look so easy and the music you create is beautiful. I even went to the jazz club one night to hear you play and I was blown away."

"You did?"

"Yes, I did and I almost waited out by your car to tell you all of this then, but I didn't have the courage to do it. You're truly remarkable and I love you with every fiber of my being. I can't stop thinking about you. Crap, I'm repeating myself but this bears repeating. I try to focus on anything else to keep my mind off of you, but you always come back. I have poured myself into different elements of my life – acting, painting, running – anything to get my mind off of you but I just can't. But tonight, on the beach, I looked at you and knew that I just had to tell you."

This feels familiar.

"Z…"

"And I know you've moved on! I mean, I know how crazy some of those girls at the jazz club are about you, I could tell just how they acted around you. But I'm crazy about you, too. I have been ever since you sat next to me at Cocoa Beach in the sand almost a year ago today. I love you, Jack, and I want to be with you."

My heart is racing at this point.

"Z…"

"And I know! I know I hurt you. We hurt each other. So why would you want to get back together with me? I know we might have missed our shot at being together and I don't want to ruin the friendship that we have re-cultivated in light of all of this, but I need you to hear me and believe me when I say that I love you with all my heart, askim. I do."

"Z…"

"Please don't hold this against me. Please keep being my friend. We can even pretend I never said any of this and we can go on with our lives. I just needed to tell you, Jack. I hope you can see how desperately I needed to tell you."

"Z…"

"Jack, please just…"

Nick's advice to live in the moment floods my head. I remember all the times that I waited too long to express myself. I remember all the times where there was an opportunity and I just let it slip by. I remember that night I hesitated to kiss her on this same beach.

But not now. No more waiting. No more hesitation.

"Z, please stop talking."

I step into her space, pull her close, and kiss her.

She gasps as I step in, but once our lips meet and hold their meeting, I can feel her sink into it then rise to meet me. Her arms fling around my neck and she pulls me as close to her as possible. I wrap my arms tighter around her lower back and feel myself sink into the kiss as well. We separate only for a moment to simply kiss again and again and again. Her hand runs through my hair and her scent overwhelms my nostrils yet again – lavender, just like at the Steinmetz. I remember how she felt slender, but not fragile and realize that she feels the exact same but also so much more familiar than ever before.

When we finally separate, I don't move away from her. My nose still touches hers. Her hand is still in my hair.

"Z, I am still madly in love with you too. And I would rather not be friends when we both want to be so much more to one another."

She smiles and nods, her hand wandering through my hair again.

"Good, that's what I was hoping you would say."

I kiss her again and this time it's more passionate, more earnest. Like we are making up for the lost months of not being able to kiss one another.

We finally take a step back from one another, but we take each other's hands and laugh and smile.

"So," Z says, tears welling in her eyes, "will you be my boyfriend again?"

I smile wide. "Absolutely, Zendaya. Absolutely."

She giggles, pulls me to her again, and kisses me. When we part, I wrap my arms around her and we stand there hugging in the cool night air.

"I guess we should talk about what our relationship is going to look like now, huh?" Z asks quietly.

I nod. "Yeah, especially going off to college. Open and honest communication."

"Not putting one person's dreams in front of the other."

"Being as understanding as possible with the other and supporting them in their endeavors."

"Making time for one another."

My heart, despite riding a new high that I've never felt before, sinks.

3000 miles.

44-hour drive.

6-hour flight.

"I'll start looking at flights tomorrow morning out to LAX. See if I can't head out there over fall break."

Z steps back and gives me a light smile. "About that."

I raise an eyebrow. "About what?"

Z gestures to the patio loveseat and we sit down. I quickly start the outside stand heater since it's getting cold and I figure that we will be out here for a while.

"Okay, so, don't be mad."

I shake my head. "I promise, I won't be mad."

"I'm not going to UCLA anymore."

I'm taken aback. She had been talking about UCLA ever since she got accepted. Her dad was super excited for her to go and I knew her mom was looking forward to her being home for a change.

"Really? Where are you going?"

A smile creeps on to her face. "Harvard."

Harvard.

I quickly pull out my phone.

"What are you doing?" Z asks, putting her hand on my phone.

"I was going to see how close Harvard and MIT are!"

She shakes her head. "You don't need to. Just over one mile. Six-minute drive. Twenty-minute walk. And there is a shuttle that brings kids back and forth between Harvard and MIT too."

Just over one mile.

Six-minute drive.

Twenty-minute *walk*.

I smile wide. "Z, that's amazing."

She smiles back at me. "I know! The admissions office called me about my unfinished application. They encouraged me to complete it and then come out for a private tour around campus. I got there and just fell in love with the place, Jack. It's so beautiful and there's so many creative minds there. When they offered me a spot in the fall, I instantly said yes."

"Were you going to tell me at some point? Even if we were just going to be friends?"

She nods. "I was going to tell you on Saturday at the cookout. But now seems like a much more appropriate time."

I lean in and I kiss her. We're together again. And she'll be so close.

We separate and smile at one another.

She jabs me in the chest with her pointer finger. "But, that doesn't mean you get to come to Harvard all the time and hang out with me. We both still need to be social and make new friends."

I laugh. "Of course, we will absolutely do that."

"Do you think you'll find all your nerdy friends?"

I playfully drop my jaw. "How dare you insinuate that I will only make nerdy friends?"

She gives me a look that I can't tell if its serious or jokingly asking me 'are you serious?'

"Yeah, that's fair, they'll all be nerds."

We laugh and she snuggles up to me. I wrap my arm around her and smile. My heart is happy. This feels different, but so familiar all at once. I take a second to process exactly what just happened. Z and I are back together. She's going to Harvard. We'll be so close.

Z and I are back together!

I can't believe it. My heart is soaring to new levels and I couldn't be happier.

"Z?"

"Yes?"

"Pinch me."

She pinches me playfully. "Why?"

"Just to make sure I'm not dreaming. You're 100% sure that Harvard is the way to go? You're not making this decision based on anything else?"

"Yes, Jack, I'm absolutely positive. I made this decision without anything else in mind. It's a phenomenal school and has a great business program. You're sure about MIT?"

"Absolutely."

She lets out a deep sigh. "Good. I'm so glad."

"I can't believe this is happening."

"Me neither. I wasn't sure if you still felt the same way."

"I will always love you, Z. Whether we were together or not wasn't going to change how I feel about you."

She looks up at me. "Promise, askim?"

"I promise, hjartat."

"I think this is the start of something really great."

"Me too. Something far greater than I could ever put into words."

"I love you, Jack."

"I love you too, Zendaya."

We kiss and it is sweeter than any kiss we have shared. It's sweeter than any words could describe. I can't believe it's all happening. And I have the weirdest thing to thank for all of this. For bringing Z into my life. For finding happiness that no words could describe. For finding the love of my life.

It's all thanks... to Florida summers.

EPILOGUE

Every day I feel like I couldn't fall in love with Jack any more than I already am, but every day I prove myself wrong.

My name is Zendaya Thompson-Connors. No, not O'Connor. Not Connor. Not Corners. It's Connors, like a bunch of guys named Connor walked into a room. Connors. Zendaya Thompson-Connors. I used to be a pretty famous actress, but now I'm a talent agent for the next generation of shining stars. I still have cameos here and there, but only when I have time. Which is pretty rare. Especially since we have two kids to take care of.

It's been about twenty years since the beach where Jack and I decided to be together again. I look back on that night and I always smile, knowing that last night before college was the best way to not only end that summer, but to start the journey he and I are on. Sure, things weren't always easy. I mean, I went to Harvard and he was at MIT, we had tons of homework and requirements to meet before graduation that kept us busy. There would be weeks where we wouldn't be able to see each other, but we would always, *always* make sure that was remedied as soon as we could. We had our fights and our squabbles, but nothing we couldn't overcome.

I was worried that we wouldn't be able to at first. Many high school sweethearts don't make it through the first year of college because people grow and change so much. And we did too. I started to get very much into business and talent requisition and took it as far as starting my own agency the summer after my junior year. Probably shouldn't have done that as I was then so insanely busy during senior year between balancing these emerging actors and actresses from Massachusetts and still finishing strong – top 10 of my class – at Harvard. Jack grew, too. He got really into fencing with Dr. Thurmond – I mean Ryan – and developed a really healthy social life with a bunch of his classmates. I loved seeing that happen. He would introduce me to his friends with pride since most of them knew who I was from *APL*, but he would introduce them to me with the same amount of pride. He loved having this new and improved social life. He and a couple of his friends worked on their senior project together and ended up getting insanely high remarks and accolades for their work towards more sustainable cars and fuels. They even started to plan a business together to create new modes of transportation that were green and efficient. He was busy, but I loved seeing him work and fell in love with his passion all over again. And that's how we grew. And what was beautiful is that as we grew individually, the more we grew together.

That business didn't stop him from planning something behind my back. In April of our senior year, a knock at my door pulled me out of my studies and I opened it to find Lydia standing there. She asked me if I could join her for a quick errand before meeting up with Jack and Simon for lunch. I loved how often she visited me, despite her health beginning to decline that year. I agreed and her and I went to a small theater venue on campus. We sat down and were joined shortly by Simon. I was kind of shocked – generally he and Jack fence for a few hours prior to joining us ladies for lunch. But there he was, dressed up and not sweaty at all. Before I could ask any questions, the sound of a familiar song began to ring out through the hall.

It was *Jeux Deux*.

The song that Jack had played that night at the Steinmetz.

The song that made me fall in love with him as he played.

I quickly realized that it was Jack actually playing, but it wasn't when the lights came on to illuminate him at the piano. It was before that. I knew it was him because the music immediately filled and melted my heart all over again. It was beautiful. I had heard him play it a dozen times since the Steinmetz, but this time was different.

Oh, how I wish I could describe it. How I wish there were words that would even come close to the wave of emotion and love and joy and yearning that filled my soul. Tears quickly streamed down my cheeks as the song continued to its build and I am, once again, in awe of my boyfriend.

When the last notes ring out, I launch to my feet and start applauding and cheering. Then I realized that it was just us in the theater, so I got out into the aisle and ran to him. I launched myself in the air and collided with him, hugging him as tight as I could while still crying at the piece's beauty.

"It was that good?" Jack asked.

"Yes, askim, it was," I replied.

"Do you remember how I play that piece?"

I nodded. "You daydream. Usually about me."

He nodded back. "This time, I daydreamed of you again. But this time, not as my girlfriend. But what it would be like if you were my wife."

My heart exploded when he said those words. Before I could even reply, he was down on one knee with a ring box in his hand.

"Zendaya, I have been crazy about you since the day we met on that beach all those years ago." He had called me Zendaya, so I knew he was being very serious. "We've been through so much together and I can't ask for a better someone to go through the rest of my life with."

My heart began to race as he opened the ring box to reveal a diamond surrounded by sapphires set in a silver ring.

"Zendaya Thompson. Will you marry me?"

I said yes before he could even finish the question. It had been one of the happiest moments of my life up until that point.

We ended up getting married in Scotland on the banks of Loch Lomond – a favorite spot of ours to travel to during our time in college. The ceremony was small and personal, but the receptions we threw back in the states were not. Nick and Lisa, still our close friends after all these years, threw us two. One was for the more sophisticated parts of our lives – professors, former coworkers, friends of parents, assorted family members, and former teachers like Ryan and Genevieve. The elegance matched the more cultured attendees thanks to Nick's excellent taste in decorating and his phenomenally successful interior, exterior, and event decorating business. The second was for close friends and was a party full of music, dancing, games, and laughter.

Needless to say, we both enjoyed the second one far more than the first.

Our marriage has been relatively easy for the most part, but tragedy struck a few months in. Lydia's cancer had returned and this time it had targeted her colon and intestines, metastasizing faster than treatment could treat. Jack and I quickly moved back to Florida from Massachusetts after graduation to be close to her in her final days. I painted with her while she could still hold a brush and Jack played all the piano she asked him to. We were hoping that a miracle would happen and she would be around for a long time.

But we didn't get that miracle.

She died peacefully at home in the early hours of the morning. Simon had woken up to find her not in bed with him, discovering she had gotten up, wrapped herself in her favorite blanket, went into her creative space, painted one last sunrise, then passed away.

Lydia had a smile on her face. Even at the very end.

Simon struggled with her death. He lost weight rapidly and it was hard for him to do just about anything. Jack and I managed to talk him into an early retirement – he had more money saved up than he could ever spend. He agreed to retire only if he could live close to us which we happily obliged to. Jack was really the only family he had left, other than his sister in Maine which he didn't see all too often. I wanted them to stay close, both physically and emotionally.

It was also a good thing once I got pregnant. We had agreed to wait a few years after getting married to start a family – Jack wanted to finish his designs and prototype and his Doctorate of Engineering and I wanted to make sure my clients got a good start on their careers. So, about five years after we got married, we started trying and I gave birth to Andrew Thomas Connors in September of that year. He was a bundle of joy and happiness and we instantly loved him. Two years later, Emma Kirsten Connors joined her big brother in May. They kept our hands full, but they also kept Simon busy and happy. We were, and still are, a happy little family.

When Emma was about six, Jack got a job offer at a pretty large company in Minnesota to design more energy efficient power structures for large businesses and schools. It paid more than we could ever ask for and I wanted to become a silent owner of Thompson's Talent and focus more on our kids. We moved to Andover, Minnesota, buying a house outside of the city on a few dozen acres. When the kids started school, I decided to take out Lydia's paints and began to paint to honor her memory.

I love our house. I love where we are at. And I love my family dearly.

It's a Sunday afternoon and Emma and I are painting. I had placed a bowl of fruits on the table for inspiration, but little Emma has quite the imagination and is painting a scene from a book she has been reading – ironically by Farrow McNiler, the owner of Lucy's and still a close friend of Jack. The painting depicts a man and a woman dancing in a courtyard, glowing in candle light while men and women dressed in armor watch. I'm not sure how she does it, but Emma has painted it in just the right way that I swear the woman is leading the dance instead of the man.

Her imagination is so vivid sometimes.

Jack is in the middle of a piano lesson with Andrew. I love watching him teach our son to play. I have to admit, Andrew is very good and plays wonderfully. I'm sure he'll rival his dad's skill one day. I smile as Jack feels me looking at him. He gives me a playful wink and I giggle.

He's such a goof sometimes.

I feel an elbow bump my side. I turn and Emma is looking at me with one of her eyebrows raised – it's her classic 'I have a question' face.

"Yes, Em?"

"Remember when I was over at Lyla's house the other day?"

"Yes, of course, dear."

"Well, she asked her parents how they met and they had a really cool story. I was wondering if I could know how you and Dad met?"

Jack looks back at me and smiles. "Do you want to tell her?"

"I can, unless you want to, askim."

"You tell it so much better though, hjartat."

I roll my eyes and laugh at him.

"Yeah, mom, please!" Andrew chirps in from the piano bench.

"Fine, fine!" I exclaim, setting down my paintbrush and moving to the couch. Emma and Andrew hurriedly join me as Jack pivots on the bench of the piano and leans back against the keys. I wrap my arms around our two children and look at Jack.

Good lord, how I love that man.

"Okay, so, this happened more than twenty years ago. I had just moved to Orlando and was out with some friends. We were out at Cocoa Beach and went to a small tiki bar called Lucy's. Your dad was our waiter. I wasn't really in the mood to talk to someone new, but Dad was different. We started talking and we ended up bonding over something that I don't think either of us expected - our common hatred of Florida summers…"

About the Author

Mitchell J. De Haan—Mitch to his friends — is a social studies teacher from central Minnesota. He is married to his beautiful wife, Ali, and they have two dogs. Although much of his time is taken by his graduate work and teaching position, Mitch likes to spend his free time writing, reading, gaming, spending time with loved ones, and relaxing while watching a good TV show or movie. He has been writing for over fifteen years and hopes the words on the pages of his books will touch the hearts and lives of those who need it most.

www.ingramcontent.com/pod-product-compliance
Lightning Source LLC
Chambersburg PA
CBHW061428150726
47987CB00001B/138